IN PRAISE FOR JENN LEES' ARLAN'S PLEDGE SERIES

"Perfect for anyone who ever wished *Outlander* had dragons."
—**Beatrice Grasso**, *Book for Thought*. 5-STAR review *Of Warriors and Sages: Arlan's Pledge Book Two.*

"*Arlan's Pledge* is a book of forbidden love and yearnings, battles against evil, honour and restored heritages. So rich and complex, woven into each tartan plaid. If you are searching for a time portal book, or the Scottish highlands where dragons once swooped, or timeless love restored, then this is for you."
—*Elizabeth Klein Award winning Fantasy author.*

"Jenn Lees' world building is like none other. Rich landscapes and almost tangible settings. But it's her characters who take centre stage. No one does romantasy like this author. Read *Murtairean: An Assassin's Tale; Of Myths and Portals; Of Warriors and Sages* and *Of High Kings and Mages* and be transported into an alternate world .... epic battles and passionate romance."
—**S L Dooley**. *Award Winning Fantasy Author of Portal Slayer Trilogy and The Delgara Duology.*

"This trilogy is unique and has so much heart. The magic is inspirational."
—*Fantasy Author* **PS Patton**

"The detail... for this story, not just this one, but the ones that precede it, is amazing. This is clearly well-thought out... I hope to see this story sitting amongst others of its genre, like LOTR."
—**Shreya Gopaulsingh** *Ink & Insights Competition Judge 2022*

'What a fantastic story from start to finish! Jenn Lees is an expert at world-building, and the world of Dál Cruinne comes alive with her gorgeous and evocative writing.'
—Amazon UK 5-Star review of *Of Warriors and Sages.*

Of High Kings And Mages: Arlan's Pledge Book Three (unpublished manuscript) achieved Semi-Finalist in OZMA Fantasy Fiction Awards 2024 CIBA's (Chanticleer International Book Awards)

Of HIGH KINGS And MAGES

Arlan's Pledge

BOOK THREE

JENN LEES

OF HIGH KINGS AND MAGES

ARLAN'S PLEDGE BOOK THREE

Cover by Fiona Jayde Media
www.fionajaydemedia.com

Map by J I Rogers, Mythspinner Studios

www.mythspinnerstudios.com

To my husband, Frank.
Always.

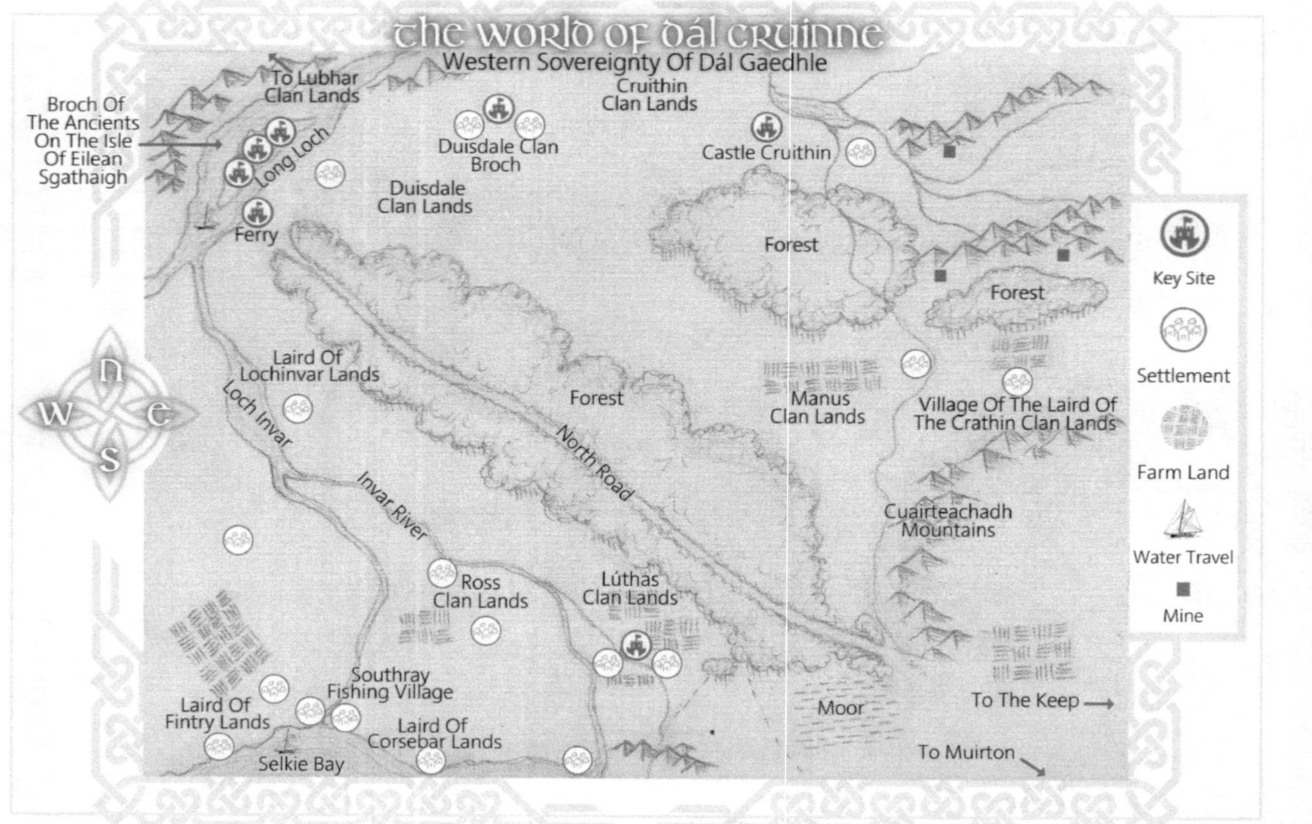

the world of Dál Cruinne
Western Sovereignty Of Dál Gaedhle
Broch Of The Ancients On The Isle Of Eilean Sgathaigh
To Lubhar Clan Lands
Cruithin Clan Lands
Long Loch
Ferry
Duisdale Clan Broch
Duisdale Clan Lands
Castle Cruithin
Forest
Forest
Laird Of Lochinvar Lands
Loch Invar
Forest
Manus Clan Lands
Village Of The Laird Of The Crathin Clan Lands
Invar River
North Road
Cuairteachadh Mountains
Ross Clan Lands
Lúthas Clan Lands
Southray Fishing Village
Laird Of Fintry Lands
Laird Of Corsebar Lands
Selkie Bay
Moor
To The Keep
To Muirton
Key Site
Settlement
Farm Land
Water Travel
Mine
n
e
s
w

The World of Dál Cruinne
WESTERN SOVEREIGNTY OF DÁL GAEDHLE
EASTERN CLANLANDS OF DÁL GALLAIN
Cuairteachadh Mountains
Creagach Mountains
Boggy Moor
Meadhan Mountains
Dragon Boulders
Ancient Derelict Fort
The Keep
Gallawain Clanlands
Sage Hold of the Healers
Ancient Broken Stone Henge
River Ruairidh
Loch Fioreun
Lúthas Clanlands
Caisteal Gallawain
Muirton Trade Port
The border
Burnt Village
Lord Ciarán's Tower
Inlothian
Callaghan Clanlands
Craegrubha Broch
MacEnoicht Clanlands
Caisteal Monsae
Muir Gaedhle
Muir Gallain
N
E
S
W
LEGEND
Important structure
smaller Landmark
village
Guard Tower
Ship
Forest
Mountains
Snowcapped Mountains
Farms & Cultivated Land
Swamps & Bogs

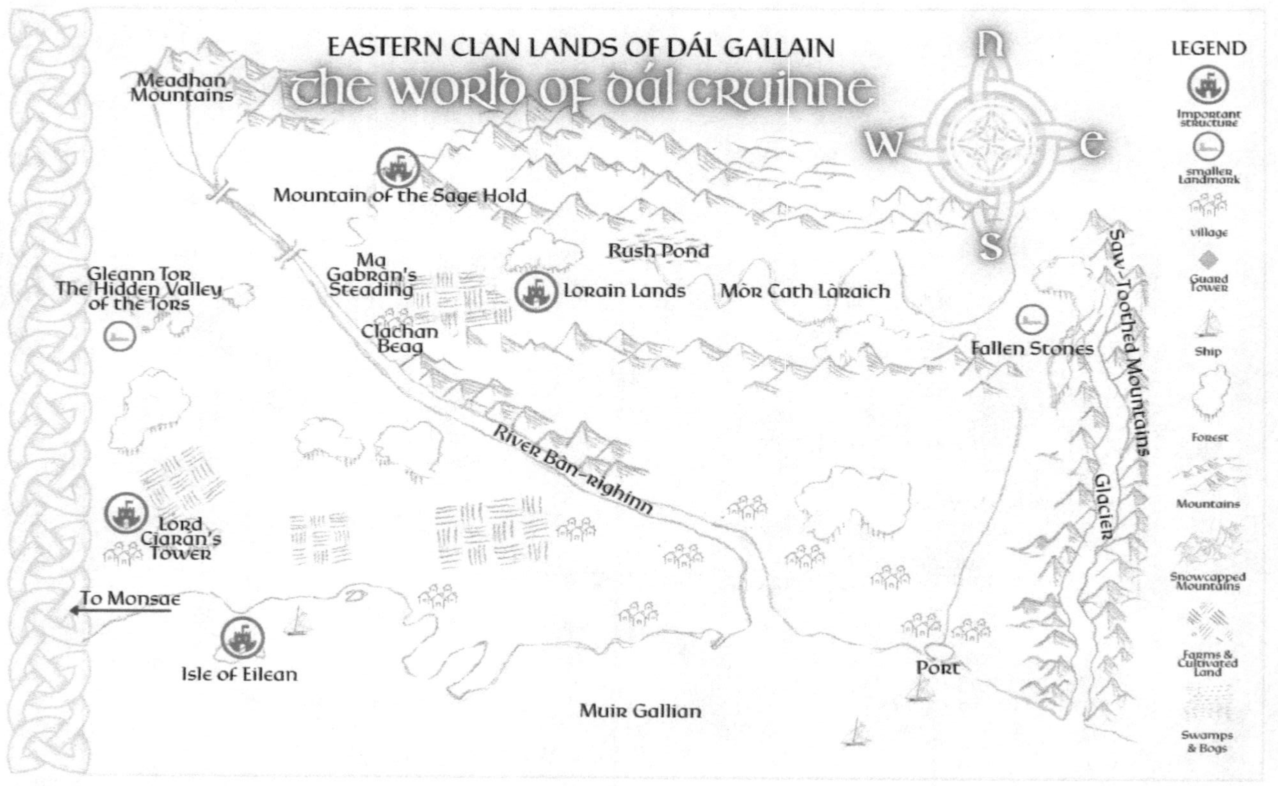

EASTERN CLAN LANDS OF DÁL GALLAIN
The World of Dál Cruinne
Meadhan Mountains
Mountain of the Sage Hold
Gleann Tor
The Hidden Valley of the Tors
Ma Gabrán's Steading
Clachan Beag
Rush Pond
Lorain Lands
Mór Cath Làraich
Fallen Stones
Lord Ciarán's Tower
River Ban-righinn
To Monsae
Isle of Eilean
Muir Gallian
Port
Saw-Toothed Mountains
Glacier
N
S
E
W
LEGEND
Important structure
smaller Landmark
village
Guard Tower
Ship
Forest
Mountains
Snowcapped Mountains
Farms & Cultivated Land
Swamps & Bogs

Contents

Summer flourished, as did womb
And we for gathered harvests stored, made room.
The enemy we all did spy
In preparation, then low did they lie.

Autumn passed and evil gave rest.
From dire intentions we were blessed.
In quietness the foe did ponder
And through worlds' portals they did wander.

Winter's grip came all too fast.
Cold, ice, and blizzard did long last.
When crocus through the snow did peek
'Twas past its time by many a week.

Then did the warmth of spring burst forth
And gathered shields with spears
Joined swords.
For with belated spring, we saw
When armies march,
And kings... to war.

THE BLIND LADY SAGE

PROLOGUE

Let not your fear mould your life.
Ye must grab it by the throat,
Silence its lies,
And parade your conquest in triumph through the streets of your own history.

POETRY OF THE WARRIOR
WARRIOR SAGE TAPAÌDH
(4009-4059 POST DRAGON WARS)

Our World, 2036
Oxford
Historical European Martial Arts Practice Hall

"Rhynne Wilson. Approach the floor, please."

My martial arts instructor's voice echoed off the wooden floor and bare brick walls of the practice hall. He had taught me Ju Jitsu since I was a kid, but here he looked so out of place amongst those who taught Historical European Martial Arts.

Not our usual dojo.

A wave of coolness flashed over me. It could've been relief at my sensei's presence, as he was here for my support only. The HEMA instructors had stipulated no conferring.

Three years. Three long years to get to *this*.

I'd worked my way through Japanese martial art classes throughout my childhood and teens to gain a second dan black belt. But that was only the beginning.

Hand to hand fighting. *Tick*.

Small weapons and disarming. *Tick*.

My gut tightened. *Something* in me yearned for the sword. And I was uncertain as to why, but a double-edged sword appealed to me more than a katana. In any eventuality, the way of the blade would be my *way*, and *they* needed to know it. They *must* allow me admission into this elite HEMA club.

Now they'll try me out, test my skills… and judge.

My opponent for the try-out stood in the middle of the hall, as straight and as unyielding as the thick wooden practice pole in the corner, his gaze resting on me while I stood at the edge of the floor.

My heart knocked against my ribs.

Why him? The guy with the old Gaelic name. Just a glance from Bàn's blue Highland eyes in his lightly tanned face caused a spike in my heart rate.

Always had. Well, for the three months he'd been at martial art classes, anyway.

Muscled and fit, Bàn could fight. I had no chance of beating him.

That's not the point, Rhynne. They want to know what you're made of.

Bàn nodded. I held the blunt practice sword in both hands and marched across the floor to him.

Damn. The handle's damp already.

Wiping one hand on my thigh, I got to two sword lengths from him and halted, gripping tight once more. He raised his broadsword, flat side to his face, and touched it to his brow.

It was on.

He came at me with an arc of blade moving so fast. Just a flash in the sunlight spearing through the tall windows. My muscles tensed. A wash of air from his sword hit my face.

Move girl! This is it! Watch him. His eyes, not his weapon. That's where it starts.

I jerked into motion with a block to his sword, sending a juddering right through me, then followed through with a counter. Bàn's eyes lit up, and without pausing, he drove down more blows.

Our blades clashed, and the energy shuddered up my arms, jolting into my shoulders. My peripheral vision now distant. Non-existent.

This man and his blade—my entire world.

I pushed forward with clanking blows and thrusts, my pounding temples drumming out the murmured comments of the instructors assessing me.

Bàn stepped back, blocking each one of my parries. My forward momentum carried me to him. I locked his sword with mine then pushed up.

Metal screeched against metal. Jumping a leap, I landed my foot on his midriff.

Like kicking a concrete wall.

His brows flicked a fraction, then he pelted me with more blade swings. I caught every one. He stood back and ran his sword through some arcs on either side of his body, with his vision on me and droplets of sweat on him.

At least I'm making him work for it.

My grip shook around the practice sword, its hard handle digging into the soft flesh webbing between my thumb and forefinger.

His right shoulder lifted. I readied for a counter. He moved to his left instead and his spinning arc slowed.

I stepped in, countering each of his strikes, each one setting my teeth clunking. I moved closer.

Is he letting me?

More fool him. I'm within kicking distance now.

One to his knee. It gave slightly. His grunt blew close to my face and his breath tore past my forehead. I lifted my body and snapped my leg out for a chest kick. His widening eyes corresponded with one hand leaving his double grip on his sword, then encircling my ankle and clamping on it.

I twisted my whole body, wrenching my ankle from his grasp as I spun, then ran out of his reach.

Damn!

I turned after three paces. He was there, sword raised high and bearing down on me. I danced back. He ran forward, his breath and body heat coming closer with each step.

My back's gonna hit the wall any second.

A crease formed above his nose, and he crossed his sword over his chest, pushing mine aside. My heart sledge-hammered my ribcage.

I'm wide and exposed. Vulnerable!

The brick wall thumped into my back. I lifted afoot against his abs, pressing him to a halt. His torso heaved beneath my foot, sweat dripping down the side of his face.

He's still workin' for it.

His frown relaxed and his face softened, dimples pitting in a tight grin, but eyes looking down at me.

"Ye know if I had a dagger, ye'd be dead." He spoke low, his left hand in a mock grip now resting just below my ribs.

My breath came hard, matching his. I pushed my foot against him, straightening my leg, thigh muscles screaming. It didn't budge him. He leaned in. His left cheek had a silvery scar that crossed the dimple there.

"Fancy kicks are fine, but when the blade is real"—his broad Scots accent came through his panting— "dinnae waste your time on them, unless your opponent is a slow, old man."

I released my foot from his chest and dropped it to the floor, leaning forward off the wall. But he moved in closer, pressing my hips and shoulders into the cold, hard brickwork, blue eyes intense, and as serious as death.

"*Never* turn your back on your enemy."

ONE

I see you in that thin place,
Where kings meet with gods,
And I hold my breath
While eternity reaches out
And touches time.

VISIONS AND SAYINGS OF THE BLIND LADY SAGE

The World of Dál Cruinne
Western Sovereignty of Dál Gaedhle
Summer, Year 6083 Post Dragon Wars
Bhienn an Rìgh a'Dèanamh
Mountain of the Kingmaking

Arlan cast his vision down the side of the narrow, winding cliff track. A sheer drop lay beyond small patches of gorse clinging to rocks. Ahead rose the highest peak of this mountain range encircling the wide valley, Bhienn an Rìgh a'Dèanamh. Clouds gathered below him where The Keep sat small beside the River Ruairidh. From here it seemed but a shallow brown burn winding its way through the wide glen. Clouds continued to pour their generosity on the land, for it had been a wet summer and the harvests would be bountiful.

Ciarán Gallawain's raiders had harried plantings near the border, yet the warbands Arlan had sent to protect the steading holders had held them at bay for now.

Harvests must occur, for he would have an army to feed. Arlan had ordered the clan chieftains to prepare their warbands, readying them to join his own and form that very army. All watched from the border forts for the movements of Gallawain's warriors. The foe—Mother's own cousin—had been quiet for a week. Arlan grunted.

The foe had been quieter than he'd expected all summer!

Was that not when armies warred? Gallawain prepared, but for when? There was no sign of recent war-like mustering, or so Sage Eifion, his faithful advisor, had said after his many occasions of *seeing*—what he named looking afar in his spirit form. Arlan shook his head fractionally. Still so strange that Eifion was a mage, and had been so for all Arlan's days, and now only recently revealed.

Gallawain would not restrain his ambitions for long. With this seeming lull, and almost half the summer passed since the Quest, Eifion announced that *now* would be the time for his kingmaking ceremony. Sages and clan chieftains would gather and pronounce Arlan the Àrd Rìgh of Dál Gaedhle, their high king.

Horses could only walk this muddy track single file, and at these heights, stone no longer lined the path. The horses slipped with almost every second hoof-fall. Eifion had anticipated this and instructed the team to bring the tents and provisions on the small narrow carts trailing behind the pack mules. The group of warriors, including his troop, plus sages and clan chiefs able to attend his kingmaking, followed him and Eifion to the top. Many distant clan chiefs had had to decline due to the urgency of the invitation.

They'd never get here in time. Let them continue their preparations for war.

He twisted in the saddle to face Rhiannon behind him. Bàn, his sword-brother and most faithful friend, rode close behind her. Douglas, Muir, Adele, Angus and Morrigan, his closest warriors followed. Rhiannon looked over the valley below, a dreamy smile on her lips. Her rosy cheeks glowed with a vitality and her amber hair, a mass of curls and waves, spilled out of its clasps and fell about her like a cloak. He laughed softly to himself, for she'd often complained how it made her look a mess and not like the wife of a high king. But to him, her loveliness surpassed them all. He dropped his gaze to her belly, now a small, round bump.

"Ye are well, my wife?"

"Of course. Don't be so worried, Arlan. I'm not the only woman in the world to have a baby." Her eyes widened, and she shook her head at him.

"Aye, but ye are my woman and I'm meant to—"

"I'm fine and relieved I didn't take the rickety option." She flicked her head, indicating the carts of supplies rattling behind the mules. "Bridie is a much smoother ride."

Drayce flew overhead, the dragon now the size of a horse, circling high in a sky turning dark grey. Arlan let out a short chuckle, for he had regarded his dragon as male from a hatchling. But Eifion maintained she was, indeed, a she, and very much protective of Arlan. She dived low, close over Arlan. Horses shied and whinnied. His stallion, Mengus, shook his head vigorously, flicking his long, black mane into Arlan's face, then snorted his annoyance.

The track had wound back and forth on itself as it ascended the mount. It now appeared to finish at nothing as it rose with the incline ahead. He reached the end of the rise and Drayce landed in front of him. To his right and stretching far, spread a great plateau that backed onto further peaks. A grey granite standing stone circle sat on the flat ground, the sarsens topped with lintel slabs except for an opening gap.

"Wow! An original Stone Henge." Awe echoed through Rhiannon's voice. "Or how it once would've looked."

"Aye." Eifion pulled his horse up next to Rhiannon's. "The place where kings meet with gods."

Arlan dismounted, and the others followed suit. Bàn beckoned Muir, the oldest and most experienced of Arlan's personal warband, to organise the camp and set up the pavilion tents for the guests.

"So, you really stay out all night in the middle of the circle?" Rhiannon tucked her plaid tighter around herself. "It feels like it's going to pour again." She twitched her head towards the deep grey clouds now piling high over the valley and heading toward them.

"Aye." He stepped to her and finished tucking her plaid around her waist, his hands resting gently on the small mound of her belly. "But you shall be warm in a tent."

"I hoped I could stand with you in your vigil."

"I shall be the support for your husband." Eifion, slower to dismount, drew nearer.

"But you can't stay out all night in the cold, Father!" Rhiannon reached out for Eifion's gnarled hands.

"You need not, Sage Eifion," Arlan agreed, using Eifion's official title, for it *was* an official occasion, after all.

"But I shall." Eifion pulled a rolled fur from the back of his saddle. It fell open to reveal a thick cloak.

"Bàn, will you ensure my lady is comfortable and dry while I spend a sleepless, wet night?"

"Aye, my sword-brother and king, for by the look of the weather, you will not just receive a shower of blessings, but a drenching." Bàn's dimpled cheeks pitted deeply.

Arlan returned a wry smile.

The hollow thunk of wooden hammers on tent pegs soon filled the natural arena, followed by clanking pots and the garlicky aromas of a lentil stew. Arlan sat with the company in their campsite and ate, barely tasting any of his meal. The stone henge filled his vision.

"It is time." Eifion's orotund voice rang out on the plateau.

Arlan placed his half-eaten meal beside him, then turned to Rhiannon. He gathered her into his arms and kissed her, her warm lips returning his love.

"I love you, my wife," he said when their lips parted.

"And I you, my husband. See you on the other side."

"Aye." He slipped his baldric holding his sword, *Camhanaich*, over his shoulder, straightened his plaid and kilt, then nodded to the gathered throng.

A sea of faces, his warriors and close troop among them, looked back at him. Some clan chiefs were not so familiar, although he recognised their tartans. Mother's uncle, Adomàn, a tall man, stood slightly stooped, with the angular nose and wavy hair of a Gallawain. A guard of his warrior clansmen surrounded him. Warriors of the other clan chiefs surrounded their leaders too, the ones able to make the journey at such short notice. The officious sage, Cénell, who had protested Arlan keeping Drayce alive, scowled from the middle of a cluster of sages Arlan recognised from the sage council, the Sàsaichean. The expressions of all varied from expectation, to wonder, to pride.

All present to witness his kingmaking.

What kind of show are they expecting?

They bowed to him, then raised their faces.

Standing close beside Bàn, Rhiannon held his gaze the longest, the corners of her mouth curling in a tentative smile.

"The clan chief of MacEnoicht"—Eifion looked at them all with a serious expression—"and winner of Tòireadh, the Quest for our new high king, will now go forth and vigil. May it please *Tobraichean na beatha,* the spirit who is the source of all life, to meet with our àrd rìgh."

Eifion led him to the ring of stones while Arlan dragged his gaze from Rhiannon, who remained with the throng of witnesses. Drayce took flight, landing ahead of him into the middle of the henge. Arlan followed Eifion and walked through the opening to a perfectly flat area of green dry grass, where all else lay soggy from the heavy summer rains. Eifion led him to the very centre, where he stopped. Drayce ambled closer, tucking her wings neatly behind her.

"Kneel, Arlan Finnbar MacEnoicht." Eifion stood tall, straightening his shoulders and masking a flinch.

Arlan bent to one knee, the ground cool where his bare skin touched it.

"Both knees, Lord Arlan. Ye are on hallowed ground."

Arlan kneeled fully and unsheathed *Camhanaich*, placing her tip onto the earth by his knees and holding tight to her grip. Eifion stepped closer and placed his hands on Arlan's head. The gentle tremble of Eifion's hands shook his head slightly.

"Eternal light that brightens the mind

Free this man's mind's eye.

Evaporate mist and burn away fog by the warmth of your light.

Clear his vision's blindness of things unseen.

Make crisp the contemplation.

Sharpen the image of what is real.

Truer than thought or substance

More tangible than touch

More valid than all vain pursuits."

Eifion removed his hands, leaving a warmth on Arlan's bowed head, then stepped away, walking backward a few paces. He bowed from the waist, turned, and strode to the nearest stone, then faced Arlan.

Arlan swallowed and gazed around him at the silent stones. Naught moved, except for Drayce, who had settled with her head resting on her front claws and her longtail, now grown black with a barb on the tip, snaking around her in a manner reminiscent of her mother dragon.

The grey stones, solid, and three times the height of a man, seemed to examine him. He let his vision drift toward the camp. People—his people—had moved away from the entrance to the henge and packed up after their meal. Some stood in groups or milled about the tents, preparing for their night's slumber. The two youngest warriors of his own warband, Angus and Morrigan, stood with their backs to him, pointing away.

The clouds were closer, thick, black, and angry, tumbling over each other in an earnest desire to reach the mountain and his camp, and empty their bellies of rain.

Aye, Bàn was correct.

He moved to stand.

"Nae, stay where you are." Eifion's voice rang from the stone to his left. "All will be well. Trust *Tobraichean na beatha.*"

Arlan grunted, but he dared not move after the sage's admonition. He closed his eyes.

That was what he was meant to do, aye?

Close my eyes and ponder being a king.

He did so for a while, but naught happened. No brilliant ideas. No noble thoughts. No visions of grand things.

Och, but I need wisdom.

Tobraichean na beatha make me wise and enable me to defeat the evilness threatening my kingdom.

Arlan held his mind in silence.

Nothing came.

What did he expect? A voice from the heavens? A flash of lightning? A vision?

He stilled his soul. What kind of high king would he make? He would not spend the wealth he could gather on his own needs. Nor use position to dictate his own desires. That was cousin Ciarán, through and through.

He huffed. He desired to defeat Ciarán Gallawain and any other threat that would enslave his people.

My people.

Wasn't that why he'd become their leader? *Why I'm king over the clan chieftains?*

He opened his eyes. Beyond the ring of stones, horizontal rain lashed through a grey world. No fires glowed, and the drenched tents flapped in the wild wind while dark figures hastily tightened tent ropes.

Around him, all remained calm. Not a breeze stirred within the circle of the stones, nor a drop of rain. His plaid draped over his shoulder provided enough warmth for him with the air as balmy as any summer's evening. Eifion stood before one of the standing stones in the wide ring, himself sentinel-like. He must have seen Arlan looking about, for he gave a sharp glare, glanced toward the campsite—or where it should be, for now grey stormy rain filled the view—and shook his head. Arlan leaned his forehead on his hands, which rested on his sword's pommel, and settled back to his contemplations.

A grinding came from all around him, vibrating the ground beneath him and the very mountain itself. He shot open his eyes, stood, and readied his stance to fight. Drayce rose onto her hind legs and flapped her wings.

Surrounding him, where were once stones, now stood warriors. But no Eifion. They were tall, as tall as the sarsens, and all wore armour. Each held a sword, downward pointed, and their feathered wings—for that was what they were—spread from behind each being and touched the wingtip of the warrior to either side.

"Hail, mighty warrior." The salutation came from one wearing blue armour.

Drayce settled and gave a soft, high-pitched click.

These warriors are no threat, then?

Arlan eased his stance a little. The warrior in blue stepped forward, his deep red hair flowed around him like water, and his beard sat plaited at his chin in the same manner as Muir's. Arlan's neck strained to see all of him. The warrior knelt in front of Arlan and reached out to *Camhanaich*, inclining his head to the blade.

"May she ring true in justice." His voice was gravelly. "May she be wielded to bring forth peace." He touched Arlan's sword, and the blade's edge turned blue.

He returned to his place in the circle and rested his wingtips to his neighbours'.

Arlan held his breath while thrumming vibrated his hands. His sword glowed blue, the runes speaking *Camhanaich's* name along the fuller were now etched in darker lines.

A warrior to Arlan's right stepped forward. Her skin was as black as night, and her hair so curly it rose in a glorious dark fuzzy crown above her head. She wore animal skin for armour, like a *felid*'s, only spotted. She slinked toward him, her movements as graceful as a wildcat's.

"Hail, mighty warrior." She raised her hands, then traced an outline of his physique. "May your movements be lithe. May your body and mind be agile, out manoeuvring all foes."

A shimmer travelled over him, each muscle in limb and torso lengthening, and a new strength coursed through him. The warrior bowed, returned to her place, then set her wingtips to touch her neighbours'.

A third warrior broke his place in the circle. His garment shone like silver and wrapped around him like a robe. Tucking his weapon in its sheath at his belt, he knelt on one knee in front of Arlan. Beneath straight, black hair, and through almond-shaped lids, deeply intelligent eyes locked with Arlan's.

"Hail, mighty warrior." He withdrew his sword and, in one smooth motion, brought its edge to *Camhanaich*, which Arlan still held extended. The swords touched and sang together. The warrior then raised his single-edged blade to rest above Arlan's head. Arlan held his breath, not daring to move.

"May your mind be in the way of the master warrior, at one with your blade."

Arlan's scalp tingled as the warrior bowed his head, sheathed his weapon, rose from his knee, then returned to his place.

Another paced toward him wearing leather armour, sheathing his curved sword, then pressing his palms together as though in prayer. He wore a cloth wound about his head. This brown skinned, brown-eyed warrior with a dark beard, reached out for Arlan's hands. A band of silver adorned his wrist, and a gentle smile rested upon his mouth. Arlan placed *Camhanaich* beside him and surrendered his hands to the warrior's grasp.

"Hail, mighty warrior. May these be the hands of a servant. May they be willing to give aid whenever required." He released Arlan, bowed and returned to his place.

Heat filled Arlan's palms and, turning them over, his jaw dropped.

His palms glowed.

A tall warrior approached next, her long blonde hair braided and sitting neatly over her shoulder. An armour of shiny metal covered her torso, like that he had seen with

Rhiannon at the caisteal in Edinburgh while in the Other World. She rested the flat of her sword on her collarbone, in the manner Bàn often did, her green eyes sparkling. She walked right up to him and planted a kiss on his mouth.

"Hail, mighty warrior. May your lips speak the truth always. May you command with authority."

She winked, nodded a bow, then returned to her place.

Arlan blinked and touched his lips, which were still buzzing from her chaste kiss.

A movement came from behind him.

"Arlan." It was Father. Love and tenderness harmonised in his voice, and this single word—his own name—was melodious.

Arlan's heart sang. He pivoted. Father strode to him, his long hair raven black as in his youth, beard like coal, and his face held not a wrinkle, apart from those fanning his eyes like sunrays, bought from his humour.

Strong arms surrounded Arlan and held him fast. One arm slid upward, and Father's broad, heat-filled palm rested on Arlan's head.

"Hail, mighty warrior," Father said into their embrace, his voice cracking with emotion. "May ye have the wisdom ye so desire. May ye rule our people with discernment and lead them in the right ways."

Arlan's whole body trembled, his eyes moistening with forming tears. "Father—"

Father stepped back, a finger to his lips.

"Wait for him," he said, then walked to the opening of the henge. He turned briefly and smiled, his chest expanding as though swollen with pride.

Then he disappeared into the rainstorm.

Two

—·—

War, famine and flame
Open the maws of the grave.
That rapacious plunderer
No bloody battle can assuage.
When all that remains
Is to fall with warriors slain,
I will resurrect for you an army
For this, my world, to reclaim.

SECRET SACRED WRITINGS OF THE SAGES

The World of Dál Cruinne
Summer, Year 6083 Post Dragon Wars
Western Sovereignty of Dál Gaedhle
Bhienn an Rìgh a'Dèanamh
Mountain of the Kingmaking

Arlan blinked away tears.

Father...

It *was* really Father. He swallowed past the thickness in his throat and slowly rotated on his heel. Outside the circle, rain fell. Within the circle, stones looked silently on, the winged warriors now nowhere in sight. Neither was Eifion. His survey of the henge complete, he picked up his sword and returned his gaze to the opening.

What now? Night had fallen beyond the stones, but where he stood, it was as bright as midday. He paced to the centre of the henge and patted Drayce, who nudged him, her knobbly head rough against his cheek.

How I long to still be with Father.

"Yes, he's a great man, Arlan. Donnach is one to be proud of."

Arlan spun to the voice.

A tall man stood behind him. Warrior-like, wearing kilt and plaid of the àrd rìgh's tartan, his blue tattoos covered his left arm in the emblems of this world. Drayce clicked a welcome in Arlan's ear and bounded over to the man, who reached up and scratched her head.

"It was great to see your father again, aye?" The warrior's voice belonged to a young man but held a strength and resonance of someone much older.

Arlan nodded mutely as the man chuckled and stroked Drayce.

"What did you think of the others? Awesome, yes?" The man had no weapon that Arlan could see, and his skin, clothes and hair were dry.

"Ah, aye." Arlan's brow tensed. *Who is this?*

"So, you and Rhiannon?" The man's cheeks dimpled with his smile. "She's incredible." He shook his head gently, as though in wonder.

"What do ye know of my wife?" Arlan's chest tightened a touch.

"A lot."

Arlan tilted his head. "Are ye friend or foe?" He hardened his voice.

Drayce leaned into the stranger's hand, emitting a purring-like noise.

"I'm the lover of your soul." The young man shrugged. His long brown hair fell back over his shoulders.

Arlan adjusted his grip on his sword.

"I'm so proud of Rhiannon. She sought and sought until she found. Admittedly, she had you to help her." The man smiled. "I knew you'd both like that. And she waited for you." He gave a brief shake of his head once more, then said softly, "Wonderful."

"Who *are* you?"

The young man opened his arms, inviting a hug. "I am the Source of all Spirit. The Fountain of Life. The one who sages name *Tobraichean na beatha*. You know this, Arlan, deep down inside." He closed the space between them, avoiding *Camhanaich*, and rested the flat of his palm on Arlan's chest. "In here."

At the touch of the man's hand, a joy entered Arlan. A cry of delight escaped him. It was as though the light of the purest goodness filled him, and life's energy coursed through his body.

It was a warm summer's day. Childhood embraces from Mother. As strong as the bond of a sword-brother. Like the promise of life in spring, a full womb, or a new born colt. Solid as the mountains, as constant as waves on the seashore, and as permanent as the seasons.

It was light on a dark night. The rightness of justice. The goodness of compassion. Love that gentled, supported, strengthened. The sentiments of a noble act gone unnoticed and unrewarded but given in generosity and self-denial all the same. And the soul connection he experienced in the love he shared with Rhiannon.

This flooded Arlan, swirling within him, searing past his body, and grabbing his soul in the embrace the man had invited.

Arlan dropped his sword and wrapped his arms around the man. A glowing and peaceful warmth enveloped and infused him. It trickled through the spaces in between his thoughts and emotions, then went deeper. Into the space where the real *him* resided. Where no one else, not Father, nor Bàn, nor even Rhiannon, ever saw.

Here, he was *known*.

And loved.

He fell to his knees, warm tears wetting his cheeks, and he rested in that place.

The rarest of places. Somewhere he'd only vaguely sensed in the best parts of his life. With Rhiannon—his wife. With Bàn—his truest sword-brother. With Father.

Acceptance. *Aye, that is it!*

Arlan stood and faced the reassuring and knowing gaze of the young man who grasped his shoulders in both hands, forcing him to look him right in the eye.

"I've something really special for you to do, Arlan. And I know you can do it."

"Be àrd rìgh?"

"Of course. But more than that." The man gently shook Arlan's shoulders, his eyes alight and his whole body vibrating with an energy.

Arlan blinked. *What is this man on about?*

"Come on, you know," he coaxed.

Arlan shook his head, fumbling for ideas.

"I gave you a big enough hint from your mother-in-law, before she even became your mother-in-law." He spoke through his laughter. "It's a really special and seriously important job."

The words lit up in Arlan's mind like one of those electric light signs he'd seen in the Other World.

"Warrior King?"

"Yes!" The man raised his hand, inviting Arlan to slap his palm. "It's not just something Eifion and Bàn have hooked on to."

Arlan slapped his hand. Then the man's expression dropped, and his gaze lowered to the ground, his eyes misting.

"He went wrong... Ciarán did." His voice held an ache. "Everyone has a chance... But you, Arlan." His speech sped up and he fixed his intense gaze on Arlan. "*You* I pin my hopes on. You and all who trust what I'm doing."

He grabbed both of Arlan's shoulders again, his face close to his. "It won't be easy. Nothing really worth doing is. You just have to listen."

The young man slid his hands from Arlan's shoulders and pulled him into a hug. The sense of peace and purity surrounding Arlan intensified, so he closed his eyes and allowed himself to float in it.

Time seemed not to *be* in this place.

But how long would this hug last? If only it would never end.

"I must listen, ye say?"

"Aye. You'll hear it on the wind," the young man said, and a breeze blew, stirring the balmy air around them.

It grew stronger, jostling Arlan, and a heat filled his left arm. He opened his eyes and turned his arm over. The triskelion glowed golden amongst the blue inked symbols on his forearm.

The man had gone, but the peace lingered. The wind swept through the circle, tugging Arlan's hair out of its clasps and swirling long black strands about his face. His plaid came loose from his shoulder, flicking and snapping around him. Drayce's clicks came fast while she fought against the wind's lift.

The swirl of wind grew tighter. Now a cylinder of motion touched the centre of the henge and reached the sky above.

It lifted and rested at the height of the henge, drawing the rain clouds that surrounded it and had kept the camp in a grey drenched squall. It ascended, taking the rain and clouds with it.

Outside the henge, dawn broke, glistening raindrops on tents. His people emerged, gazing around and their mouths dropping open.

Rhiannon ran toward him through the henge entrance, Bàn on her heels. Eifion stepped to him, appearing from the side, and beckoned to those who followed Rhiannon into the standing stone circle. They gathered around Arlan and Drayce. All except his troop wore uneasy expressions and moved to the far side of the crowd, away from the dragon.

Arlan swept his hair away from his face, straightened his plaid and tucked *Camhanaich* in her sheath. Rhiannon crept to his side, her fine eyebrows meeting almost in the middle. She had stopped a pace away and clasped her hands in front of her, but her gaze roamed his body, as though she saw him for the very first time.

His muscles held strength, and with his body more alive, a vitality ran through him. He felt different...better. Arlan glanced down at himself.

Perhaps I look it, too.

Through the lingering peace, he reached out to Rhiannon, drawing her into his arms, ignoring the quiet surprised exclamations of those gathered. He sought her mouth and kissed in earnest, her hesitant breath brushing his cheek. Tears spilled from her eyes, and he let her go.

"Lord Arlan Finnbar MacEnoicht, Àrd Rìgh of Dál Gaedhle, kneel." The powerful voice of Eifion rang behind him, echoing through the henge.

He faced Eifion and knelt on both knees. Eifion held Father's silver torc and raised it above his head.

"As a sign of your position, I place this torc about your neck. It is but a symbol of your high kingship. It does not make you a king, for *Tobraichean na beatha* has designated ye as such. May its touch at your neck be a constant reminder of your duty and obligation to all who would put their trust, hopes, and very lives under your rule."

Arlan raised his chin and Eifion pulled the ends of the torc apart then placed it around his neck. Cool at first, it warmed almost immediately. He stood.

Those about him now kneeled, including Eifion, and Drayce lowered her head in her version of a bow. Arlan's mouth pulled at the corners, then he stifled a chuckle as the gravity of his position impressed itself upon him. The torc sitting tight around his neck thrummed.

The hiss of drawn swords came from Bàn, his troop, and other warriors who knelt at the back of the crowd. They stood and raised their blades in the air.

"To our àrd rìgh, Arlan MacEnoicht." Their shout echoed around the stone circle.

The clan chiefs, sages and other guests stood also, with fists raised, and joined their voices with the warriors. Their shouts changed, melding into another chant.

"Laoch Righ! Laoch Righ! Laoch Righ!"

Arlan swallowed. Their passion for him, their *warrior king,* was so real he could reach out and touch it.

THREE

—·—

A king's life is never his own
But belongs to those he governs,
Who share their life and breath with his.
Give him moments of freedom, though,
When the rìgh is but a man with a woman,
Father with a son,
Dadaidh with a daughter.
Then the kingdom pauses and holds its breath
While the àrd rìgh is a man living life.

WISDOM WRITINGS ON KINGSHIP
SAGE GLIOCAS
(2870-2962 POST DRAGON WARS)

The World of Dál Cruinne
Spring, Year 6084 Post Dragon Wars
Western Sovereignty of Dál Gaedhle
The Keep

"I swear she's fluttering her eyelids at you." Rhiannon peered over Arlan's shoulder.

Rhynne gurgled and cooed in his arms, grasping at his hair and tugging at a handful of his long, black locks, sending a laugh rippling through Rhiannon.

"Ouch. Our babe is barely two moons old." Arlan twisted to look up at her. "She has only just learned to smile."

Arlan sat on the couch by their fireplace, deep cushions hugging his muscled arms, their private chambers an oasis in the hustle of activity that seemed to be constant in The Keep.

War preparations kept everyone busy... and on edge.

13

A broad grin encompassed Arlan's face, distorting the paling scar on his cheek, slashed there by Ciarán Gallawain on their one and only encounter.

It could never diminish his handsomeness.

"But, aye, she's magnificent. Ye have done us proud, Rhiannon." He reached up and placed a soft kiss on her lips. "And a braw mother ye make."

A gentle warmth filled her, pushing through her heavy limbs and cloudy mind that'd dogged her daily since the birth.

Maybe Rhynne will sleep through the night soon.

She grunted and walked around the couch to face them both, her back to the fire, its distinct peaty scent surrounding her. "I think she's going to be a *daddy's girl.*"

Arlan's eyelids appeared half closed as he gazed down at their daughter, his mouth softening to a smile. Rhynne's tiny hand reached out to her father's neck and fumbled a grip on his silver torc glinting in the firelight.

Times like these would be rare. Ciarán Gallawain would surely rear his ugly head again soon.

Thank heavens for the severe winter.

It'd shielded them from whatever he'd planned. The sages and warriors were getting twitchy, and like now, Arlan snatched every opportunity he could to leave the Àrd Rìgh's Council meetings and come to spend precious moments with her and baby Rhynne.

Rhiannon sighed. Life had changed and having a child *upped the ante*. She had so much more to lose now. Rhiannon clasped her hands together, squeezing tight. She'd never felt more protective of *anyone* in her life.

Other issues had seemed an irrelevant blur in the past few weeks, and only now could she muster the energy to think of anything apart from Rhynne.

A squawk came from their balcony which faced the valley behind The Keep. Drayce landed on the railing, then poked through the heavy curtain covering the balcony entrance and pushed it aside. The dragon's deep red scaly hide shone in the light, which reflected off the last of the melting snow that still lay in the private gardens below.

"Soon your dragon will be bigger than a war horse and that balcony won't take her weight."

"Och, no," Arlan chuckled. "This is a sturdy caisteal. Moreover, she's an animal of flight, and her bones will be light, such as a bird's."

A firm rapping echoed from their chamber door. A servant opened it and Eifion entered, his purple adviser-sage robe rustling with each step and a look of expectancy on his face. Rhynne stirred and whinged in Arlan's arms, and Drayce clicked softly from the balcony.

"I will return to the council soon, Eifion." Arlan shushed Rhynne, who shifted in his arms, then settled back to sleep. "Please allow me a few more moments."

"She loves the sound of a deep male voice." Eifion stood beside Rhiannon in front of the fire and considered Arlan and Rhynne. "The reassurance of strong arms keeping her safe."

Arlan chuckled. "But she'll be able to defend herself if my wife has anything to do with it."

Rhiannon placed her hand on her hip. "Would you disagree?"

"Nae. I dare not."

"Once she is grown"—Eifion continued as if he hadn't heard them— "she will look for a man who will protect her and make her feel safe. A man like her father. She will not go wrong if she listens to the voice of her inner self."

Rhiannon glared at Eifion. "She'll find him in the practice yard."

"She will be clever." Eifion straightened his back, ignoring Rhiannon's gentle rebuttal. His eyes never left the sleeping bundle in Arlan's arms. "Maybe even a sage, considering her heritage."

"Ye sound like a doting grandfather," Arlan said.

Rhiannon caught their reflection in the large, polished bronze mirror that stood beside the heavy blue tartan curtain hanging across the balcony, which Drayce had pushed aside. They were the picture of a family, three generation's worth. She'd found her roots, her man, and her home in this world of Dál Cruinne. *Her* world now. Her hand slid away from her hip.

Oh, let Eifion have his grandfatherly say.

"I have discovered there is a portal nearby," Eifion announced.

Rhiannon raised an eyebrow at Eifion's subject-change. "Where?"

"How?" Arlan's question collided with hers.

Eifion grinned and put up a staying hand. "I have spent some time searching outside as far as the horrendous weather has allowed. It has confined me... *us* for so long. I walked as far as I could yesterday, and on crossing the bridge out of the village, I felt a thrum."

"Ye mean a power?" Arlan leaned forward. "Where did it concentrate?"

The hairs on Rhiannon's arms lifted.

"It thrummed most strongly in the centre of the ashen circle," Eifion said. "Where stands the memorial to your dear father, our late àrd rìgh."

Gooseflesh shimmered across Rhiannon's skin. Arlan's eyes rounded, and the crackling of the fire filled the silence Eifion's answer had left.

"I have gained helpful information regarding portals." Eifion spoke into the stillness. "I have fellow sages who are of the same mind as I, and yestermorn a rider arrived who had made his way through the snowmelt from the Broch of the Ancients, up on the Long Loch. The rider brought a parcel for me from Àrd Gliocas. It contained copies of a scroll, hitherto locked. I had requested this during my enquiries regarding you, my lovely daughter." He looked at Rhiannon, the creases around his eyes crinkling further, then abruptly returning to their *normal* as his hoary eyebrows lifted. "Ye will be fascinated to hear this." He leaned closer. "The scrolls record that portals can be directed by those who seek entry. A traveller can go anywhere from any portal if they know when and where they desire to go. The *desire* is the key."

"Wow." Rhiannon did a double-take. "Any place? Any time? From any portal?"

Eifion's lips held a mischievous smile. "Wonderful, is it not?"

Arlan raised his head from Rhynne and placed his frowning stare on Eifion. "I only desired to pass through and return home."

"To your own world, in your own time." Eifion spoke with a hint of confirmation in his tone.

"But what about when he came through to me at the Celtic Festival in the grounds of the Highland Estate?" Rhiannon asked.

"Ah yes, but Arlan had been previously, so he sought you then." He turned to Arlan. "Did you not?"

"Aye, but prior to that I sought no entry... the first time, in the midst of that skirmish..." Arlan's words trailed to nothing, a crease deepening his frown.

Eifion paused for a moment, chewing his cheek as though he chewed over his next words.

"What is it, Father?" Rhiannon stepped closer.

Eifion's face burst into a grin. "My daughter, do you remember helping an unwell, elderly man in a park near the place you worked in the Other World? The South Inch, if I recall correctly."

Rhiannon's mouth dropped open. "You! I thought so. Didn't I mention that to you, Arlan, when I first arrived? But Father, it seemed you hadn't gone through a portal to the South Inch at that time."

"Aye, for me, that was yesterday. I grew to know the world you lived in through our conversations in which you shared recollections of your previous life. Hence, I knew of the Last Chance Book Shop in the City of Perth, and"—Eifion's eyes twinkled— "I *stalked* you."

Rhiannon's cheeks tugged in a smile, recalling Eifion dressed like a cool professor in a tweed jacket with brown leather elbow patches and his hair in a ponytail.

"I had to be certain that what I have read of this scroll still holds true," Eifion continued. "And it does. I sought to find you, and I did." His face crinkled in a smile filled with pride and eyes holding her in love. "As you see, I am home after filling my will with the desire to return to you all."

"You took a risk, Eifion." Arlan's tone held a reprimand. "I remember being admonished by yourself after making a similar journey..."

Eifion slid his hands up his sleeves and made a noise in his throat. "*I* had the knowledge of the Ancients found in the secret locked scrolls to guide me. You had the blind courage of a man in love. One who also had a Quest to win." His serious glare flicked to Rhiannon, then rested on Arlan.

"Aye, Sage Eifion. And I won the Quest. *And* gained my love." Arlan looked Rhiannon in the eye, a gentle smile on his lips, then his gaze dropped to the sleeping bundle in his arms. "That's how it worked for me then"—Arlan gave an uncomfortable cough—"when I purposefully sought Rhiannon and met her at the Celtic Festival. But still, I didn't know of Rhiannon when I *first* went through during that skirmish near the border."

"Oh"—Eifion stirred his fond gaze from Rhiannon to face Arlan— "the ancient scroll reports, on rare occasions, a person can be *called* through a portal." He turned back to Rhiannon. "Were you seeking Arlan when he came to you the first time for him?"

Rhiannon screwed her mouth to the side. "I was walking the track to the ruins of the Iron Age Fort, then that young guy attacked me." She repressed a shiver.

"And before that? Your thoughts?" Eifion encouraged. "Were they of Arlan?"

Rhiannon's lips pulled in a grin, warmth tainting her cheeks. "Yeah, well. I was drooling over the man who'd kissed me at the Celtic Festival."

Arlan chuckled. "That was I."

She locked her gaze with him, so easily mesmerised by his navy-flecked blue eyes, then she snatched in a breath. "But that doesn't explain all my failed attempts at going through after Arlan. I'm sure I had the right spot, although I never saw a portal as such, just had an idea of its location from where I saw Arlan disappear."

"Oh, you will never see one." Eifion shook his head for emphasis. "By all accounts it is only a very gifted mage who can see a portal. And that would be when it opens at dawn or dusk. Just as yourself, I have never seen, only ever sensed where one might be positioned."

"Wow," Rhiannon replied. "Well, anyway, I tried a million times to go through that portal... but I couldn't." She shook her head gently. "It... stopped... me. Each time." She gave a quick shrug. "So, I didn't try any longer. Father, why did it prevent me from going through?"

Eifion's gaze went into the middle distance, like he did when trying to untangle a problem. The fire crackled in the hearth.

"I wasn't there anymore." Arlan's deep voice broke the pensive silence. "It must have known the one you sought wasn't on the other side of it." He spun to Eifion. "Could that be so?"

Eifion tilted his head from side to side and pursed his lips. "Aye." His tone was almost of surprise. "It may be. But also this: Rhiannon knew not where you were—your location in Dál Cruinne with its geography unknown to her at the time—to think of the place required to find you." After a thoughtful pause, he huffed. "I shall seek access to the locked scrolls in the library here at The Keep. Sage Cénell guards them fiercely."

Footsteps ran to their door, then a hand pelted heavily on the wood. Bàn let himself in, his kilt swinging with his stride, and a scowl sharpening his brow, accentuating his striking features.

Maybe one day I'll get used to how healthy and handsome everyone here is.

Rhynne woke and emitted a low, whining cry.

"Pardon my intrusion." Bàn halted a pace from Arlan and winced, having glanced at Rhynne, whose hands now flew about her, her gurning increasing. "But that Findlay cur is here, seeking an audience with you."

"He is alone?" Eifion asked.

"He has a dog." Bàn lifted a shoulder and let it fall. "But he came on foot. The guards searched him. He's unarmed."

"No horse?" Arlan squinted an eye.

"Here, give her to me." Rhiannon took Rhynne from Arlan. "Find out what it's about."

"Nae, Lady Rhiannon"—Bàn looked at her—"but he specifically asked ye to be present."

Rhiannon's feet froze to the floor, and she held Rhynne closer.

"Ye should come." Arlan nodded once. "We shall discover what he desires."

Rhiannon sat next to Arlan, and Bàn stood on his other side. Her hard wooden chair, now softened by a cushion, wasn't as elaborate as the horse throne of the àrd rìgh.

Arlan's throne.

She glanced at the gold knotwork on the horse seat. Her seat was still rather impressive, though. No horses, but intricate knotwork. It must've taken ages to carve. The Great Hall with its Celtic knot-like carvings, tall windows, and tapestries still sent a tingle to her middle.

"So, we're going for intimidation, then?" She leaned aside to Arlan, her arms empty and feeling odd without Rhynne.

"Aye. Findlay needs to respect the position of àrd rìgh, even if he continues to see me as your *boyfriend*." The corner of his mouth twitched, then he adjusted the ermine collar of the cloak he'd slipped over his shoulders.

Rhiannon's gaze slid to the silver torc sitting around Arlan's neck. He looked so *kingly.*

The tall double doors at the entrance to the Great Hall opened. Two warriors led a man wearing leather armour and mud-stained breeches beneath a thick sheepskin coat that flapped open with each step. His weapon belt held no blade, with a slight gut hanging over it. He pulled off his cloth cap and his hair stuck up, and he walked with his head slightly bowed.

It was Findlay, alright. The detective from the Other World who had followed her, Angus, and Morrigan through the portal. She'd fought him, sort of, at the battle of Monsae. That seemed an age ago. A dog, like a Staffordshire bull terrier, walked at his heel. The guards led him to the plinth where she and Arlan sat, then he kneeled.

Arlan said nothing, but gripped the throne's arms, his knuckles whitening.

Findlay's dog yawned and gave a short whine. Findlay turned his head a fraction and whispered a command for silence.

"Why do you seek an audience?" Arlan's voice rose to the ceiling, and Rhiannon stifled the impulse to flinch.

Findlay kept his head bowed. "My Lord Àrd Rìgh—"

"Ye would name me your sovereign?"

"My lord king, I come begging your mercy. I've been the victim of circumstance. I accidentally joined Lord Ciarán, through innocence. And now I see him for what he is, and I wish to be on the side of right. Your side, Lord Arlan MacEnoicht."

Arlan ran his fingers through his beard at his throat. "You requested my wife, Lady Rhiannon, be present. Why?"

Findlay lifted his head, eyes wide and mouth agape. "I didn't know...you had married." He smiled at her. It seemed genuine. "Congratulations to you both."

"What do you want, Findlay?" Rhiannon wouldn't acknowledge his well wishes. He was a puzzle. He'd seemed a nice policeman in the Other World, honest even. But here, taking up with Ciarán Gallawain. *And now this flip?*

"How do you ascribe innocence to your joining with Gallawain?" Arlan asked, like he'd just read her mind.

"I came through the opening half a day after you, Lady Rhiannon. At sunset." He looked at her. "I longed to be in the beautiful world I spied behind you as you walked through and disappeared with your *cousins*. When I entered Dál Cruinne, in my disorientation, I went down the road, not up it. To the mountains, instead of the sea, ending with myself in Lord Ciarán's service and not in your own, Lord Arlan. I was ignorant of the politics and what was at stake here."

"Ye were at the battle of Monsae. You escaped. You expect me to believe ye have turned?" Arlan's deep voice vibrated in his throat and echoed through the throne room.

"I beg you." Findlay took a step closer, moving to be directly in front of Rhiannon, his raised hands grasping his cap.

The warrior-guards beside him drew their weapons.

"By my blade, he'll betray us if he's allowed into your confidence, my king," Bàn hissed, then moved to Rhiannon's side, grasping his sword hilt.

"No, I won't. Miss Ferguson... Lady Rhiannon, please remember how I endeavoured to keep you safe from the Glasgow gang by organising police protection—"

"Aye, and I nearly lost her to your safe house!" Arlan jolted forward in his seat and Rhiannon placed her hand on his arm.

In the Other World, Findlay had been doing his job and seemed to truly care. Maybe he *was* lost and had thought Ciarán to be okay until he'd been involved in the Monsae battle—on the wrong side—and discovered otherwise. She tightened her grip on Arlan's arm. He faced her, and she raised her eyebrows.

Give him a chance to prove himself. He may be genuine, she willed her face to say.

Besides, he would prove to be a fountain of knowledge on the enemy. Arlan would know this.

Arlan narrowed his eyes. "Where is my brother, Lord Kyle? Ye took him from the aftermath of the battle for Monsae, aye?"

"He's with Lord Ciarán, who wishes to discuss a ransom for him."

No surprise.

"Place Findlay in the dungeon," Arlan ordered the guard. "I will question you at my leisure to discover why Ciarán Gallawain is so slow to advance. If ye have any useful information," he said to Findlay as the guards grabbed him, "it may help sway me."

"There is an imminent dragon attack." Findlay's words jostled through the warriors manhandling him.

Arlan shot out of his seat. "When?"

Rhiannon's gut clenched, and her baby's face filled her mind.

"I don't know," Findlay said. "But soon. I overheard Lord Ciarán speaking with his mage. He can control them."

"Of this, we are well aware. The death of my father, our late àrd rìgh, is the proof of your claim." Arlan lifted his chin in dismissal and the warrior guards dragged Findlay away. "Bàn, organise the placement of hunting bows on the battlements and order our best bowmen to ready themselves."

FOUR

Scattered through the worlds
Are doorways each to the other
Sentient and yielding
Bent to the will of those who seek their access.

LOCKED SCROLL 72
GRAND MASTER LLEW'S SAFE LIBRARY
ISLE OF INNESFARNE

The World of Dál Cruinne
Year 6084 Post Dragon Wars
Western Sovereignty of Dál Gaedhle
The Keep

Warmth brushed away the cold on Rhiannon's cheeks, and she raised her face to the clear spring sky. Their balcony was a sun-trap of a morning. Tucked away at the peaceful side of The Keep that faced the River Ruairidh, their chambers avoided the hustle and bustle of the village and the market below. Rhiannon held Rhynne close, her heart spilling over with the intensity of emotion her baby brought on.

Love. Happiness. She shrugged. Whatever it was, the strength of it brought tears to her eyes.

Rhiannon tucked Rhynne's baby rug around her, tight against the breeze—she slept at last—and placed her in the cradle sitting in a pool of sunshine. Rhiannon sat beside her, tilting her face to the sun once more and resting her arms on her chair. Her limbs grew heavy and warmth seeped in.

Arlan had conferred with sages all morning. Findlay had proven his worth over the past few days and Arlan seemed resigned, if not pleased, that he'd received the man into his service.

A wide *w* of a silhouette approached in the sky above. Drayce must have flown far today in her search for food. They fed her sheep after sheep, but she still went hunting. Arlan often repaid a steading holder for his loss, once proven his dragon was the cause.

The shape grew larger. Definitely a dragon's profile now. So majestic in flight. And faithful to Arlan. Still protective. Her screeches were nearer now.

Odd. Drayce's screeches came from somewhere closer than the creature flying rapidly toward her.

Rhiannon narrowed her eyes, focusing.

That isn't Drayce.

This darker one seemed enormous. Its flight now took it over the river nestled right below The Keep.

It soared close to the curtain wall and headed directly for the battlements. Each downward thrust of wing raced the beast ever nearer.

Shouts rose from the archers along the wall head as long, solid, hunting bows lifted high, their iron arrow-tips glinting in the sunshine. Arlan's dark head, with Bàn's blond hair close beside him, peeked between the crenulations.

Arrows flew from the battlements. Thick, sturdy, hunting arrows with wide white fletching bounced off the side of the dragon. Its long, deep-blue neck seemed to stretch toward the battlements. And Arlan.

Rhiannon lost sight of its head. The dragon's long tail and wide wings were her only view.

Arlan would be burned to death if it was a firebreather and it let go its flames. Her mouth dried.

The beast flew past the corner of the tower and out of Rhiannon's sight.

What's happening?

She leaned over the balcony and peered to the side, now able to see the animal again. It let out a roar, the walls of The Keep seeming to shudder with it. Men yelled, arrows flew, and the dragon soared over the archers. Warriors ducked. Arlan held his head high, his face tracing the path of the beast.

It turned in her direction and followed the wall, which skirted The Keep then ran along to the living quarters.

Closer now, it stared at her with small eyes and never diverted its new flight path.

Very close.

Her hands clenched the balcony masonry, immobile and refusing her brain's command to *move!*

A chill, cooler than any wind the past winter had sent, ran down her spine. She spun, grabbed Rhynne from her cradle then ran inside.

A powerful rush of air blew against her back, and a shadow darkened the balcony. The long back legs of the beast followed her into the chamber, stretching toward her. Reaching from behind, cold, thin, curling talons slid around her waist. The arctic reptilian grip surrounding her midriff intensified and tipped her forward, the thick wool rug of their chamber floor filling her view. With gusts of wind from soundless deep blue wings, her feet left the floor.

"No!"

She let go of Rhynne, dropping her onto the rug with a thud. Rhynne startled awake, her cries growing fainter as the voiceless beast dragged Rhiannon out from her room.

"Arlan!" She grabbed the heavy curtain that covered the balcony entrance to their chambers.

The dragon wrenched her through the balcony, but she held on with a death grip to the bulky curtain fabric, ripping it from its rail hoops. The beast's flight yanked her backward, the drape still in her hands. She let go. Two storeys from the ground, the curtain dropped, landing in a heap.

Rhiannon gritted her teeth, her hair flying wildly about her face, and a seething heat stirred inside. *It will* not *take me.* The dragon's flight whirled her around. Clawed tips of leathery wings caught the edge of her vision while the ground blurred beneath.

"Ahhh!" The cry flew from her mouth, then she swallowed down on breakfast.

Her baby's squeals were now a distance away. "Rhynne!" The wind snatched her cry.

Will I see you again, my baby?

And Arlan... where was he?

I don't want to leave you.

She shook her head, clearing the dizziness, and grabbed the talons around her waist to pull them away from her body. She would rather risk a broken limb crashing to the ground than go wherever this beast wished to take her. Ciarán would be behind it, for certain. The muscles in her forearms burned, but the claws stayed tight.

Drayce's squawks rent the air, her cries loud and right beside Rhiannon. The dragon holding her jolted and spun, dizzying her even more with its spinning flight.

Drayce flew up from beneath her and nosed-punched the dragon's legs. It hissed and snapped back at Drayce, who dodged.

An arrow flew past Drayce, just missing her neck.

Rhiannon thrashed her legs, kicking at nothing. Her fingers curled around ivory-hard claws and her knuckles cracked with the strain.

Shouts wafted over from the battlements, Arlan's voice among them.

The ground sped beneath her—green patched with dirty-grey old snow yet to melt. Nearer to the ground now, the dragon's flight took her toward the river.

Drayce's screams grew earnest. The dragon jolted, harder this time, its grip on Rhiannon's waist loosening. The river wasn't far below. Rhiannon pulled at the talons at the same time Drayce pummelled the dragon again, distracting it. She twisted out of its grasp.

"Drayce!" *Catch me!*

Now only air surrounded her. The dragon's claws and Drayce's squawks receded above, while air blew past, tearing strands of hair away from her face. The ground pulled her towards it. River Ruairidh rushed coldly along its course below, rising to meet her.

Will I survive this?

Water thumped into Rhiannon, knocking the wind from her lungs. Cold enveloped her and the river, freezing from the snowmelt, turned her vision into a brown monochrome.

She surfaced, gasping. Shivering. Her gown dragging her down. Her solar plexus aching while she sucked in air and recovered her wind. She kicked and kept her head above water. Thank heavens the river wasn't deep as it passed below The Keep.

Drayce hovered over her, spreading her wings like a shield, and screaming like a banshee. Above her, arrows rained on the fleeing dragon, bouncing off the massive beast's tough hide. Arlan's shouts came to her from the parapet, punctuated by Douglas' curses.

Damn it, they wasted their time with arrows.

Rhiannon gained purchase on the riverbed, her slippered feet crunching on pebbles. The Keep's granite curtain wall rose ahead of her while she dragged herself through the water. The water-logged material of her gown tangled her legs as she splashed up the bank. *If only I'd worn my breeches.* Her teeth chattered.

Bàn came running to the riverbank. "Get the Lady Rhiannon some blankets and order her servant to stoke the fire in her chamber," he yelled at the nearest caisteal staff while sheathing his sword.

"Where's Rhynne?" Rhiannon's shivering added to the fear in her voice.

Bàn glanced over to the balcony, then down. Rhiannon followed his gaze. No bundle of baby blanket lay in the garden.

"It appears she's safely in your quarters, my lady. There's nae sign of a bairn on the lawn beneath your balcony. Nor do I hear a cry." Bàn took his wool plaid off his shoulder and wrapped it around Rhiannon. "Come, we'll take the shortest way in."

Bàn held her arm in a gentle grip and angled her to the farthest edge of this side of the caisteal to a nook in the stone wall, where a door stood unnoticed.

Huh. Of course Arlan's best friend would be privy to the secret passages of The Keep.

Rhiannon stumbled along, water sloshing out of her shoes. Bàn opened the creaking door and ushered Rhiannon up a narrow staircase to another door, which opened toward him. A tapestry covered the doorway and he pushed the heavy drape forward and edged around the side.

Rhiannon followed, her teeth chattering and her bones as cold as the water, like the burn had flowed into her very marrow.

She stepped out from behind the tapestry into her and Arlan's chambers. Their maidservant stood just inside from the balcony, jiggling Rhynne, whose cries had turned to shrieks and tore at Rhiannon's heart. The maid turned, hastening toward her, but stopped two paces away.

"Oh, my lady, ye are drenched. I shall get ye dry garments." She handed Rhynne to Bàn, who grasped her awkwardly, and scrunched his face at her screams.

Morrigan ran into their room. "Lady Rhiannon, go by the fire and strip off your garments!"

Morrigan took Rhynne from Bàn, who'd held the baby out to her with a tight expression. Morrigan cooed softly, rocking her from side to side. Rhynne's screams settled to upset hiccoughs by the time Rhiannon handed Bàn his plaid and peeled off her skirt. She dropped it by the fire and grasped the hem of her soaked shift, now stuck wet to her torso and legs.

"I shall leave." Bàn fiddled with his soaked plaid, averting his eyes.

Arlan burst into the chamber. "Rhiannon!" He glanced aside to Rhynne in Morrigan's arms as he passed Bàn, then strode straight for Rhiannon, coming to a halt and wrapping his arms around her. She buried her face in the blue tartan plaid of the àrd rìgh sitting across his chest. Her knees gave way with her shivering, his solidity the only thing holding her up. His warm lips covered her face with kisses, intense and relieved.

"I thought I'd lost you." His voice shuddered, then he kissed her some more, seemingly oblivious to her shift and hair soaking his blue tartan kilt and plaid.

"I'm fine." Her teeth chattered less. "Thank heavens for Drayce."

"Aye, I do thank *Tobraichean na beatha* for our wee beast's attachment to ye." He gave a serious, breathy laugh, then he frowned. "A hunting arrow nearly pierced her. That would've killed her. We aimed at the larger dragon... but you were in its claws." He gathered her to himself once more and held tight. "Och, I hope not to see *that* again."

"It was Ciarán's mage, wasn't it?" She spoke into his warmth.

He rested his chin on her head. "I can only assume so from what Findlay says. It didn't appear to be a fire breathing one. Seemingly it had no desire to kill, either. The creature only wanted *you*."

"It nearly got Rhynne, too." A shudder ran through her, from her head to her toes. "Never again."

"Ye must dry and warm yourself." He looked her in the eye. "Ye are well if I return to the council? We have much more to discuss with this new development."

"Aye, go," she said softly.

His forehead remained furrowed, and he stared into nothing, still holding her.

"Arlan?"

"Och." He snapped his attention back to her. "Findlay has spoken of much. Ciarán Gallawain has been quiet over winter regarding movements toward Dál Gaedhle, but the man has forced the allegiance of many more Dál Gallain lairds to himself." He gave a sharp grunt. "He has cannon, of a sort. Plus many other weapons, some beyond comprehension. Och, I must entreat the sages and metalsmiths to hasten their devising of gunpowder and cannon. Now the roads have opened, we can access the coastal caves where Eifion assures me we will find bat droppings for the potassium nitrate George said we require."

She nodded. He pressed his warm lips to her mouth in a gentle kiss, then rested his forehead on hers, his spicy male scent perfusing the air within their embrace. "I love you, my wife." His deep voice caressed her.

"And I you, my husband."

He let go, strode toward the door, pausing by Morrigan to plant a kiss on Rhynne's head peeping out of her wrappings, then left. Bàn nodded in Rhiannon's direction then followed him out.

The room blurred and darkness danced at the edges of her sight.

"Lady Rhiannon!" Morrigan's voice came from a long way away.

She walks through a door that hums, and steps onto green grass within an old ruin. She's been here before. It's the old nunnery on the suburban outskirts of Oxford.

Rhynne cries. Rhiannon looks down at her baby in her arms.

"I'll take her." It's George's voice. "I don't mind, really. It will be like still having you around."

George pushes his glasses up his nose and smiles, his cheeks pinking.

Soft furs cushioned her, warmth seeped into her bones and more furs touched their soft caress to her bare skin. She opened her eyes to the sturdy wooden cross beams of her chamber's ceiling.

"Oh, ye are awake." Morrigan hovered over her. "Ye concerned me for a wee while there." She smiled. "I must return to the council. I will let Lord Arlan know you are fine. And your baby wants to be fed. I shall leave." Morrigan strode out, her tall straight back disappearing through the doorway.

"Here's your wee lass, milady." Rhiannon's maid placed Rhynne on the bed beside her. "I have chores tae do. Ye'll be alright if I go awa' the noo? I'll be back at bedtime, aye?"

"Yes, of course. I'm fine now." She sat bolt upright to prove it. "You can take your leave."

The maid bowed and bustled to the door, shutting it behind her.

Rhiannon turned onto her side, and Rhynne latched onto her breast, ravenous, her little jaw wiggling in time with each mouthful. Soft black lashes, as thick as her father's, sat on her cheeks, fanning from closed lids. Her fine baby hair, a black mat, covered her head. And maybe she'd imagined it, but Rhynne's new born blue eyes had now taken on a mauve hue.

That'd been close.

A bolt, like an electric shock, ran right through Rhiannon.

Dragons. Plus, a war brewing. A war like none she'd ever seen. But with Ciarán's access to other worlds... who knew what those weapons *beyond comprehension* were?

And now it's on our doorstep.

And it'd just got personal. Ciarán Gallawain would stop at nothing to defeat Arlan. Even attacking his family.

Her gaze focussed back on her baby. Her precious child. What if he sent a dragon for *her*? A heat stirred inside.

Not anger... no, I know anger.

When the dragon had lifted her away from Rhynne. That was anger.

This was different—a protective instinct she'd read about. Since Rhynne's birth, it'd flowed through her daily like a raging river. Now this river boiled. All her emotions had honed her warrior skills in on this one tiny person... Rhynne.

But her brawn wasn't enough. She had to use her brains...and other skills.

Eifion seemed certain, and Father was a wise man.

He'd done it too. She remembered well helping him on the South Inch a few days before the Celtic Festival where she'd first met Arlan. There, in the Other World—her world at the time.

She could trust Eifion was right... *Would* trust him.

Bloody Ciarán Gallawain. He'll never get his hands on this *child.*

FIVE

In crafting deception to shine,
Ye do mark the light as lighter
And deepen yet the darkness.

SAGE GLIOCAS
(2870-2962 POST DRAGON WARS)

The World of Dál Cruinne
Post Dragon Wars Year 6084
Eastern Clanlands of Dál Gallain
Lord Ciarán's Tower
The Mage's Workshop

Bram released the power flowing through his *source* and slowly took his hands from the water in the bowl. The room spun, sheaves of hanging dried herbs blurring as he clutched the rim of the stone carved divination bowl, gasping. His legs gave way, all strength gone, and he slid down the side of the pedestal. Hard wood flooring belted his knees, his elbows, and finally his cheek.

Damn Lord Ciarán.

He was not the one risking his life each time they called a dragon into play. Things would be different if that were so.

And blast that Findlay.

He took deep breaths and regained control of the shaking deep within. Thankfully, this dragon, one smaller than the previous dragon he'd controlled, was not a fire breather. It had seemed to require less energy and not taxed him so much.

The room stopped spinning, so he got to his knees, grunting, then used the side of the sturdy divination bowl to pull himself to stand. He grabbed his walking stick from where it leaned against the wall, passing a shining pan base hanging above it. He peered closer.

More grey streaks through his long, dark hair. Magic took its toll, as it was wont to do.

He stepped down the stone stair, grasping tight to the rope that passed for a banister rail. His bones were as wax, and if he fell, they were sure to not bend but snap. If only he had a mage assistant, an eager acolyte like he himself once was. But Innesfarne had been displeased. The mage masters had refused his request, their disapproval of Lord Ciarán's efforts to rediscover portals explicit in their scribed reply. His second request to provide information on the magical workings of portals, firmly rebuffed.

So here he stayed, as ordered by the mage masters themselves, sole pursuer of Lord Ciarán's assigned task without the resources to fully achieve it. Perhaps he had been a fool to think he would have the support of the venerated Grand Master Llew.

Bram coughed and spat the phlegm into a cloth. He'd had an autumn and a winter searching for and deciphering this magic himself, accompanied—as usual—by the hot breath of Lord Ciarán continually in his ear. The man pushed him so. Patience was not one of his attributes. And how he'd ranted when deep winter hindered the search. Bram forced out a breath. He'd only wished for a reprieve from the lord's curses, but that had led to a day in a snowstorm near a suspected portal site. Bram coughed again. Aye, it lingered, and his lungs, now scarred from the winter fever, still ached.

He finally reached Lord Ciarán's library, the man's inner sanctum.

Murmurings came from behind the door, which opened. Lord Kyle sat by Lord Ciarán's desk, his head bent in the perusal of a scroll. Not in a dungeon like any other prisoner would be.

Nae, this one held for ransom had a special place in Lord Ciarán's heart.

The place of sonship.

Bram knocked, and foot tread echoed on the wooden floor, approaching the open door.

"Ah!" Lord Ciarán's hand rested on the handle, his eyes dark and long greying hair in a plait down his back. "Come. Tell me all." He spoke in clipped tones. "Particularly why I do not see the Lady Rhiannon in my courtyard having been deposited there by your pet." He slid his hands behind him.

So, he endeavoured to control himself, then. Good, I wish not for a slapping.

Bram shuffled in, using his stick in a heavy manner, and leaned on it to remain upright while he faced Lord Ciarán.

"MacEnoicht's beast attacked the dragon, worrying it like a terrier until it dropped—"

"But you control the animal, do you not? Or so you, and those hoary heads on the Isle of Innesfarne, have led me to believe." Lord Ciarán tapped his foot.

"If the animal is under any stress, it will not always comply."

Lord Ciarán need not know the whole truth. At times, Bram had made use of the man's arrogance. Too proud to enquire further on the subjects that he gave the impression of expertise. Bram stifled a scoff. How this lord considered himself an expert on magic, Bram would never comprehend. Promised as a child to the arts, Lord Ciarán now scorned magic as beneath him. The man was an enigma.

An ache of the head clamped Bram's temples, joining one already there.

Nae, Lady Rhiannon's baby had cried, and she herself had struggled with a might almost animal-like from the grasp of the dragon in his control. It had torn at his heart. He could not do it.

"Ye have failed me, Bram," Lord Ciarán said.

"I ask for your pardon." He placed his gaze on his feet. "Findlay is there at The Keep. I saw him on the battlements as hunting arrows flew. The animal was bruised from such."

Lord Ciarán grunted. "Ensconced himself already, has he?" He snorted out a breath and spun to his bookshelf. "He *was* of use with regards to portals but that fount of knowledge soon dried. His life is forfeit if he reveals one iota—"

"I have made contact with the mages in Dál Gallain." Bram lifted his gaze. "We meet through our—"

"Yes, yes, your *magick goblet*." Lord Ciarán flicked a dismissive wave, hiding none of his disdain. "But we require closer contact, and those self-designated morally upright lords in Dál Gaedhle deign not to employ mages."

Bram blinked, his heart speeding its pace. Now would be the time to use his idea. Mayhap it would secure Lord Ciarán's favour once more.

"There are many refugees. We can employ mages in the guise of such who can enter the village of The Keep, or anywhere that hints at the activity of ... war... preparation." Bram shut his mouth at the wide-eyed expression on Lord Ciarán's face.

"A spy *network* within enemy lines." Awe filled the lord's tone. "Findlay spoke of such occurring in the Other World when a war was cold. *Brilliant.*"

Bram's shoulders eased.

"Well, go!" Lord Ciarán's shout echoed right through him, jolting his shoulders back to stiffness. "Totter on that stick of yours to your bowl and get on with it!"

"The mages will wish payment, for they risk much."

Lord Ciarán leaned closer, so close his breath brushed Bram's face, revealing his luncheon of a dish containing onion.

"They will be *well* rewarded."

Six

— • —

Marriage is a journey two walk together.
It is a story of forgiveness and redemption,
Mirroring all of life.

SAGE GLIOCAS
(2870-2962 POST DRAGON WARS)

The World of Dál Cruinne
Year 6084 Post Dragon Wars
Western Sovereignty of Dál Gaedhle
The Keep

Arlan walked along the corridors of The Keep to his and Rhiannon's chambers, his spurred boots clicking with each step. Through the open archways, the mountains darkened to purple while the last of the sun's light left the sky and bird chatter filled the deepening dusk. Kingship weighed heavily on his shoulders, as weighty as the cylindrical tube of cast metal the sages had presented to him. It was *almost* cannon-like. There had been progress, but the appearance of the dragon today had sent a surge of urgency through him. Cannon balls would wound the beast. Perhaps even enough to kill.

Hunting arrows are mere toothpicks!

He grunted and opened the door to their chamber where Rhiannon and Rhynne, and all the joys of being husband and father, would greet him. Just inside the room, the fire's heat hit his face and bare arms, matching the warmth within. He surveyed the room; glowing coals filled the hearth, Rhynne's cradle sat empty, and furs piled high on their bed. He stepped closer. The bedding smelled of heat, baby, and warm Rhiannon. He pulled back the furs.

Empty.

A light tapping came from the door and the servant woman entered, curtseying.

"Begging your pardon, lord king." She stayed by the door. "How is the Lady Rhiannon?"

He breathed in through his nostrils. "Where *is* the Lady Rhiannon? For neither she nor the babe are here."

The woman started. "I know not, lord." She hurried to the privy and returned, shaking her head.

Arlan treaded to the door, an unease rippling between his shoulder blades, and ordered a guard to fetch Bàn.

"I shall enquire of the other servants, my lord king." The woman curtseyed and hastened past him down the hall.

A scuffling came from inside his room, and he raced back in. Rhiannon appeared from behind the tapestry that covered the hidden passage. She wore breeches and leather armour with a plaid of the àrd rìgh's tartan loosely over one shoulder.

He strode to her and gathered her to him. "Where have you been? I was worried." Her body held warmth, apart from her cool arms. Her shoulders trembled. He drew her closer and placed his lips on hers. She returned the kiss, though her lips held a tremor. "Come to the fire, ye are cold." He walked her to the hearth, its heat enveloping them both. "Where's Rhynne? Were you outside? I see ye found our secret exit."

Rhiannon remained silent.

"Have you given her to a nurse maid? Ye must have needed rest after your ordeal." He snorted a laugh. "Our babe is too young to know what danger ye were in. Thank *Tobraichean na beatha.*" He sat her down on the deep cushioned couch, then slipping his arm around her sat by her side. "I'm so sorry the beast lifted you, and I see it has affected ye so. I promise—"

Her trembling shoulders stiffened. "No. You can't promise. Not safety. Not that there won't be any more dragons. Not that a war won't hurt our baby. Not now it's here. A dragon was right in our home, and all our defences did *nothing!*" Her words held vehemence.

Arlan's mouth went slack.

"Not when mages control dragons at Ciarán Gallawain's command." She jumped out of his arms, then faced him as she stood at the hearth. The fire light gave her hair a glow and outlined her muscled physique now returned to her pre-pregnant definition. "The man has a vendetta against you, Arlan. Taking Dál Gaedhle isn't enough for him. He wants you. He wants me. He wants our baby. We can fight back, but she can't."

The hairs on his arms stood on end.

"Where is our baby?" He rose and grasped her upper arms. Her whole body felt rigid and immovable beneath his hands. "Where have you been, Rhiannon?"

"It is the best solution."

"Ye aren't making sense." He leaned in closer. "Tell me, where is my daughter?"

"Safe"—she lifted her face to his; her gaze, direct and close, held a hint of defiance—"in the Other World."

"What?" Arlan's vision filled with the mauve of Rhiannon's eyes. The crackling fire, the murmur of voices outside their door, and Drayce landing on their balcony, were all drowned out by the thudding in his temples. "You took... How? *Why?*" Rhiannon blinked at his words in her face. "We will never get her back!"

The fire's heat seeped past Rhiannon's body but did naught to halt the chill stepping determinedly down his spine.

"Yes, we will." Rhiannon held her tone level. "It worked. I did what Eifion said and thought of where and when to go. *And* come back. I've been gone from here only moments."

"For how long were you there? Nae"—he shook his head— "I care not! Tell me, where is my *Rhynne?*"

Servants standing at their open door flinched at his shout.

"George is caring for her until—"

"George!" His word lifted the stray hairs at the side of her face. *Why him?*

"Until it's all over here, then I'll get her," Rhiannon said. "It'll only be a couple of hours there."

He let go of her and stood back—he had to—otherwise, he would have gripped her harder.

"Ye do not trust me to care for *my* child?" A deep, dark pain, like something solid, sat in his chest. *Nae, in his soul.* "You think so little of me as a husband and father that ye would give our babe—the child of *my* body—to another man to protect?"

"Arlan. It's safer there. George is nowhere near a war. Or *dragons!*"

"Ye said I have always made you feel safe."

"This"—Rhiannon waved her hands around her in an all-encompassing manner— "is bigger than *you.*" She yelled the last word.

His breath came in starts, so he willed it to a rhythm.

"Ye have betrayed me," he ground out.

Her eyes widened. "But Arlan—"

"Bàn! Where is Bàn?" His shout filled their room.

He stood away from her; his desire to keep his searing insides from striking out kept him from nearing her. Rhiannon stood tight-lipped, head held high, and arms straight against her sides. Shouts rang down the hall, then footsteps arrived at their door.

"I'm here, Lord Arlan." Bàn spoke from the doorway.

"Come in, sword-brother." He didn't lift his eyes from Rhiannon. "I have a task that only you, my truest friend, can accomplish." He turned to the guard at the door. "Summon Sage Eifion! And shut the door."

Rhiannon stood stock still, the trembling now sneaking into her core.

"Please understand," she began, but Arlan raised a hand, palm out. *Is he shushing me?* Her insides boiled. "I'll not be silenced!"

"Ye have had your say. Done your deed." Arlan's nostrils flared. "Now I must *fix* it."

Bàn stood by his side. He looked from Arlan to her, then back again.

"Lord Arlan, ye wished to see me?" A crease sat between Bàn's brows, and his shoulders twitched.

"Aye, Bàn, I need you." Arlan spoke low, his voice barely audible.

Bàn stepped closer. "Arlan, if it's something between you and your wife, I dinnae think I have a place—"

"Bàn, Rhiannon has taken Rhynne to the Other World."

Bàn's twitching stilled, and he turned to face her. That crease deepened. *That's right Bàn, be your usual judgemental self.*

"I need you to get my baby girl back," Arlan continued in his quiet voice.

"But surely her mother—"

"Nae, Bàn, I need you, my sword-brother and someone I can *trust*, to bring her home to me." Arlan's voice seemed hollow, and he stood motionless, his scowl never leaving her.

Bàn fiddled with the handle of the dirk at his belt and his cheek danced as he chewed it. He turned to speak into Arlan's ear. He would've meant to be quiet, speaking out of her hearing, but his voice came over to her all the same.

"Arlan, I do not wish to be the one in between ye and your wife. Besides, I know not that world."

Arlan snapped his head to face him directly, and Bàn shifted his weight to his back foot.

"Bàn, I know you can get my daughter for me. Eifion will gift ye with the tongue." He faced her. "Rhiannon will tell you where she is."

"I will go," Rhiannon said, then pressed her lips together hard.

Arlan glanced at her mouth and continued. "Nae, you will not."

"But—"

"You will do as this àrd rìgh orders." Arlan's voice vibrated in her ribcage. "Ye will inform Lord Bàn how to get there from the portal that opens at my father's memorial stone."

Bàn started. "There's one so close? I still dinnae wish to be—"

"Ye will do this for me, aye?" Arlan reached out and placed his hand on Bàn's shoulder, gripping it gently. "Not as a laird serving his king, but as a friend."

Bàn bowed his head. "Aye, sword-brother."

"Thank you, Bàn," Arlan said in a husky voice, then his gaze slid back to Rhiannon and lingered.

His forehead creased and his eyes narrowed in that universal expression of pain, and the soft gulp as he swallowed reached her by the fire. His shoulders rose and fell in time with his breathing, and he stood in utter muteness.

Rhiannon's limbs shook, and she still held her fists curled, with her throat closing in on itself.

He didn't get it.

Rhynne is safe there! She'd yell it at him—again—but his glare kept her mouth tight.

Eifion opened the chamber door, eyeing all three of them.

"What is amiss?" He surveyed the room. "Where is my granddaughter?"

Arlan didn't turn, but kept his piercing stare on her. Bàn rubbed his upper lip with his thumb and looked at the floor.

"Ye summoned me, my àrd rìgh." Eifion walked to stand in between Arlan and herself. "What do you require of your advisor-sage?"

"Ask my wife." Arlan spoke through his teeth. "Your daughter."

A shiver ran through her, the skin on her scalp crawling.

Eifion turned and raised his brows, his mouth slightly open. "Rhiannon?"

"Eifion, Father, you'll understand this." She took a breath, gathering her thoughts while Arlan's pain stabbed at her resolve. "I've taken Rhynne to a safe place till this war is over. Dragons, and whatever Ciarán has found weapon-wise from my world—the Other World... means it will be a tough war." The darkness sitting around Arlan's eyes and the tightness to his mouth tore at her heart. "It will be a dangerous war. I want our baby to live, Arlan..." Her voice dried up.

What have I done?

But I couldn't ask you. You would have said no.

She turned her gaze to Eifion, his expression undecipherable. He frowned, his mouth dancing, like he wished to say something, then he folded his hands in his robe, blanking his features to neutrality.

"What do ye wish, my lord king?" He turned to face Arlan as he spoke.

"Gift Bàn with the language. Send him through safely to get Rhynne and return. I'll tell him what he needs to live in that world for the brief time he'll be there." He nodded to Bàn. "I shall give ye jewels to sell for the money they use in the Other World. Ye can do this at a shop named *Pawn*. And my *wife*"—he forced the word out. *Could he not even say my name?* — "will tell ye, Bàn, where George lives." Arlan strode to the door.

But I love you, my husband. And *our precious, precious daughter.*

Eifion followed Arlan, leaving her alone with Bàn.

Arlan stomped out through the door, servants scattering in front of him, hastily finding tasks to attend. Eifion's steps followed while Bàn's deep rumbles floated through the doorway behind Arlan.

"Arlan." Eifion spoke in a gentling manner.

"She has gouged a chunk from my heart, Eifion. My baby girl is not *here*. The joy and all that is good and innocent in my life, removed by the love of my heart." His voice crushed to a whisper.

He had no actual words for it, his thoughts only a jumble. He opened his mouth to speak, but nothing would come out, and what he wished to say sat, churning there. A sigh was all he could utter.

A thin hand rested on his shoulder. "Arlan, son of my heart, she was scared—"

"Of course, ye will defend her. You who are her father." His voice came out like gravel.

"Try to understand her actions. She was concerned for her child's safety. I... perhaps am to blame for informing her of a near portal and how to use one accurately."

"Nae. To use it was her *choice*. She trusts me not, Eifion. She gave me no say in this. What kind of father... *husband* does she think me?"

He let his breath out slowly. He would blow the heated emotions away. They were of no help now the deed was done. "I'm angry at her."

"I know."

"She has hurt me."

"Aye, she has."

"She has taken my baby girl from me." He clenched his jaw in a vain attempt to crush the overwhelming emotions.

"You must allow her to explain." Eifion angled his head. "Perhaps when both of you are less stirred." Eifion stepped in front of him, looking him in the eye. "You know what ye must do."

"But—"

Hoary eyebrows rose.

"Aye. Forgive her." Arlan's answer came out harder than he'd intended. "Forgive the one person I believed would never betray me."

"Work on it, for it will take time." Eifion nodded his encouragement.

"My faithful and true brother, Bàn, will go. I am too involved with this impending war to even look for my babe myself!" His voice broke then, broken by the hot tears on his cheeks. "I dare not send Rhiannon. I am unsure of her intentions. If she went, I may never see either my wife or my child again." He swiped the tears from his face. "I must inform Bàn of George's fondness for Rhiannon. How the man competed for her affections. Och, he may resist. Refuse Bàn's request to return Rhynne! Wanting a part of Rhiannon to be with him always." He swallowed. "I ken I would."

"Arlan, I know not the man but—" Eifion patted his shoulder. "Aye, each sunrise and sunset will be an anxious awaiting until they return."

The heat from the fire pelted Rhiannon's back. Arlan stormed out the door. Eifion shut it, giving her an unreadable look through his thick, grey eyebrows. He would be practicing diplomacy, but as her father, she'd put him in a difficult place.

Damn. The two men she loved the most *both* angry at her.

Bàn hadn't trotted after Arlan like a faithful dog. *That's a first.*

"Where do I go once in the Other World?" Bàn looked at her from beneath a tight brow, and his deep voice had a force to it.

Rhiannon held her chin high, squaring her shoulders and pressing against the tremble in her core. "I don't want to tell you."

"The high king has commanded you. So, whatever ye had desired your actions to achieve—"

"I know! Okay?" She had only wished for Rhynne's safety, but that was now immaterial compared to the order Arlan had given Bàn. She blinked, willing the tears not to come. "If you end up where I did"—she began, reluctance spilling into her tone—"when I set all my thoughts on George, you'll be in Oxford. Well, just outside of it at an old medieval ruin. Godstow Nunnery. I'll write instructions for how to get to George's place from there."

"And George's woman caring for the bairn... What is her name?" He stepped toward her.

"George isn't married. It didn't look like he had a girlfriend, either."

Bàn stopped mid-stride. "Ye would give your bairn to the sole care of a man?"

"George is a good man. He's quite capable. The women of the Other World don't always spend their entire days minding children, even their own."

Bàn crossed his arms, tucking his chin and accentuating his scowl. He opened his mouth, sure to offer his opinion on their behaviour. *And on mine!*

"Don't you judge me, Bàn Lùthas! You're not a parent."

His mouth remained open.

"You're always so quick to criticise. Anyone would think you were jealous. You've got a real man-crush on my husband."

His nostrils flared and his arms tensed, just like they did before he clouted someone with that sword of his. He wouldn't dare touch her!

"Your husband is a far better parent in this instance. How dare ye take his bairn from him." He didn't raise his voice, but his whisper held a menacing tinge, sending shivers marching down her spine.

His rapid breath brushed her face, even from where he stood a pace away. He stared at her, looking from one eye to the other. She repressed a flinch.

No, I won't let him intimidate me.

If she were back in the Other World, she would tell Bàn where he could place his comments.

"Where I was raised, women don't let people or circumstances force them into anything," she said. "If they can improve things for themselves and their children—like being safe—they do. They have rights when it comes to their children—"

"And fathers do not?"

I huffed. "Look. I know... I acted in haste. I'll admit that. And I won't go against my husband's wishes—"

"Ye should have thought o' those in the first place."

She shut her mouth, pressing down on her lips and the sting from Bàn's whiplash words.

Bàn stood there, mouth hard but eyes softening. Although at this moment he seemed quick to condemn, she'd always sensed his fondness for her. Her thoughts flashed back to the impressed widening of his eyes when they'd first met at The Keep, his dimples revealing themselves with his smile when she'd mentioned Arlan had spoken of him, and his almost flirty comments, gentle brushes of his hand and lingering looks when he'd stood close to her while he'd taught her sword skills—these all now did a replay in her mind. She blinked.

Oh, the man has a crush on me, too.

If her baby had to come back, then she must always be protected. Guarded throughout her return journey through a portal. And what better warrior, apart from her father, was there to bring her home?

"My husband insists on retrieving our daughter. He's the high king, so I won't contradict his orders to you." She stood closer, then whispered right into Bàn's face. "If you love me"—he started at her comment, fractionally, but remained close, his Adam's apple bobbing— "don't mess up. Bring back my baby Rhynne and protect her with your shield arm and sword, in the Other World as well as ours."

SEVEN

For the heart of a true brother
Shirks not at discomfort,
Sneers at pain,
Endures shame and scorn,
And would give his very self for the other.

SAGE GLIOCAS
(2870-2962 POST DRAGON WARS)

The World of Dál Cruinne
Year 6084 Post Dragon Wars
Western Sovereignty of Dál Gaedhle
By The Memorial Stone

Bàn shucked on the black leather jacket Angus had acquired during his time with Morrigan retrieving Lady Rhiannon from the Other World. He fastened the garment using the *zip*—as Angus named it—with difficulty, for it pulled tight across his chest. But it would have to do.

The night had been long, with Arlan, Angus and Morrigan's instruction on Rhiannon's world and Eifion laying his hands on him, to gift him with the foreign tongue.

Eifion had used magic and Bàn had gritted his teeth... and submitted.

Only for my sword-brother. Arlan, only for you.

Bàn secured his sword at his waist for readiness and concealment. Arlan had described that world to him—a dangerous place, but he'd warned against displaying his weapons.

Bàn closed the door to his moonlit chamber in The Keep. He would be back in a short time.

He rode through the grey pre-dawn with Arlan, Rhiannon, and Eifion. A round moon sat above the mountains in the east, its light still shining on the path while they rode in silence through the sleepy village and over the bridge to the stone memorial of the late àrd rìgh. Arlan's face imitated the stony sarsen, and Rhiannon held herself tight on her white mare. They dismounted then Bàn followed Eifion to the dark, shadowed rock looming before him.

Chill air touched his skin, his arm hairs rising. He'd faced wild beasts as a boy assisting the youth of the clan to protect the cattle, fought cruel warriors—now one himself, and pulled his best friend from the flame of a dragon.

But to travel by the means of *magic* to another *world*. He shook his head, steadying his pumping heart.

'Twas incomprehensible.

But go he would, for the sake of those he loved.

"Stand there, Lord Lùthas." Sage Eifion pointed to the very base of the standing stone. "Be ready when I direct."

The sun spread its glimmer along the western horizon, now edged in silver.

A warm, strong hand squeezed his shoulder. "Thank you, sword-brother. I am indebted, for I ken ye have... misgivings when it comes to things of magic. But return soon with my precious treasure, I beg you."

"Go!" Eifion's voice held command and urgency.

Bàn stepped closer to the rock and glanced aside to Rhiannon's tear-filled face glistening in both the light of the sun and the light of the moon.

Then he stepped into a rock and passed through.

Into nothing.

It swirled, and noise collided with sound.

He thudded on all fours to green, grassed earth, grunting. He stood, staggering, surrounded by aged stone walls, empty windows, and nae roof.

"What?"

He waited till the world stopped spinning, then walked along neatly clipped grass to a gap in the ancient walls broken by time, then on out of the shell of a building.

"Aye. Rhiannon said it was a ruin."

A green meadow sat to his right where, on the fence bordering it, dew drops on a neat spider's web glistened in the strange golden light of this world's dawn. He followed a path, passing a stand with pictures and words. He read it.

Godstow Nunnery.

"Och! It makes sense. I can read it. Eifion, I am indebted to you."

He walked past a closed tavern, then along beside a road that traversed a larger bridge over four long lines of a shiny metal. Then across a canal and onto wide streets with houses. He adjusted his sword, tucking it further into his jacket so its scabbard only showed a touch at the hem. None here appeared armed. They walked quickly past him, all with faces bent over an object in their hands. Some even spoke to it. They did not look up, but still avoided colliding with him as they passed on the narrow dark strip on which he walked beside the road.

The moving cart they named a car, sat in front of most houses and some passed him in the street. Angus had spoken of these in depth. Some made a whine, but others, such a grumble. He recalled the growling of the armoured jeep they'd encountered at the portal where Arlan had fought Gallawain.

Bàn squeezed his eyes tight, shaking his head. Nae. Never.

A horse for me!

He walked a ways, following Rhiannon's directions, then came to the street and the house she'd shown on her map. It would be George's. A car sat on the hard paved yard of the dwelling, and the door of the house squeaked open. He hid behind the wall of tall leafy shrub that fenced the front of the dwelling, securely out of sight of the young woman who now stood on the paving by the car.

So, George did have a woman. A wave of relief washed over him. She would have cared for the babe. Rhiannon's comments on the attitude of women in this world came to mind. Och, if George's woman did not care for Rhynne herself, she would have ensured *someone* minded her, surely? He peered through the leafy foliage. The woman leaned her tall frame against the car and looked down at an object glowing in her hand.

A *mobile* phone? It must be.

She smiled at it. Young, with dark hair tied back, she wore the same kind of jeans he'd borrowed from Angus. The bag on her shoulder slipped off and landed on the ground, but she didn't notice, absorbed as she was with the phone in her hand.

Was a woman so easily distracted suited to the responsibilities of a caring for a bairn?

The door opened again, and a man of middle age stepped out, then locked the front door. A short man—Angus had warned him that the men of this world were mostly smaller—with grey peppering his hair, and his clothes were not fine. Not, in any sense, noble-looking. Arlan worried this man would resist. But to take the babe by force, he wouldn't do. It would be too unfair a contest.

The man turned and pushed gold-rimmed spectacles up the bridge of his nose with one finger while he held a small object in his other hand. Lights on the car flashed orange, the car itself emitting a *click*.

Bàn covered his mouth, smothering his exclamation.

If this was George, and his description fit the one Rhiannon had supplied, who cared for baby Rhynne while he and his woman were absent? For George now stood at the car, opening a door to enter it.

"So, Rhynne." George spoke the English clearly. "Do you want me to pick you up after college today and drop you off at martial art class?"

"No, Dad," the young woman answered him across the top of the car. "I'll find my way to the dojo tonight. Thanks." She opened the car door and got in.

Bàn's cry escaped him, the clunk of shutting car doors covering his yelp. The car came out of the drive. He spun and turned away as the car went along the road past him.

Rhynne.

The street returned to quiet. Honking came from the far distance. Dogs barked.

Bàn closed his gaping mouth, clunking his teeth together, his brow tightening by the moment.

She was not a bairn?

He rubbed his thumb briskly across his top lip, grazing the skin in his effort.

I have come too late.

That lovely, but distracted, young woman was Arlan's offspring, fully grown.

He ran back to the ruin, sweat dripping down his temples. The light from this sun, now gaining its height above the horizon, had warmth in it. He ran all the way, unzipping the leather jacket, for it held his body's heat too well. The ruin sat in long shadow, and he stopped in the centre, in the place he recalled he'd landed.

"Take me back!" he yelled with arms outstretched.

Naught happened. He remained.

He looked at the sky, now a bright blue. "I have failed ye, Arlan." His voice cracked. "Before I have even begun."

He leaned over, resting his hands on his thighs.

He would wait for sunset and return to start again at the right time. When Rhynne was still the squealing babe in arms.

His gut tightened. Nae, if he stepped through the stone empty handed, it would hurt Arlan and worry Rhiannon beyond distraction.

He was here. And so was Rhynne. He would devise another way. Regroup and re-plan, as any warrior would.

Rhynne was a young woman now. From Rhiannon's comments, the women here would not easily be swayed to do aught they did nae want to.

"Ah, a young woman brought up in the ways of *this* world."

Dad? Rhynne had called George *dad*. Perhaps it was a term of endearment here. It sounded so much like *Dadaidh* in his own tongue. So, they were close. Of course, she had most likely spent all her life with him. He would be her protector, her provider... father.

He could rip her from George, take her back kicking and screaming, and present her to her real father, distraught and rebelling.

"Och. No!" That was not the way. Not *his* way.

So, he must encourage her to go with a stranger.

"Nae simple task." It will take time.

Regroup and re-plan.

He would require a place to stay, and a thing named ID. *Hmm.* Angus spoke of those who could forge the plastic card required. He would discover them and seek to obtain the cards needed in *this* time in the Other World.

He would follow her to this dojo, and learn her martial art.

"And so, I will make myself her friend."

EIGHT

Beware a greed-filled heart,
It is apt to overstretch the mark.

SAGE GLIOCAS
(2870-2962 POST DRAGON WARS)

The World of Dál Cruinne
Year 6084 Post Dragon Wars
Eastern Clanlands of Dál Gallain
Lord Ciarán's Tower

The map laying atop Ciarán's desk brought a smile to his lips. He had slowly shaded almost half of Dál Cruinne—the eastern portion, Dál Gallain. He leaned over the map, tapping his teeth with a fingertip. Some lairds near the border had still not taken him seriously. The mages with whom Bram had connected in his bowl would do their work for him here in the northeast. His next campaign, though, would be across the border to the west. To Dál Gaedhle.

Now he would begin his push. He would have his faithful lairds gather their warbands, for soon it would be time to move to Mòr Cath Làraich, the wide glen that would be the site of his great battle. But it would start with something grand. Perhaps the retaking of Monsae.

That still stung. *How dare they.*

In time, he would regain it. He had more faithful warriors than ever. Aye, they knew from whence came their reward.

But first he had something more grand and more pertinent than Monsae, and a greater snub to the nose of that whelp, MacEnoicht.

The approaching clatter of horses' hooves caught Ciarán's hearing, and he strode down the stairs two steps at a time, shading his eyes from the glare bouncing up from the paved courtyard. Galan rode his steed. At one time an assistant to Bram, he now did for Ciarán in the special tasks he assigned. The warriors who had assisted Galan in this particular one ambled behind him, sitting shambolic in their saddles, and covered in much red dust. A mule dragged a cart on which sat a cannon. It was the *light artillery* of which Findlay had spoken on Galan's first return from his journey through the portal Bram had discovered in the east of Dál Gallain. That world had been a land of heat, curious animals and a Zulu war, as Findlay had named it.

"Success this time, young Galan." He left the sneer in his tone. The imbecile needed to think when gathering these weapons. He glanced at the abandoned jeep from the war of the Gulf, or so Findlay called it. He grunted. At least a cannon on wheels did not require the liquid they named *petrol* to make it move. The chunky-wheeled jeep, now left untidily in the corner of his courtyard, remained a constant reminder of the many setbacks that had occurred.

"Take it straight to the smithy," he said to the lad.

"We have travelled far these past days, lord." Galan eased himself off his mount.

Ciarán held his stare. Galan's shoulders dropped a fraction, then he bowed his head, turned to the warriors dismounting, and ordered them to assist in wheeling the cannon.

Ciarán rubbed his hands. He would now utilise the alchemists Bram had sequestered. Apparently, they were *not* mages. Ciarán pursed his lips. This gunpowder not magic then? He cared not, as long as it worked. The caisteals of Dál Gaedhle would not withstand a bombarding.

"The blacksmith has devised a method to ensure the cannon balls are spherical. So, they do not jam in the tube and cause it to rupture." Bram's voice approached from behind.

Ciarán flinched. "Do not sneak upon me in such silence, mage," he spat at Bram, who now stood beside him. *The mage is wont to take liberties.*

"Pardon, lord." Bram gave a slight bow. "The mages are on their way to Dál Gaedhle."

"Very good." He glared at Bram. "At last."

"Ye will be interested to know," the mage continued, "MacEnoicht has commissioned his sages and metalworkers in the making of cannon."

Ciarán sucked in a breath. "Ah, inevitable after his sojourn in the Other World, of which"—he cast his gaze around him then changed what he would say— "your informant reports." He ground his teeth. "We must hasten our progress on the matter. What is the latest on the falling out between Dál Gaedhle's high king and his spouse? It is such a gift that servants talk."

"He has sent Lord Bàn to retrieve their daughter."

Ciarán lessened his glare. "Through the newly discovered nearby portal?"

"Aye, but he has not yet returned, and it has been many days."

"Discover her whereabouts." Ciarán jiggled his hands clasped behind his back. "I shall order Galan to send his best warriors through. Also, one with intelligence enough to seek and find a babe in a strange world. They must get her before Lord Bàn of House Lùthas. He must *not* return her to her parents."

Bram faced him, a dark eyebrow cocked.

"What!" He spat the word.

"Lord Ciarán, ye do not ask for much." The mage's tone held a sardonic note.

He stepped closer to his servant, lowering his voice. "Ye are the one with *magick*. Make it work! I would have MacEnoicht weakened by grief over his lost babe. And when I produce her, 'twill be more power to hold over him."

A sheen covered the mage's forehead, and with eyes lowered, his look froze.

Chatter echoed out of the circular tower and spilled into the courtyard, soon followed by Lord Kyle and his man. Ciarán eased his shoulders, purposefully bringing them down from his ears. The comments from young Kyle were constant some days. The lad often spoke drivel, and he seemed to have no sense of when to shut his mouth!

Son or no, it was an irritation.

He turned his face away from him. *I have no time for this today.*

"Bram, have you heard any dissention in the ranks? Surely there are some who are not happy with their new high king?"

"I shall enquire of our mages once they are in place." Bram observed the warriors who dragged the wheeled cannon past on their way to the smithy, a scent of rotten eggs accompanying it. "I have sent most to The Keep and the nearest lords."

"That is a waste of time." Kyle spoke in Ciarán's other ear, and he and the mage faced Kyle.

"And why?" Ciarán's breath stalled in his throat a touch. *At times, 'tis as though I look in a mirror at my younger self.*

A pity the young man had nae idea of battle strategy.

"All those faithful to my brother are situated in the lands closest to the high king's seat, The Keep. It is those who are not geographically close who are not so enamoured with him. I think particularly of Clan Callaghan. The clan chief lost his heir in the Quest. It is rumoured they blamed Arlan directly for it." Kyle leaned closer and whispered in a conspiratorial manner, "He left a door open, apparently. Also, my brother spurned the advances of the second daughter of the Duisdale clan chief."

"Ye will work on them, Bram, with your network. Ensure a *refugee* enters the caisteals of those who grumble against their new high king."

Bram nodded.

Galan approached from the direction of the forge and gave a curt bow. "The blacksmith sets to his task. He has employed the services of a man who is an expert in making moulds for molten iron, my lord."

Ciarán grunted a brief acknowledgment. "I have another task, young Galan, but I need you here, so ye must entrust it to a worthy warrior. But ye shall enter more portals for me"—he spun to Bram— "for which *ye* shall search."

"Aye." Bram gave a deferential bow.

"Whereupon"—he faced Galan once more— "ye shall return with not only weapons but those who know their use. Bring me mercenaries, armed and with ammunition sufficient for our task. Offer them gold, jewels, or whatever they desire. My army would be superior to that of the àrd rìgh of Dál Gaedhle. Choose the best warriors and weapons from whichever realms these portals lead."

NINE

'Twas no dream, only thoughts in colour.

VISIONS AND SAYINGS OF THE BLIND LADY SAGE

Our World, 2036
Oxford
Three Months After Bàn's Arrival

George closed the backdoor behind him and plonked his briefcase on the kitchen table among a pile of bills and a magazine on ancient warfare. He scrunched up old, scribbled sticky-notes from himself to Rhynne—the most frequent mode of communication between them since she started her part-time job.

Apart from texting. *Hmm.* Young adults these days. Noses in their phones worse than he'd been.

He wandered toward the lounge room where the television blared, echoing loud grunts and slaps into the hall.

Another martial arts movie.

Standing in the doorway beside Rhynne, who sat on the couch eating snacks, he sighed.

"Don't you ever watch *chick flicks?*"

"Dad." Rhynne's lips curled in a snarl, and her eyes remained on the TV. "You know I hate soppy stuff. How was work? Oh"—her hand stopped half way between the packet of crisps and her mouth— "Sophie's coming over soon."

"That's okay. Um, work's fine. Thank you for asking. Got papers to correct."

"But you always have papers to correct, professor." She wiggled her head in mock appreciation of the supposed status the position held. Her mass of long, black, wavy hair spilled around her.

Beautiful, like her mother... A sting hit his chest. If only some things about her didn't remind him so much of her father.

"I got that weekend off, so the HEMA camp is on." Her eyes lit up, mauve sparkling in the glow from the television.

"Oh, good. I suppose... How much is that, again?" Academic penury hadn't allowed for him to provide all he'd promised Rhiannon. The Gaelic had been fun. A special way of connecting with her since early childhood. His lips lifted, unable to repress the smile. As a youngster, she'd giggled every time they'd used their *secret* language in public. A warmth stirred—she spoke it fluently and without an accent.

And martial art. No force of nature could've prevented that.

"I've got it, Dad." She smiled her smile that could light up the room—*no, the whole world*. "That's why I've been doing those extra shifts."

His chest warmed. *That's my girl.* Never expecting nor demanding that he, her parent, provide it all.

"So, who's going to this camp?" he asked.

"The people who do HEMA," she said with eyebrows raised in sarcasm and a *who else?* tone.

"And you really want to do that? Learn how to fight with a sword?" He bit back the emotions that swirled. She was *so* shades of Rhiannon...

"I want to improve my fighting skills, especially with a sword." She dropped her phone, and turned away from the television, her expression so intent and fixed on him. "There's more to this."

"Which *this* do you mean?" he asked.

"This world. Life. The universe"—she flung her hands in the air— "everything."

"Hmm. So, you want to study philosophy?"

"No. I want to know what it's all about. Who's in control... 'cos that plague in the 2020s showed us *no one* is!"

George's breath gushed out. "I'm proud you're a deep thinker. Just don't go too deep... It's a real rabbit hole."

"I need to be ready when it's time to fight against it."

"Against what?" He forced his face to screw up in an incredulous expression. "Who are you going to fight against with a sword? That's a bit gruesome, don't you think?"

Don't be like this—like Rhiannon and her cause. Please don't.

"I'm not sure... but I'll find something." She shrugged. "Yeah, you're right. Perhaps not with a sword. But that's such a cool skill to have." A crooked smile came to her lips and her cheeks pinked. In a flash, her expression turned serious. "But I won't be a sheep, Dad. There's a bigger picture here, and most people don't look up enough to even glimpse it."

George swallowed hard. "Do I know anyone on this camp apart from Sophie?"

"Um... Yeah, you know the guy I had to fight at the HEMA try-out. Bàn. He's come to my martial art classes for a couple of months now. I think you met him at my last grading."

"Did I?"

"Yeah, the blond guy."

"Oh, yes, he's blond and his name means?"

She frowned. "You're not checking my Gaelic comprehension, are you?"

"Aye. What does his name mean?" he asked in the Gaelic.

"Fair. *Huh.* His parents didn't have much imagination," she answered, also in the Gaelic.

She'd never realised he'd actually taught her ancient Gaelic.

I'm lucky a trip to the Isles has never interested her.

"I think it's a good, sound name. I remember him now." He leaned forward and stole some crisps from the packet in her hand. "He seems of good character. I'll ask him to keep an eye on you."

"No, Dad! That's *so* embarrassing!"

He turned away, a chuckle shaking his ribs as he walked to his bedroom, crunching on the crisps.

It only seemed a short while ago that Rhiannon had knocked on his door dressed in leather armour with a sword over her shoulder like a warrior, and a baby in her arms. She'd begged him to care for Rhynne until she returned, and she'd promised she'd be back in moments. Said something about a war and Rhynne being in danger because of her father, Arlan. She was so upset, she'd made little sense.

Time had dragged on, and he'd had to make up a story about an abandoned baby.

They'd taken Rhynne from him then. The authorities. He closed his eyes against the pain and anguish that'd caused. Only through his impeccable conduct, pristine record, and—he gave a sardonic chuckle—his way with words, had he been accepted as her foster parent. His mouth tugged in a rueful smile. Being a nephew of a once member of the House of Lords had assisted his cause. He couldn't deny that.

The legal fees involved in her adoption had swallowed most of his inheritance. He'd done it all for Rhynne. And he'd do it again. She'd needed ID in this world, and health checks and immunisations, a birth certificate for school entry and so on.

I had *to do it, Rhiannon. Make her a citizen of this world and make me forget about any possibility of her returning to you.*

He halted by his double bed—one half never filled. The life of a single father wasn't bad. He'd struggled without the inheritance money, but Rhynne herself was all the reward he'd needed.

He grunted.

Rhiannon... She'd never come back.

Rhynne hadn't asked for a while. The fabricated story of a mother returning to the Orkneys then losing contact had hurt her as a young teen. He'd vowed to never let her feel abandoned. He'd seen how that had hurt Rhiannon, and he wouldn't do it to his Rhynne. She seemed resigned to having a single parent.

He stood tall, throat thickening and vision blurring.

He'd been enough for her.

Rhynne

Phew. The HEMA camp issue hadn't been an *issue* after all.

My phone buzzed. It was Soph, so I ran to the front door and let her in.

"It's okay for the weekend." I grabbed her hand and dragged her to the couch. "Please say your mum said you can go."

"Yeah. Fine." Soph waved dismissively. "Does your dad know without me there you'd probably be the only girl among a whole lot of men?"

"No. Because I won't be. Women do it too, you know. And don't let my dad hear you say that." I curled my hands into fists, tucking them under my armpits and hugging myself tight. "I've worked so hard for this, and I really don't need Dad saying no at the last minute. For *any* reason."

"Would he?"

"Probably. He'd do his usual *because I said so.* Humph. There's been so many times he's used *that.* It was okay when I was a kid."

"But you're not a kid anymore. Where's the food?" Sophie asked. She jumped off the couch, so I followed her into the kitchen.

I opened the freezer and pulled out a frozen pizza. "If he says no, he's gotta tell me why." I ground my teeth. "I never got *why.*" I tore the pizza out of the cardboard box and ripped off the plastic, then threw the pizza into the microwave. "Why I *had* to learn the Gaelic. Why I *had* to study herbal medicine. I don't mind either of them. Quite enjoy them both, actually."

"Speaking of herbs." Sophie cocked her head.

"No!" I widened my eyes at her. "Dad's home." I thrust a bottle of fizzy drink into her hands. "He knows what weed smells like. He's a professor, remember. His students probably reek of it." I got glasses out of the cupboard and rested them on the bench, still clutching them in my hands while my gut clutched tight to my grievance. "Why doesn't he get it that I need to know the big picture?"

And I need to know why crushing bergamot while saying Ciamar a tha thu was an essential part of my education.

Sophie grinned awkwardly and turned to the living room just as the microwave pinged.

Because I said so. Dad's voice echoed in my mind. I waggled my head, dropping the pizza on the plate and cutting it. Soph walked into the living room, and I followed with the pizza, then sat on the couch beside her.

"Have you ever kept asking?" Sophie took a bite of pizza. "Like 'ill yoo het a mecent hanswer?" she asked around the mouthful.

Dad's footsteps came down the hall from his room, and Soph's chewing stopped. He flashed a wave as he passed on his way to the kitchen.

"He'd always clam up if I insisted," I whispered. "Once we had a stinking argument. It was terrible. Couldn't speak to him for days after that." I forced back the prickling behind my eyes. "That was *so* bad. Never want to fight like that with Dad again." Clanking plates and the clinking of cutlery came from the kitchen. "He says I need to trust him.

Well, maybe he needs to trust me! It's like there's something he's always kept from me. And not just about my mum, either." I crossed my arms tightly and pressed down on my tongue, *and* the heat in my chest.

I was spoiling my evening with Soph.

"Yeah. Parents!" Sophie rolled her eyes, then got the movie going, munching pizza in my ear. She'd chosen a girly chick flick romance.

Gag.

Voices came from the kitchen.

Sophie turned to me. "What's going on in the kitchen with your dad?"

George sat at the kitchen table, laptop open and a very wordy essay on his screen.

Another student wishing to impress.

He wrote a comment on his notepad beside his computer. A flyer about the display of da Vinci's war machines at the local museum poked out from underneath.

"Oh yes, can't miss that." He shuffled the notepad aside for a better look and his hand nudged the salt shaker still tabled from his dinner, tipping it over a hardback on the development of ancient Goidelic and other forms of the Gàidhlig.

"Damn." He got up and turned to the sink, brushing the grains off the book and down the drain.

A face peered at him through the window. That man, Bàn. His brow crinkled, but he put on a smile and pointed to the backdoor beside him.

Okay, you only needed to knock, not be weird.

George went to the door and opened it. "Hello." He held out a hand. "Bàn, isn't it?"

The guy's hand was large. Same as the rest of him. And muscled.

"Aye, pleasure to meet you, Professor Wilson." Bàn had a very strong Highland accent—*along with his grip*—like he came from the Isles.

"I'm so glad you dropped in." *If you could call it that.* "I hear you are going to the HEMA camp." He ushered the man in.

"Aye." Bàn stood in the kitchen, his broad shoulders squared, looking like a soldier, with a serious expression on his face. "I wish to speak to ye about it, and..." He glanced past George in the direction of the living room, where the dialogue of a movie echoed into the hallway.

It seemed to be a romance. *For once.*

"...your *daughter*." Bàn's voice dipped with the word.

"Yes, she's here with a friend." George took a step, heading for the living room.

"Nae, I dinnae want to speak to her. I wish to speak with you."

"Well, then, please have a seat." He waved his hand at the other chair by the table strewn with papers and left-over dinner condiments.

"Nae, I will stand, for what I must relay is of great importance."

"Okay..." George stretched the word out and remained standing.

"I think ye should sit, for ye will not like what I have to say." Gravity filled Bàn's tone.

What? She wasn't about to go on this camp, then? Disqualified somehow? She'd lied and wasn't really going there, but somewhere else? *No, she's never lied.* What, then?

Bàn's stare locked onto him like an Exocet missile.

George sat.

"I see it has been some years in this world's time since the Lady Rhiannon put baby Rhynne into your care."

George's heart seemed to stop, a solid lump dead-centre of his chest.

"I'm Lord Bàn Lùthas, and I have come to return Rhynne to her world and her parents."

Frigid tentacles traced a track down George's spine, and he couldn't open his mouth. He strained to shout, *No, never!* but nothing even remotely near the vicinity of his voicebox moved.

Bàn searched his face. "I see ye have expected this, although the time is well past when she should have returned." He now spoke in ancient Gaelic. "Here is a letter from the Àrd Rìgh explaining my charge and proving my right to do so."

He handed over a neatly folded calf skin in an envelope-shape and sealed with wax. The round seal pictured a horse rampant with a chain of knotwork around the edge.

"Why do you need permission from the high king?" He broke the seal and opened the letter.

"As ye will read, Lord Arlan thanks ye for your service to him in caring for the bairn but wants her back at once." Bàn placed a calloused hand on George's arm. "He knows not that so much time has passed. He thinks her still but a babe."

"Arlan's the high king? She didn't mention that. That means..." *Rhiannon.* He almost whispered her name, but shut his mouth tight.

"Aye, the Lady Rhiannon is his wife, and the young woman in your home is a noble princess. I have seen how ye are with the lass. How ye are fond of her. I wished to give ye warning and time to say farewell."

George let out the breath he'd been holding in.

"I will take her with me after the HEMA camp. She looks forward to it so." Bàn gave an embarrassed laugh, and his cheeks pinked. "She will be pleased to be with her parents at last, aye? Ye have taught her well in the language. And she is a braw fighter. So like her mother..."

He followed Bàn's gaze to the letter in his hands. The vellum, as soft as a kid-leather glove, was now a scrunched mess.

"Ye have told her of her parents and heritage, Mr Wilson?"

"No." George's voice came out small.

"But ye have ensured she has the skills required to go home." Bàn's forehead now crumpled like the vellum. "Surely ye have—"

"Rhiannon disappeared. It's been eighteen years! I couldn't...*wouldn't* tell Rhynne of something that may never happen. Hold out hope for some *illusion.*" His neck heated.

"Dad?" Rhynne's voice came from the kitchen doorway. "Oh, hi, Bàn." There was a ring of curiosity in her tone, but she didn't say more.

Bàn nodded to her, almost a bow from the neck. George blinked, then breathed deep, steeling himself.

He'd put it from his mind. Pushed the possibility so far back, it had ceased to exist for him.

But it did.

Niggles had caused him to send her to herb medicine school, so she had the skills to look after herself in a backward world. Just in case. Luckily, she'd loved it.

And now this Dál Gaedhle warrior standing in his kitchen was proof his time with Rhynne would soon be over and his hope that it would never happen, just a delusion of a lonely—and now old—man.

"Bàn says he'll make sure you have a good weekend." He smoothed the letter, and forcing a smile, turned to Rhynne.

"Oh, Dad. You didn't!"

Bàn laughed and George joined in. *It'll wipe the strain off my face.*

"We'll have a braw weekend, Rhynne." Bàn's voice held affection. "Be ready to fight like never before."

Rhynne smiled and tucked in her chin, like she did when feigning shyness.

So, she feels okay about this guy?

Bàn stared at Rhynne while George fiddled with the letter. Rhynne looked from him to Bàn and back again through an uncomfortable silence.

"I'll just go and..." Rhynne chewed her lip and pointed over her shoulder, then returned to the lounge room and Sophie.

Bàn's sturdy grip clamped on his forearm. George spun back.

"Ye will tell her." The warrior's voice, now low, held a hint of threat.

"After the HEMA camp. Let her enjoy that. I'll explain everything next week."

"Aye, then I'll come for her." Bàn paused, as though he waited for an answer.

Did he think I'd rejoice at the thought of him taking Rhynne? Her going to another world through a magic portal? It sounded so...*fantastic* in the truest meaning of the word.

He hung his head. He couldn't deny Rhiannon of her beautiful, incredible, gifted, wonderful daughter... Cold gripped his heart.

Boots filled George's vision, and he lifted his head to the stern features of Lord Bàn Lùthas, the official emissary of the àrd rìgh of another world. A blond eyebrow slowly cocked.

"Okay," George said, his insides so numb his voice seemed to come from somewhere else.

Bàn turned, strode through the open door, then was gone.

The door framed the night outside—dark, like the prospect of a future without his girl.

TEN

He stands beside me
A fearless warrior,
Though the garb of one he wears not.
For it is the heart that makes him so.

WORDS OF RIEINMELLTH
ANCIENT WARRIOR QUEEN OF DÀL CRUINNE

Our World 2036
The Cotswolds

Bàn jogged ahead of me, perspiration soaking his back. The dark patch of sweat in the middle of his T-shirt formed an elongated Rorschach pattern. Drops gathered on his neck just below the hairline and on either side of his ponytail—a mass of tight blond curls—where shorter hairs grew wisp-like. I forced myself to take my eyes off him.

Grimacing, I sucked in more air.

They said nothing about a five-mile run each morning of the camp.

Sophie jogged beside me. Beads of sweat gathered on her forehead and ran in rivulets down her face.

"What're you looking at?" Sophie spoke between breaths. "You're the same."

I smiled. "Legs like jelly and a stitch in my side putting me off breakfast." *But it's invigorating.* "What more could a girl want?"

We'd reached the mess hall in the converted barn, and I slowed my jog, then paced back and forth, shaking out my tight calf muscles. Sophie did the same, eyeing the rest of the campers. She sidled back to me.

"Hmm..." Her tone sounded dreamy—puffed, but dreamy. "Ever believe you'd be at a camp full of men?" Her eyes remained on the youngest guy there. HEMA seemed to be for older and more serious males than Sophie usually went for.

"

"Soph, there *are* other women here, or are you just ignoring that fact? *I'm* here to improve my sword skills. They've accepted me for their classes."

"I know."

"They're holding try outs again this weekend if you're interested."

"I'll see." Sophie's gaze wandered across the campers.

"You don't seem..."

"What?"

"Did you just come for the guys?" I left the accusation in my tone.

"Me?" Sophie faced me, tilted her head, and lifted a shoulder in mock innocence. "I wouldn't do that."

I rolled my eyes. We followed the group in for breakfast, then sat at a long table. Sophie plonked herself beside me. With her bottom barely on the seat, she grabbed two pieces of toast and a packet of breakfast cereal from the centre of the table. Bàn approached on the opposite side and placed both hands on the table, leaning in.

"Rhynne, after breakfast, there's a theory session." His arm muscles stretched his T-shirt tight. It only covered the top of his inked sleeve. "Then we'll spar," his said, his accent was mesmerising. *Bet he speaks the Gaelic.* "You'll partner me, aye?"

Sophie nudged my elbow, jolting me.

I blinked. "Oh, yes, that'd be great. Thanks."

He smiled, and I dropped my gaze to his dimples. One day I'd have the guts to ask him how he got a silver scar-line through the one on the right cheek. He left our table and made his way to the servery.

"He's got the hots for you," Sophie whispered into my ear. "Bàn!" she shouted at his back.

"What're you doing?" I hissed, my face flaming.

"How old are you?" Sophie shouted, ignoring me.

The guys at the next table lifted their heads in our direction, looked at Bàn, then went back to buttering toast while Bàn turned and strolled to our table.

He crossed his arms, biceps bulging. "I'm in my twenty-ninth year."

"How long did it take to grow your hair?"

Bàn tilted his head, a *v* appearing above his slightly crooked nose.

"So that it's long enough to have a ponytail?" Sophie clarified.

"I've always had long hair."

"How old were you when you got your tattoos?"

"Sophie!" I glared at her.

"Oh, good. Never mind." Sophie dismissed Bàn with a wave. "Go eat."

He frowned, pivoted on his heel, then resumed his wander to the bain marie for the cooked breakfast selection.

Sophie faced me.

"What?" My face must've been glowing red. Soph could be *so* embarrassing.

"Do you like older men?" Sophie's right eyebrow curled.

"That's not old."

"So, a ten-year difference is okay?"

"Soph, I'm here to fight, not pick up guys, so just leave me out of it."

"Okay. Just sayin'. The man has the hots—"

"Shush." I poured milk over my cereal, keeping my eyes on my cornflakes. *Hots for me? I wish.*

I trod out from the mess hall, my tummy full of dinner and my legs heavy. A slight burn remained in my arms and thighs from the built-up lactic acid. I smiled to myself. Earlier, Bàn had beaten the crap out of me while the other campers had watched and cheered. They thought Bàn was great. Some came up to him after he'd killed me a few times and asked him for pointers. Like he was the expert, even though he'd only been with them for a couple of months.

But he *was* a pretty awesome swordsman. And kind. He'd taught me heaps and had even let me hit him back—now and then.

Clouds wisped through the sky, and the moon had already risen, but the sun hadn't even reached the horizon on its way to setting. Both celestial bodies brightened the evening enough to see the path that led away from the converted barn.

I took in a deep breath, the cool Cotswold air softly chilling my throat and lungs, then let it out slowly. The gentle hills around me were a rolling monochrome, and the honey sandstone they used to build almost everything in the Cotswolds now dimmed to a dusky yellow. Conversation spilled from the barn, Sophie's cheeky laugh amongst it all.

I'd gladly left Soph to her flirting, but I needed air and solitude. Too many people for too long overwhelmed me. Crowded me. I was better on my own. My mouth stretched into a grin. I took after Dad with that.

Footsteps came behind me. "Rhynne, do ye want tae go for a stroll in that wee wood?" It was Bàn.

My heart raced a bit. *Settle down.*

"A walk through the forest at night?"

"It's not quite night yet, but it's the best time." He caught up and walked beside me.

My phone vibrated. 'Where are you?' It was Soph.

I shoved my phone back into my pocket and turned to Bàn. A sword handle rose from behind his shoulder and a strap ran across the front of his leather jacket, looking like it held a leather baldric in place. I'd seen him carrying the sword-shaped bundle when he'd arrived at the camp, bunched with his other belongings. The guys had already ooh-ed and ahh-ed over its contents.

"Where did you get that?" I pointed to the sword. "It looks real."

"Aye, it is. Family heirloom."

"Wow, really? It must be old."

"I thought you might like to look at it." He reached back and pulled it from its sheath, accompanied by a silky metallic whisper.

Oh, wow! The soft snick of a real sword went right through me, touching something deep. I halted, my mind grasping for...*what?*

Bàn held the sword loosely across his palms, handle resting on one, and the flat of the blade across the other. The edges shone silver, and its tip had a defined point. Down the centre of the blade, along the fuller, symbols etched the metal. I stroked them, the indentations thin beneath my fingertips. Not English. Not even the Latin alphabet. More like the writing in one of Dad's books.

"They used to name swords. Has it got one?" I asked.

"Aye, this one is called... *Dìleas do do mhaighstir.* It's the Gàidhlig."

"I know. It means *faithful to your master*. And that's Ogham script."

Bàn's grin filled his face, and in the fading light, his eyes seemed to sparkle. "Very good," he said softly.

I squashed the tightness of a too-enthusiastic smile that threatened, then faced the path to the woods.

"But it's a mouthful." Bàn re-sheathed his sword. A tingle ran along my spine. *Ooh, that sound again.* "So I call her *Dìleas.*"

He walked beside me, and we ambled along, the silence comfortable, with a scent of apricot soap wafting across from him.

Heavy footsteps came from behind us, in the opposite direction from the barn, where the distant laughter of the campers still echoed out the door.

I turned in time with Bàn. A group of roughly ten people marched toward us, almost shadows now the sun dipped at the horizon, but they all carried weapons. One of them spoke in a low voice, giving orders to the others, who then spread out. They wore leather jackets, and they all had long hair, either braided or pulled tight behind them. I double blinked.

Their blades glinted. *Real* blades.

The leader spoke again. In the Gaelic.

Bàn tensed beside me, Dìleas singing from her sheath, and I turned to him. His stance changed; he looked ready to pounce and he held his sword steady.

"Get ye to the woods, Rhynne," he said in the Gaelic.

"What—?"

"Dinnae argue. Go!" His deep voice thundered through me.

I turned and ran, heart thumping fast, and Bàn's foot tread falling in behind me. I stole a backward glance. Bàn held his blade up as one of the group strode directly behind us on the track that now narrowed into the wood. Thick-trunked trees lined the path. Bàn gripped my upper arm, ringing a tight band around it, and steered me into the forest.

"Get behind a tree." He shoved me. "Dinnae move."

So, was this a LARP-ing game? Adding some realism to it all? My hands trembled and itched to hold something. I should have a sword!

I huffed. They could've given me notice. Even a wooden practice sword would be better than nothing. Although... against Bàn's real sword...

Why does he have a real blade with him, anyway?

Metal rang against metal. I peered from behind the tree. Bàn pounded a woman dressed like she'd just come from the set of a fantasy movie. She fought well and was a match for Bàn.

Had the guys running the camp set this up? Maybe they were jealous of Bàn's fighting skills. Perhaps they hoped to teach Bàn a thing or two with a realistic LARP. These fighters were serious-looking.

Grunts, like an animal's, came from both Bàn and the woman he fought. She was definitely not one of the campers.

Bàn's striking arm came down on her, his sword running across her throat, leaving a deep gash. Blood poured out of the darkening slit, and the woman's eyes opened wide. Bàn continued his flowing movement and sliced her neck again on the backswing. She grasped her throat with her gloved hand and gurgled something, blood spurting through her fingers, then she dropped to the ground.

I ran from behind the tree to Bàn. The woman lay at his feet, twitching. A spray of dark crossed Bàn's T-shirt.

"You killed her." My hands were numb.

"Aye." His voice was calm and steady as he picked up the woman's abandoned weapon, then held both swords in his massive grip.

"No. You've *really* killed her." Stomach acid lifted into my mouth, but I pushed it down.

"Aye, and we must go." He faced away from the camp, grabbed my wrist, and ran, dragging me with him.

"Wait. Why aren't we going to the barn?" I spoke to his back. "You've really killed her?" My voice came out shaky with my running, my disbelief jolting in my ears.

Really.

A place in my chest went numb.

"I must get ye out o' here, Rhynne."

A man grunted behind us, where the woman's body lay. Bàn pushed me to the nearest tree and spun to face the man who stood snarling by the dead body. Tall like Bàn, this guy wore— *yep*—leather armour, with a blade the same style as Bàn's. He spoke in the Gaelic. A word or two, in a guttural growl, caught my ear.

Ribhinn... It meant princess or beautiful female.

Bàn bolted toward him, blades ready, one in each hand. The man lifted his sword and Bàn, now a couple of paces away, leaped slightly to the man's left, hitting the man's weapon with the woman's sword in his left hand, thrusting it away from himself. Bàn's left foot landed on the man's thigh, and dropping the woman's sword, Bàn raised himself into the air, climbing the guy, and pointing his sword tip downward. He'd changed his grip to double handed, bringing his sword straight down on the man, point first, stabbing through the collarbone, right into the man's chest. Bàn drove it down with his bodyweight as he spun past. The man dropped as Bàn landed on the ground behind him.

What? It had only taken seconds. My mouth dried.

Bàn pulled his sword from the man's body, then ran toward me, his face filled with a dark expression in the shadows of dusk. I turned to run in the same direction as Bàn, but skidded to a halt.

On the path ahead, a round shimmering blocked my way.

"We're going to take the princess from you now, Lord Lùthas." A cocky voice came along the track, speaking Gaelic.

I pivoted on my heel, hardly able to take my eyes from the shimmer. It was like a swimming pool stood on its side and I looked at its surface. A brackish odour, like murky pond water, wafted over to me. Bàn had turned and faced the direction of the shout—a group of guys dressed like warriors from a fantasy movie. The Gaelic words finally registered.

Lord Lùthas? Princess?

"Run," Bàn whispered heavily from the side of his mouth.

"I can't. The shimmering's in the way."

"What?" Bàn glanced at the path. "Naught there."

Metal clattered and booted feet pounded. The group ran forward, blades flickering in the last of the daylight angling through the branches.

Bàn was good, but those people tearing toward us fit my definition of *outnumbered*.

"Bàn, look." I tapped his shoulder. He glanced to me, then past me, then back again.

"Ye see something?"

"Yes. Don't you?"

His eyes grew wide. "Nae." He turned back to the crowd now swarming toward us.

Bàn looked me in the eye again and, in that fraction of a second, decision rippled across his face. The guys in the front of the group started yelling, screaming. It tore straight through me, shuddering my spine. Then they surged forward, blades glinting shiny-edged, and coming for us.

"Take us through, Rhynne," Bàn yelled.

"What?"

"Guide us through the portal, lass! Now!"

ELEVEN

Time goes round and round.
I see myself once more.
What I have lived.
Where I have been.
And I ponder my journey back to myself.

CONTEMPLATIONS OF A TRAVELLER
GRAND MASTER LLEW
(POST DRAGON WARS 6000–CURRENT)

The World of Dál Cruinne
Spring, Post Dragon Wars Year 6083
Eastern Clanlands of Dál Gallain

Bàn grasped Rhynne's hand. Och, that was right. He must think of the destination and those he wished to be with.

Arlan. Rhiannon.

Ahead of him, Rhynne gasped. Whiteness hit his eyes, so he shut them. Harsh sound battered him; not only his ears, but his whole body vibrated with it. He held tighter to her hand.

The onslaught ceased then cold, wet water surrounded him, and his feet touched a slimy base. He held his breath and stood, breaking a pond surface, water-drenched and chilled.

Beside him Rhynne rose, dripping wet, gasping and coughing, then dragged in air.

A reed-fringed pond. A rocky shore. A sunset glowing through a rising mist. A silver sun descending.

Home.

Nae other warriors... yet.

"Ye okay?" he asked Rhynne, still holding her hand and surveying their surroundings.

Rhynne nodded, so he pulled her through the water, stumbling on its slippery floor, and headed for a large natural rock formation just past its shore and close to a small wood.

Behind them, the pond water stirred. He dragged Rhynne to rocks large enough to slide between while darkness descended quickly. The cool air thickened with water vapour as a fog rose from the pond.

He leaned his back against the rock, breathing deep, trusting the night and the developing fog to cover their wet footprints.

"Where—?" Rhynne spoke in the now dark of night, seemingly loud compared to the stillness surrounding them.

He clamped his free hand to her mouth and tilted his head, while warriors' yells and gasps burst through the pond's surface. Bàn followed the distinct *scush scushing* of their steps as they strode through the water. Choking, coughing, and cursing rang around the pond.

Rhynne nodded, eyes wide, so he took his hand away and grasped his sword double handed and readied.

"That bastard killed Merline," one coughed and spluttered.

"Dearg didn't make it."

"What!"

"He cannae swim," another said.

"Search the place," a gruff voice ordered.

Swishing blades against tough marsh grasses, more *scushing* through water, and the crunching of boots on pebbles ensued.

The noises receded to the far side of the sizeable pond, the comments gruff and angry.

Bàn placed a finger to his lips and indicated their rocky exit. Rhynne gave a curt nod. He made a run for it to the nearby wood, dragging Rhynne behind through a swirling mist, and flinching at every footfall that seemed to crash through the undergrowth. He scurried low and only stopped on reaching the depths of the wood, then shoved Rhynne behind a tree and peered around it. The coarse comments, laced with heated commands echoing through the night, continued to come from the other side of the pond.

Rhynne fumbled in her pocket and retrieved her phone. "Ah! It's wet," she hissed.

He covered her hand, holding the phone with his. "Ye will nae need that now."

Her mouth dropped open.

"We must run, Rhynne. Silence on our part will be our friend." He kept his grip on his sword and placed his other hand on Rhynne once more.

They ran on through the wood, leaving the warriors and their search behind. The wood was larger than it first appeared, and it took a good wee while to pass the last tree. Ahead of them lay a plain where the fog thinned, and a standing stone circle stood in the middle of it, illuminated, glowing in the light-scattering mist. It was ancient, its lintels stones absent, and the edges of most sarsens rough shadows.

One section sat aglow, the grunt of an engine coming from near the light.

An engine? A *car* in Dál Cruinne?

Bàn focused, tensing for flight.

Two men spoke. One drove the vehicle... a jeep. The vehicle's headlights, conical beams trapped in the moist air, lit an older man's face. He yelled at a younger man in his tongue.

"Maybe those guys can h—" Rhynne began.

Bàn dropped his sword and covered Rhynne's mouth again.

"They may be our foe," he whispered, putting the index finger of his other hand to his lips, willing her to understand she must be silent for now. A fine line appeared above her nose, but she nodded, then he guided her to the nearest tree from where he could still see the goings on at the stone formation.

The henge seemed familiar. A lantern stood to the side of a gaping open... was it a portal? Yet it was now night. He concentrated on the conversation between the driver of the jeep and the older man, who spoke with authority and abruptness.

Dragon's breath! It was Ciarán Gallawain!

And this would be last year, when Arlan had faced Ciarán. If he wasn't mistaken, Arlan would arrive with himself and Rhiannon from the other direction, plus most of their warband. He swallowed, then leaned back beside Rhynne behind the tree.

"I have been here," he whispered.

"Good, then you know where we need to go." Her whispered words were quick, and she moved to leave.

He leaned closer, gripping her arm, preventing her flight. Her body's natural scent filled his head—lilac—and her hair tickled his lips.

"Any moment now, your father and mother, plus myself, will come here," he whispered into her ear, "to this very stone henge."

"My father—?" She raised her voice.

Bàn clamped his hand over her mouth and frowned her into silence.

"Your father will fight the older man," he continued, "who is our enemy, Ciarán Gallawain." He took a breath to tell her more, but she turned her head, nudging his hand from her mouth.

The whites of her eyes glinted in the moonlight, and she placed her mouth so close to his ear her soft lips touched him, and her breasts brushed his arm.

"We've gotta go. You can't be in the same place as yourself in the past. The universe will implode. Time Travel 101." She leaned back, then pressed against his ear again. "I'd really like to know where we are!" Stress wove through her whispered voice. "And what you mean by my *father?*"

He moved to look her in the eye. She should know, but the need for silence made it impossible at this moment.

"Once we are far from here, I will explain all."

The vehicle's engine roared in the night. Bàn peered back into the wood behind them. There was no sight nor sound in the silent mist of those pursuing them.

Bàn searched the surrounds of the stone circle. A dark-robed figure of the mage, as in this situation of his past, stood waist deep in the waters of the burn, thick vapour rising from the water swirling around him. He'd learned since that this young man had held the portal open by his magic.

Movement caught Bàn's eye. He focused beyond Ciarán Gallawain arguing with the young warrior who drove the jeep, to where figures approached—himself amongst them.

"We must go while the noise covers us." He picked up his sword and grasped Rhynne's hand.

He kept Rhynne close. If he recalled correctly, the warrior would drive the jeep to the southeast. And Ciarán Gallawain would soon best Arlan, slice his arm and jeopardise his chances of becoming àrd rìgh, even though Arlan had won the Quest. How thankful he was that Gallawain's plan had been thwarted. Bàn recalled with a slight shudder that he and Arlan's troop had then taken their lord to the sage hold in the northwest for the ministrations of the healer sages.

So, northeast would be the safest direction now for himself and his charge.

He slunk away in the darkness with Rhynne, keeping the shouts of his own warband—himself included—plus the clash of swords, to the far right. Rhynne turned to look, creeping backward for some paces, until they were far enough for her to see no more. They walked through the dark in silence, until the echoes of his past were far, far in the distance. He led her into a stand of pine, the forest floor soft under his feet and the tangy scent wafting up from their footfall.

Rhynne... She'd guided him through the portal...

His arm now jerked with her sudden stop.

"You killed people!"

"Rhynne, I did it to save you." He spoke calmly to her.

She huffed, then put her hands on her hips and faced him full on. She was a silhouette in the night... Rhiannon's silhouette. "Okay. So, you owe me some explanations. No, in fact, one big one. Like how did we get here and what was that up-ended swimming pool all about? Where are we, and what did you mean by my *father and mother* would soon be here? But most of all, when will you take me home?"

He sighed. "Lady Rhynne of Clan MacEnoicht, ye *are* home."

I stared up at the pine branches waving in the breeze, the fine needles flicking like my thoughts. Bàn lay beside me, his hand resting on his drawn sword by his side.

My body was heavy, sleep drawing me, but my mind spun. Bàn had spent most of the night explaining it to me. *It* being my real parentage, life, and world.

But Dad... I may never see him again.

I swallowed and brushed away the trickles running down the side of my face and into my ears.

It had been noisy, dead serious fighting at that stone henge thing. Bàn said he'd been there, and he was. With a massive guy with long black hair. That guy had fought the old man who'd been yelling at the guy in the army-type jeep. I'd watched until I couldn't see them anymore through the fog.

That black-haired warrior was *awesome*. And my *real* father. I couldn't deny it when Bàn had told me. Same hair. But apart from that, I recognised myself in him... more than I ever had in Dad... *George*.

I pressed my lips tight.

Bàn had smiled. Well, I'd heard it in his voice, when he said I could see the swimming pool portal. He hadn't seen it, but had believed me and, apparently, I'd saved the day, and he'd thanked me for it.

And I was a *princess*. *Wow!* I grunted a soft laugh. And there was magic in this world. Not just portals.

"So, my grandfather has special powers?"

Bàn shifted his arm resting against mine. "Och, are ye no' asleep? Ye need to rest, for we have a long journey ahead of us." He wriggled beside me.

I sat up. "You tell me *all* you've just told me and expect me to sleep!"

He sighed. "I ken it's a lot—"

"Understatement! And why can't I go to the castle that's supposed to be my home?"

He sat up now. "Because ye have nae been born yet."

I scrunched my brow, and Bàn made a sympathetic sound in his throat, like he sensed I didn't get it.

"We have come to Dál Cruinne, to the Eastern Clanlands of Dál Gallain—*not* where we live—in a time before I went through a portal to get ye. We must bide until the time that I left is upon us. So that neither of us meets ourselves in our past. The *101* to which ye referred."

"How long will that be?"

"After the winter to come has passed." He grunted. "A very long, hard winter."

"But that's months away."

"So, while this summer gives us sunshine and warmth, we must find a suitable place to see the winter out in safety."

"You don't sound happy about that."

"Aye, well, I dinnae ken this part o' my world. I'm as much a stranger as you are."

The face of another stranger to this world—Dad's face—flashed in my mind. I sighed heavily. "Dad knows where you've taken me?" The skin on my arms cooled. "He knows you planned to take me. Right?"

"Aye, he was aware, although it was to be after the HEMA camp."

"And he's okay about it?" The cool on my arms seeped into my chest.

"Nae, not really, but he knew what he had to do. That he must let ye go. He was to explain all to ye after the weekend but..." Bàn's shoulder lifted in the shadows, then his warm hand covered mine. "I ken this is hard on ye." His voice was gentle, close. "But ye must endure and get to your rightful parents. They are..." His voice cracked.

I shuffled on my pine needle bed. *Is he being emotional?*

"I love them both. They are the best people I know. Your father, my sworn sword-brother, and your mother..." He swallowed. "They will miss ye dearly and..."

I gently shook his hand holding mine, encouraging him to finish that thought.

"They know not ye are nae longer a babe."

TWELVE

A warrior's word is a warrior's life.
A sworn oath, a bond
Only broken by death or treachery.

ADVICE TO WAR CHIEFS
WARRIOR SAGE TAPAÌDH
(4009-4059 POST DRAGON WARS)

The World of Dál Cruinne
Post Dragon Wars Year 6083
Eastern Clanlands of Dál Gallain

I woke to a full moon ghosting the trees in silvery light. The leaves soughed in the breeze and night sounds caught my hearing. Soft padded footsteps trotted nearby.

Bàn jerked beside me, jolting me fully awake. He rose, flying to a stand as the reek of dog swamped over me.

Bàn roared, stepping away from our pine-needle bed toward a savage growl.

A shiver creeped across my scalp, joining gooseflesh crawling along my skin. The growl sounded *insane*. I jumped to my feet, kicking a dagger sitting where Bàn had lain. I picked it up.

Bàn waved his sword around. It glinted and flashed in the moonlight. A grey blur collided with him.

How did it miss his blade?

The massive animal, a wolf, thudded Bàn to the ground. He grunted, like he was winded. Moonlight flashed off white spikes of teeth as the wolf went for Bàn's throat. Bàn's arm connected with the open jaws, holding the powerful animal away with his leather-clad forearm, but only just.

Bàn was strong. Surely he'd get this savage dog off him?

Snarls and growls sent shivers to my guts. Man and beast rocked and churned the dirt, both grunting and growling, striving for supremacy. I gripped the dagger handle tight, digging it into my palm. My thigh muscles tensed, springing me into action.

Standing over the beast, I raised the dagger high. It seemed to not notice me, Bàn its only concern. I forced the dagger down with all my might and thrust the blade into its furry side. I gulped for air. Dog reek, metallic blood scent and pine dust filled my mouth.

The night echoed with the yelp of a wounded canine. Bàn rolled over, now above the wolf with a dagger hilt sticking out from its side. With his arm free of the wolf's jaws, he grabbed it by the scruff of its neck and ran his blade across its throat. The yelps ceased and its last gurgle rang out in the cool breeze.

"Are ye alright, Lady Rhynne?" Bàn, still breathless, dropped his hand away from the wolf, then grimaced.

"Am *I* alright!" My words came out strangled. "It... *You*..." I dropped my hands by my side. Stickiness covered the fingers of my right hand, now stained dark with wolf blood.

"I thank ye for your assistance." Bàn stood grimacing and leaned his sword against his thigh, then pressed his hand to his left shoulder and scanned the immediate area. "I see nae more beasts. Must hae been a lone wolf."

"They're a real thing?" My hands shook. "You're injured." I blinked at the calmness in my voice. "I know first aid."

"Of course ye do." Bàn surveyed the woods.

"I'm serious. Sit. Let me see. You might've broken something."

Bàn stopped looking around at the moonlit forest and rested his gaze on me, then sat.

"When the beast landed on me, I felt a crack here." He pointed to his collarbone. "I have broken a bone there before. It healed well enough. Only grateful it was not my sword arm."

I wiped the wolf's blood from my trembling fingers with some dry pine needles, then squatted. My legs went from beneath me, so I knelt instead, then pulled his jacket aside. He flinched and pressed his lips tight. I gently prodded along the line of his collar bone and reached almost where it joined his breastbone. There it crunched, and he gasped at my prodding.

"Sorry." I scrunched my mouth. "I think it *is* broken. You need to sling it. A collar and cuff."

He looked directly at me, and in the moonlight, one eye seemed to squint. "I require two arms to protect ye, if ye have nae noticed. I'll not incapacitate one tied up in a sling."

"Protect *me*? Who stabbed the wolf?"

His lips parted, though no sound came out.

"I'll find something to help it heal quickly." I rose from my knees and walked to the edge of the forest. "Knitbone. I'll make a poultice."

"Dinnae wander far," Bàn called, and grunted as he stood.

I stepped into the woods. The sky lightened with a silvery glow tingeing the horizon. The trees, rocks, and bushes were gradually fading from their night time black, white, and grey, and taking on their daytime colour. I scoured the woods around me while birds twittered in nearby trees. Rich soil sat beneath the trees of the forest's edge where low bushes and clumps of plants grew. I waded in through a knee-high leafy patch and found the gently curving, broad, textured, deep green leaves of the comfrey plant.

Bàn's footsteps padded behind me. "And ye ken herb lore too." It was a statement, not a question.

"Yeah. Dad insisted I know that stuff for some strange reason. I mean, *insisted*. But now it all makes sense." I plucked some leaves from the plant. "And I was a Girl Scout."

"Ye memorised the *handbook*, I expect," he said under his breath.

"I need to mush these up and press them onto your collarbone." I stood straight, ignoring his comment. "Hmm. I should make it into a tea, too. Can we have a fire?"

Bàn looked around again, eyes narrowing. "But why would we require a fire when we have nothing in which to boil water and make this tea?"

"Oh, yeah. We have *nothing*." I followed him back to where we'd bedded down for the night, letting my shoulders slump as the implications of our lack of resources hit me.

I crushed half the comfrey between my fingers, pressing out the juices. *Hmm.* I'd need a cloth to hold the mush onto Bàn's shoulder.

Blood patched red on Bàn's once white T-shirt. I didn't have anything else.

"Bàn, I need a strip of your T-shirt."

Taking off his leather jacket, Bàn held his mouth tight and flinched slightly as he eased it over his shoulder.

I grimaced for him. "Here." I took his jacket with one hand and laid it on the ground, placing the mushed-up comfrey on it. The wolf's body still lay a couple of metres away and I stepped to it. "*Eww.* I need this dagger."

"I can hear a burn past that line o' trees. Go wash it. I'll watch ye from here." Bàn ran his hand along his sweat-glistened brow.

I pulled the knife. The wolf's corpse groaned with air moving through its sliced throat, but dead eyes stared, a pink tongue lolled from a slack jaw, and nothing else moved. I strode past Bàn in the direction he'd pointed.

The track was moist and springy, the morning air cool and crisp in my lungs, and I headed for the burbling. The water in the burn was *so* clear. I washed my hands, then scooped a handful and drank, the cool sweet water soothing my thirst. Daylight now came fully, but it had a strange silver tinge. A dove cooed softly nearby. I ran my vision over the rocks lining the burn, and along its length. Then to the leaves of the birch trees on the other side, their definition sharper than anything I'd ever seen. I raised my eyes to the sky—a brilliant cornflower blue. Birdsong rang from the trees, a constant chatter as they continued their melodic dawn chorus.

But it was different. Clearer. More beautiful. Or maybe, I'd just never looked at nature like this before. I rested back on my haunches, the tremor from my ordeal gone. Peace surrounded me here. I could've stayed forever.

The pristine water from the burn had quenched my thirst—we hadn't had a drink or eaten since we left... the Cotswolds and my world. I grunted and washed the dagger, careful of its edges sparkling sharp in the crystal water, then walked back the way I'd come. Bàn sat cross-legged on the ground where we'd slept.

"I need a strip of cloth, and well..."

"Aye, modesty prevails upon me. I cannae have you baring flesh to all." Bàn eased his T-shirt over his head, grimacing and baring his torso.

I turned away. I could *not* let him see what my face would surely show.

The man is built like a Greek god.

"Do ye want this?" he said through his teeth.

Smoothing my face to neutral, I turned, not looking him in the eye, and took his T-shirt from his hand. The material was still warm when I cut a strip off the bottom, enough for a makeshift bandage, then I handed his T-shirt back to him. I applied the paste of comfrey to the strip I'd torn, then placed it over his collarbone, where the bone had crunched under my fingers. He put his T-shirt back on, his mouth shutting down on groans, then shrugged into his leather jacket and slipped his sword in its baldric over his right shoulder where it usually sat.

"We require warmer clothing. T-shirts and jeans will not be sufficient in the cold weather ahead of us, but I have little coin and only a few gems left for trade." Bàn stood and did a half stretch, cradling his injured arm to his side, and his back joints popping. "Ye shall assist me in skinning the wolf."

"What?"

"Its pelt will do ye for a winter coat. For as ye have already observed, we have nothing. And we require horses."

"So that's how people get around in this world?" I turned slowly on my heel. A narrow gulley with steep cliff sides led away from us and wove through the trees. Not a house in sight. It would be a long walk *anywhere* to buy a horse. "Wait. We have to ride?"

"Surely ye know how."

"No. Well... I had a couple of lessons..." I shut my eyes tight for a second.

So, that's why Dad had been so insistent on riding lessons.

"A couple?" Bàn faced the narrow valley as he spoke. "It will be enough."

"I don't like horses."

Bàn spun round, his eyebrows raised, and his face tilted down to me. "*Don't. Like. Horses?*" Disbelief hung in his words.

"I... fell off." My face heated. Bàn was sure to be an expert rider—along with everything else he seemed to be *gifted* at. "And when my friend came to help me up, the... horse..." Two back hooves, their shoes shining, flashed in my mind. I shuddered. "...kicked her. It bruised her kidneys, and she had blood in her pee for days. I never went back."

Dad gave up trying to make me, but Bàn didn't need to know that.

Bàn placed a fist on his belt and his head moved in short, sharp shakes. "Well, ye had better get to liking them, for this world runs on the back o' a horse."

I groaned. Dad's face filled my mind, and the sound I'd made caught in my throat while my legs wobbled and wouldn't hold my weight. I sat down hard. Bàn stood in front of me, his boots a step away.

"Rhynne?"

My breathing stuttered, like someone shook me on the inside.

"What if I don't want to?" My voice came out small.

Damn. I've never sounded so weak! I balled my fists, crossing my arms over my chest.

"Lady Rhynne, ye must come..." He sighed heavily.

I lifted my gaze to his face. He was frowning, and his good shoulder jolted downward. His hair had come out of his ponytail and the breeze picked it up, blowing blond strands past blue eyes creased in... *Was he concerned or desperate?*

"Your mother came from the Other World—"

"My world!" I interrupted.

"She loved your father and came to fight in his warband for Dál Gaedhle." He opened his mouth like he had more to say.

"But she *wanted* to come here." Man, my voice came out snappy. "You've not given *me* a choice. Take me home, please." *What did he expect?*

A muscle jumped in his jaw.

"Take me home, now!" I stood, legs hollow, and marched off in the direction we'd come the previous night.

He ran and reached paces ahead of me in seconds. Spinning, he knelt in front of me on one knee, right in my path, grimacing a little, then bowed his head.

I skidded to a halt.

"Lady Rhynne MacEnoicht, child of Dál Gaedhle." His deep voice filled the air between the trunks of the tall pines. He lifted his face to mine and pulled his sword from its sheath.

I stepped back. A flash of cool went through my lungs, but he pointed the blade-tip into the dead pine needles under our feet. Just like a knight would do, only this one wore jeans and a tattered T-shirt.

"I have vowed to your father, my sworn sword-brother and my àrd rìgh, that I will return to him his only child. I beg you, allow me to be faithful to my promise. Permit me to guard ye through this winter and bring ye to your parents."

"But you're talking about months!"

"Then, I promise you, I shall do all in my power to advocate for ye to visit the man ye call *Dad*." His eyes were serious, and mouth held tight.

The trees creaked in the wind and pine's tang filled my nostrils... and Bàn stayed on one knee.

I swallowed. *What choice do I have?* How could I go back through that swimming pool? And this warrior kneeling in front of me was dedicated to returning me to the parents I never knew.

I nodded in silence, tears sliding down my cheeks.

Bàn's broad shoulders eased a little, then he stood. He walked me back to the wolf where we spent some time skinning it and washing the pelt's hide-side in the burn. I pinched my nostrils against the stink. It was worse with the blood adding to the wet dog stench. Once it dried enough to roll up, we left the makeshift camp.

Bàn led me through the gulley, his hand on his sword and his head turning from side to side as his gaze roamed everywhere. The dagger handle peeked out from the back of his belt. I looked up at the top of the cliffs on either side where squat plants grew. What looked like heather, ferns, plus grey rocks covered in moss lined the gulley.

"Are we in Scotland?" I asked Bàn's back.

A chuckle rose from him. "Nae, but your father tells me it's the nearest in beauty to Dál Cruinne."

The day wore on, and a distant roar of water drew closer.

"Are we approaching a waterfall?"

"Nae, we approach the River Bàn-rìghinn. If I remember the geography taught me by the sages, this is the shallowest section of the river. Her name means white queen, for its grandness and the rapids one encounters as it nears the ocean. We can cross ahead."

"Do we have to cross it at all?"

"It cuts the land. No way around it."

"What's on the other side?"

"I know not."

"Then why—?"

"Because it's away from Ciarán Gallawain... and myself." He turned to me then, with an encouraging smile on his face. "We shall find a place to stay over winter."

We continued on and the roar of the river grew as we approached, the noise like a crowd at a football match. A man in a shabby coat sat on a large rock on the riverbank and turned to face us.

"Good day, friend." Bàn stopped a bit away from the man, who looked him up and down, then raked beady eyes over me.

I clenched my teeth and shuddered.

"Is it that ye are wishin' to cross the Bàn-rìghinn?" The man lifted his chin, using it to point to the wide river. Further along to my right, water, white with foam, churned and poured over rocks.

"Aye, that we are, friend," Bàn replied.

The man spat at his feet. "Need a horse."

"I dinnae have one at present." Bàn stood still.

"Ye are from the west." He leaned forward. "Are ye a *friend*? That is at issue, but in truth I care not for I need the coin." The man's gaze went to Bàn's sword. "Weel, I can offer ye passage on ma wee barge, for a price. What can yoo offer?"

Bàn sighed. "Tell me your price."

"Two gold pieces."

"What!" Bàn ground the word out. "Do ye think I'm a wealthy man?"

"Dinnae ken nor care what ye are. Times they be tough. Just cast yer gaze over yonder at oor poor village. Pillaged, it was, not a week since. We need coin for wood and stone for repairs."

The grubby man pointed to a group of houses sitting close to the other bank. I supposed it could loosely be called a village. Some houses were roofless, and rubble piled at the base of what would've been the wall of a larger building. Mud filled the one and only street, and a cow—no, an ox—dragged a cart along it, slipping every two seconds.

"If ye get us to the other bank"—Bàn dug into his belt pouch— "I shall give ye this coin and seek to assist with repairs in the village."

"Yer woman, too?" The man squinted at me.

His woman?

"Aye." Bàn glanced in my direction.

Thanks for asking.

The ferryman ushered me onto the rickety barge.

Barge! Logs roped together.

"This better make it," Bàn said under his breath.

"I'm not your woman, FYI." I lifted my chin to him.

Bàn tilted his head down to look into my eyes. "Ye may be safer if people think ye are," he whispered.

"*Piff.* I can defend myself." Despite my legs being heavy with fatigue. Same with my arms. *And* I'd only had about three hours' sleep in the last twenty-four.

"Aye well, from my experience of this side o' the border"—Bàn spoke into my ear— "there are those who dinnae care the breadth of a felid's whisker if ye are with a man or no'. Just be ready with your fancy kicks, then."

THIRTEEN

Despise not the humble folk with simple lives,
For in these lowly places do true riches lie.

SAGE GLIOCAS
(2870-2962 POST DRAGON WARS)

The World of Dál Cruinne
Post Dragon Wars Year 6083
Eastern Clanlands of Dál Gallain
Clachan Beag Village

Bàn's wet jeans stuck to his calves and the spray from the rapids had soaked his T-shirt by the time they reached the other side. He took Rhynne's hand and helped her off the poor excuse for a barge. Her teeth chattered, dark circles sat under her eyes, and her usually neat hair was a frizzy halo about her face. She looked at him with her mauve eyes and gave him the same accusing glare of her mother's.

"Where may we seek lodgings?" He handed coin to the ferryman.

The ferryman grunted, his lip curling. "Wherever ye can. An' good luck tae ye." He wandered back to his barge where a lad with a goat waited to cross.

Bàn faced the main street ahead, where the clang of a smithy's forge rang out. He shrugged, gave a flick of his head to Rhynne, and walked toward it.

"So, you know where to go?"

"Nae, I aim for the forge, where folk usually gather and discuss the goings on." He turned to her. "We must take care, though. The moment we open our mouths, they will ken we are not from here."

"*Ahem.* But jeans aren't the local dress either, Sherlock. And that's not leather armour you're wearing." Rhynne stood with her hand on her hip, the rolled wolf's skin sitting over her shoulder.

"Aye, ye are correct." He took the pelt, shook it out and wrapped it around her. "You must keep far back from the crowd when we reach the smithy."

She nodded.

He lifted his baldric from his shoulder and tied it around his waist. A blade sitting at his hip would be less conspicuous. He eased his leather jacket and the stained T-shirt from his body. His collarbone, as Rhynne named it, seared like many daggers stabbed their pointy ends directly in. Dragging his clothing over his head with his good arm, he tied both the T-shirt and leather jacket over his shoulder. He gave a quick nod. The poultice that Rhynne had applied stayed in place, and his leather jacket looked like a plain plaid of sorts.

He walked on, Rhynne close by, beside charred stumps where once vendors would have sold their wares. The village cross came into view. A wooden structure, appearing hastily built, dominated the small square. Two bodies dangled from it, attached to the crossbeam by ropes; necks at angles, eyes popped from congested faces, and breeches wet at the crotch.

Rhynne drew in a shaky breath. He grabbed her hand, hushing her, and strode past.

A percussive clang grew louder, and Bàn soon faced the smithy's forge. People milled around and the warmth hit him from many paces out. He moved to the back of the gathering crowd, manoeuvring Rhynne to stand behind him. She may wear a wolf's coat and her hair be a mess, but her beauty stood out—as it did wherever she was.

"Aye, we will rebuild." A squat man spoke to another.

Bàn viewed the smithy's forge over the heads of those gathered. The blacksmith's assistant hung tools, horseshoes, and cooking utensils on hooks from his wall. Tidying up from the recent disturbance, no doubt. He was but a boy, and the men who gathered were older, well past the age of strength and energy.

"We return to our work then. Safe now?" asked a woman, her skirt hem mud-soaked.

"Aye, now that warmonger has the last o' oor young lads," growled an elderly man.

"And oor laird under his thumb," the smithy commented. He stood by his forge with a hammer in one hand and glowing rod of metal in the other. "Lorain submits to Lord Ciarán for our sakes, he says, ken? But what will that bring us in the end?" He belted the rod with his hammer and sparks flew. "Naught but servitude."

"Aye, the laird is safe. But oor young'uns..." The woman burst into tears and the older man with her put his arm on her shoulder, then ushered her out.

The smithy looked up, his gaze followed the weeping woman, then roamed those gathered. Bàn ducked his head. *If only I wore a hoodie!* He took hold of Rhiannon's arm and steered her away from the back of the crowd, then walked in silence until they reached the edge of the charred and blackened dwellings.

"We're not staying long?" Rhynne whispered from the side of her mouth through her chattering teeth.

"Nae. They will recognise me for a warrior—"

"You're not kidding."

"—and think us with Ciarán Gallawain."

"Not their favourite person, from the looks of it."

"Nae, as I have told you. The townsfolk are desperate and would easily give up a warrior from the west to stay any harm to themselves from Ciarán Gallawain." He increased his pace, and they soon walked a road flanked by green fields, and past those on his right sat thick forest hugging a bank of hills, the village now a small cluster of buildings far behind them.

He breathed heavily through his nose while Rhynne walked silently beside him. He was supposed to get a bairn and go straight back to Arlan. Now here he found himself with a beautiful grown woman to protect in enemy territory. And he *their* enemy, or so they would think. *Aye,* he nodded to himself, *she was rather good in a fight, and so-so with a blade.* Yet she had come across naught like the fighting of this world. *Real fighting.*

"Are you talking to yourself, Bàn?" Her voice held a tinge of uncertainty. "You're nodding your head like you're speaking to someone, but not to me, right?"

Bàn's cheek pulled to the side in a half-smile, but he didn't answer her.

"It's a little weird," she said under her breath.

Ahead to the left, a steading cottage sat by the river, its thatched roof torn off at one corner and sections of the surrounding drystone wall gaping with piles of rocks scattered at its base. Sheep gathered across their path, directing their bleating at him.

He guided Rhynne to the left of the sheep, examining the steading house as he did so. Thin smoke arose from the chimney and chickens scratched in the dooryard. Rhynne's teeth chattering rang in his ears and his stomach growled, drawing his attention to their hunger.

"Come. We shall see who lives here. We require sustenance before we attend our journey further."

"But you don't know—" she began.

"The state of this steading tells me a man has nae maintained it for a while. I trust a woman will be more approachable. But ye discern rightly. Stay back until I gather the sense of the occupant."

"You know you speak really *olde worlde posh* sometimes?"

He turned and blinked at her. "And have ye realised ye have spoken the tongue of Dál Gaedhle since ye arrived?"

Her mouth formed an *o*, but no sound came out.

He tugged her forward, and they walked with care along a muddy track to the door of the cottage. Chickens scattered, clucking loudly, then the door to the dwelling creaked open a crack.

"Greetings, steading holder." Bàn bowed from the neck. "Would ye be so kind and able to provide a meal for two weary travellers? I can pay."

The door opened further and a slight woman, her hair covered in a scarf and wearing a skirt in a tartan of the east, took a step to fill the doorway. She looked at him, then her gaze slid past to Rhynne, and the narrowing of her eyes lessened.

"Or if ye wish, I can attend to some chores." He put on a broad smile. "I have experience with drystone. And I see your roof needs attending. I can cut the thatch if you point me toward the rushes."

"What would a man of nobility from the west be doing on this side of the border?" Her voice was strong, and one eye narrowed as she spoke.

"We are merely travellers."

Rhynne stepped beside him. "We have seen the village nearby. We're sorry for whatever misfortune that attack caused you. We can help you clean up. We're just *really* hungry." Rhynne's pleading face beetled into a frown and she pressed her hand to her stomach. A grumble came from that direction.

The semi-charred aroma of porridge reached him then, and his stomach joined in with Rhynne's.

The woman tilted her head and pointed to the woodpile by the far side of the small yard.

"Seat yourselves. I shall bring it tae you. I will hae to water it down, mind. 'Twill be thin."

"Oh, thank you." Rhynne clasped her hands to herself in a posture of gratitude.

They wandered over to the pile where a chopping block and a stump were suitable seats, then sat.

The woman soon came with two wooden bowls and handed them to him and Rhynne.

Aye, thin indeed. The tinge of burnt flavour tickled his tongue as the watery gruel went down, but the warmth sat full in his belly.

"Thank you, gracious lady." Bàn returned the bowl to her. "That is the best meal I have had in days."

The woman's hand rested on her hip. "Where do ye travel to?"

"We are far from home, as ye have so rightly discerned, and seek a place to over-winter."

The woman looked up at the sky, then back down again, resting her gaze on Rhynne.

"Do ye wish for more parritch? I have but one serving left."

Rhynne looked at him, her eyes still hungry.

"Aye, the young lady may have it, if it is truly to spare. I wish not to deprive you of food, madam."

The woman grunted, took Rhynne's bowl and walked back to the cottage. Bàn stood and picked up an axe by the small pile of short cut logs. He spun it in his grasp, then ushered Rhynne off her seat.

"'Tis the chopping block," he said to her questioning expression. "Grab me that thick log there." He pointed to a short but chunky piece. "Place it on the block, please."

Rhynne stood the log on its end on the block then stepped back. He thrust the axe down with his right arm, slicing through the wood and splitting it in two, the pieces flying either side and landing with a clunk on the hard packed earth. Pain shot through his injured collar bone and he breathed deep, pushing it away.

"You shouldn't be doing that." Concern edged Rhynne's tone.

"Och, a sharper blade would help." He retrieved his whetstone from his belt pouch, sat and, holding the axe handle between his knees, sharpened the axe head one-handed.

The woman returned and gave Rhynne the bowl of sloppy oats. "A neat pile would pay for your vittles."

Bàn nodded, putting on a smile as he lifted his focus from sharpening the axe. "Gladly, madam."

He resumed his one-handed wood chopping while Rhynne ate the gruel and the woman returned to her dwelling.

"I'll get this back to her." Rhynne twiddled the empty bowl, then walked to the cottage.

The axe swung down, and he gritted his teeth. This could be an ideal place... if only he could win the woman's trust.

"Hello?" I tapped on the door, and it opened at my touch.

The woman had her back to me, leaning over a deep bucket, hands moving vigorously as she washed a cooking pot. A fire burned in the hearth at one end of the only room, and metal racks and pots hung by it.

"Come in." The woman turned abruptly and hurried over to me, taking me by the arm and leading me to the table in the middle of the tiny room where a candle flickered. The place had one slim window, a box bed by one wall, and shelves on another. Apart from the chair at the table and one by the fire, that was the only furniture. The woman peered at me, her forehead creasing, and her cool wet grip still on my arm. "Tell me, does the warrior hold ye against yer will?"

I took a short step back, then giggled. "No!"

"Truly? Ye are no' sayin' that 'cos ye are afraid o' what the warrior will do tae ye?"

"No, he's my father's friend"—*Boy that sounded weird*— "and he's taking me home."

"I see ye are an innocent one. Is he a good man?"

"Yes."

"Would ye trust him with yer life?" The woman's stare was intense.

I blinked. I'd not really considered it in that light, but... really... *I already have.*

"Yes." I put all my conviction into my tone.

The door shuddered open and Bàn strode in, sword in hand. The woman gave a small cry of alarm, raising a hand to her face.

"Bàn, it's okay." I put my palm out to him. "She's just making sure I'm safe with you."

"Put your sword away, warrior," the woman said. "I have had enough hurt from a blade to last two lifetimes."

"Aye, madam." Bàn re-sheathed his sword.

"Ye may call me Ma Gabràn." She sighed and sat heavily on the rickety chair by the hearth. "Ye seek a place to stay for the winter."

"Aye, Ma Gabràn." Bàn stepped closer.

I joined them both by the fire, its intense heat seeping through my still damp clothes and melting the perma-chill that'd sat beneath my skin since the river crossing.

"And a bad yin of a winter 'twill be," Ma Gabràn said.

"Aye, I ken." Bàn rested his left hand on the pommel of his sword by his waist, the lines of his face easing a touch. "Where are your kin?"

Ma Gabràn's bosom rose and fell with a sigh that seemed to come from deep within her. "My son and his wife died in a battle. Trained to be warriors, though not of noble stock. Forced to fight for that Lord Ciarán." She spat out his name with such force that I flinched. "And now"—she sobbed— "ma wee boy... grandson... their lad. Taken by them warriors the other day." She picked up the edge of her skirt and wiped her face. "He's too young to fight, I said—*shouted* it at them. But they took him for their chores in camp, they said. Train him to fight, they said." She sniffed deeply. "If he lives that long."

Bàn knelt in front of her. "I can go and find—"

"Nae, ye have this noblewoman to protect and take to her faither. I have had enough of young people dyin'." She sat taller. "My grandson will live his fate, as you will live yours."

Ma Gabràn sniffed, her snuffles filling the air of the small room. Bàn stood and looked at me, his expression holding a decision.

"Ma Gabràn, we would stay with you this winter. Help repair your steading and prepare for next year's plantings. Care for your sheep and so on in return for lodgings. Ye have my shield arm also."

"Aye, agreed." She peered up at him. "But that broken shoulder of yours needs to mend first, does it not?"

Fourteen

Fate, destiny, purpose, calling.
Name it what ye will, for naught will cease its inescapable pull.

GRAND MASTER LLEW
ISLE OF INNESFARNE
(POST DRAGON WARS 6000-current)

The World of Dál Cruinne
Late Summer, Post Dragon Wars Year 6083
Eastern Clanlands of Dál Gallain
Ma Gabràn's Steading

Rain fell overnight, pattering softly but continually on the dooryard outside. Clanking buckets roused Bàn from his mat by the hearth as Rhynne picked up yet another full pail.

"Here, let me take that." He took the handle from Rhynne. "It's surely my turn. Ye go rest."

"So, it rains here in summer like it does in Scotland." Rhynne pushed her hair behind her ear.

"Aye, so I'm told. I must get the thatch to fix this roof before we all drown." He shucked on his leather jacket, barely grimacing at the soreness in his shoulder, and stepped out into the rain. Perhaps gathering rushes for thatch would not take him too long away from his proper mission of keeping Rhynne safe.

A cloud-darkened dawn greeted him, and chickens clucked their curiosity as he strode past on his way to the trough that watered the sheep in the meadow nearest the house. He smiled. It had been many a year since he had dry-stoned, but his repairs to the fencing walls seemed to be sturdy enough and now confined the animals securely in the meadow. He'd managed it all one-handed. Mostly. He rubbed his collarbone, now knitting nicely, but the ache had seemed stronger just prior to the rain. He would tackle the wood pile again today.

"Chook, chook, chook!" Rhynne shouted behind him.

He emptied the pail, splashing the nose of the lone sheep interested in a drink in the rain, and turned to the cottage. Rhynne stood at the shelter where the chickens had gathered out of the weather. Her face lifted and her mouth spread in a grin. He trod back that way and stood by the entrance to the rickety lean-to, watching her. She held a bowl and scattered old grain and mouldy bread. Brown and white chickens scurried to her, heads bobbing as they pecked at the ground for their morsels. She giggled.

"Ye love the wee beasts, do ye not?" He couldn't keep the delight from his voice.

"They're gorgeous."

"Nae, they are ugly."

"Aww, don't be so unkind," she huffed. "There's something about birds. I've always liked them. They're the descendants of dinosaurs. Did you know that? Do you have dinosaurs here?"

Dragon's teeth!

His hand froze on the way to scratch an itch in his beard. The animals from the Other World's past named *dinosaurs* were similar to dragons. Or so he had discovered while watching the TV during his sojourn there. He'd avoided mentioning the dragon attack that had led to Rhiannon taking Rhynne as a babe to George for safety. It may have scared her to know such dangerous beasts were alive and well. Awoken from myth here in Dál Cruinne. He moved his hand—which finally obeyed him—and covered his mouth to hide any uncertainty in his expression. He chewed his lower lip.

What to do?

She had asked few questions, and not spoken of returning to George since the wolf attack, seeming content to discover her new world. And these beasts were part of this world.

He coughed. "Aye. But we name them dragons."

"*Dragons!*" She dropped the bowl, and it landed on a chicken's head. A scattering and frantic clucking ensued. Rhynne's eyes rounded as she drew in a gasping breath. "Wow! Awesome!"

"What? Ye are nae scared?"

Her mouth closed, and her brow drew in. "Why? Should I be?"

"Ah... your grandfather, Donnach MacEnoicht, the late Àrd Rìgh of Dál Gaedhle, was killed by a fire-breathing dragon."

Rhynne's eyebrows were lost in her hairline, and her jaw dropped. "Oh." She surveyed the chickens that had returned to her feet, then her gaze flew up to him. "So, they have *that* kind here? None you can make friends with and ride? Like in a fantasy novel?"

"Um. Well, your father, Arlan, has a dragon. A small one, mind."

Rhynne dashed toward him. Chickens squawked, and feathers flew as she shook her hands out beside her.

"My real father has a pet *dragon!*" She reached him, grabbing his upper arms. Mauve eyes filled his vision. The heat from her warm hands seeped through his sleeves.

He swallowed. "Aye, well, not a pet as such, but she is very attached to yer father and mother. Protects them both. Quite fiercely, actually."

"Can he ride her?"

Bàn frowned. "What? Ride Drayce? Och, no!"

"Drayce." Awe filled her voice, and her breath brushed his face. "What a cool name."

Her natural perfume—reminiscent of lilac—overpowered the unpleasant smell of chickens and their droppings, and her loose hair tickled his cheek. Her eyes regained focus and her gaze lowered to his mouth. Rhynne stood so close it would take but little movement to place his mouth to her own. Her moist lips glistened.

Her gaze flicked to his, eyes widening slightly, then she took an abrupt step back. Heat rose from his neck, setting his cheeks ablaze.

He spun to the woodpile and, snatching an armful of chopped firewood, willed his hammering heart into submission while he walked back to the cottage with her in silence. He returned the pail to its place beneath a heavy drip, then stacked the wood neatly on top of the pile near the hearth. Ma Gabràn sat by the sliver of window with a lighted candle, working on the same garment she had started just after they arrived. She looked up at them, grinning.

"'Tis nearly done and ye shall be warm and dry this winter, lass." She lifted the heavy cloak of thick woven black wool with a wide collar of wolf fur almost half the length of the garment. She had just about sewn the pelt completely to it.

Rhynne stepped to her and ran her fingers through the soft silver fur. "Oh, it's glorious. How did you stop it from smelling like wet dog?"

"Just cured it, lass." She looked up at him then. "And warrior lord Bàn, I have pieces of leather to make ye a cuirass and armguards. They will nae take me long, though the hardened leather is difficult to work with. Mayhap I should fasten it together with studs. I would have ye kitted oot afore this winter sets in." She lifted her chin in the direction of the door. "Although ma bones tell me tha' rain will soon turn tae snow."

"Ye are so kind, Ma Gabràn. How can we repay ye?" Bàn asked.

"Ye are. Ma steading ne'er looked sae good. Oh, and I hae drawn ye a map o' where tae go tae get the rushes for thatch." She lifted a scrap of leather from her work basket. "Now that yer shoulder bone is well on the mend, ye can make the journey for it."

He took the leather piece from her. On it she had scratched a crude map in charcoal.

"I will need a mule or such. I have coin," he said. "When ye were in the wee village purchasing the leather, did ye see what was available in the stock yards, by any chance?"

Ma Gabràn scrunched her mouth to the side, wrinkles surrounding her lips like sunrays. "Nae, but I shall go today and see what is at market. 'Tis mid-week, is it no'? Aye. Market day." She shoved her work aside and gathered her shawl from her bed. "The sooner ye go, the sooner ye return, I always say." She took the coin from his hand, winking at him, and trotted to the door.

"Here, Ma, take my jacket. It will be some shield from the rain." He handed it to her.

Rhynne found an extra shawl and raced to the door with it.

"Thank ye, young'n," she said to Rhynne. She shucked on Bàn's jacket, then covered it with the shawl she wrapped around herself. "The rain will cease soon."

"But you said it would then be snow. One of us should come with you."

"Nae! Ye'll be seen as a foreigner. Dinnae fash. 'Twill nae snow for a wee bit yet." She smiled, the gaps from her missing teeth showing, then trotted out the door.

"I had enough left over to buy some studs to fasten yer chest armour." Ma Gabràn held out to Bàn the halter lead of a mule, a sturdy-looking beast.

But a lowly animal. Such a change from his own stallion. His chest pinched. If only he had his steed right now. It would mean a faster journey and less time away from Rhynne.

"Ye must stay inside the cottage while I'm away." He spoke sternly to Rhynne. "No one must see you."

"Aye, I have a place in which she can hide if ought take note of her." Ma Gabràn placed a hand on her hip. "Or ye dinnae go."

"Nae, Ma. I promised to repair your thatch. And I shall." He waved a finger an inch from Rhynne's nose. "Ye stay oot o' sight, aye?"

She raised an eyebrow at him. He widened his eyes at her, then she nodded.

"There is a tunic of my sons ye must take," Ma Gabràn said. "'Twill be a touch tight, but ye need more than the tattered thing ye came in, being oot in this weather an' all."

"Dinnae worry about me, Ma. I'll make quick the journey, be about my task in haste, then be back afore ye ken it." *I must.* He would leave Rhynne without his protection for as short a time as he could make it.

He hurried inside, changing into the offered tunic and his leather jacket Ma Gabràn had returned to him. He tucked his sharpened dagger in his belt at the back and settled his baldric over his shoulder. The handle of *Dìleas,* her edge also freshly honed, sat proudly above his shoulder. Ma Gabràn stood back, eyes glinting in her survey of him.

"Aye, ye are a grand warrior, I am certain." She gave a short laugh. "Now go and be a humble thatcher for me, aye?"

I stood among the chickens; their gentle cluck and *tuk tuk tuk* told me they were content with the food I'd scattered around for them.

"Man, I never thought I'd be a farm girl."

The rain had stopped for a bit, so I ambled to the drystone wall where I could look down the road. Ma Gabràn said he'd be half a day getting there, a day cutting. Then the same to come back. That was two in total. He'd been gone a day.

Why am I counting?

A sheep bleated at the fence right in front of me. I jumped. It bleated again.

"What's *your* problem?"

Other sheep joined in, their hooves mud-caked from the meadow, which was now almost bare of grass. Perhaps I should move them to a meadow that had grass. Didn't you need a sheepdog for that?

I strode back to the cottage to ask Ma Gabràn, but clanking and hammering came from one of the smaller outside buildings, so I walked to the doorway of the drystone-built shed where candlelight flickered from inside. I peered in. Ma Gabràn belted some leather with a hammer.

"Come in, lass. I'll be having a wee *stooshie* with this hardened leather till I get your man's armour made, ken."

"He's not my man."

"Oh, is he no'?" Ma Gabràn looked up from her work, one eye squinting. "If ye say so."

"He's my father's best friend."

"Ye must hae a young faither."

"Don't you believe me?"

Ma Gabràn placed her hammer on the garment, walked around the bench and took my hands in her own. "I ken ye are a noblewoman, tho' ye seem somewhat unfamiliar with our ways. Like ye are no' frae around here. And your man's—Bàn's—accent is strongly from the west. I dare not think who ye really are, but ye have been good to me and I am fond of ye both and I wud never want harm tae..." Ma Gabràn's grip tightened, and her focus seemed to wander, like she now looked right through me.

"Ma Gabràn?" The hairs on my arms stood on end.

I shook Ma Gabràn's hands and called again.

The old woman's eyelids fluttered, and she gasped as she opened them fully. "Who are yoo?"

"What do you mean?" The question wouldn't stall the woman for long, but what should I say? How much could I risk telling my new *old* friend?

"Ye are a body of importance."

"It may not be good for you to know," I said.

"I dinnae mean yer family. I mean, *who* ye are. *What* ye are. Och, come inside." She grabbed the candlestick in one hand and my arm in the other, then marched me to the cottage, where she sat me in front of the fire.

Ma Gabràn stoked the fire, swung the kettle over the flame, and sat on the stool opposite me, taking my hands in her own again.

"I have nae always been a steading holder." Ma Gabràn's throat worked, and she blinked rapidly. "I was once a mage." Her gaze darted to me, her deep brown pupils locking with mine, and she seemed to wait for a reaction.

Mage? Magician? Sorcerer? I swallowed. *Witch?*

"And you're not one now?" I spoke slowly.

"Aye, ye are right. I suppose I am still one, but I have not practiced my art for many a year. But I still sense things. Such as ye and Lord Bàn are good people and ye needed my help. And... that ye have a gift. And ye must grow it."

I pulled my hands away. "No, no, just wait a minute. I'm a king's daughter and my mum's a warrior woman, but that's it! Oops." I smacked my hand to my mouth so hard I split my lip. A metal tang seeped onto my tongue.

Ma Gabràn tilted her head, a warm smile encompassing her features. "Aye lass, I kenned ye were noble. But ye are also gifted. Ye must embrace it. Cultivate it." She stood and pulled me to stand with her. "Come." She tugged gently and walked me out the door to the yard. "Look."

I followed the line of Ma's arm to the mountains that sat just behind the steading. White-capped and rocky, they glared down at me. I pressed my teeth onto my lip, sucking away the metallic taste from where I'd split it, and took in as much detail as I could. A dark strip of path zig-zagged up the side of the mountain.

"When they come"—Ma Gabràn's spoke soft and low in my ear— "for aye, they will, ye and your warrior must flee to the sage hold atop this mount. There ye will be safe for as long as ye need be."

I spun to Ma Gabràn, her face so close it blurred. "You'll come with us."

"Nae, it is not my fate. But *that* mountain is yours."

FIFTEEN

Among the verdant meadows,
Where those sleeping quiet lay.
Their task complete, their lives cut short,
The warrior price did pay.

POETRY OF THE WARRIOR
WARRIOR SAGE TAPAÌDH
(4009-4059 POST DRAGON WARS)

The World of Dál Cruinne
Post Dragon Wars Year 6083
Eastern Clanlands of Dál Gallain

Ma Gabràn was correct, *Tobraichean na beatha* bless her soul and her wee knitted woollen stockings.

It had taken the best part of the day to arrive at a swampy marsh where water reeds grew plenteously. Bàn eased himself off the mule, every bone of his rear telling him of its presence and unhappiness that a saddle hadn't been included in the old woman's purchases at the market. He pulled his jacket from the animal's back. It had sufficed for a makeshift saddle.

Only just.

The body of water shimmered silvery-white under a cloudy sky, and thick, long grass sprouting through the water encircled the bank. More rushes than he could carry if he cut all. His gut twinged. How much would be enough? He had not enquired.

Och, a full load on a mule's back would have to do!

He staked the lead rein and let the animal nibble, pulled his dagger from his belt, and adjusted his sword while he surveyed his surrounds. None near. None interested in thatch, then. 'Twas late in the season to be clambering over a roof for repairs. And late in the day, but he would make a start.

He chuckled. Aye, the sooner ye start, the sooner ye will return.

Bless you, Ma Gabràn.

Bàn rubbed his nose, but the tickle remained. He sneezed, eyes opening wide to a glaring sunrise and sheaves of rushes, his makeshift bed and blanket, falling awry. The mule brayed a morning welcome, ears pricked in expectancy.

"Aye, I'll move ye to more feed." He pulled the stake to which the mule's halter lead was attached, then walked a ways to some verdant growth on the rise of a hill. The mule followed, nibbling rush straw stuck to the back of Bàn's jacket. "Soon be there, pal. The grass looks sweeter over here. Ye will thank me, aye?"

He strode to the side of the hill where the long grass, lush and a deep green, dragged on his lower legs, then he bashed the tether stake into the ground with his booted foot. Rummaging in his bag, he brought out the cheese and dried bread Ma Gabràn had wrapped in a cloth and dropped in at the last moment. He climbed the gentle slope to the hilltop then sat.

His teeth crunched down on the hard bread. He had finished his water bag on arriving yesterday and had naught to sodden it. The swamp pond water was too muddy. He would not risk bad bowels.

He surveyed the land for a clean water source and breathed in deep, the meadow's heady scent lifting his soul. By all that was good, 'twas grand to be home in his own world. To his left sat the Central Meadhan Mountains, white with snow. Some of their highest peaks rose not far behind Ma Gabràn's steading cottage. Here, they were farther away, and a wide valley began at their base and continued in front of him as a moor. It seemed to go on forever. Wide and flat, with a river snaking silver through some peaty sections of it, and grassy knolls spread to the side, here and there. Like ready-made redoubts.

Bàn squinted, searching for the end of this vast natural arena. It went on a fair ways, but far in the distance sat snow-capped mountains, his vision funnelled by the rocky bens either side.

What would Arlan make of this? A battle ground made by nature. And here in the east, Ciarán Gallawain would be sure to know of it.

He hit his fist to his forehead.

Of course the *bassa* does!

This would be his Mòr Cath Làraich—aye, a place for a significant battle.

Bàn strained his vision again to see the end of the valley. Sages taught of a mountain range cutting between the edge of Dál Gallain and the foreign lands beyond. An army pressed to that end would be trapped. Blocked from escape.

Cornered.

Then annihilated.

He ground his teeth against the cold forming in his gut.

So, if Ciarán Gallawain planned to use this plain, it would involve such a tactic.

Bàn breathed heavily, nostrils flaring.

Where was that piece of leather of a makeshift map? He had the cloth wrapping the cheese also.

His mouth pulled tight in a grin. He lifted the borrowed tunic he wore and poked into a hidden pocket in his jeans from the Other World.

A pen, they named it, and its ink went on and on.

Good. For he required such to map every detail of this battlefield.

The sun angled toward the eastern horizon, speeding its journey home. Bàn scribbled in the fading light, hatching areas to note the marshy places that would bog horse and cart, and other drier areas suitable for caltrops and stakes to impale and maim a horse or foot warrior. A trickle of a burn flowed across the area too. Yet another water source for thirsty warbands. The dryer places ran well along, so wagons could bring supplies once further in the field. There were areas of forest skirting the glen—timber for field fortifications and such. He would patch the hide and the cheesecloth together. They made one large map of the land he had surveyed as best he could whilst riding the mule as far as he dared into this valley in one day.

He grunted. He had stayed an extra day and was yet to load the mule with the cut rushes and return. But 'twas essential he mapped. The valley spread before him would sure to be a place of significance to Gallawain's battle plans. It could be one of many possible contingencies. Even so, Arlan must know this one well enough to be prepared and have the advantage.

Ma would keep Rhynne safe. Rhynne could hide. Fight if she had to.

His cartographic task was almost as imperative as Rhynne's protection.

He pushed against a cool flash that ran across his neck. Ciarán's warriors had taken all from the village. Surely, they would not return so soon. Ma Gabràn had hidden Rhynne and himself as well as she could, but one or two villagers who had passed by had kept their gaze on the steading longer than one would expect.

No, he must hasten back now. He would memorise all he could of this valley, for he had nae more makeshift parchment.

Rhynne would be there to greet him.

A warmth sprang into his chest, catching his breath. He longed to be near her again, and enjoy her smile, or even risk his arm brushing against hers in some chance moment. He rubbed his upper lip. What would his sword-brother make of his growing fondness for his daughter?

Soft rain pattered on his head, the air cooling with summer rushing to autumn. He rolled his map up tightly and tucked it into his jacket and, unpinning the mule's tether, walked back to the pile of rushes he'd placed beside the pond the previous day. He made quick work of loading it, then stood by the reedy lake, sipping from his water bag filled with fresh burn water from the wide glen. Raindrops landed on the water's surface, stirring the silence with a tinkling. Circles, ever increasing—the water's version of the endless knot—expanded and crossed each other, impeding their own journeys across the surface. The air was still, only the water spoke.

How peaceful. And what a contrast to the war that raged in these parts and sent its circles of disturbance toward Dál Gaedhle.

Serenity surrounded him, as though daring the future to lie about its history that was yet to be. Deny the truth of an evil man wishing to obtain all, but who would consume all in the process.

He shook himself. Time to return and resume his duty. Protect the precious daughter of his sword-brother, sworn liege, àrd rìgh, and dearest friend.

Aye, and he would do so with his life.

Sixteen

— · —

**The World of Dál Cruinne
Post Dragon Wars Year 6083
Eastern Clanlands of Dál Gallain
Clachan Beag Village**

Ma Gabràn leaned on her walking stick, bunions heating, and hips creaking like dry wood rubbing stone. 'Twas nae a far walk to the village, but her joints shouted that snow would fall soon. Aye, an early winter was upon them, impatient to turn their world to cold and ice. Extra mouths meant more supplies needed to be stocked for when the clouds above opened, and their contents blanketed the world. Rhynne stayed at the cottage. Ma dared not defy the warrior lord Bàn's orders, nae matter how many bags o' food she must carry home hersel'.

The girl fretted. Her man had not yet returned. Should have by yester-eve.

Nae. *Not her man.* Ma tutted to herself. The lass had fooled no one as she had glued her doe eyes to the road on which he would come home. Ma Gabràn had forced her to stay inside. There were strangers in town and the need for stores provided an excuse. She would discover why Lord Ciarán had sent more warriors to the village.

Liquid mud seeped through the gaps in her boots, cold trickled through her woollen stockings, and squelched between her toes. She had meant to repair them, but warrior lord Bàn's leather vest and arm bracers held greater urgency. She nodded her satisfaction at not only completing the task but sewing together for him a woollen cloak with a sheepskin collar.

Aye, he would need it.

She passed the butchery, the walls almost restored. She craned her neck to see ahead. The road remained mud-mixed rubble, and only half the buildings were returned to their previous wattle-and-daube. Murmurs came from ahead, where the smithy plied his trade. He had received little abuse when Lord Ciarán's warriors had cleared the village of men.

She spat. Boys, ye mean!

Her heart clenched... *My boy.*

Gossip told they were nae the only village to receive such treatment.

If only the fighting would stop. Bàn, a fine man and fine warrior, to be sure, would be of the likes to win against the badness of Gallawain and his ambitions. But it did nae always go that way. She had seen it too often.

Mayhap Bàn fought for the new àrd rìgh of Dál Gaedhle. If so, why was he here with the maid? The maid who had let slip her faither was a king. But many a laird regarded hissel' a king. She would never speak her wonderings out loud.

"Greetings, Ma Gabràn." The reek of the unwashed reached her. She lifted her head to see who she already knew it to be.

"Greetings to yersel', barge man." She walked on, but he stepped beside her.

"I see the two who crossed a while ago have aided your repairs. A few have commented on the blond warrior type who knows the ways of a drystone."

"What of it?" She kept her stick in its rhythm.

"Och, naught. 'Tis only that"—he bent closer, his unwashed male scent wafting in her nose— "a warrior faithful to Gallawain is in town, and I ken your visitors are from the west. He may be interested."

She straightened, pinching her nostrils tight against his stench, and speared him with her glare.

He held up a hand, palm out. "Not that 'tis any business o' mine, like. But others, well, they be still so scared o' that lord an' all he took. Well, tae keep the peace and him awa' frae us. Some might..." He shrugged. "Well..."

She hurried along, slipping slightly in the mud, a piercing pain shooting out of her hip and down her thigh. She stopped and leaned on her stick to catch her breath, then walked at a slower pace as she approached the blacksmith's. *Nae sae much of a crowd today.* But, aye, a warrior with a sword handle sitting over his shoulder and dirk at his belt, and someone whispering in his ear.

She turned without them noticing her—with luck—and hastened her pace, grimacing at the complaints of old joints.

After her numbered paces, when she would be near home, she raised her head to view the road. A tall, slim figure stood a wee way down the road, just past her gate. Long thick black hair, shining in the midmorning light, fell in graceful waves down the back of young Rhynne, who faced the direction her warrior man would return.

Ma Gabràn stepped behind her. "Ye need tae be aware of yer back. Your man will nae thank ye if the warrior of Lord Ciarán, who prowls the town the noo, finds ye sae easily."

Rhynne spun at her words, mouth open.

"And dinnae continue to deny ye have feelings for warrior Bàn."

Rhynne shut her mouth tight on whatever would have come out of it.

"Go gather yer things, and his. Ye must leave as soon as he returns. They are here."

Rhynne's eyes widened, but her mouth firmed.

She would be brave, then.

That's ma lass.

"And the last o' that cheese." Ma Gabràn tucked the chunk into the hessian bag.

I folded the tunic Ma Gabràn had given me, its coarse fibre cloth rough beneath my fingers. I must be the same size as her daughter-in-law.

The same size she *was.*

I gulped and leaned on the table. It creaked. My mother, Rhiannon, had taken me to Dad to keep me safe from this war when I was a baby. It was still the same war, and I wasn't a baby anymore. *So I'd better stop acting like one!*

I could fight, and Bàn was brilliant. We'd be okay if anyone came after us. I had to admit that my father, Arlan, knew what he was doing sending Bàn for me.

Where is he?

Ma Gabràn had come home all churned up, with no supplies from the village, then trotted around the cottage getting out the cloak she'd secretly been making Bàn and some more blankets, saying we'd need a saddle on the mule this time. Could a mule gallop? We needed speed, right?

"Ma Gabràn, are you sure?"

"Aye." She didn't look up from the folded blanket she'd placed on the table by the leather armour and arm bracers for Bàn. "Ye must go. Even if not this warrior of Gallawain's, then 'twill be another. And they never come alone." She rested her hand on the pile and turned watery eyes to me. "The snow comes."

"What about you?"

"Nae, child. It is all about you, aye?"

"But they'll hurt you."

"Better me than—"

"Don't say that, Ma." I wrapped my arms around her stooped shoulders and tiny frame. "We can stay and fight them before we leave."

"Nae, child." Ma Gabràn breathed her frustration into our hug, then released herself from it and looked up at me. "They will either slaughter ye or take you to their laird, and once they find oot ye are of nobility of the west, they will demand a ransom. They'll hold you in their dungeon till your relatives pay a ridiculous sum. And kill your warrior for certain. 'Twill be one against many. Is that what ye wish?"

I hung my head and shook it in silence.

The *clip clop* of hooves approached, and Ma Gabràn took a sharp intake of air.

A mule brayed and I let out a breath. I raced to the door and pulled it open. The sky had darkened and the chill breeze blowing earlier had now warmed a touch. Bàn lifted his leg over the beast and landed on the wet ground, shaking his legs out in a stiff manner. His gaze shot to me, and his smile erupted. Giving me a nod, his eyes slid to Ma Gabràn, who bustled past me.

"Get that beast unloaded. Gather yer things."

Light from the freshly lit lantern Ma Gabràn held shed gold on Bàn's features. They hardened as he followed her progress toward him.

"A Gallawain warrior is in the village. Time to leave," she said.

His jaw worked and his hand on the rushes curled tighter. He glanced at me, then heaved the bundled rushes from the mule's back. The beast hung its head low and seemed only interested in eating the rushes Bàn threw at its feet.

Ma Gabràn spun to me. "Dinnae just stand there, lass. Get yer gear and help him load up. You'll away at once. Nae time tae waste."

Pressing my lips tight, I pivoted on my heel. There wasn't much to pack, and it all sat on the table. I put my cloak around me, the luxurious, silky wolf's fur caressing my cheeks, then grabbed the cloak for Bàn, the blankets for a saddle, and the leather armour. Slipping the bag of food over my shoulder, I hurried out the door. Tiny white spots fell from the sky, silent and cool. They stuck in Bàn's hair and speckled his shoulders and left a cool kiss on my cheeks.

"Yer saddle." Ma Gabràn took the blankets from me and threw them over the mule. "Yer armour and cloak." She lifted her chin to me, and I handed Bàn the leather chest armour.

He emptied the pockets of the leather jacket he wore, then threw it over the makeshift blanket-saddle. It slipped, and Ma grabbed it before it reached the ground. He shucked on the leather armour, stuffing a rolled wad of something in between the chest piece and his tunic. He slipped the arm bracers on and held out his arms while I tied the laces.

"Hurry," Ma Gabràn growled, and took the thick, heavy wool cloak from me and handed it to Bàn, whose jaw dropped.

"I want nae thanks, just you twa safe and oot o' here." Ma Gabràn's tone hardened. "Get yoursels up that mountain afore this snow blocks the track." She made shooing motions with her hands as Bàn threw on the cloak.

"What's up the mountain?" Bàn secured his cloak about his shoulders and adjusted his sword for easy access.

"A sage hold." Ma Gabràn gave a curt nod. "The lass kens."

My throat tightened, and I stepped up to Ma and flung my arms around her. Beneath her tartan wrap, bony shoulder blades pressed against my hands.

She leaned into me, and I held on tighter. "I won't forget you. Keep safe," I said.

Ma Gabràn gently eased away. "And you promise me ye'll do what I said, aye?"

"Aye." I nodded and let go.

Bàn's arms flew around the woman, surrounding them both in his new cloak. "I ken ye dinnae wish for thanks, but I speak on behalf of the Àrd Rìgh of Dál Gaedhle when I thank ye for all ye have done for his daughter."

Ma Gabràn took a sharp intake of breath, then turned her stare on me.

Bàn placed a kiss on the old woman's forehead, released his embrace, then turned to me, cocking his head to the mule. "Up ye get." He held out his hands for a leg-up.

I knelt in his clasped hands and my shaky thigh muscles got me part way. Bàn's thrust did the rest, and I found myself astride the mule. Bàn lifted himself behind me. The mule brayed and trotted forward a pace and Bàn grabbed the reins, pulling it round.

I looked over Bàn's shoulder. Ma Gabràn clutched Bàn's leather jacket to herself. I waved, my vision blurring, my heart cracking, and soft, wet snow splodging on my face.

More snow fell, dotting Ma Gabràn in white, then a gust sent more across my line of sight. Bàn kicked the mule, and it jerked to a trot down the lane leading out of the steading, the figure of Ma Gabràn getting smaller and smaller while the world got whiter and whiter.

"She was so good to us," I whispered.

"Aye." Bàn's answer was curt but edged in softness, his voice right beside my ear. "Well, pal, let's see what ye can do. Ha!" He kicked the mule again.

It brayed and did its version of a gallop, following the track to our left.

The mountain sat ahead of us, silent and covered in a swirling snow-globe cloak.

The dull *clop* of unshod mule hooves travelled to the north. Ma Gabràn pressed her face into the jacket. The young man's aroma embedded in the warm leather filled her nostrils. It spoke of bravery, dedication, loyalty.

Aye, goodness emanated from the warrior.

Keep them safe, o' god of this world, for ye are the one who made the humble beast they ride. Get it and its precious load up that mount, I beg ye.

The sharp *clip clop* of shod hooves approached from the direction of the village. She stood tall and grasped the jacket tighter to her breast. A dark horse, coming at a trot, headed down her path, followed by three more, snow beating their long faces and flecking their riders in white. The cloak of the leader flew open in the breeze, revealing an orange Lorain clan tartan. Sword handles on the backs of all glinted in her lantern's light.

Lorain. Their laird's clan. And now he belonged to Lord Ciarán Gallawain.

"Ho, old woman." The lead warrior pulled his horse up sharply, its hooves slipping on the snow-sludged pathway.

Ma Gabràn's stomach churned. 'Twas the same clansman warrior whose ear bent to those who would whisper.

"What do ye seek?" Her voice was clear and strong despite the dampening effect the falling snow had on the sounds around her.

The warrior rested a casual arm over the pommel of his saddle, while his horse snorted and flicked its head, tack jingling. Another war horse gave a whinny.

"I hear ye have sheltered a couple from the west."

"Just travellers passing through."

"Passing through long enough to repair yer drystone wall, old woman." His gaze lowered to her hands. "What have ye there?"

Ma Gabràn's stomach sank. *Fool.* She still held the proof of Bàn's recent presence, and the oddity of his attire, ensuring some took note. She swallowed and narrowed her gaze.

"Where are the warrior and the young woman?" the clansman demanded.

"Not here. Now go." She lifted her chin. "I'll waste ma breath on ye nae longer." She turned her face to the sky.

The warrior snorted.

It had been many a year, but aye, there are some things a spirit never forgets. Ma Gabràn concentrated on the snow, each crystal pattern unique and close. In her cleared vision, white fingers extended in shapes and lines. She drew in a quick breath.

So beautiful.

The frozen falling water spoke of ancient glaciers, their long slow path marking millennia, and her life's breadth a mere dot in the epoch of their time.

Power surged, that for too long was but a memory, shunting the air from her lungs. In her urgency and using a skill long dormant, its flood into her soul rocked her, but she held firm.

"What are you doing, old woman?" The warrior's voice filtered through the roar in her head. His companions echoed his question with their grunts.

Silence, you fools!

Ma Gabràn raised her arms; the dark garment she'd held in her grasp now fell to the snow.

"Oh, power of the storm

Of wind and snow and cold,

Send forth thy chilly blast

With white their world enfold." Her voice rang true.

"Stop woman!" The warrior's tone held command.

"Cover with thy blanket crisp;

Hide them safe from all who seek."

"Stop it, I say!" Fear edged the warrior's words and metal rang, his withdrawn blade flashing in the lantern light.

Unsheathing swords sang as his companions followed suit. The wind picked up, swirling around her and the warriors. The men gawked as snow bounced from the ground and lifted, joining the frozen water in the air, thickening its presence, and impeding their view.

"Strengthen legs and will and sight." Ma Gabràn raised her voice above the commanding cries of Gallawain's men. *Naught will silence me!*
"While blinding eyes of those
Who might,
With dire intentions
Deepen plight."
"Argh!" The warrior nudged his steed closer.
Ma Gabràn locked eyes with the Lorain clansman warrior. Metal whistled, flashing down, slicing her neck, severing head from torso.
A gust of wind brought a wall of white, knocking the warrior from his horse and scattering the jumpy mounts of his companions. Riders shortened reins and shushed their steeds.
Ma Gabràn's soul lifted. She looked down at her body now blanketed in white and sending a fountain of steaming red in rivulets throughout. She rose to face the mountain. A snowstorm whirled around it, the track at its base now covered, blocking any chance of pursuit. The warriors emerging from the snow dump would have nae chance to follow.
Ma Gabràn's soul smiled, her last task complete, then lifted to glorious realms above.

Seventeen

The snows have come, and aye, with a vengeance. We are cut off from the lands below till nature's frigid breath turns to warmth and melts our world. Now begins our time of quiet meditation. Of honing skills and keeping bodies and friendships warm.

FROM THE JOURNAL OF COMGALL
APPRENTICE SAGE AND MAGE CANDIDATE
SAGE HOLD MOUNTAIN

The World of Dál Cruinne
Post Dragon Wars Year 6083
Eastern Clanlands of Dál Gallain
The Mountain

Bàn grunted. He'd pushed the poor animal. The mule had tired from his urgent ride home to Ma Gabràn's steading, but he still dug in his heels each time it slowed or faltered. With the snowfall so dense, it would be impossible to hear riders to their rear. Bàn estimated the mule had got them halfway up the mount, though it was hard to tell. A wall of mountain sat by his right and a drop to his left, then a sharp horseshoe bend, and the drop was to his right and the mount to his left. This had alternated three times so far. The track remained discernible, but for how long that would last in this thick fall of snow he cud nae guess.

The wind gusted, flapping Rhynne's cloak open.

"Tuck in your cloak, Rhynne," he yelled over the roaring wind. "Ye'll die of the chill."

"I know." She shoved the end of the cloak into her side. "Exposure."

"What?"

"First aid." She twisted her face to him, shouting into the wind that would snatch her words away. "But my cloak is saturated. It's only making me colder."

The mule staggered, bumping her face against his. Her cheek touched him, ice cold.

"Pull yer collar up. Ye are frozen already."

She nodded, lifting the wolf fur around her neck and face, and holding it tight with one hand, but the top of her head remained exposed. Her other hand rested against his where he held the reins. It was glacial, so he rubbed her fingers with his own free hand.

"I can hardly feel that." She leaned back into him, her voice muffled through the fur, brushing her ice-stiffened hair locks against his face. "My head's numb too."

She stayed there, as if to share his warmth. His teeth chattered, and he blinked away the flakes that would land on his eyelashes, for to clear his view of the snow-covered track ahead.

The mule stumbled and tripped, almost unseating them. Rhynne's wolf's fur collar fell away from her face, and she did naught to pull it back. The mule groaned and gave a weak bray. He kicked it on, urging its ever-slowing pace. He steered the mule around another sharp bend in the zig-zag track. White covered most of it with only a narrow ditch in the middle of where the path would lie.

"I hate to say it, but are we there yet?" Her voice held a whine.

"I dinnae ken. What did Ma Gabràn say?"

"Only that up this mountain there's a sage hold. I think she meant right at the top." Rhynne's voice now sounded hollow, sleepy. "Ma Gabràn pointed to above the snowline when there was a snow line. Not like now when it's *all* snow."

Rhynne had kept her sarcasm. *Good.* Still, a sting hit his chest. They *must* make it.

The shiver in his arms moved to his core.

The mule grunted. "Come on, pal. Keep going. *Gee up!*"

The animal's feet splayed beneath them, tossing Rhynne into the snow beside the track. Bàn jumped off, tugging the reins to get the animal to its feet. Rhynne grunted and stood up beside him, brushing snow from her jeans and cloak. He shook the wet snow out of his hair.

"I can't feel my feet." Rhynne's teeth chattered.

Bàn gave up pulling the mule's head by the reins and stepped behind it, stooping to nudge its rump with his shoulder. The mule moved not, and, like a rock, it stayed there. He came away from it, one side of his cloak wet from the animal's snow-soaked coat. It gave a weak bray. Pitiful.

A *clump* and a *crunch* came from behind him. He pivoted. Rhynne lay in a drift, sinking deeper, eyes closed, mouth lolling. His gut clenched.

"Rhynne!" He crunched the sparse steps through the snow to her and shook her shoulder.

Her eyelids fluttered.

He cradled her in his arms, then lifted her. "Rhynne!" He shook her again. She moaned. He rested her on his knee and rubbed her cheek. Icy still, though he barely felt it, so cold were his own fingers. Behind him, the mule groaned, then became quiet.

He closed his eyes and swallowed. *That was its last breath for certain.*

Bàn opened his eyes and patted her face. "Rhynne, wake up!" He rubbed again, harder this time.

She shook her head, flung a hand around to push him away, whimpered, then her head lolled forward.

"Dragon's teeth!" he cursed through his own. "Stay with me, Rhynne!" Don't die. *Leave me not in this world without you, now I have found you.*

He laid Rhynne gently down, then took the drier saddle blanket off the mule, still with some warmth from the beast, then stepped back to Rhynne. Pulling her soaked cloak aside, he wrapped her in the blanket, re-wrapped her cloak around her, then picked her up in his arms.

The snow lay deeper here, and the wind blew wilder, but with less snow in it. He stepped forward and sunk knee-deep in the drift. Holding Rhynne close, he followed what he could make out of the track. It was straightforward at this section as the sheer drop sat to his left. Wind roared chill through his cloak and battered his ears with a wildness.

He stuck close to the bank on his right. One foot after the other, sinking knee-deep each time. For how long he did this, he could not tell. His head had ached at first, but now was numb, and an icy cold sat in his teeth, blown there by the hollering wind.

He shook Rhynne again. She was a dead weight in his arms. She mumbled some incoherent words, and a glacial spear tore at his guts.

Oh, get us to this sage hold, I beg you.

His shoulder muscles burned. He must be the only warm being in this snowy oasis.

He plodded on, eyes narrowed, viewing the track now making yet another sharp turn. The snow squeaked with his footsteps, yet he heard it here where the wind slowed and it was more sheltered. Through a now dying wind, he eased the squint of his eyes, for the chill no longer touched his eyeballs with frosty fingers.

His legs were heavy. He couldn't move either limb to take another step. Brilliant white filled his view, but central to his path and in the distance, a many-turreted caisteal arose from the rock of the mountain. Yellow light glowed through much glazing and smoke spilled from chimneys dotted throughout. Steam rose from a burn that rushed from the base of the rock and travelled along beside him and to his left, between ice-edged banks.

His breath left his lungs, misting about him. His numb arms dropped Rhynne in the snow, and shaky legs could hold him up no longer. He collapsed, landing on Rhynne's inert form.

"Rhynne!" He shook her vigorously.

She groaned.

A *creak* broke the quiet, followed by the rattle of chains and a *clunk*. He lifted his numbed head, his temples crashing into his brain. Figures clad in animal skins poured over the caisteal's drawbridge, now sitting across the steaming burn. They headed toward him. He lifted his arm to his sword, touching something solid. It could only be *Dileas'* handle, for in truth, he felt naught except for fingers so cold they burned. He peered through the haze. The figures appeared to be weapon-less. Breath staggering, he tugged his blade from her sheath.

He held his sword aloft, muscles trembling.

Then fell forward over Rhynne, planting his face in the snow, gasping at the icy cold gripping his eyes, nose, and lips.

Eighteen

Look at the heart, my child.

VISIONS AND SAYINGS OF THE BLIND LADY SAGE

The World of Dál Cruinne
Post Dragon Wars Year 6083
Eastern Clanlands of Dál Gallain
Mountain Sage Hold

A drip, drip of water. A trickle, then a gurgle. I opened my eyes to soft candlelight glowing through a haze of water vapour and reflecting off dark stone walls misted by steam. A hint of minerals tinged the moist air.

Silkiness covered my skin. And warmth. Soft water caressed all of me, except for my head.

Oh, I can feel my toes again.

My hair floated on the surface of steamy water like a black fan. Heat touched my back, right along my length. I must've been resting on something soft but bony in places, and in spots it had the coarseness of body hair.

I peered closer at my black locks floating in the water. They moved in a gentle current, falling away to the side. A blue tattooed arm lay across my belly. Celtic knots and a triskelion. And the tree of life. A strong hand, wide palmed, and knuckles grazed, rested around my waist, my own abdominal tattoo peeking beneath it.

I jerked my head and hit something hard.

"Ouch!" Bàn's deep grunt rang in my ear.

I pulled away from him, hot water sloshing as his arm slid from my waist leaving a sensual tickle in its wake. I spun, stirring the water to splash over the sides of the sunken tub we were in. He still reclined where I'd lain, his long, wet hair slicked back close to his scalp, curls lost in their wetness. Dark circles sat beneath his eyes and the lines of his face etched deeper. He managed a weak smile as a rosy hue crept up from his neck to cover his face.

And he was totally naked!

So am I!

"What did you do?" Accusation filled my tone, but I didn't care. I covered my breasts with my hair.

"He saved your life, young woman." An older woman's voice came from the side of the cave-like chamber. "So, ye should change your tone to one of gratitude."

I faced the woman who wore a dark robe, her pale skin shining with fine beads of mist. Her mouth held a gentle smile, and she inclined her head to me.

"He has not left your side since we brought you in from the mountain pass. Both of you suffering the effects of too much cold." The woman stood. "Now I know you are well, I shall leave you to give your thanks." She gave a curt nod, then left.

I wasn't in a tub, but in a natural pond in a cave. A thermal one, by the feel. The water was gloriously hot, and its heat had seeped into my bones. Water sloshed and splashed, nudging me with a gentle current. I moved further from Bàn, and pressing my back against the opposite side of the pool, I crossed my arms to cover my breasts.

Bàn now sat, leaning his back against the edge of the shallow pond, and his muscled chest rose above the water with tufts of hair sitting between his pectorals, while his knotty arms rested on the edge of the pool, and pink dusted high on his cheeks. He leaned his head back and closed his eyes, relaxing in the water's heat. His firm jawline cut angles through the steam rising from the thermal pool, and his arm muscles curved in strength, holding him in place.

"Thank you."

"'Twas my duty." He remained leaning back, eyes closed.

"The mule?"

He shook his head. "Not my duty."

"So, we're at the sage hold?"

"Aye."

"We can stay here?"

"Of that I have nae enquired. But it seems snow blocks the pass, and the sage who assisted us into this thermal pool is of the opinion it will not clear for some months." He opened one eye. "And from what I ken, she is correct in her estimation, for that will nae be till a late spring begins." His voice rumbled gently, the vibrations travelling through the water and across to my insides where it joined the warmth—a warmth that wasn't from the hot spring water. I opened my mouth to speak and closed it again.

Should I even say it?

Bàn opened both eyes and raised a blond eyebrow, all his hair now darkened by the damp. He was a handsome man, but Dad always said that a man was only as handsome as his actions.

If that were so, Bàn was gorgeous. How could a guy be so nice? None of the boys—and they were only *boys*—I'd ever vaguely considered going out with were a fraction as noble as Bàn. Was *noble* even the right word—

"What are ye thinking? Ye seem to be struggling." He sat further up in the pool, taking his hands down from the edge. "And ye look like ye are speaking to someone, and it is not I. I am told that is *weird*." His mouth lifted at one corner and his eyes creased ever so slightly at the sides.

"I missed you, Bàn. When you went to collect the thatch."

Bàn's eyes softened, and his shoulders seemed to relax a bit.

"Oh!" I covered my mouth with my wet hand. "Ma Gabràn's leaky roof." I sighed. "How will she manage the winter? No one in town will help her. And what if—"

"Ye need worry not for Ma Gabràn," a deep voice said from one side of the steamy cave.

Bàn jerked to sit taller, eyes widening, and doing the tensing thing he did when getting ready to fight. I spun to the voice. A man in a dark, hooded robe sat in a shadowed corner.

"I apologise for not alerting you to my presence, but I have observed your recovery." He stood, pulling his hood back, revealing a good-looking dark-skinned man of maybe middle age. "I am so pleased ye have survived. It was a delicate time for you, young lady. Only the *handsome* actions of this *noble* man have kept you in this life." Stepping to the pool, he stopped by its edge.

I put my hand to my chest, ensuring my hair covered me.

The man looked at me and smiled, not in a creepy way, either. Like nudity in front of a stranger was okay. "I am Eochaid. I jointly run this sage hold with my wife, Saoirse." He bobbed a bow.

Water scooshed with movement, and I faced Bàn, who stood and walked through the shallow spa pool to shake hands with the sage. My eyes stretched wide, and I turned away.

"I am Bàn Lùthas. I am grateful for your care." The water scooshed again.

Oh, no! Don't tell me he's turned to face me now.

"The lady is Rhynne MacEnoicht."

I turned my head, peeking through a half-opened eye. Long pale tapered thigh muscles and smooth skin were all in view.

"Hello," I said, then snapped my eye shut.

"I see ye are not used to our bathing customs. We bathe in the hot spring regularly here. Its heat warms the rock and, therefore, our home. We could not abide here if it were not so. We are like family, and we hide naught from one another."

I gulped. *Oh, he means literally.*

The water gurgled and swirled around me with Bàn immersing himself. I opened my eyes again.

"Once ye are finished, dressed and have eaten, I would be pleased to introduce you to my wife in the main hall." Eochaid gave a curt nod then left, the foggy air swirling in his wake.

My vision slid to Bàn, who sat back in the water, a smirk on his face.

"What?"

"Ye are going to have to overcome your shyness if we are to winter here."

My breath stalled for a second. "So, no private bathing?"

Bàn shook his head slowly, the smirk transforming into a full grin. "Does nae seem that way. And why would ye want to hide that tattoo of the tree of life ye sport on your belly? I am surprised George allowed ye to make the permanent inking."

I flicked my head. "Dad doesn't know."

Bàn pressed his lips together, a crease flashing for a second between his brows. "Och, well, I shall dress mysel' now." He rose to a stand.

I shut my eyes. Dripping water tinkled, then his bare feet padded on stone.

"There are clean robes here. Nae weapons, though," he said.

I stole a look. He stood at the bench seat where Eochaid had sat, with his back to me, drying himself. His muscles flowed along his back, and that intricate dance of sinew, muscle and bone rippled over his shoulder blades, sending a shiver coursing through me. He slipped on buckskins and a long plain shift, then tied his still damp hair back in a ponytail.

"I shall leave ye to dress, Rhynne." He kept his back to me. "I'll be just outside the door." He walked out.

I stepped out of the hot pool, the mineralised water slipping off me like warm silk, then I dried and dressed hastily in similar buckskin leggings. They were soft and moulded to my body. I pulled a shift over my head. It went to just above my knee, not so close-fitting and definitely not flattering. I wandered out of the bathing area where a young sage in a dark robe waited with Bàn.

"I'm Comgall." The sage smiled a crooked-toothed grin, and his voice came out a husky squeak. "I am to take you to the room we dine in." Now his voice was deeper.

Yep, his voice is breaking. I pressed my top teeth on my tongue. I wouldn't be impolite and laugh at his boy's voice alternating with a baritone.

I padded barefoot behind Bàn and Comgall. Heat came through the stone floor, warming my toes and the air had a dry feel on my exposed skin. Rooms ran off the long, raw wood partitioned hallway. I stumbled into Bàn's back. He'd stopped in the open entranceway to a large room where thin mats covered the floor and weapons sat racked against the opposite wall. There were so many weapons of different types that the bare wood hardly peeked through.

"You may have heard we practise and train in the martial arts." Comgall's teeth splayed through his smile.

"Nae." Bàn shook his head. "I have heard nothing of your sage hold."

"Aye well, ye are from the west." Comgall's lips pulled to the side. They ran over his teeth, doing their best to cover them. "We are contemplative and prayerful sages who fight but also give succour."

"You mean like the Knights Templar?" I stepped in for a closer look.

Comgall gave a blank expression, but Bàn turned to me and nodded.

"We train daily, after prayers"—Comgall resumed the tour— "and seek to help those who come for healing in our waters. That will nae be any now the pass has closed for winter. Ye were such a surprise to us all. Come."

He led us to a large room with two long tables running parallel. At one end, a door swung open. Clanking metal pots and shouted orders came through behind a tall man carrying a tray of food. He smiled, placed the tray on the end of one table, tilted his head in an inviting gesture, then returned to the kitchen.

I reached the table ahead of Bàn and took an oat cake, sliced a piece of very dark hard cheese and placed it on the biscuit, then bit a large mouthful. The dry oat cake stuck in my mouth. Bàn poured a drink from the pewter jug and offered it to me. I sculled it down. Watered down red wine, but the best drink I'd had in a long time. Bàn ate also, and when we'd done, Comgall led us further down the long hall to a large room with a rug-covered floor, seats at the far end, and cushions scattered in clumps throughout. A fire blazed in the hearth by one wall and candelabras added to the light, for a dull glow came through the windows.

"Still snowing," I remarked.

"Aye, it will snow continually for nigh a month." Comgall shrugged. "Well, that is the usual way of it."

"Thank you, Comgall." A familiar female voice came from the side, and the woman who had spoken to me in the spa stepped along and sat. "Please join us."

Eochaid followed and sat beside the woman. I approached, Bàn close beside me, and Comgall left the hall.

"My wife, Saoirse." Eochaid's rich voice rumbled deeply as he gestured to the woman.

Bàn bowed. "A pleasure to meet ye both."

"We are pleased to have you, Bàn and Rhynne, as our guests. You will gather from the weather that, unless you wish to risk the elements, you will be with us for some months until the snow melts with the warmer weather, thus clearing the pass."

"Aye, we had surmised such and are grateful for your hospitality," Bàn said. "We will help you in anything ye wish. Give us a list of chores, if ye please."

"Of course." Saoirse inclined her head. "You may make use of our practice hall. Your weapons will be returned to you, also."

My insides jumped. The hall stood chock o' block with weapons, and I had months ahead to learn and hone my sword skills. It made the HEMA camp look like nursery school. My mouth stretched in a grin I couldn't stop.

"You are most welcome to join us in prayers as well as training sessions." Saoirse's gaze rested on me.

Bàn turned to me, his eyes softening and the edge of his lips curling upward. "Thank you, Sage Saoirse. It would please us both to attend classes. And prayers."

What? I let out a quiet grunt, my grin freezing.

Bàn nudged me to silence with his elbow.

"It pleases us to hear this," Eochaid said. "We differ from many sage holds of the east. Here we do not worship the many gods—only the one. *Tobraichean na beatha.* The Fountain of all Spirit." His orotund voice took on a reverent edge.

"Very good." Bàn's elbow still rested on me, and at Eochaid's words, his arm muscles seemed to relax.

"We sup early, retire soon after, and rise in the wee hours. The short days of winter make many hours of darkness, but we have light." Eochaid set a smile on his lips.

Comgall returned and took us to our allotted accommodation far from the main hall, but our rooms stood across from each other. I stepped into a narrow room with a single bed, a small cupboard, and one whole wall bare. A small window sat in the thick stone outer wall. Outside, all was white except for the babbling of a steaming river with icy sides. My clothes lay folded on the bed and my cloak with the wolf-skin collar hung on a peg by the cupboard.

I turned. The door to Bàn's room stood open. It was just as bare. His sword and knives were arranged on his bed beside his neatly folded clothes and cloak. Comgall waited between us, grinning like he'd just shown us the master suites of a grand hotel.

"I shall collect you for our evening meal. In the morning, prayers, then practice." His toothy grin spread wide, then he spun and marched along the hall.

My arms were heavy, and I could barely hold my head up. Bàn looked at me. Dark shadows remained under his eyes, but he walked with his usual lithe gait.

"What?"

"Ye will keep our hosts happy and come to their worship hall with me, aye?" he asked.

"Yes." Reluctance slipped out in my tone. "I suppose it's a prerequisite for attending practice."

Bàn lifted a shoulder and let it fall. "Seems so."

"I need to rest." I closed the door as he remained at his, with his eyes fixed on me.

I pivoted and leaned back against the hard wood.

Okay, Ma Gabràn, I'm here. What now?

NINETEEN

My lover is a warrior strong
Brave in conflict, fearless, dreaded.
Yet his yielded love caresses me,
Nae sign of battle when we've bedded.

WORDS OF RIEINMELLTH
ANCIENT WARRIOR QUEEN OF DÀL CRUINNE

The World of Dál Cruinne
Winter, Post Dragon Wars Year 6083
Eastern Clanlands of Dál Gallain
Mountain Sage Hold

Sweat drenched my clothing, sticking to me in awkward places. It dragged my linen tunic under my arms and dug my breeches into my groins. The stale, sweaty-sock smell of a gym changing room had nothing on this practice hall. The tiny window in the corner let in a little fresh air. I strode over and sucked in the icy cool from outside.

With hands resting on hips, I continued to breathe in deep.

"Oh, wow, it's gorgeous."

"You show promise, young Rhynne." Eochaid spoke from behind, his rich tones vibrating through me. "In your short time with us you have made remarkable progress in your sword skill."

I turned. "Thank you. I have great teachers here."

"Aye, but your best teacher is the warrior with whom you arrived. He has great skill. And patience."

My cheek pulled in a half smile, then my gaze slid beside Eochaid to the doorway where Bàn waited for permission to enter. Eochaid followed my gaze, then turned and nodded at Bàn, who bowed and walked onto the floor.

"Rhynne has just warmed up and may be ready for a spar with you, warrior Bàn."

Bàn spun his practice sword in his hand and raised his brows. I picked up my sword, touched the blade to my forehead, and Eochaid stepped out of the way.

Steel rang against steel.

Bàn's sword stung my left upper arm.

Focus!

I threw an overhand slice and Bàn countered it, his sword spearing near my face. I stepped back in retreat.

"Nae. Keep coming but move your head oot the way. Take a step to the right, then push against ma blade to your left and up." He curled one blond eyebrow upward. "If ye have the strength. Start again."

I sliced, he thrust again, and I moved my head and body a step to the right while pushing his counter up, naturally turning my sword over with it, keeping his low and virtually locking it in place.

"Ahh, that's good, but put the thumb of yer forward hand slightly along your blade. Makes a stronger grip when ye turn it. Try again."

I repeated the actions and lined up for a thrust to his neck, hesitating.

"Why do ye stop?"

"The end's pointy. You're not wearing armour. I don't want to hurt you."

He tilted his head to the side for a second. "Aye, I appreciate yer desire to cause me nae harm. But dinnae hesitate when ye are out there, lass. It's you or them. Nae other choices." He gave a rueful smile.

"They won't let me, will they?" I held my voice firm, not letting my disappointment at the inevitable answer slip through.

"Your parents, ye mean?" He skewed his mouth to the side. "Ye may be surprised."

I thrust forward, and he countered, my arms jolting like always when fighting him. I hit his sword again, and he returned it. We disengaged, then he went on the attack with swift, swiping arcs. Sweat dripped down his face and trickled into his whiskers. My tunic clung and dragged with my movement and my breath came hard.

I glanced around for a nanosecond. The others had left, and Bàn and I sparred alone.

He hit me with force, stepping in and pushing back. The wall thumped into my back as his face loomed closer. My arms shook, and he swatted my sword aside left-handed, as if it were a broken reed.

He leaned closer, his body against mine—the whole length of him—his free hand resting on the wall above my head, every muscle tense, rib cage expanding and contracting. His heart thudded beneath my palm pressed against his chest, and his breath blew in my face. Golden curls flowed over his shoulder. His beard was a two-day growth of bristly blond. His eyes were like the clear, blue sky on the day I'd arrived, and every inch of him as real and vibrant as everything else in this new world in which I now found myself.

With *this* man.

I dropped my sword, which landed with a clang on the wooden floor, then grabbed his face between my hands. His lips were red and healthy, blood coursing through with a masculine vitality.

His sword clattered onto the floor as his gaze dropped to my mouth. I ran my fingers up into his hair, grasping some golden strands, then grabbed his lips with mine. Warm, soft, and responsive.

This man—my entire world.

I curled my legs around him, tugging him closer, so there was nothing between us.

Lean muscled torso pressed against my thighs, and his mouth played hard with mine. Devouring me.

Moaning, he wrapped his arms around me, lifting me from the wall and holding me close to him—heart beating against heart.

I held his lips with mine, tasted his mouth, played with his tongue. He answered, running his hand to my hair and pulling out the tie. My hair fell down my back and he grabbed a handful, then slid fingers onto my scalp. Hot and probing, his touch sent shivers to my core.

He broke our kiss and moved his head enough to look me in the eye.

"Rhynne." He breathed my name. There was love in it. And desire.

I ran fingers through his facial hair, down his slightly crooked nose, then across his blood-red lips. His shoulder muscles arched in their act of holding me. I returned my gaze to his eyes, his own searching my face, like he was drinking in everything about me.

He was incredible. *Too much.*

My heart sledge-hammered my chest and warmth spread right through me. An intoxicating feeling. I would never let go of it.

A sharp cough came from the doorway.

Bàn froze for an instant, eyelids flaring wider. He eased me to the floor, giving me a soft, quick kiss before stepping away as sages entered the hall and selected weapons.

My heart still hammered, my breathing came short and sharp like I'd sprinted a mile, and my face heated.

Bàn left the practice hall, his eyes staying on me, but his smile was faint, and his forehead wrinkled.

TWENTY

Do not seek a magic that is greater than the wisdom and skill you possess to use it.

GRAND MASTER LLEW
ISLE OF INNESFARNE
(POST DRAGON WARS 6000-current)

The World of Dál Cruinne
Post Dragon Wars Year 6083
Eastern Clanlands of Dál Gallain
Mountain Sage Hold

I opened my eyes. Clear, weak light shone into my room from the pre-dawn, not the glowing hue caused by falling snow that'd filled the sky since our arrival. I jumped out of bed and peered through the window. Though it was early, the glare bounced from the lying snow blanketing everything except the steaming burn that flowed from beneath the castle. The pale blue sky was edged silver strongly to the west.

The sage hold rested in early-morning quiet. They would've finished prayers by now. The sages hadn't insisted I go, and Bàn hadn't made me.

That was great. So was the extra sleep.

I dressed and walked to the mess hall, which sat almost empty.

Unusual. Normally, it would be packed by now with big, burly men and taut, muscled women. Warrior sages filling their stomachs with protein before the day's fighting practice began.

I scooped a bowl of porridge from the nearly empty pot and sat down. Comgall walked toward me, wooden bowl in his hand, spring in his step, and teeth protruding in his version of a smile. He sat beside me, eyes wide and his breakfast ignored.

"They go on a hunt," he said.

My gut clenched. "Who are *they*? Hunts are dangerous."

"We restock our larder when we are able. The snow has ceased, for now, and the game will be out."

"Where's Bàn?"

"Warrior Bàn gathers with our warriors who wish to hunt—"

"Where?"

"At the stable gate."

"Stable? You have horses here?" *Wow.* There was so much to this rambling sage hold I'd not yet found.

"We have many animals here. They stay on the lower floors and outhouses near the warmest reaches of the thermal waters." His gaze stretched up to me as I stood.

"Take me there." I abandoned the porridge.

Comgall rose and tripped along, grinning and being his usual helpful self. I followed close. He took me to an unfamiliar flight of steps, then skipped down them. I grabbed the rope-excuse for a banister, and trod with care on steps wet with boot prints. Horses' neighs and deep male voices echoed up the stairwell, along with a cold breeze. My nose chilled and I sniffed, my exhaled breath misting. Comgall led me around a corner to an open door where brightness glared in, hitting my eyes. I squinted against it.

Comgall strode out into a crowd of horses, who stomped and pranced, stopping beside one of the massive animals. I halted at the doorway, grabbing the door jamb hard with my fingers. The horses snorted and nodded their long heads, but Comgall never flinched. The men who gathered seemed to be the biggest guys among the inhabitants of the sage hold. They all wore furs and held either bows or spears. One strode toward me.

He wore furry boots laced around his calves in a criss-cross fashion. His knee-length coat looked something like fox fur, and a hat of the same gold-orange fur covered his head, leaving his face barely visible. He looked like a trendy caveman.

It was Bàn. The hairs on the back of my neck rose. His sword wasn't peeping over his shoulder, but a sheathed hunting knife hung at his hip. He held a long spear, way taller than him, its leaf-shaped tip silver-edged. His face nearly cracked with his grin.

"Why're you going?" I couldn't hold the question in.

He reached me, still smiling. "To *hunt*, lass." His tone held an edge. He moved closer, whispering, "I have lived through this winter once before, cooped up for months. I'll no' do it again."

"What if you get gored by a wild boar?"

Bàn looked at me beneath his eyebrows. "We hunt mountain goat today, Rhynne."

"They have horns."

"All will be well. Worry not. I shall return." His eyes opened wider. "With fresh meat."

"Yeah, goat." I screwed my mouth to the side. "That's weird."

"Nae, it's delicious. Wait till ye have tasted roasted goat." He licked his lips. "It will be for the Midwinter Feast." He pecked me on the cheek. "We leave. Go inside afore ye freeze."

He spun on his heel and strode to a large grey horse. It had enormous hooves with lots of fur on them, like a Clydesdale. I stuttered out a gasp into the cold air. It was the biggest horse I'd ever seen. It flung its head and whinnied, dark grey mane flicking around. Bàn got right next to it, then one of the other men gave him a knee up, while another held his spear. He settled in the saddle, took his spear from the guy who'd held it for him, then nudged the horse with his legs. It moved and joined the rest who'd started trotting over the drawbridge. I stood there until the group of horsemen were dark dots in the snow.

"Come, Rhynne." Comgall spoke into my ear. "Sage Eochaid wishes to speak to you." He tugged at my elbow.

"To *me?*" The back of my neck prickled. "Why?"

He shrugged. "I know not."

I followed Comgall into the caisteal, my guts tickling, as though flakes of snow swirled inside them. He led me up the stairwell, my nose losing its cold tip as the warmth of the sage hold surrounded me. He came to the landing and walked in the opposite direction to the mess hall.

"Where're we going?" I asked.

Comgall put a finger to his teeth in a shushing manner. "Ye shall see."

He took me to another long hallway, a mirror image of the one I was familiar with.

Yep. This caisteal is much larger than it looks.

At the end of the hall, Comgall opened a door and ushered me into a round room, part of a round tower of the caisteal. Strong aromas hit my nose. I blinked as recollections from my herbalist classes came crashing to the fore. Sharp heady lavender, rosemary, and thyme were the strongest. A deep, thick mustard scent of some sort too. But subtle aromas tickled my nose.

A scent with vague hints of oranges. *Bergamot?*

I took another step in. Tall windows let in blocks of light, with muslins draped beside them and across the ceiling in between racks of drying herbs. Comfrey, sage, and row upon row of vervain.

It must be a favourite.

A large stone basin stood in the centre of the room, like a baptismal font at the church Dad had sometimes taken me to.

Huh?

Shelves lined the spaces on the walls between the windows. Most held books, but some had clay pots and others clear jars with—I peered closer, narrowing my eyes —*dead things* in them.

What is this place?

"Welcome, Rhynne." Eochaid's voice resonated from my right.

I snapped around to face him and Saoirse. Another woman stood beside them, black robed and grey hair dyed purple. My legs faltered mid-stride. Her eyes were mauve.

"May I introduce Maebh?" Saoirse indicated to the woman with eyes the same colour as mine.

"Hello, Rhynne." Maebh nodded a bow and extended her hand.

"Are... we related?" I took her hand. It was cold at first, then grew so warm I let go.

The woman tilted her head, and her lips pursed in thought. "Not closely. But we have a clan connection somehow, for purple irises only occur in Clan Cruithin."

"Is that my clan, then? No—" *Wait. My father is MacEnoicht—*"my mother's maybe?"

"Aye, it must be," Maebh answered.

"Um, where am I?"

"This is *our* part of this sage hold," Eochaid said. "It is the mage hold." He chuckled.

"Mage... like witches?"

Saoirse sucked in a slow breath. "No, not exactly. We are mages of good intent."

"Good mages. Are there bad ones?" The skin on my arms crawled.

"Not here," Eochaid said. "But in the land of Dál Gallain, there are many. Most now work with the troublemaker, Ciarán Gallawain."

That name again. The hair on my scalp lifted. The bad guy here.

Correction, the *really, really* bad guy here.

"What did you want to see me about?"

"Come, sit." Saoirse waved her hand toward couches off to one side in a cosy boudoir-looking area of the tower room.

I sank into a deep velvet cushion while the mages seated themselves on the surrounding cushions. Saoirse smiled. Maebh's mauve eyes, filled with curiosity, never left me. Eochaid rested his elbows on his knees and leaned in my direction. Three pairs of eyes locked on me. The skin on my forearms rippled with gooseflesh.

"So, do the sages know about you guys?" I asked.

"Aye, they do." Eochaid clasped his hands. "Now that you know us, may I tell what I know of you?"

The crawling, hair-lifting thing my scalp was doing now crept down my spine. Eochaid's eyes opened wider.

"I beg you to trust me, Rhynne MacEnoicht. For I will only tell of what you have revealed to me."

I squinted. What had I told him? *Nothing.*

"May I?" he asked again.

Okay, go on then. "Yes."

"Ye are the daughter of the Àrd Rìgh of Dál Gaedhle. Lord Bàn Lùthas—although he omitted to inform us of his nobility—seeks to protect you and bring you again to your father, his sworn sword-brother, Arlan MacEnoicht."

Maebh gasped, but Saoirse didn't flinch.

I clenched my hands in my tunic. "So, I'm askin' again, what do you want to see *me* about?"

"You tell us." Eochaid spoke low and calm.

I blinked.

"Come now, you have gifts, and you know it," Maebh said, resting an elbow in her palm, and touching the corner of her narrowing eye with the forefinger of her free hand.

"Well, Ma Gabràn told me I had but..." I shrugged. *These people are intense, and how does the big man know all this about me?* "You need to ask her, 'cos I don't really know what she was talking about." *If only Bàn were here.*

"Ma Gabràn can speak no longer," Eochaid said. "She has passed from this life."

"What!" My chest tightened and my eyes stung with tears. "Was it our fault? The warrior after us in town..." My words stuck in my throat.

That poor old lady.

Eochaid reached out, his large hands surrounding mine now balling in my lap. "She did it for you and Bàn. Don't let her efforts go to waste." He paused while I sniffed and wiped my nose on my sleeve. "What did she tell you?" he asked.

"To grow my gift." I huffed a choked laugh, wiping my eyes to cover it. "Whatever that is."

"Tell me of portals." The dark-robed mage still held my hand, his voice coaxing.

"That's how we got here."

"Here in Dál Gallain?" Maebh asked.

"Nae." Eochaid turned to her. "Here in Dál Cruinne from the Other World."

Maebh pressed her hand to her lips, seeming to stifle a gasp, and fixed her eyes on me.

"Where did it arise?" Eochaid asked.

"On the HEMA campgrounds. In a forest."

"Bàn took you through?"

"No... I did. He couldn't see it."

Maebh's eyes rounded, Saoirse raised her eyebrows, and Eochaid leaned further forward.

"And you could?" he asked in measured tones.

"Yes. Why? Don't you mages see them?"

The mages sat in silence, and only Comgall's mouth-breathing behind me broke through it.

"Not all of us," Maebh said at last.

"None of us here." Eochaid laughed, then his face grew sombre. "Aye, Ma Gabràn was right. Ye need to nurture your gifting. We have a short time to teach you what will be a little of much. It will be a start. And this winter will soon pass."

Yep, it does eventually. Then I'm born, and Bàn can take me to my parents.

Eochaid sat straighter, stifling an exclamation.

I jerked my vision to him.

"Ye came through from the Other World prior to your time?"

"You can read minds, can't you?" I couldn't keep the accusation from my tone. "That's how you knew... How you know everything."

The mage hung his head for a moment. "I sat in the hot spring cave while you recovered because we needed to know who you were and why ye came up our mount."

I sat straighter, snatching my hand from his. "Why did you send Bàn on a hunt? Are you planning to kill him?"

"Oh no, dear child. We wish the man no harm. But..." Eochaid glanced at his wife. "Having been brought up in the west, where they only remember the mages who fought in the Dragon Wars, Bàn does not like mages,."

"*Dragon* Wars?" *That sounds awesomely scary.*

"They see us as evil," he continued, "and ye will discover not all of us are."

"How can I be sure?"

"Are *you* evil?" he asked.

"No!" I shook my head so hard it hurt.

"Well, then."

"It depends on whom you serve," Saoirse said, "and here we serve the Source of all Spirit. Goodness. Light."

"We will show you," Maebh said.

"Bàn won't like it." My stomach curled inside itself.

"His bias is against us, and he may try to stop us training you." Eochaid sat back, glancing to the other mages, his eyebrows drawing together.

"He need not know," Saoirse said.

Not tell Bàn? My stomach curled further as I slid my stare to Eochaid.

"As you wish," he said to me. "You decide what he is to know."

TWENTY-ONE

When conversation turns to argument,
Choose the yielding way
And let it lie.

SAGE GLIOCAS
(2870-2962 POST DRAGON WARS)

The World of Dál Cruinne
Post Dragon Wars Year 6083
Eastern Clanlands of Dál Gallain
Mountain Sage Hold

Fresh air and sunshine, weak as it was, were the best things to touch Bàn for a while.

Apart from Rhynne's lips—and her body.

He shook himself away from *those* thoughts and sat straighter in the saddle.

The mountain goats were wily. The hunters had chased them over boulders and flung their spears only to send them clattering over the rocks. Bàn laughed. Such fun. Especially as his spear ran true for the first kill. Now six goats hung from poles carried between three pairs of horsemen. Aye, 'twill be a braw Midwinter Feast. He would show Rhynne how they celebrated here in Dál Cruinne.

His chest warmed. Then it seared.

What will Arlan say?

For he had tried—and oh how hard he had tried—to *not* love his sword-brother's daughter. He swallowed.

He'd had to wrench his body away from hers on the practice mats the other day. He sighed. The door to her chamber sat temptingly close to his on these long winter nights.

Would Arlan be angry about his feelings for her? Och, he knew the man, every nuance of his character, every thought. He could anticipate Arlan's actions, good and bad. But know his mind in *this*? He gave a wavering shrug, shaking his head at the same time.

It changed naught.

He loved Rhynne. And it would use all his self-control to wait until he asked Arlan for her hand before he made love to her.

Nae... it would require begging for her hand.

And if he made love to her... Arlan would kill him... perhaps. His chin sunk to his chest.

"Why so glum, warrior?" A brawny arm thudded his back. Bàn faced Reece, the burliest warrior sage among them. And their fiercest fighter. "Woman troubles?" He nudged his war horse closer to the grey Bàn rode.

"Och, no."

Reece's laugh bellowed. "Dinnae lie. All know ye pine for the beautiful young warrior lass." He leaned in closer. "Take her. She'll have ye. All see that as well."

"Och, but it is so much more complicated than all could know."

"Nae, 'tis nae, man. Ye love her. She loves you. Simple. Ye are both noble." He winked. "Aye, we see that also." He leaned over from his horse, who nickered and flicked its ears at the weight shift. "Life is too short. And with a war... much shorter for some." He shook Bàn's shoulder, then nudged his own horse on.

Bàn ground his teeth and sunk into the saddle.

If only it were *simple.*

The track turned a bend, then the sage hold caisteal came into view, revealing the other side to his original approach with Rhynne over a month ago. A round tower, perhaps of four storeys high, faced this way, light glowing out from tall windows. *Hmph.* Airier than his quarters by far.

He followed the line of horses to the door by the stables, then dismounted. Footsteps sloshed through the sludgy, half-melted snow churned up by hoof-prints. Someone came up behind him. He turned. Rhynne threw her arms around him. Slipping, he caught her and his balance at the same time.

"Oh, you're back." Her warm breath came in his ear.

"Of course I am. Did I no' tell ye?"

"Come inside." She grabbed his hand.

He threw the reins to a young lad who handled the horses, then followed Rhynne's earnest tugging.

"What's the hurry, Rhynne?" Bàn passed Reece, who winked at him.

His neck heated. He did not wish any to think along *those* lines. The young woman's reputation was at stake. Rhynne drew him up the stairs, tugging with each step.

"What—?"

Rhynne spun. "Shush." She spoke low, and her mauve eyes pierced him.

He clamped down on his tongue. So much he would ask. Perhaps Reece was correct and the day without him had strengthened her ardour. His step lightened. Her reputation? *All knew,* Reece had said. Their want for each other—*all knew.* His chest heated. He pulled off his gloves and hat while she continued to drag him along the hall.

She turned left down the corridor to their rooms. He loosened his coat. Would he let all restraint flee? Where had gone his resolve? Her hand so warm and soft in his. Her long black locks streaming behind her as she faced forward, intent on directing him to her room. She dragged him in, closed the door and spun to him.

He reached her first, pressing his mouth to her blood warm lips and knotting his fingers in her hair. He played with her mouth, tasting of something sweet. Her breath brushed his face, sending a shock wave thundering through him.

Her hands pressed into his chest... pushing him away.

"Bàn!"

"Aye." His voice came out husky.

"I have something important to tell you."

Was that annoyance in her tone? He opened his eyes.

She stood there, placing her hands on her hips and her fine black brows meeting above the bridge of her nose.

"Oh, aye." He swallowed. "What, then?"

"They contrived the hunt to get you away from me today."

He jerked back from her, all ardour of his own gone cold. "What did they do to you?"

"It was Eochaid and his wife and another one called Maebh." She pressed her lips together, now standing back and wringing her hands. "They know everything. Who I am. That I come from... the Other World." Her eyes went round. "That Arlan is my father."

Bàn's vision lost focus. Were they safe? Was she safe! They were trapped here. Such a risk to steal a horse and go. His guts clenched in a knot.

"How do they ken?" he asked.

"Eochaid reads minds."

"How?" *Och, no!* "They are mages."

She nodded, then her features hardened. "You should've told me sooner about the whole mage thing."

"But I did. That your grandfather is a mage—"

"No! About the good and bad side to it all. How can you expect me to trust you when you keep important things from me like Dad did?" Her words held pain.

The silence in her room closed in on him. He shifted his weight. How to answer that accusation? He could not.

"I know naught of these ways of magic."

Rhynne blinked at his ignorance. "There's a whole other part to this sage hold." Her voice sounded tight. "It's twice as big as it looks."

"I ken." He breathed out slowly, grateful for the subject change. "I saw a different round tower section today."

"That's where they took me, and where they want to teach me."

He clenched his jaw. "Teach ye what, Rhynne?" He steeled himself, for her awkwardness could hide not her wishes.

"To—" she began.

"Be a mage!" he exclaimed.

"No, to—"

"No!" he interrupted. "I forbid it."

She blinked, her chest rising with a breath, then she stepped away from him. "You can't *forbid* me."

"Aye, I can, and I do."

"But—"

"Your father has put you in my charge." He would stifle her protests. "And I say nae. You'll no have anything to do with magic. 'Tis evil."

Her nostrils flared, then her frown deepened. "I don't get it. My grandfather's a mage."

"Aye, Sage Eifion is a good man and uses his"—he flung his hands around— "*magic* for good."

"So do they."

"How can ye be sure?"

"They believe in the good god here. You know that. You go to their church!"

"Their *church?*" He frowned.

"Yeah." She wiggled her fingers, raising her hand in the air. "Morning prayers."

He pressed his lips together, flinging off his coat and putting his hands to his belt, staring her down. His breath came fast.

Och, if only I knew what my sword-brother wished.

Eifion would want her taught in the ways of a mage, but would wish himself to be her teacher, for certain.

"Nae," he finally said.

"Really?" Her inflection rose. "You're sticking with that?"

"Aye."

"Get out of my room, then." She crossed her arms tight over her breasts and looked beyond him. "You're biased and prejudiced. Where I come from, that doesn't go down well." Her voice was a soft growl.

"Rhynne?"

She curled a dark eyebrow but spoke not.

He picked up his coat and walked across to his room, her door slamming shut behind him.

TWENTY-TWO

On the cross-quarter day, when shadows darken the ancient doorways of the tors, then will we celebrate. We trust the light to come again and save us from the grip of winter darkness.

ANCIENT HISTORIES OF DÀL CRUINNE

The World of Dàl Cruinne
Post Dragon Wars Year 6083
Eastern Clanlands of Dàl Gallain
Mountain Sage Hold
Midwinter Feast

Snowflakes fell outside, soft and silent, covering the old icy snow that had lain without addition for almost a week. I stood looking out the narrow window of my room. A gentle blanket of frozen flakes settled itself over the old snow, covering dirty footprints, now patchy darkness on the ground.

A gown lay on my bed. I was supposed to wear it to the Midwinter Feast tonight. Made of a finely woven black material, it looked hand stitched. I chuckled.

Of course it had been stitched by hand. No clothing factories here. A woollen plaid of an unfamiliar tartan in blue sat beside it. Not that I knew many tartans. I'd once bought a mini skirt of Royal Stewart. A laugh bubbled up. Dad always scowled and gave the *be careful what you wear* lecture when I'd worn it for a night out. The bubble of laughter turned to a choke.

Dad.

Wet warmth slid down my cheeks.

Bàn better keep his promise to let me see him again!

I dragged the tears from my face with the heels of my hands, my veins heating. Well, maybe not as much as they had in the past few days since my argument with Bàn.

If that's what you'd call it.

I was an adult, for heaven's sake. Who did he think he was? I could do as I chose and didn't require *his* permission. Bàn wasn't my *dad*. Dad would let me weigh up the options and allow me to make my own decisions.

I huffed. It was all still so weird.

They would teach *me* magic?

Like... *real* magic. Not sleight of hand magic but *use-your-power* magic.

Butterflies—no, mini dragons—flew around in my stomach. What form would the magic take? Maebh and Eochaid hadn't shown me any yet, apart from Eochaid's mind reading.

Man, that had been rude and intrusive.

But portals. And maybe dragons? I clutched at my chest. No—dragons were animals, not magic. Like dinosaurs, Bàn had said. I sighed heavily.

They'd quizzed me on herb lore. Some things I'd told them were a surprise to the mages. But, man, the vervain! They used it for enhancing visions.

Hmm. I'd never had a vision. *At all.* That'd worried them.

Maebh wanted me to discover my *source*—something like a conduit you channelled the power through. That's how I'd have visions and be able to *move* and *see*, they'd said, but hadn't explained further. They insisted the power they'd teach me to use came from good, from the god of this world, and not the bad. I'd asked what that was, and they gave a weird answer.

"Not what, but whom," Eochaid had said in his mystical way.

My guts niggled, swatting at the mini dragons. Maybe Bàn was right to be against it.

But my grandfather was a mage. I always came back to that fact. *Hmph.* He'd be proud if I learned magic, wouldn't he?

I still didn't get why Bàn was so *anti*. This world had real magic in it. Why didn't he embrace it? Sophie would be so jealous if she found out that I was an apprentice mage.

Soph... Would I ever see *her* again? Something twinged in my chest.

Footsteps padded down the hallway and someone knocked on Bàn's door, then mine.

"Ye should be ready for the feast, aye?" Comgall said. "The players are here. We will have grand entertainment this night."

Bàn's door creaked open, and his voice rumbled low in the passage, then Comgall's footsteps retreated.

A light tap came on my door. "Rhynne?"

I steeled myself and opened the door. Bàn stood there, looking like a Highlander in the full regalia—sort of. Well, Dál Cruinne's version of it. He wore a kilt. Knee-high boots. For once his sword handle wasn't sitting above his shoulder, and a plaid crossed his chest instead of a leather baldric. He wore his hair out, and tight blond curls sat at his nape.

The rest of him was bare. Smooth curves and plains of healthy male for all to see.

I stifled an appreciative murmur.

"I'm not ready yet." I kept my tone clipped, like I had for the past six days. "You go on. I'll go when I'm dressed in my outfit."

His shoulders lowered a fraction, and his face hardened a touch. "Very well."

He turned on his heel, pleated material swirling, and marched down the passage, his kilt swinging with each step, and broad shoulders holding steady in counterpoint.

It was stupid. *His* stubbornness.

"Argh!" I slammed the door, stripped off my breeches and tunic, then pulled the gown over my head. It fit snugly. I smoothed the velvet-like material down, its fine weave clinging to my shape. What about my hair? And should I carry a weapon?

No. Tonight, I'd be a *lady*. Bàn called me Lady Rhynne.

Why not?

I raked through the small pile of belongings I'd had on me when Bàn brought me through. No—when I'd brought *him* through. The item I looked for sat at the bottom of the bag Ma Gabràn had given us—a necklace with a Celtic Cross hanging from it. I clipped it closed at the back of my neck. On a long chain, the cross itself dangled just above where my cleavage started.

Hmm. I threw the plaid over my shoulder and trod down the passage, following my nose. Approaching the main and largest hall of this sage hold caisteal, the barbeque aroma of roasted meats grew stronger.

Music blared from the wide doorway to the hall. Loud voices and rifts of laughter followed, and light spilled out. Sages, both warrior and mage, milled about the hall entrance, illuminated by many candles. I trod on the soft tips of short pine branches, passing candle-trees packed with lighted beeswax candles. Holly branches, their bright red berries sitting in clusters amongst the deep-green spiky leaves, adorned the doorway. It smelled like Christmas that time Dad had bought a real pine tree, and we'd decorated it in our living room.

I stepped through to the main hall where swathes of pine and holly hung from the walls and clusters of lighted candles sat in sconces. The tables were arranged in a horseshoe, with stumpy candles surrounded by green foliage arranged down their centres, and platters of cold meats and cheeses, oatcakes, bannocks, and dark breads in between.

The musicians, a guy playing an Irish harp, a drummer with a bodhran, a woman on a recorder-looking whistle, and another playing something like a fiddle, sat to one side of the open end of the horseshoe. The music they played was... different. Like something I'd heard in a Scottish pub the time I went to Edinburgh on a school trip and snuck away with Sophie.

People were taking their seats, so I followed the crowd.

"Rhynne." Saoirse's voice came to my ear. "Ye and Lord Bàn will sit with us this Midwinter Feast." Her grip came around my arm.

I tensed, either from the woman's bony grasp, or the idea of having to sit next to Bàn. I put on a smile.

"Thank you, Sage Saoirse." *Manners.* I would be a *lady* tonight, after all. "That's so nice of you."

Saoirse led me to the top table where Eochaid, Maebh, Bàn, and some senior sages sat. There were two settings in between Eochaid and Bàn, and Saoirse led me to the seat next to Bàn.

He nodded to me as I sat, his eyes lingering on my dress, then loitering on the Celtic Cross. His gaze flicked up to my face, locking briefly with mine, then darted away, his cheeks going bright red.

I pressed my mouth tight on a grin.

So, he likes my outfit.

"You look nice tonight, Bàn," I said. "Is that your clan's tartan?"

"Och, nae. I borrowed it. I had nae such luck as you."

I started, looking down at the plaid I'd thrown over my shoulder. "This is Arlan's plaid? MacEnoicht tartan?"

"Oh, no, Lady Rhynne." Eochaid leaned forward to speak past Saoirse. "We have a bolt of nearly every tartan in Dál Cruinne stored in our archives." His smile broadened. "You wear the tartan of the Àrd Rìgh of Dál Gaedhle."

Wow.

My hand went to the soft woven wool material draped over my shoulder. "But am I allowed to wear it?"

Eochaid tilted his head. "Only for this special occasion. We shall return it to our archives after tonight. But I... we... thought it would do no harm for you to have a tactile demonstration of your roots, and your position here in Dál Cruinne."

I shuffled in my seat, blinking, then scanned the room to avoid the stares of those seated next to me. All others sat facing my direction, intent on the head table. Eochaid rose and cleared his throat.

"Fellow sages and friends. Family." His vibrant voice seemed to fill the far corners of the room. He bowed his head and all in the room did also, even Bàn. "O Tobraichean na beatha, giver of all that is good, from your loving hand you sustain us with all we require. We thank you for the depth of your goodness and the greatest gift of all—relationship—with you and with each other, from which our lives derive their meaning and joys. We ask, O Source of all Spirit, Fountain of Life, your blessings on our winter feast and our time together this night."

Shuffles came from either side of me. I opened my eyes, Eochaid's rendition of *grace* now over. Servers streamed into the hall carrying large platters of carved roasted meat, the aroma filling my nostrils and my mouth answering with saliva.

"Roasted goat." Bàn spoke into my ear. "Now ye shall ken what I mean."

His eyes glittered in the candlelight, and his bare arm brushed mine with his body's warmth. The corners of his mouth lifted in a tentative smile.

So, he was being nice now? Trying to pretend it was all okay. Then why was he still stone walling me when it came to mage training? This was the most we'd spoken since *we'd spoken*.

"I'm still not happy with you." I ignored the drop to his mouth. "I'm having lessons."

"How?" he whispered harshly. "I have kept watch on yer room. Ye have nae left it in a week apart from meals and"—he pointed to my middle somewhere— "personal needs."

I stifled a laugh. "You mean bathing, etc?"

He gave a funny nod, and his face flushed red again.

"I've booked a time to bathe when no one else is there." That hadn't been straight-forward, but Comgall was either an easy bribe to stand guard, or just plain too eager to please. Especially as he'd told me, with a hopeful grin, that everyone knew Bàn and I had fallen out.

"I'll let you in on a secret." I couldn't prevent the smirk. "One complete wall in my room is bare for a reason."

He sat up straighter.

"Caisteals have secret passages, yes?" I said.

"Nae!" he said, but his expression told me he knew what I meant.

I wouldn't tell him it led straight to the round tower.

"Yes." I took a sip from the pewter mug at my table setting. A rich red wine filled my mouth. I rolled it around with my tongue then swallowed, my eyes fixed on Bàn's. "You. Can't. Stop. Me."

The lines of his face etched deeper, and his eyes narrowed. "Your father—"

"Is not here."

"Your grandfather, Sage Eifion, would wish—"

"Is also not here." *My* turn to interrupt and not let *him* finish a sentence!

A server plonked a platter of roasted meats at our table settings, frowning at us. A plate of roasted root vegetables followed. Another server refilled our wine cups as Bàn pressed his mouth tight on whatever he was going to say.

The aroma of barbequed meat wafted from the platter. Eochaid and all at the table served themselves and ate. I stabbed some meat with a knife, the only cutlery at my setting, and placed it on the wooden plate in front of me. Juices dripped from the glistening portion. Bàn chewed, *hmm-ing* and *ah-ing* around a mouthful of goat, his muffled exclamations loud in my ear. I took a bite of the chunk—salty, warm, and very much like lamb.

Mmm. Bàn was right.

I offered him a smile. We'd still have to be friends... if he didn't take his guardian responsibilities too seriously.

Bàn drained his cup as I skewered a roasted parsnip, and the musicians played a loud short piece while people in costume marched in.

"Ah," Eochaid said when they'd assembled. "The entertainment. This joyful band of troubadours journeyed through the snow and reached us this afternoon. Friends, your attention on the players, if you please."

A light applause rang from the people seated, apart from those who had their hands full of food. I faced the opening of the horseshoe table arrangement, where one of the troubadours stood in the centre of the gap and gave a flourishing bow. He took a deep breath to begin, his grey hair sticking to his damp forehead.

"Time, it travels on and we but journey too.

This night of Midwinter Fest, we players wish to bring to you

Fair lords and ladies, and warriors... mages." He bowed low.

"A reminder of our times past.

For whom but those who remember and recall

Do make the lessons learned to last?" He coughed and cleared his throat.

The musicians played a tune as the players jostled to their places. A woman walked in front of the troupe carrying a sign that read: *The Dragon Wars*.

Bàn stirred beside me, picking up his cup that a server had refilled. "Aye, this ye should pay attention to, Rhynne," he said in a firm voice.

I faced him. He leaned close, with a crinkle above the bridge of his nose, and eyes earnest. The narrator still spoke, but I couldn't take my vision from Bàn. So, he still cared, even though we were in the middle of an argument. Or maybe the subject of the performance would make *him* seem in the right.

Bàn took a long drink from his cup. The narrator's scratchy voice broke through to me, so I returned my attention to the performance. Gasps and applause burst from the audience. A man stepped forward with daggers in his hands and juggled the flashing blades.

"The west, skilled warriors and true, fought back." The narrator coughed, then continued, "Their iron mines a source for tools, weapons and trade."

The warrior sages, and all present, leaned forward in their seats, apparently waiting for the juggler to stab himself. Bàn drained his cup then sat with his mouth part open, seeming also eager for an injury. A server brought the narrator a drink, and he took a sip.

"Mages lived equally in both lands," the narrator said, his voice a little less croaky after his drink, as players in black robes wandered across their makeshift stage.

"Vassals of lairds and chieftains. Healers, teachers, wisemen all, respected, deferred to, and honoured."

The players bowed, and those seated roared a cheer.

"They with special gifting wrought their patrons valuable service.

Some could see for many a league,

Others heal from any disease."

At these words, my breath caught as a spark flashed within me, connecting with something deep inside... even deeper than my yearning to master the sword. I blinked and refocused on the performance.

"Some could control animals," the narrator continued, "and of these, only but a few could tame a beast of size."

A robed actor walked past, tugging on a lead attached to the bridle of a pantomime-style donkey, the two actors in the costume dragging their feet. The crowd laughed. My heart twinged for the poor mule who'd carried us up the mountain until it had dropped. Bàn's cup clunked beside my hand resting on the table.

"Prized these mages were, for seeing through a greater beast's eyes," the narrator said.

A player ran into the room holding a puppet-like, papier mâché dragon's head on top of a pole.

"From battlefields spied from the skies, they would bring the enemy's plans,

And know their intentions down to the man."

Bàn's arm, still resting against mine, tensed. I glanced down. He grabbed the edge of his seat, knuckles whitening.

"The dragons, graceful, powerful, grand
Were used for clues, then strategy planned.
Though never was a mage to wield,
An animal to harm a man."
The dragon puppet 'flew' around the room, dipping close to warrior sages, who pretended to swat it. Laughter echoed from the tables. Bàn sat stony faced beside me.

"With battles fought, and closely so
The anger of each side did grow,
Until the way all good things go.
A laird had found his mage did know,
To command and make teeth and talons go,
The way they wished, and wanted so,
To turn the beasts themselves on men,
And use the graceful creatures' power,
To tear, and wound, and ruin tower."
The players did a comedic dragon attack and death scene. The hall filled with laughs and guffaws.

Bàn grunted. "'Tis nae funny, Rhynne," he whispered hoarsely. "This is our shameful history displayed before ye now. The reason mages cannae be trusted." He held out his cup to a server for a refill.

The narrator staggered. One of the troupe grabbed his elbow and helped him remain standing.

"And warriors brave, though one sliced the oth',
Wary that maiming and death now came from above." The narrator paused, his eyes rolling back into his head, and he leaned heavily on the man supporting him.

His friend lowered him gently to the rush-covered floor, and I joined those around me in an exclamation. The players stopped and stared at their leader. A woman of the troupe ran to him and beckoned another, then they, with the help of a warrior sage who had joined them, carried him away. Saoirse, already risen from her seat, followed them out.

"Too much drink already?" Bàn whispered loudly in my ear.

"Friends"—a young woman of the troupe dressed in a black mage's robe costume raised her hands, gathering their audience's attention— "stay seated, if it please you. We will finish our tale while our leader is ministered to." She pulled a tattered parchment from her robe pocket, her eyes searching it for her place.

"Those lairds who fortune looked upon with mage and beast to order, gained supremacy.
And oft was said the good by evil was overcome in pledge,
With deeds awry, then badness reigned.
'Twas made worse by one found who flamed."
A burst of fire came from a player's mouth.

I started, then laughed at myself for jumping. The man put a candle to his mouth, made to spit, and flames flew out again. Those around me squealed with delight and I clapped, joining the loud applause.

I peered past the actors; they'd moved the collapsed man out of sight.

"Incendiary the land laid waste," the new narrator continued. "Until the people gathered to one man,

Who rose from ashes phoenix-fire

To lead them all and to peace aspire.

And banished did this western king,

All mage and dragon beast and kin."

"Aye." Bàn's voice rang loud in the narrator's brief pause.

She resumed her rhyme. "A truce agreed—to fight no more,

To share and trade with farther shore,

The East did settle with many lairds." She spoke quickly now, her fellow troupe peering at her and those without a costume mask, frowning.

"The West, a rìgh to rule the clans,

And to this day, one king serves all."

Bàn stood and cheered, a slurred, drunken cheer, interrupting the new narrator. Everyone turned to him. I grabbed his arm, pulling him back onto his seat.

"Shush," I hissed. "They've not finished yet."

So embarrassing!

The woman narrator cleared her throat and glanced at the bottom of her script.

"We humble players be,

But our wishes are for all to see.

Be not fools who ignore the past.

Seek now peace and make it last,

Before it is that time has passed

And good will hath slipped into lost 'portunity."

The troupe lined up and gave a hasty bow as those seated around the table, plus the servers, whistled and cheered. Bàn grunted something negative, a muffled rumble amongst the applause. The actors ran out of the room, frowns on most faces.

"They worry for their leader," Eochaid said through the cheers. "I shall go attend." He rose and left the table.

Bàn followed Eochaid's progress out of the room, then lifted a finger to my face. "Ye should pay attention to what ye just saw. For mages *ruined* our past."

Bàn's voice rose, and I put my finger to his lips and my face closer to his. His breath of goat and wine blew in my face, and his bloodshot eyes looked at me through drooping lids.

"You'll be rude to our hosts if you say any more. I thought you had manners, Bàn."

He burped and the stench of food with an acidic tinge invaded my nostrils.

"I think I should take you to your room."

His eyebrows rose, slowly reaching to his hairline. "Really?" he slurred.

"No. To go to bed." I helped him stand.

"Aye, okay." He smiled crookedly.

"To sleep off your..."

He burped again.

"Phew." I wedged my shoulder under his armpit. Warm damp soaked onto me.

He leaned heavily on me while I guided our walk out of the hall, saying goodnight to those I passed. Reece stood at the exit with a big grin on his face, leaning his broad frame against the doorway.

"Ah, warrior Bàn." He slapped Bàn on the back, nearly knocking over both of us. "I thought ye would be a one to hold your drink." He did a fake punch. "Perhaps I am wrong."

"Nae." Bàn stood straighter. "Just a wee bit tired frae assisting those players with their kit earlier, after thrashing *you* on the mats." He poked his finger into Reece's muscled shoulder, then swayed. I struggled to keep my balance. Reece grabbed Bàn's other arm.

"I'll help ye, lass," he said to me. "Man, ye are hot," he said to Bàn. "Are ye drunk or unwell?"

Bàn's head lolled forward, a drip of sweat running down his cheek. Reece and I walked him toward the passage to our rooms, dragging him mostly. Mages bustled past us, faces lined and tight. Comgall was among them, his cheeks flushed.

"What's going on?" I put out my free hand to Comgall. A fine sheen covered his forehead.

He coughed. "The troupe leader lies ill. Saoirse attends. Others of the troupe fall sick as we speak." He coughed again.

"What is it, lad?" Reece asked.

"The troupe leader struggles to breathe, and he burns with fever." Comgall's face paled while he spoke.

"Are you okay—I mean, *well?*" I asked as we crawled past him. "Did you have much to do with them?"

"Aye." Comgall's voice was hoarse now, not his usual squeak then deep croak. "So did your man, Bàn."

Reece looked at me over Bàn's bowed head, his eyes widening, then he swallowed. "We shall get him to his bed, lass. Then a healer can tend to him."

TWENTY-THREE

'Tis but a breath's breadth.
That space between
This life
And the one beyond.

VISIONS AND SAYINGS OF THE BLIND LADY SAGE

The World of Dál Cruinne
Post Dragon Wars Year 6083
Eastern Clanlands of Dál Gallain
Mountain Sage Hold
After the Feast

Perspiration dripped down Bàn's face and neck and drenched his armpits. Reece helped me lay him on his bed. I pulled the plaid from his shoulders and rivulets of sweat trickled between his pectorals, soaking the mat of his chest hair.

Reece hovered, clenching and unclenching his fists.

"Help me remove his kilt," I grunted and lowered Bàn's head onto his pillow. "It's pure wool and he needs to cool off."

Reece unbuckled the belt that held the yards and yards of pleated material around Bàn's waist, then tugged it from beneath him. Kneeling, I manoeuvred the blanket he lay on, so it came away with the kilt, ensuring Bàn now rested on cool sheets. I draped the top sheet to cover his modesty but left the rest of his skin bare to the room's air.

"What can I do, lass?" Reece asked.

I tilted my face to Reece, whose forehead crumpled.

"You could get me cloths and a bowl of cold water."

"Very well." He spun, his own kilt flicking in my face, then his loud footsteps hurried down the passage.

"Rhynne." Bàn's voice came out weak, not his usual strong, manly voice that stirred things deep inside me. "Go away. Dinnae stay near me lest ye get sick."

I shook my head. "I'm fine."

He grasped my forearm, his grip scalding and surprisingly strong. "Nae. I mean it."

"And *I* mean it." I spoke into his face. "I'm staying with you. You're roasting. I've got to get your temperature down."

Muffled voices echoed along the passage, but apart from that, this end of the caisteal sat in quiet.

So, a fever and breathing difficulties. There seemed to be no other symptoms, so I'd treat it like a flu. I tapped my teeth with my forefinger, willing my recall of herb lore. The racks full of herbs in the mage hold weren't just for spells, or whatever they did with them, were they? They used vervain for visions, and they were into herbal medicine here, too.

Good! 'Cos antibiotics aren't an option!

Once I'd cooled Bàn down, I would go to the tower and raid their herbs. What did I need again? *Hmm.* Garlic for stimulating his immune system. That would also reduce his fever. A tea of honey and ginger would be helpful, too.

Footsteps trod along the passage and Reece appeared in the doorway carrying a bowl, a jug, and cloths tucked under his arm.

"The place looks deserted," Reece said, his expression grave. "The sages hover in the infirmary."

The bowl clunked on the floor beside me as Reece bent over and placed the jug next to it.

"Thank you, Reece," I said, taking the cloths from him.

"Comgall says the one they carried off at the feast has died."

Ice flew through me. Was it like the Middle Ages here? No medicines, and plague wiping out whole communities?

I spun to Bàn. His eyes were partially closed, and his face flushed.

"How did the actor die?" I asked.

"Comgall said he had so much phlegm in his lungs, 'twas as though he drowned."

The ice became a finger that traced the line of my spine.

So quick.

My herbalist teacher had said the Spanish flu epidemic was like that. Healthy young men returning from the First World War, having survived that horror, got sick in the morning and were dead by lunchtime.

I lowered my head onto the bed and closed my eyes tight.

Please, not Bàn.

"Lady Rhynne?" Reece's voice wavered.

I snapped my head up, dunked a cloth in the bowl. The water chilled my fingers. It must have come from the well outside, where they collected not thermal water, but melted snow.

"Help me," I ordered the warrior.

I mopped Bàn's face, neck and chest while Reece wet his arms and legs. Bàn grunted and pushed Reece away.

"Bàn, let us." I spoke firmly into his face.

His eyes flickered, then he lowered his hands, arm muscles slackening.

"You keep this up, Reece. I'm going to the mages' tower."

He nodded as I hurried past him.

I ran across to my room and pressed the niche in the wall that opened the hidden door. The passage sat unlit, with no candles burning in sconces like they usually did when the mages were expecting me. I placed my hand on the wall and felt my way along until I came to where I'd estimated the door to the tower to be, then ran my fingers across the space. Coarse stone, then smooth wood in the rough shape of a door. I pushed and it swung open.

No light shone through the tall windows from the night outside. A lone candle sat on the workbench in the middle of the room. The racks that held the drying herbs and usually hung from the ceiling were now lowered, and there were gaps in the rows of bunched herbs. A mortar and pestle rested abandoned on the bench amongst the crumbs and herb dust scattered on the surface.

I grabbed a tapered candle and lit it with the stump of candle on the bench. Holding it up, I surveyed the tower with its weak light. I screwed my mouth to the side. Come to think of it, I'd never noticed garlic, or even ginger, in this herbalist-like section of the mage hold.

What did they use, then?

I searched some more, coming to a halt at the jars of specimens. The *dead things*.

"Eww! Hope they're not using anything like *that* on anyone."

Hmm. Where would I find anything like...?

Of course. "The kitchen!"

I ran out the door, exiting the normal way, then turned down the corridor to the regular dining hall, which sat dark and empty. A quiet clatter came through the door that led to the cooking area. I stepped to it and pushed gently on the door. The cook and his assistant stood by an enormous fire in a just as enormous fireplace, big enough to be a small room on its own. Standing so close, both men had beads of sweat on their foreheads. They stirred large cauldrons that hung over the coals, with steam rising up from them and the aroma of... *chicken soup?*

"Hello?"

The tall man turned from his stirring. "Och, we have a well one, aye?"

"Yes, and how are you both?" I asked.

"We are hot but nae from a fever." His assistant gave a gap-toothed grin.

"There are those who heal, then there's those who keep the healers"— the cook leaned toward me— "and those recovering, well fed."

"If they recover," his assistant murmured under his breath.

"Now, now. We'll have nae o' that." He gave a slight slap to his assistant's head. "Keep stirring." He looked at me. "Ye wanting some broth. Nae quite ready yet."

"Thank you. I'll get some when it's done. For Lord Bàn. He's... unwell." I blinked at my forlorn tone.

The cook's assistant gaped at me for a flash, then returned to his stirring.

I swallowed, pushing down the dark pit rising from my guts and threatening to engulf my heart. "Do you have garlic and ginger? Oh, and some honey?"

The cook turned to face me fully then, one hand still stirring his pot. "Garlic?" He raised his eyebrows. "Ah well, some garlic a drying, hangs on the wall by the sacks o' grains in the store there." He nodded in the direction behind me.

I hurried to the pantry-like section of this large kitchen and stopped at the sacks of grain. Onions and wild garlic hung from pegs on the wall. They were plaited together into long ropes like in a French kitchen. I took the bottom three bulbs of garlic, then hastened back to the cooks at the hearth.

"May I use a small pan? I need to make an infusion."

The cook's assistant got a small pot, filled it with water, hung it on a pole, then swung that into the space above the coals. I found a wooden board and a broad-edged knife and crushed the garlic, then scraped it from the board into the pot.

"Garlic soup?" The assistant laughed, and the cook tapped him on the head again.

"It's proven to be good for reducing fever and stimulating the immune system." I put my hand over my lips.

"*Immu*... pardon?" The cook's mouth remained open.

"It will help the sick get better," I said.

"Put some in this chicken broth, then lass." He stood aside and pointed to the cauldron he stirred.

I crushed more garlic and scraped it in.

"Ginger? Honey?" I asked.

The cook squinted, then shook his head. "Honey we have, aye, but the other thing." He shrugged.

Oops. I'd used the English word. "Ah, you may know it by another name." *But what?* "Oh yes, *asair,*" I said using its Gaelic name.

"Oh. Aye. Why'd ye no' say?" The cook smiled. "I hae some ground dried asair in that wee pot on ma' shelf o' flavours." He nodded to a row of shelves on the far wall. "And the honey is nearby. Help yoursel'."

I made an infusion of ginger, using the drizzler to add a spoonful of honey from the pot, then poured some of that and the garlic infusion into separate mugs, thanked the cook and his assistant, then ran along to Bàn's room.

Reece knelt by Bàn's bed, holding a damp cloth to Bàn's forehead.

"He shivers so much the bed rattles, Lady Rhynne." Dark circles sat under Reece's eyes, made ghoulish in the weak candlelight.

"Thanks Reece, you go rest now. I'll be fine from here. It's his fever. It needs to break." Reece stood. "How does a lady like yourself ken sae much?"

"I was taught." *At herbalist night school 'cos my dad insisted. Thank you, Dad.*

"Aye, well, it seems a gift much needed now." He stepped out the door. "Send for me if ye need me, aye?"

Bàn opened his eyes but seemed to look at nothing. His skin was hot and dry to touch. I dipped the cloth in the jug of cool water, squeezed it out, then wiped him down again.

I grabbed the mug of garlic infusion.

"Here. You need to drink this." I lifted Bàn's head, holding him steady, and put the mug to his mouth.

He took a sip and swallowed, scrunching his face, but eventually finished it all.

"Really? Garlic is an essential ingredient in some menus."

He looked at me through narrowed lids.

"Don't believe me? Didn't you eat Italian in the Other World?"

He groaned, his mouth curling faintly on one side.

"So, you've still got a sense of humour? A good sign, I suppose."

Bàn's arms trembled, and he lay back further, moaning. Then his limbs shook so much the bed rocked, just as Reece had said. I put my hand on Bàn's forehead. His skin sat dry and *so* hot beneath my fingers. I placed the damp, cool cloth there and made soothing sounds while he rode out the rigours.

He lay quietly for a few minutes, so I made him sip the ginger and honey. He pressed his lips tight after the first mouthful.

"I know it's sharp. You need it. Drink! Boy, you're fussy."

More footsteps came along the passageway. They were heavier than Comgall's, and Reece shouldn't be back so soon.

"My Lady Rhynne." It was Eochaid, his deep voice resonating and serious.

I stood.

"Ah, ye are well, and I see ye tend to Lord Bàn. Do you require any assistance?"

"No, thank you. I'm fine so far."

"Very good," he said, his voice grave. "Tend him well. Keep him comfortable. I will send someone to check on you regularly." He looked at the floor, only glancing at me and Bàn once or twice the whole time he spoke.

"How is everyone?" I asked.

A wind had picked up outside and whistled quietly through the crack in Bàn's window.

"I am sorry, my lady"—he took a heavy breath— "but many of the troupe of players have succumbed to their illness."

"Oh!"

"Now some mages who attend are unwell." He put up a staying hand at my further gasp. "My wife is well, as is Maebh. Saoirse is the only healer sage currently in residence. She tends as many as she is able, though it exhausts her so. But I'm sorry to say young Comgall... has passed from this life."

"What!" My voice came out as a breath, my hand coming to my mouth. A wave of cold, like it blew in straight from outside, flowed through me.

"Aye, so quick. Young, yet... He helped those who ministered. Such a good lad." Sadness ached through Eochaid's voice. "I shall leave you. Tend your man well."

He left.

Twenty-Four

I will love ye with my all. My breath, my thoughts, my heartbeat, my days and beyond... even with my very soul.

POETRY OF A KING
ÀRD RÌGH RHONAN IUBHAR
(4030-4090 POST DRAGON WARS)

The World of Dál Cruinne
Post Dragon Wars Year 6084
Eastern Clanlands of Dál Gallain
Mountain Sage Hold
Turn of the Year

The whole caisteal sat in an unnerving silence. All occupied with the ill or being unwell themselves... or dying.

It could wipe out this place.

I marched along the passageway to Bàn's room. Over the past thirty-six hours, I'd only left Bàn's side for minutes at a time to get more garlic, ginger and honey infusions—and some whisky.

I swallowed. But I was well, not even a sore throat. That's how it started. I stopped mid-stride. I'd had my flu vaccination this year.

Maybe that's why.

I turned into Bàn's room. He lay silent and still. A flash as sharp as razor blades sliced through me. I ran the couple of paces to him, dumping the mugs of infusions on the floor and sloshing their contents over the sides. The liquid puddled on the floor. I placed my hand on his chest. It rose and fell, accompanied by a faint wheeze. I let out my own breath, only now realising I'd held it in.

He was still hot but not roasting and had slept soundly since his last sips of infusion. I knelt on the floor beside him. The warmth from the thermal spring-heated rock took the discomfort from the hard stone on my knees. My arms were heavy, and a dullness dragged me toward sleep.

But I wouldn't. Not until Bàn was awake and well again.

The slow churning that'd sat in my guts for just over a day now rose in my throat. I leaned over and rested my head on Bàn's chest, my head lifting, then lowering with each of his laboured breaths. With my ear on his skin, loud crackles came through his chest wall, and he gurgled each time he breathed out. It was the phlegm that could drown him. An ache pinched my heart. What if he died and we'd not made up?

"We're still friends, right?" My voice seemed so loud in the quiet room.

Bàn took a rasping breath.

"I wish you'd understand. The mage training... it's something I *have* to do."

The wind howled through the cracks in the window and Bàn's gurgling breaths continued. My mind went back to the Midwinter Feast. He'd got all het up over their history and all the mages had done in the Dragon Wars of years and years ago. All red in the face, spouting his opinion that everything about mages was bad.

"I suppose you know more than me about how it really is here."

Maybe Dad knew the bigger picture for me back... home. I gulped. Perhaps Dad hadn't spoken about who my real parents were because it had been too hard for him to face... the fact that I would leave him eventually. How would he have explained it, anyway? Who I really am. Where I originally came from.

I probably would've laughed at him.

My shoulders shook, my breath stuttering around quiet sobs.

Dad had his reasons and maybe so far there hadn't been a *right* time to tell me. Or for me to know everything.

Perhaps Bàn had his reasons for not wanting me to learn mage-craft. Magic.

"Okay, I wish you didn't hate it so much. I'll not let them train me, then. I'll wait for my grandfather. Only... please live."

His chest rose again, and halted like he was just about to speak, then it fell. I lifted my head from his chest and shook him gently. His head lolled, then he groaned, and his eyes remained shut.

My lips trembled and my heart rocked my rib cage, tears blurring my vision. I rested my head against his chest again. His heart beat steadily beneath my ear.

"Don't die..." I whispered into his chest. "I love you."

I reached for a mug of herbal infusion, my fingers touching the liquid on the floor around the mugs where it had spilled. Now wet soaked my fingers and palm.

Ahh, damn. I returned my attention to Bàn's heartbeat. At least that tapped out a constant rhythm and a good pace, although a little fast. I let the *lup-dupp* wash over me, and eased myself a little into my fatigue, allowing that not-quite-in-your-body sensation to surround me. The same kind of dreamy state I'd experienced previously when Soph and I had stayed awake on purpose for two whole days and nights just to see if we could.

My thoughts swam around between Bàn's warmth, the sharp, hot scent of ginger, and his heartbeat.

Oh, be well. Please.

A gust of golden warmth came into me from my hand still resting in the spilled herbal infusion. It spread throughout my body, like it flowed from the herbal liquid on my fingers, and not from the heated stone floor. It filled my mind with light, with a sense of growing things. Of plants, sentient and watchful while the world changed around them. Like an ancient tree observing time pass. The lives of people and animals only seconds compared to its own long existence. Ginger's sharpness and garlic's solidness swirled around me and through me. Not just in my nose, but inside me.

I saw myself lying with my head against Bàn. There was a darkness in him. I sent out the warmth, directing it to that dark. It seemed that was what I was meant to do. The warmth pushed away the dark and settled in its place. His heart beat stronger. And even though I didn't sense I was actually *in* my body, I could no longer hear the crackles and gurgles of phlegm in his chest.

He breathed deeper, clearer.

I raised my head from him. The warmth left me in a rush, the room spinning in its wake and washing the aromas of garlic and ginger around me. I grasped the bed with my wet hand to steady myself, ginger and honey tea dripping from my fingertips.

Bàn grunted. It echoed loudly around the chamber. His eyes opened wide, clear, and no longer bloodshot.

"Rhynne," he said, his voice strong and deep, his tone raised in surprise, but with no hint of accusation. "What did you do?"

Twenty-Five

Keep this charge to yourself, for this missive belongs to your eyes and none other. The woman, her aura touched with things foreign yet the very blood of Dál Cruinne runs through her veins, holds a gifting unusual. She is of intrigue and great import. If she will come, bring her forth to the Isle.

I, Grand Master Llew, write this with my own hand.

The World of Dál Cruinne
Post Dragon Wars Year 6084
Eastern Clanlands of Dál Gallain
Clachan Beag Village

Talorc left the warriors at the edge of the village, then limped along, ignoring the stares. His stiff right leg, which bent not at the hip, produced an awkward gait. He sneered at a dirty child, its pale eyes peering out of a mud-grimed face. It wore a thin tunic over tattered breeches. *Ha.* At least this one *had* a tunic.

He scanned the surrounding buildings. Smoke-charred beams abutted reclaimed stone mixed in with wattle-and-daube in the walls of rebuilt dwellings. The percussive clang of metal on metal rang out ahead of him. It arose further along the mud-sloshed path the locals named their *high street*, made slippery by the coming of spring and melting of the ice and snow that had kept all confined to quarters and only now allowed him to fulfil his designated task.

Lord Ciarán had made his mark on this wee village also. Not an able-bodied male in sight.

But he would grumble not. The lord paid well. And Bram, his mage, was an obliging one with which to work, with ideas that sent the mages out of their workrooms. Talorc rubbed his hands against the cold, but he glowed within.

What a change to his own life.

Such purpose. To be part of the *master plan*, as young Bram had named it. 'Twas about time he himself saw more of the world than that which he spied in his divination flames.

His lips tugged with a smile. *Now free to roam.*

The other mages in the *spy-network*—an odd but intriguing term—of which Lord Ciarán so proudly boasted, had infiltrated the service of Dál Gaedhle lords. They had used their many gifts of influence to lure the minds of lesser lords and warriors. Two warbands, once faithful to MacEnoicht, now sped their way to assist Lord Ciarán. 'Twas enough for the current purposes.

He ticked his head to the side. Bram... he had a touch of something, though. It hovered around their communications in their divination bowls. In those moments, Talorc had sensed the lingering malevolence.

Aye, we mages in the east are not known for our source to be of the light, but this one's spirit lord made the usual darkness seem as day.

Yet at times Bram was such an innocent lad. Or had been on Talorc's recollections of him at Innesfarne—that famous isle of the learned. He gave a wee grunt to himself.

What of the missive sent from there? An order from the very Grand Master Llew himself. This young woman with the Dál Gaedhle warrior—one gifted. With his work and roaming for Laird Lorain, Talorc was to seek her out. Verify the inklings of those on the learned isle. That a mage of some talent, but no skill, had arrived in the land. Her power a beacon to the *seeings* of the masters on that pinnacled rock arising from the ocean.

Hmm.

He reached the smithy. Here, they had advised him, he would garner the exact information required. He entered. The ear-piercing rhythmic clatter ceased on the blacksmith's acknowledgement of him. The man downed his hammer, left the glowing metal rod, and stepped close to him.

"Greetings, my lord mage."

Was that a dip of the head? A bow of respect? Good. The man knew his place.

"Smith, I come from your Laird Lorain. Ye have information for me that ye must tell."

The man's muscled throat convulsed, and he peered past Talorc to the muddied path beyond.

"Ye wish to speak in private, smith?" Talorc tilted his head.

The smith's bulky shoulders lost their tenseness and the tightness to his brow left his face flushed from the heat of the forge. He guided Talorc to the farthest end of the three-sided hut the smith would name an establishment, then nodded expectantly.

"You know of the strangers who graced your humble village afore this ghastly winter set in?" Talorc spoke in lowered tones.

"Aye, lord mage, but I ha' told all to those who came afore the snows."

"And you shall relay to me now. I am certain your recollections shall improve with the telling."

"I wish it known I had nae part in their actions. 'Twas a crying shame that what 'appened to Ma Gabràn."

Hmm. An interesting report had been sent by the surviving warriors. One piquing his interest, for it smelled of *magick.*

"Tell me of the blond warrior who repaired her drystone walls. All know of him, so you shall not be held culpable for idle chatter." Talorc glanced at the entrance to the smithy's establishment, where those waiting for his services gathered. Gossips. The source of the man's concern.

"'E was just that, lord. A warrior, if ever there was. But not familiar to these parts. I spoke not to 'im, but those who did hear him speak say he had an accent of the west. And the young woman with him—a beauty I am told—spoke in tones even more foreign."

"They disappeared about the time of the first heavy snows?" Talorc asked.

"Aye. None seen 'em since."

"At all?"

The smithy nodded, his mouth a thin line.

"What lies up that mountain?"

The smithy's mouth continued its line and his eyes hardened.

"Come now. It is more than a mere goat track." Talorc had searched far and wide on commencing his service to Lord Lorain. It had not been clear what was on this mountain, but a magic of some sort always blocked it from his *sight.*

The man's bulky shoulders rose in an intake of air and beads of sweat formed on his brow, yet he did not speak.

Talorc narrowed his eyes, drew a touch of power from the heat of the forge, proximity to the bright coals enough to draw his own source. Warmth poured into him, along with its strength. He directed it to his hand, at the same time grabbing the smithy's. Hard callouses rubbed against his own smooth palm.

The man yelped and tugged to release his hand from Talorc's grasp, but could not disengage. Talorc held steady to both the blacksmith's hand and his source. The blacksmith's face contorted.

"The steep track to the top leads to a hot spring, lord mage." The smith grimaced. "Many take the climb in the warmer seasons to bathe in the healing waters."

The man's aura was pure, and he spoke the truth he knew. But there was sure to be more.

"Who tends to this spring?"

"No one, lord mage—"

"Then how is it maintained? Surely some enterprising soul would gain a few coin by holding the garments of those who dip?"

Sweat dripped down the man's face, despite standing in the coolest area of the smithy.

"I beg you, lord mage, do 'em no harm. They be good folk."

"Who?" Talorc twisted his grip, the man's finger joints popping through the heat.

The blacksmith let out a cry, then bit his tongue, shaking his head. Talorc lifted his free hand toward the glowing forge.

Damn the man. He desired to hurt him not. If only he would cooperate. Talorc drew a touch, an infinitesimal spark from the volcano's worth of heat available to him.

The man screamed.

Talorc shut it off. He needed the information. The smithy baked from the inside would be useless to him.

The man groaned and slumped to the floor, resting his back to the wattle-and-daube wall, nestling his broken hand in his other. He panted, raising his head, one eye open to Talorc, glaring.

A tough one.

Talorc squatted in front of him. "There is more. More I can give and more I must receive." He tilted his head, endeavouring it to appear a compassionate gesture. "I wish to harm ye not."

"Harm *them* not, for my cousin lives there. She kens the magic as ye do, sir. But heals folk, aye?"

"Ah. Healer mages." Talorc grunted. "Thank you, smith. Be about your work. Ye have served your laird well." Talorc limped out the forge-hut, pausing at the edge of the gathered crowd until they parted, then stepped with care on the slimy path heading out of the village.

He did not stop for breath, but turned down the narrow track that led to the ruined steading not far from the village. Ahead, his warriors waited by a broken gate post, mounted and holding his steed. Behind them sat a mountain majestic, its cloak of snow hugging tight, but a thin grey line, a clearly defined path, zig-zagged its way up the side.

"So?" the Gallawain warrior asked.

"Aye. The generosity of healers." Talorc snarled. "There can be nowhere else for two strangers to over-winter." He mounted his horse, the ache in his hip dissipating as he relieved the joint of his weight with riding long in the stirrup, as was his custom. He spun to face the mountain, his vision rising to its peaks. "We go."

TWENTY-SIX

The fore of battle may be a shield wall,
A charging destrier,
Or the slicing swing of battle axes.
But braver still and faithful yet,
Is the one who risks their life against the invisible foe
Who rots the flesh, or drowns the lung,
And sends even the strongest to the world of the dead.

ADVICE TO WAR CHIEFS
WARRIOR SAGE TAPAÌDH
(4009-4059 POST DRAGON WARS)

The World of Dál Cruinne
Post Dragon Wars Year 6084
Eastern Clanlands of Dál Gallain
Mountain Sage Hold

Bàn leaned in the doorway, his limbs heavy with fatigue from the practice mat. He huffed.

I need to get back to full strength.

Rhynne's healing had rid him of the phlegm and fever, but his body still took its time to leave the weakness behind. In the past weeks, once recovered, he had helped where he could, cutting wood, tending the horses, and even assisting in meal preparation when the cook had taken ill. Of the troubadours, those who had brought the plague, all but two had died.

He'd returned to training. He would head back to Dál Gaedhle, and who knew what battles with Ciarán Gallawain's warbands stood between the mountain sage hold and The Keep.

He bit down on his back teeth. Now was past the time of Rhynne's birth in this severe winter, and a weak spring would soon determine to show itself. They should be away. A late snow melt had begun, and outside the sage hold caisteal rivers would rage and engorged burns would tear down the mountainside. The passes would clear, but Rhynne had refused to leave.

Stubborn. Strong-minded. Her chin had lifted with her announcement.

By my blade, she was determined!

She saw a need and she could help. And so, she did.

Another reason to love her. He chuckled. *As if I need another.*

He returned his focus to the room. Cots lined up in rows, and now with the worst of the plague over, most were empty. Of those lying ill, sages mopped brows and fed the sick with strength enough to drink a broth. They kept the bodies of the dead in a cold store outhouse. They would dispose of them once the permafrost receded and wood from the forest for the fire became more accessible. He swallowed. He envied not those who would prepare that pyre.

The ill lay quiet. For the past month, Sage Saoirse and Rhynne had tended any brought to the infirmary, being the only two sages with the healing gift. They had not taught Rhynne, for her healing gift had come naturally. And, for some reason, Rhynne had refused further offers of instruction from Eochaid and Maebh. There had been too few moments of calm for teaching sessions, anyway.

He grunted. He still could not say it out loud... that Rhynne was a *mage*. For Eifion would be sure to cultivate her natural talent.

Rhynne stood from tending an elderly sage, one of the last, if truth be known. For the plague had sent to their Maker most of those sages who'd resided here in their latter years, cared for by their juniors. Rhynne and Saoirse had tried their best but could not save all, despite their healing powers. Rhynne pressed her hands to her lower back and stretched.

Bàn stepped across to her and took her arm. She faced him. Dark circles sat beneath her eyes and her young face now took on lines.

"Come rest." He willed his voice to gentleness. "Ye have tended those in need for over a day."

She mopped her brow with the back of her hand. "There's still—"

"Sage Saoirse." He spoke over Rhynne's shoulder. "Ye can manage now, aye? Let Rhynne take a wee rest, if ye please."

"Of course." Saoirse stood from an elderly woman and nodded to Rhynne. "You go now. I am fine."

"Are you sure?" Rhynne frowned. "You've barely recovered yourself."

Bàn pushed down on the heat the statement kindled. The mage, weakened by the fatigue of healing others, could not heal herself, but his Rhynne had spent her energy healing the woman and now wore the evidence. Fine lines crinkled around Rhynne's eyes, and faint strands of silver sprinkled her beautiful long black locks. His hand by his side balled into a fist.

"Others assist and there are no new ill just now. It seems to have tapered off," Saoirse said. "Go rest."

Rhynne allowed him to lead her out of the infirmary. They walked down the passage to her room, and she leaned heavily into him all the way. How she had not succumbed was a miracle. One she named *vaccination*.

"Och, ye are exhausted. Ye must get to your bed, and I shall fetch ye some food." He guided her onto her cot.

She didn't resist and shut her eyes, sinking into the thin mattress. He stood by her bed, his fingers tapping his thigh, batting down a long-held belief clutched tight since childhood. Beliefs could change when presented with enough evidence.

A calmness rose in his chest, for he had experienced it.

And experience can overcome any argument.

Rhynne had used magic to heal him. A magic wrought by the woman he loved. It had not harmed him but made him whole.

Bàn turned on his heel and wandered down the narrow hallway, shaking his head. His views were softening. That was true.

But still, not *all* magic was good—it depended on the wielder. For now, this was what he would believe.

Shouts echoed along the passage, stopping Bàn in his tracks. Roars travelled to him in earnest, and not from the practice mats. He turned to the yelling and ringing of weapons. It came from the back stair, the way to the stables. Reece's deep cries were amongst the clatter.

Bàn ran back to his room, grabbed his sword and daggers, then glanced across to Rhynne. Her head tilted to the side, her thick black plait sat at her nape, her eyes were closed, and her rib cage rose and fell. He tore down the passage and headed for the back steps, then descended two at a time. Grunts of exertion grew louder, and an icy wind whirling up the stairwell chilled his cheeks.

Strangers contended with warrior sages. With his back to Bàn, Reece belted a warrior who wore an orange tartan plaid. Other warrior sages fought. Sunlight streamed through the open doorway from the clear sky shining on the stable yard outside. Swords flashed in its beams.

A flicker of maroon tartan caught Bàn's eye.

Dragon's teeth! The tartan of Gallawain. Ciarán's warriors, then.

By my blade! They would be after himself and Rhynne.

Reece let go a fearsome roar, grunting as he slashed down on his opponent. The man crumpled, then another came through the doorway, filling the gap.

How many are there?

Bàn reached the lower step, and Reece glanced over his shoulder at him.

"No!" Reece stabbed the nearest warrior in the face and stepped away, nodding to his companion to take over, then he ran to Bàn.

"Get your woman and go." His breath came hard. "A stable hand awaits you with a horse by the hot-spring gate."

"But—" was all Bàn could get out before Reece interrupted.

"We shall occupy them here." Grunts of exertion from sage and Gallawain warrior alike almost drowned Reece's voice. "Do *not* go through the village. Some have given you up."

Reece spun to a roar from a Gallawain warrior. Bàn drew his sword, his veins hot with anger at the betrayal, and together they dispatched the man.

Reece nodded his thanks and continued. "Halfway down the mountain, ye shall see a track to the right, now clear of snow from the melt. Take that track. It leads to a deep but narrow part of the River Bàn-rìghinn," he said in haste. "Mayhap a bridge still spans there. Cross and make your way to the border." He winked. "Take that young lass to her parents, then make her your wife." A roar interrupted another wink, and he raised his weapon in defence of a sword strike. "Go!" he shouted over his shoulder.

Bàn spun, climbed stairs three at a time, pulse thundering in his temples, then ran to Rhynne's room.

"Rhynne, wake." He grasped her shoulder and shook. "Get your things. Hurry!"

Rhynne's eyes flew open. "What's the noise?"

"Gallawain warriors seeking us. We must go. Reece holds them off." He pulled her wolf-collared cloak from its peg on the wall. "Dress warmly." He threw it to her then strode to his room, hastily putting on his leather armour. He adjusted his weapons and swung his cloak over his shoulders, giving a brief flash of acknowledgement to the dear woman who'd made it.

"Ready Rhynne?"

She'd dressed in warm breeches and had wrapped round her body the blue tartan plaid of the àrd rìgh still in her possession from the Midwinter Feast. A leather satchel sat on her shoulder.

"I need a weapon." She held out her hand.

He thrust the handle of a sheathed dagger into her palm.

She tucked it into her belt, then set her cloak on her shoulders. "How do we escape?"

"Out the hot-spring way. A lad will have a horse."

"How?"

"Reece. He and other warrior sages fight them."

"For us." She gulped.

"Aye, come." He grabbed her arm and dragged her along the passage to the other side of the sage hold, down the slippery steps long drenched in mineral salts, and out the stone steps to the sloped side of the caisteal's base.

Sure enough, a lad waited with the grey stallion he'd ridden for the hunt.

Och, Reece. Ye are the man!

Rhynne pulled back against his arm, staring with lips tight as he grabbed the reins. The grey stallion nickered and shook its head while the lad gave him a knee up.

"Nae time to fear horses, Rhynne," Bàn growled from the saddle. "Get ye up here." He grabbed Rhynne's hand and hoisted her onto the tall horse, the lad pushing her up also, shoving her onto the animal's back to sit behind him.

He nodded thanks to the boy, then took one last look at the caisteal. Its dark stone glistened in the bright pre-spring sun, which shone through the last of the clear icicles hanging from window ledges and eaves. Muffled mêlée shouts reached him, sending a shiver across his skin.

"Yah!" He kicked the stallion's flanks.

It whinnied and sprang to a canter; Rhynne's arms came round his waist and clamped tight. The grey war horse dug its hooves into the sodden ground, leaving the caisteal behind them.

Here do two times converge.
Where story, but a moment prior, lived two separate lines,
Now travellers' journeys re-join.
With portal's task attended,
Players, map thine own charted destinies.

CONTEMPLATIONS OF A TRAVELLER
GRAND MASTER LLEW
ISLE OF INNESFARNE
(POST DRAGON WARS 6000-CURRENT)

Twenty-Seven

— · —

I watch ye, my daughter,
As ye ponder your own wee girl,
Thinking her lost in the Other World.
Oh, if only I could come to ye,
Show you, my precious one, the vision I have of a raven-haired woman,
Safely home in our world, guarded and guided by the Warrior Lord Bàn.
But ye hear me not,
Thine own gift ignored.

VISIONS AND SAYINGS OF THE BLIND LADY SAGE

The World of Dál Cruinne
Year 6084 Post Dragon Wars
Western Sovereignty of Dál Gaedhle
The Keep

Candlelight glowed behind Rhiannon's eyelids, just like a cinema screen.

A young woman draws the edges of her torn dress together, covering molested breasts, and choking back bile at the lingering touch of unwelcome hands. She looks familiar. Rhiannon has seen her before. In the joint vision Aisling gave to her, Arlan, and Eifion.
It's Arlan's mother, Alana!
Alana sits on a stone bench in an alcove, a nook in The Keep. A man steps back. Ciarán—a lot younger. He pants and smiles; his lips curl up in a grin. The same lips that pressed with force not moments before, mirroring his force exerted on lower, more intimate parts.
"My love," he speaks through breathless pleasure. "Now we are one—"
"Nae!" Alana's voice strangles. She drags her skirts over her legs. "You fool, cousin. I was never yours to have. Go! Leave me to my shame and disgust. We'll not speak of this!"

144

Rhiannon's eyes flew open to her dimly lit bedroom, the night candle a stub burning low on the nightstand, and the vision lingering in the dark corners.

"Why...?" Her breath caught and she thrust her hand beside her.

Arlan's side of their bed—cold and empty. She groaned, easing off the mattress, then shook herself.

"I really do *not* want to remember that one!" She padded across the cold floor to the washbowl and scrubbed her face and hands. "That was too real. Poor Alana. If it were true..."

She peered at the bed. *Would I have told him if he was here?*

"No. There's more pressing stuff going on. Then I'd have to admit to my visions." She held her lips tight. "It's maybe not so weird here..."

A lone bird sung outside the window, its eager morning call floating through the balcony. She would be early, but she'd be at that portal, waiting. She dressed hastily and hurried out the door then along the passage to Morrigan's room.

The Standing Stone Memorial

Bird chatter wafted to Rhiannon's ears. She stood in the meadow past the bridge beyond The Keep, clenching her hands into fists, knuckles cracking. Five days had passed since Bàn had left. Her arms were still empty of baby Rhynne, her breasts now not so tight with milk, and the hole in her heart gaping wider.

Silver edged the horizon, signalling the time for sunrise drew near. She paced back and forth along the rim of bare ground that encircled the standing stone erected in memory of Donnach MacEnoicht, the father-in-law she never knew.

Not a thing grew in that circle and never had since the dragon's blast. She bit a fingernail, pacing, eyes riveted on the granite sentinel in the centre of the circle.

Where is he?

The words etched on the smooth, grey surface of the stone blurred.

"That's it! Come on." George's encouraging tones fill her mind. He kneels on a carpeted floor in front of an overstuffed couch, holding his arms out. A toddler in a pink, lacy dress and white tights, with a bulky nappy bulging below the short hemline, takes over-large steps toward him. A dark mop of hair encircled by a pink headband, wavers with each step. The small child thuds to the floor. A staggered cry erupts.

"Aww. It's okay." George reaches out and gathers the child into his arms. "Shh. Shh." Love fills his voice. "Daddy's here."

Sweat cooled Rhiannon's skin in the chill, early morning air.

Oh no. It'd happened again. She chewed the inside of her cheek. Did these visions mean something? Or like a dream, was it just her subconscious trying to make sense of it all?

Morrigan coughed and Rhiannon flinched, then turned to her.

Good old Morrigan.

Morrigan had glued herself to Rhiannon's side since Arlan had assigned Morrigan the task of guarding her when away from The Keep. *It's like he doesn't trust me.*

He said it would be for her protection in case a dragon returned.

So, he admitted the real danger too. He *must* realise her reasons for taking their baby to George. She couldn't take much more of his coolness toward her. He was always at the Àrd Rìgh's Council meetings... and not in their bed.

Rhiannon sighed and closed her eyes. She couldn't blame him. She'd acted in haste and fear. She saw that now. Now it was done and couldn't be *undone.* Bowing her head, her insides churned.

I'd find me hard to truly forgive too.

"Lady Rhiannon," Morrigan said from outside the ring. "The sun has risen. My brother returns not. Let us go back to The Keep."

Rhiannon's shoulders sank, then her breathing shook with her sobs, and tears slicked down her cheeks, a slow watery warmth. A gentle arm rested on her shoulder, and the earthy smell of Morrigan's leather armour surrounded her.

"It will be well, my lady," Morrigan said, hugging Rhiannon to herself.

"He hates me now," Rhiannon stuttered out.

"Nae, Lord Arlan loves ye as his own soul."

"*Hmph.*"

"Give him time."

Rhiannon spun from Morrigan's sisterly embrace. "He doesn't get it. Rhynne would be safer there, but now he's made Bàn fetch her back into *this* danger we all face. You get it, don't you, Morrigan?"

Blonde eyelashes lowered, and rosy spots of pink appeared high on Morrigan's cheeks.

"But there are no *dragons* in the Other World!" Rhiannon's voice rasped.

"Come, Lady Rhiannon." Morrigan spoke in a placating tone, steering her away from the stone and toward her mare, Bridie.

Rhiannon reached out to the white horse's muzzle, soft and welcoming in her hands. Velvet lips nibbled, seeking a treat. Rhiannon dug in her pocket, retrieving a piece of carrot, and opened her palm to her mare's mouth.

"There, girl." She leaned her cheek against Bridie's long face. At least she received some comfort from her mare. Horses didn't judge, and they accepted you just as you were.

No matter if you think you did right, but later it seems that you didn't.

She'd hurt Arlan. Believed taking Rhynne to the Other World was a good idea and the right choice—the *best* solution. And she'd not dared to ask him. Left him out of her fear-fuelled decision. *I just couldn't give him the chance to deny my wish to take her somewhere safe.* Tears spilled again and the emptiness in her rib cage returned, just like the widening empty space between herself and Arlan.

Well, she had to repair things. She couldn't stand the ache every time he looked at her.

Stirrup leathers creaked; Morrigan had mounted. Rhiannon wiped the tears away, rose into the saddle, and headed for The Keep.

Her boots slapped doggedly behind Morrigan's tall, straight back up the steps to the entrance of The Keep proper. Morrigan turned.

"Ye can go about your own business now, my lady." Morrigan spoke in a dismissive tone.

Not today. "I think I should be more involved with this war planning."

Morrigan lifted an eyebrow.

"I'm sure to learn something." Rhiannon kept her tone light. "I *am* a Dál Gaedhle warrior."

A slight crinkle appeared above the bridge of Morrigan's nose, marring her movie-star good looks. "Very well."

Rhiannon walked side by side with Morrigan through the double doors to the Great Hall. Deep-voiced discussion in tense tones blared out from the door of the side room where the war council met. Rhiannon paused at the open door to the room while Morrigan walked across to sit beside Angus. All of Arlan's warriors were present. Except Bàn.

"Ciarán Gallawain's warbands make no move in our direction, Lord Àrd Rìgh." A leather-armour-clad warrior stood in front of the àrd rìgh's seat. "Our scouts report a Dál Gallain warband to the south somewhat."

Arlan sat on the ornately carved wooden chair, his fingers tapping the arms.

"Aye, the man would prepare for an offensive move, and he will act soon." Leuchars, the war chief, stood beside Arlan. His gruff voice hit Rhiannon with its intensity. "We will send our scouts deeper into Dál Gallain."

"Aye." Arlan grimaced. He rubbed the back of his neck and glanced at Eifion, who sat with another sage.

Eifion met Arlan's gaze, and something silent passed between the two men in Rhiannon's life.

"The cannon, Eifion? Are your fellow sages and those who work with metal any further on? How have they progressed these past ten days?"

"The sages have designed an improved mould in which to pour the molten lead, Lord Arlan." Eifion spoke and the room hushed. "Those involved try once again and will test it soon. They appear happy with the perfection of the cannon balls. Your idea of rolling them in barrels to smooth them has worked."

"Lord Leuchars, how many more clan chiefs pledge their support?" Arlan asked.

"The warbands of Clan Manus and Clan Ross are but a day away, according to their scouts, and the Laird of Muirton has sent a band. I am yet to hear from Clan Callaghan or the Chief of Duisdale," Leuchars replied.

"And our arms?" Arlan asked. "The weapons masters and smiths have been busy?"

"Aye, frantic, lord. They will supply us well."

"Then we must make our move. I can delay nae longer. We will head to Gallawain's tower, dealing with his bands of raiders by our borders on the way." Arlan stood and eyed all clan chiefs and warriors present. "The current trickle of refugees from Dál Gallain brings reports of towers and caisteals raided, and the ladies and children of their lairds taken prisoner by Gallawain's warriors. Villages are stripped of men of fighting age." Arlan grunted in disgust. "Gallawain acts in desperation, forcing the reluctant to comply. This will be to our advantage." Arlan's frown deepened, and his tone firmed. "I wish to hurt not the innocent nor the coerced. We will rid our Dál Gallain cousins of this tyrant, prevent his entry into Dál Gaedhle, and reinstate those who wish for a peaceful rule. We do not go to conquer. We go to defend. Am I understood?"

"Aye, àrd rìgh," echoed throughout the room.

"We must act now. If only we knew where the man himself was." Arlan placed his hands on the dirk at his belt. "We could aim straight for him."

"I could make a strong guess at where he might be, my Lord Àrd Rìgh." Findlay stepped into the quiet gap Arlan's comment had left, his dog by his side.

Arlan looked at Findlay, examining him from top to toe. "Go on."

"He still smarts from the retaking of Caisteal Monsae." Findlay's mouth curved up on one side. "It really grates on him, actually." He chuckled. "Well, it did last I saw him."

"So then"—Arlan raised a brow in query— "it is possible Gallawain seeks to retake what was not his to *take* in the first place. Hence his warband in the south."

"It wouldn't surprise me," Findlay said. "He's a greedy bugger."

"Monsae is now better equipped since our lord war chief has trained them up." Arlan cocked his head in Leuchars' direction.

"More mercenaries and lairds join Ciarán Gallawain daily," Leuchars commented. "We should be ready if our friends request help."

Arlan sat back in his seat, leaned his elbows on his thighs and scratched the beard growth below his chin. His fingers travelled up to the scar on his cheek and traced the line of hard flesh there.

Servants entered the room, bringing bowls of porridge and plates of bannocks. Rhiannon stood aside to let them pass.

Hmm. This early meeting would go all day, if the most recent meetings were anything to go by. Well, she'd be in on it, no matter how long it took.

Arlan lifted his head from staring thoughtfully at the floor, and smoothed back his hair, looking straight at her. He blinked twice, as though he wasn't expecting her to be there.

Yes. Her shame and embarrassment had kept her from these meetings. But *not* now. She lifted her chin. So, she'd made what everyone believed to be a mistake. But who doesn't make mistakes? She wouldn't be the only one with regrets before this war ended.

A servant stepped up to Arlan and whispered in his ear.

Arlan sat bolt upright. "Bring him in, man."

A young lad, wearing mud-splattered Monsae tartan and reeking of horse sweat, entered and knelt on one knee to Arlan.

"Welcome." Arlan sat tall, his eyes riveted on the stranger. "Speak, lad."

"Lord Arlan MacEnoicht." The young man kept his head bowed. He spoke in an accent similar to those of the east, from what Rhiannon recalled of the people of Monsae. "I come from Monsae where the lady herself begs you, her ally, for assistance." He handed a small wax-sealed scroll to Arlan. "A warband of the foul Lord Ciarán approaches. It is rumoured the man himself is amongst them."

Arlan shot out of his seat, opening the scroll as he did. "Your news is a week old already!"

"Nae, lord, I rode with haste. The Lady of Monsae sent me three days ago."

Arlan's gaze roved over the scroll. "We shall gather arms and warriors and answer the call of our lady friend and sister-in-arms." Arlan faced Leuchars, who gave a nod.

He turned to the young man again. "How many warriors, do ye know?"

The lad remained kneeling, his shoulders stiff. "I know not, Lord Àrd Rìgh. All ken the man is over-confident in all things."

Arlan looked around the room at his council. "If Gallawain does indeed head for Monsae, I am determined to rout him. While he seeks revenge and feeds his greed, we will aim for the man himself. Cut off the head and the snake dies. Perhaps this is our opportunity to resolve this at last." He looked at Leuchars. "I will take four warbands plus my own warriors. You may stay here, war chief, and continue the preparation of warriors and gathering of supplies, for there will be more to come from our foe if he gains Monsae once more." He finished with a nod. "Warrior lords, those to join me, please prepare." Arlan stepped from the plinth and strode out of the council room.

Rhiannon followed him, both their footsteps tapping through the silent hallways. They entered the passage to their rooms, and he finally turned to her.

"I see no babe in your arms. So, my sword-brother did not return this sunrise."

She didn't answer, instead gritted her teeth, stepping up beside him as he stood by the door to their chamber.

"I'm coming too." She reached past him and opened the door. "I want to fight with you against Ciarán Galla—"

"And not be here when your bairn returns?" He stood in the doorway, looking down at her with hard eyes.

"If we defeat Gallawain at Monsae, then the danger is over. Rhynne will be safer here with that bastard done away with." She stepped into the room ahead of him, the back of her neck prickling with his glare following her. "I won't sit around doing nothing but wait! A messenger can bring word of their arrival. It could be days yet! Bàn obviously hasn't mastered portal travel." She grunted. "Or maybe your magic-hating friend has stuffed things up."

"Dinnae say that, Rhiannon. 'Tis bad enough I had to send him." His tone was hard.

She spun to him, pressing her hand onto her hip. "I could have got her—"

"Then I risked losing you both!" He slammed the door. "Eifion gifted his passage. Believer or no', Bàn will return, and with our daughter. Perhaps not in the timely manner ye would have, I'll admit. But he *will* come back with our bairn." His eyes held hurt.

Again.

She lowered her hand from her hip. "I'm... sorry," she said.

His face softened a touch, then he nodded slowly. "Aye, I ken ye are." He brushed past her—the closest he'd been to her since Bàn left—swirling the air with his musky scent. She breathed it in.

He strode across their room, stopped by their bed, and placed a hand on the nearest bedpost, head bowed and his back still to her. Long, dark hair trailed between muscular shoulder blades and his fingers tapped the wooden bedpost. She swallowed hard and remained where she stood. Unspoken words... ones she would use to beg his forgiveness, thickened the air in their room.

I love you, my husband.

Oh, please say it... You love me, your wife.

She had to break the silence. "So, may I come?"

He sighed heavily. "I also hate this inactivity. I ken preparation wins a war, but I detest sitting and discussing endlessly." He flicked his hand to the side and turned to face her. "Truth be known, I have longed for a reason to get out there and fight at last."

"What does Eifion say?"

"He has... *sought*, or so he names it when he"—Arlan shrugged one shoulder— "*leaves* his body and searches afar."

One corner of her lips tugged into a half grin. Eifion had let her stay once while he'd done his *meditation thing*. Almost trance-like, when he'd finished, his glazed-over eyes had sprung to life again. It had been a little creepy.

"Eifion reports being blocked by Ciarán's mages." Arlan's lips thinned.

Rhiannon jolted. *What?*

"Aye, *mag-es*. Plural. This is what your father felt, but he knows not how many." Arlan placed his hands on his belt. "With knowledge of Eifion's status as mage still secret, I cannae reveal this information to anyone, only seek to prepare for warfare as best we can. Eifion believes they watch us"—he wiggled his head from side to side— "as we watch them." His gaze wandered around the room, then returned to her. "I... dislike what ye did, Rhiannon. But ye are still my wife." He stood by the bedpost, not moving an inch, speaking in an authoritative tone.

She dropped her gaze, unable to meet his hurt-filled eyes.

Did that mean he wouldn't banish her or put her away? *Do they do that here?*

If only the hollow sensation in her gut would go. It had sat there since she'd discovered his displeasure at what she'd done about Rhynne. Plus, there was the emptiness in her arms that she'd not even considered when she'd left her baby with George.

Yes, it would be like moments for her baby, but this war could be a lifetime. She released a choked sigh. Why had she not even thought of that at the time? *I was too hasty, just wanting my baby in a safe place.*

"Ye may come and fight with me." His voice rumbled across the room to her. "But you must do as I order, whether you agree or no."

She swallowed against the coldness in his tone, now chilling the emptiness.

"Yes, my àrd rìgh."

Arlan wandered their room, gathering weapons and other items for their journey. His favourite dagger lay beside the polished bronze disc they used for a mirror. He faced the mirror, staring.

"Are you okay?" Rhiannon stood behind him, peering over his shoulder at his reflection.

On a certain angle, his cheek still had a deformity from where the scar line puckered it slightly.

"Whenever I see my face in a reflection, I recall my one and only meeting with my cousin." He grimaced. "And how he bested me." He dropped his gaze to the dagger he held. "I go to face him again." The doubt in his voice lingered in the air.

Rhiannon grasped his arms from behind, still looking at his image in their polished bronze mirror. The gouge of scar on his left upper arm ran knobbly beneath her fingertips. Ciarán's sword cut had left it there. The healer sages had worked long and hard to save his arm at her insistence. The scar wasn't neat—neither the one on his cheek—but at least he still had his arm.

"Arlan." Her voice broke the silence. "We all believe in you. You and your warbands *will* defeat him. You can do it."

He lifted his face to the mirror, shoulders straightening. "Aye. If I am to be any kind of king worthy of my people, I must."

Twenty-Eight

When dire need assails you,
With wonder, appraise your plight.

FOREST OF STRATHRÌGHINN

Eastern Clanlands of Dál Gallain
The Mountain

Slush covered the track below the snow line. The wide hooves of the grey stallion gripped the mud, only slipping now and then. I grabbed Bàn's waist tighter whenever the horse's back shifted sharply beneath me. We continued down the mountainside, Bàn's muscles lessening in tension the nearer we came to the valley below. He turned the horse off the trail and onto a narrower one with uneven stones protruding through the moisture-laden path.

"Where's this bridge?" I said into Bàn's ear.

He didn't answer as the horse trod irregularly while it navigated the track. The clip clop of its hoofs wove through the increasing roar of a river to my left.

"Ah! There." Bàn pointed to a stone bridge where the track moved closer to the bank.

Swollen with snow-melt water, the narrow river churned underneath the bridge's arch, cresting white where it buffeted and flowed over the rocks at its base on either side. We neared, and Bàn slowed the stallion. The path across it was wet, but clear of tracks.

"Looks like no one's used it for a while. Is it okay?" I asked.

Bàn slid off the horse, threw me the reins, and walked to the bridge. The animal took a step to follow him.

"Hold him back," he commanded.

I pulled on the reins, and the grey stallion nickered and stopped. Bàn walked across to the other side and back.

"Aye." He spoke deeply, with a hint of annoyance. "Hop off and we'll walk the grey. He's heavy. If the bridge crumbles, make a run for it."

"What? Really?" I asked as I slid from the saddle.

He gave a sharp nod. "Aye." He grabbed the bridle and led the horse across.

I ran over the bridge ahead of the big grey, and the war horse let out a snort. Bàn led it to the track lined with older oak trees, their thick gnarled trunks so wide it would take three people holding hands to encircle them. Green budding growth of early spring dotted their branches, pushing away bronze leaves here and there, the remnants of winter. My mouth tugged in a smile, and I turned to Bàn, my hand raised ready to point out the trees' beauty. His shoulders were set and his expression dark.

"Anything wrong?"

"Nae, just such a long way home. It will take us many days and who kens..." He stopped, placing a hand at his belt, and rubbing his upper lip with the thumb of his other hand, the reins dangling from his grip. Then he looked at me. "If we must fight, we will, but I will do ma best to keep us away from the warbands that we will surely come across." His eyes narrowed. "I'll no take any chances. If I tell you to run, ye run."

"But I can fight."

"Och! What is it with—?" He gave an exasperated grunt. "Yer mother was just the same. There are some fights for which ye are not ready."

I narrowed my eyes and bit down on the grumbles.

He straightened his shoulders. "There's a confrontation ye should be wary of, but ye are oblivious to its significance."

"What?"

"When your father meets ye and you are not a bairn. I tell ye, I'm not looking forward to that one."

"Won't he be glad I'm here? And my mother too?"

"Aye." He cocked his head with his blue stare locked on me. "But it will also be when I tell him I love his daughter."

I blinked, then smiled and released a nervous laugh.

"I enjoy hearing you say that," I said. *I'm still getting used to an awesome guy like you feeling that way about... me.* As much as I knew about love, that *was* how I felt about Bàn.

"Wait. My real father won't like it? But you're his best friend. He knows you. Knows that you're a great guy. Surely he'd be happy for you to be his..." *Son-in-law?*

My heart thudded. Was that what I wanted? To marry Bàn? I closed my eyes and rolled them beneath my lids, shutting my mouth on a groan.

There's so much going on here.

A *serious* war where I could be a warrior and fight. Really fight. A bad guy to get rid of, and my father—the real one—was the very person everyone said would do it.

But there was other stuff, too. Like meeting my parents, being the daughter of the high king... and learning to be a mage... I opened my eyes and curled my fingers into the soft material of my wolf-skin cloak.

"Bàn." My voice came out strained. "I... love you but I... I'm perhaps not ready to even think about..." I shut my mouth tight.

I might hurt him if I say more.

"It is well, Rhynne." He reached out and gently disentangled my fingers from my cloak, wrapping his big, warm hands around mine, then pressing them to his chest. "I love you. And I know you love me. For now, that is enough."

He tilted his head to me, his eyes on my lips. Hesitant. I lifted my mouth to his. He closed the space between us and filled it with the tenderest caress, placing warm lips, as soft as the water in a Dál Cruinne loch, onto mine. Gentle, not demanding. I kept my eyes open. His were closed, blond lashes covering the blue and splaying over angled, beard-stubbled cheeks. Then he lifted away.

"There's more to deal with before we think further on a future," he said. "If that is what ye want from me."

But would he be happy with me being a mage? *He's avoided mentioning that.*

I scrunched my mouth. We'd have to talk about it... sometime.

"How bad is this war? Will there be a future?" I asked.

"Your father is a great warrior and war leader. I fight with him to make this land free, and I will do it with my heart and my body." He sighed. "If I lose both in the process, at least I have tried. And I would have known your love, Rhynne, for however short a time it may be. That will be enough if that is all we have." He slid his arms around me and pulled me close, his soft lips caressing mine again.

I sighed into this kiss, wrapping my arms around his neck, his curls tickling my hands. He broke away and rested his forehead on mine.

"But I have all the more to fight for now." His voice, soft and deep, blew his warm breath into my face.

Water beneath the bridge continued to roar, and light drops of rain spattered cold on my head. On the other side of the bridge, a horse snorted, its ringing hooves joined by others. I spun out of Bàn's embrace.

Riders tore along the mountain path leading to the bridge. The one in front wore leather armour and a maroon plaid. The cloak of the one immediately behind flew open in the wind. He wore the dark robe of a mage.

Bàn stepped back from me, his eyes wide, drawing his sword and flinging off his cloak. "Get on the grey and get oot o' here."

"But I can't ride!"

Bàn glared at me past his upraised sword. "Aye, ye can!" He turned and faced the charging warrior.

I grabbed the reins—my legs so leaden it was like I moved in slow-motion—dug my foot into the stirrup then rose into the saddle. I kicked the grey's flank, and he lumbered off. Behind me, grunts and ringing swords mixed with thudding hooves. I turned the horse.

The first warrior had ridden past Bàn and spun his war horse around to charge him again, aiming right for Bàn, now a horse-length away from him.

My gut clenched, and the grey nickered with my hard tug on the reins.

The mounted warrior bore down on Bàn, who held his sword raised, ready to connect. A sharp ring erupted from their sword clash, then Bàn went with the flow of the warrior's sword and the motion of his mount. Spinning, Bàn turned and back slashed the horse's hind legs, hamstringing it. The massive war horse shrieked and slowed. Hooves flicked back, weakened but still almost reaching him. Then Bàn turned side on, running his sharp blade across the back of the animal's thighs again. He darted away as soon as he'd finished the stroke.

The horse stumbled a few paces, screaming further, blood dripping from the gaping flesh, falling and throwing its rider. Bleeding with legs now powerless, it landed in the mage's path. The mage's horse crashed into the flailing war horse and tripped forward, catapulting the mage off. He landed heavily.

A crunch and a rumble came from the river's direction. Warriors on horseback following those who'd already crossed, now clattered in the middle of the bridge. Rubble tumbled into the engorged river, the structure disintegrating under their war horses' hooves. Horses shrieked and men hollered, falling sidelong into the raging torrent. Their cries travelling down river faded by the second.

Bàn never paused at the tragedy occurring on the ancient bridge. He swiped down on the warrior who now stood apart from his flailing, stumbling horse, their swords clashing and grunts filling the narrow space between the trees on either side of the track from the bridge.

The mage stood up, staggering away from his floundering horse. He limped to a nearby oak, puffing and dragging his right leg, his forehead crumpled and eyes tight. He leaned on the tree and held his right leg, his breath gusting in a mist around him.

I gripped the reins. That mage might be out of action. *But maybe not.*

He could have some power and be waiting for Bàn to finish the warrior off and then do *something* to him. The mage looked past the warriors fighting in front of him and faced me, his eyes dark with recognition.

A shudder coursed through me, bouncing off my heart and ping-ponging around my guts.

I kicked the grey, tugging at the reins to guide it to the nearest tree, a wide-trunked ancient oak. I nudged the horse closer, dried acorns crunching under its hooves, then leaned over and placed my hands palms down on the striated, gnarled bark of the wide trunk, rough nobbles tickling my fingertips and old moss moistening my hands.

Shutting my eyes and surrounded by the fresh smell of wood, I *looked* into the oak.

Branches like fingers reached out and touched me, soft but strong. Not physical branches. Inside this tree, twigs and branches—no, *images* of them—went beyond. Beyond itself to the other trees around it. Golden threads ran along roots, a chain of communication right to the oak the mage leaned against.

Please.

A crack, like a gunshot and louder than the metallic ring of swords, echoed to my right.

I snapped my eyes open. The mage looked above him. A split second later, he set his vision on me with his eyebrows raised, eyes widening, mouth opening in the beginning of a scream.

A thick tree branch cut off his gaze locked with mine—and the cry from his mouth.

The warrior fighting Bàn stopped for a second and turned to the mage. Bàn raised his sword, levering the pommel forward, and *thunked* down on the back of the warrior's head. He crumpled to the ground like a rag doll.

Bàn grabbed the man's discarded weapon, then spun and ran to me, red-faced and teeth gritted. "Take this." He thrust the sword's handle into my hand then ran to his cloak now crumpled on the ground. "Why'd ye no go, Rhynne!" he shouted as he sprung into the saddle behind me. He dug his heels into the grey, screaming for it to move. He smelled of man sweat and blood.

I held tight to the saddle, as Bàn rode with a dripping sword in one hand and the other grabbing for the reins.

I twisted back to look.

Old brown leaves spun lazily to the ground, landing on two inert bodies.

TWENTY-NINE

The largest of the dragon beasts were black, with bellies as bright red as the flame they would draw from them.

DRAGON SCROLLS
ISLE OF INNESFARNE
DATE OF TEXT UNKNOWN

Eastern Clanlands of Dál Gallain

My teeth jolted, clunking hard while Bàn urged the grey on over the rough, uneven ground, dodging low-hanging branches on either side of the narrow track. Bàn's hard-muscled thighs dug into the backs of mine every time he kicked the horse. He held his blood-tinged sword to the side, ready to strike any more pursuers.

Bàn finally pulled the grey to a halt and spun the stallion around. It panted, giving deep throated whinnies, and spitting froth from its bit. The path behind us was clear, and through the thinning forest on either side of us, no human forms moved. Bàn slipped off the horse and strode to the grass beside the path. He wiped his sword, then took off his baldric to re-sheath it.

"Fortuitous that the thick tree branch fell on the other one when it did." He looked up at me and squinted an eye as I remained mounted on the horse.

"The *other one* was a mage." I held his stare.

He snapped his sword into its scabbard. "And ye kenned that how?"

"Huh? Didn't you see his black mage robe?"

"Nae, I was otherwise engaged with a Gallawain warrior." He stopped adjusting the baldric over his shoulder. "Give me that sword."

I handed it to him. He wrapped his cloak around the sword, then tucked it behind the saddle. "*Ye* did the branch?"

Wait a minute? "Yes. I'm not really sure how, but *I* did. And *you*"—I leaned toward him from the saddle— "should be grateful."

He made a noise in his throat. It could've been gratitude.

"Hop off." He curled his fingers at me. "I need to be in front."

I slid off, thigh muscles trembling. "I've never been on a horse for so long."

I avoided glaring at Bàn. This world was so full of magic, yet he was oblivious to it!

A gentle rumble came from ahead and to our left. Bàn had grabbed the reins, but now stood stock still, ears pricked. The rumble came closer.

Bàn pulled the grey into the nearby tree line. "Hide yoursel'!"

I ran into the trees and stood behind the thickest trunk. Bàn hurried to a space where he could stand hidden with the horse and rubbed the grey's nose to shush it.

The rumbling increased and drew closer. Down the track, where the forest cleared to a grassy moor, riders came from the left. They headed to my right, all looking straight ahead, not seeming to notice me and Bàn deep in the woods beside the moor. They rode war horses with necks and forelegs covered in leather pieces, like horse armour. The men and women were muscled and fit-looking, all with stern expressions. They also wore leather armour and had weapons strapped to their backs or belts or thighs, and shields hung from their arms.

Wow. Serious.

Various tartans flashed by me.

"I must stop thinking I'm in a fantasy movie," I whispered.

"Hush." Bàn had crept right beside me. "Watch the grey." He slid to the front edge of the forest and crouched low, peering from behind a tree at the last of the passing warriors. He leaned on his haunches for a good five minutes after the last rider, then stood and walked back to me, rubbing his upper lip.

"What?" I whispered, grabbing the grey's reins that dangled in the undergrowth.

He placed his hands on his belt, shaking his head slowly as he stared at the ground.

"Och, that was Ciarán Gallawain himself amongst three warbands. I counted maybe one hundred strong in each. They go northwest. Toward Dál Gaedhle lands... but north?" His head shot up, eyes widening. "He aims for Gallawain lands! Och, no. He will attempt to take back his old clan lands. We must return to The Keep and let Arlan know." He dragged the massive horse onto the track and flew into the saddle, holding his hand out to help me mount. "He takes the long way around by the base of the mountains, certain our scouts and those in fortresses faithful to the àrd rìgh will not see his passage. We must travel further south, then cut across toward The Keep."

I'd barely got on the horse when he dug his heels in, sending the animal surging forward. I clamped my knees to its sides and wrapped my arms around Bàn. He turned the animal to our left a bit, urging it on, leaving the mountains behind us.

The sun travelled across the sky to the left as we crossed the tree-edged moor. Bàn steered the grey horse through fast flowing burns, where in some the water reached almost to my boots. The horse snorted as it splashed through, flicking up spray and stumbling on pebbles, but Bàn kicked it on. After the third burn, we neared a small forest of tall trees where Bàn slowed the horse. The stallion panted and puffed, hanging its head.

"The grey needs a rest and so do we. See what's in those saddlebags." Bàn pointed to the bags behind me.

I got down from the tall horse, removed the saddlebags, and rummaged in them while Bàn led the stallion to a shallow burn and let him drink. Cloth-wrapped cheese and some dried meat, like jerky, sat in the bottom of one bag, also a skin full of liquid. I drew them out. The skin, resting smooth in my hands, had a spout of sorts. I pulled the stopper and sniffed. *Wine?*

Bàn returned, having hobbled the horse, and took the cheese I offered.

"There's no age limit to drinking alcohol here, is there?" I took a swig from the skin.

Bàn tore at some jerky, ignoring me, like his mind was somewhere else. He looked at the trees behind us, then walked toward them, chewing the dried meat.

I followed him, but I doubted he noticed me. The horse nickered by the burn. Bàn reached the tallest tree right at the edge of the thin forest that lined the moor, then climbed. For a big man, he was agile, grabbing branches and nimbly moving up to two-thirds of the tree's height where thick branches held his weight. He turned and looked into the distance.

I hoisted myself onto the lowest branch and levered up a few branch levels. The tree, being right on the tree line to a moor, gave a view for miles. To my left sat a group of standing stones, all higgledy-piggledy. Not a neat round one like Stone Henge on Salisbury Plain. This one looked like the teeth of a dinosaur, worn and broken, sticking out from its jawbone jammed in the ground, almost oblong, not circular.

"Are they the stones we came across when we first got here?" I asked.

"Aye," he nodded, a ghost of a smile curving his lips, distracted as he was by the view.

Bàn had kept his promise to my father. *I am safe.*

He looked ahead, frowning. Although he'd ripped me from my old life, he'd brought me to a new world where so much seemed to make sense to me, in my soul. And I'd been with him for months. He was so much more than the guy I fought at the HEMA trial.

I blinked. Wow, that seemed so long ago. I was almost a different person now. I shook myself back to the present and followed the direction of Bàn's attention.

To my far right, a long line of earth works went on for miles until the fort-towers spaced evenly along it became dots in the distance. They were just like the ridge of earthen banks and broken stone that were the remains of Hadrian's Wall. I chuckled.

Only someone my age with a dad who's into history would know that.

I sucked in my breath. *Dad.* I pressed down on the ache. Oh, how I missed him. I couldn't do anything about it now.

Bàn continued to look out, then crawled up another branch level. I grasped branches and climbed ladder-like up to stand on the branch next to his, hugging the tree trunk to stop from falling.

"Wish I had a spyglass," he mumbled.

I faced again in the direction that'd caught Bàn's concern. Some of the forts dotted along the earthworks were intact. Most were broken down and old-looking. Really old.

Like *Dad-would-love-to-see-them* old.

Bàn squinted and leaned forward, so I looked closer in that direction.

Another warband, by the looks of it. Backs of warriors and horses, five groups of them, headed away from the forts.

"Going south." Bàn grunted. "Where Monsae lands lie." A grin split his face, then he looked at me.

"That's good then?"

"Aye, for they are friends. And, if I'm not mistaken, the warband in the middle is your father's. The warband in which I fight."

A shadow passed over us. A large one, like the size and shape of a light aircraft, travelled along the ground to where the warbands were.

Bàn laughed in my ear.

"What's funny?"

"You'll see." He kept his vision forward.

A rhythmic drumming of air came above and to my right, then an animal screeched. I flinched, then strained my sight in that direction, my breath stilling.

A dragon flew overhead.

It soared above me—a dark, deep red leathery hide, so dark it was almost black except for the belly where it was bright red. Its wings were wide, and it had a knobbly head, and a barbed tail. Green cat-like eyes glanced down at me and Bàn as it passed. I ducked instinctively, the hairs on my arms rising.

Bàn's grin widened. "Ye always wanted to see one of those, aye?"

"Yes," I said when I could draw breath again.

"Och, well, that's yer father's wee dragon."

"Wee?" I stuttered. "It's as big as an elephant! And it's flying."

Bàn scurried down the tree, and I followed.

"What did you say his name was?" I asked. "Does it shoot fire?"

"Drayce is female and, so far, she has not breathed fire. Unless it has occurred since I went through the standing stone to go and get you, which, if I have estimated correctly, was ten days ago in this world."

We landed on the forest floor with a thump, then Bàn ran to the stallion. The horse munched on the grass and swished its tail around. Bàn gathered the reins ready to mount.

"Your father is most definitely with his troop in that war band." He rose into the saddle and tugged me up behind him, then kicked the horse on.

I moved with the motion of the horse, but my insides trembled. I would meet my real father soon. The tall black haired awesome fighter I saw on the night I'd arrived here through the pond portal. *What will he think of me?*

The sun continued to lower in the sky. Even after a few hours, we hadn't caught up with the warband, now not visible in the distance.

"Their mounts are fresher." Bàn pulled up the puffing grey, its sides lathered and hooves stumbling. "The warbands are battle ready. Something is amiss at Monsae."

"So, we're still in Dál Gallain, yeah? But Monsae people are on our side?"

"Aye, the Lady of Monsae, a warrior herself, and her man, Vygeas, assisted Arlan in obtaining the dragon's egg required for him to win the Quest and become àrd rìgh.

We then helped them take back Caisteal Monsae from Gallawain, thus becoming close allies."

I closed my gaping mouth. "Dragon eggs. Quests. This world is *awesome*! Wait. Is Drayce anything to do with the dragon's egg?"

"Aye. But wait till ye meet Lord Vygeas. He can sense what ye are feeling from across a room. Naught is hidden from him."

"Magic?"

"Nae, but a gift from a mage."

I shook my head, mouth stretching wide in a tight grin. "I can't wait to meet your *friends*."

"And your father. We must be... careful and not too close with each other at first. And ye must be respectful, for he is the high king." He glanced at the plaid over my shoulder. "Ye never returned it after the Midwinter Feast."

"No. I got busy." A twinge of guilt rose, and I tugged at the blue tartan cloth, soft and warm against my neck. "You mean I should bow to him?"

"Aye, down on one knee."

Bàn jolted. A second later, a gentle thunder of hooves came from our left. He'd heard it before me.

I've gotta be more aware of stuff around me.

Bàn pulled hard on the reins, turning the stallion to the right and kicking him into a sparse wood. He jumped off, dragging me with him, and pushed me to hide behind the widest tree trunk, then peered around the side of it.

I bit down on my tongue, fighting the urge to ask *what's wrong?*

Another warband, coming from the same direction as Ciarán Gallawain's, but smaller, turned away from us. I let out a loud breath.

"Be not relieved," Bàn whispered, "for that's a Gallawain warband heading for your father and our friends."

THIRTY

Thick strong ramparts doth my fortress own
Where I shelter from mine enemy.
My tower reaches to the skies
From whence my arrows fall.
My shield from the foe,
My domicile of safety.
None as secure as those who rest behind its masoned walls.

POETRY OF THE WARRIOR
WARRIOR SAGE TAPAÌDH
(4009-4059 POST DRAGON WARS)

Western Sovereignty of Dál Gaedhle
Caisteal Gallawain

Ciarán had sent the cannon ahead with those warriors and alchemists who understood its function. He followed, riding north with his warband and Laird Lorain in the lead, his faithful men beside him.

Yes, prior to that harsh winter just passed, the Laird of Clachan Beag had capitulated with little protest, submitting villagers and supplies to Ciarán's cause without a murmur. But this was no surprise, for a family in chains can persuade a man of much.

Ciarán kept the mountains still brown with last season's heather, to his right for half a day. The scouts had found easily enough the ancient double border fort with the broken gate, standing not far from the mountains of his homeland. He pulled his steed to a halt at the remains of the towers, the worn cut stone long pillaged by locals to make dwellings of their own.

Ciarán rode on, taking deep breaths of air, crisp and clear, with hints of spring blossoms floating on the breeze. It had been thirty-one years since he'd smelled Dál Gaedhle and, oh, how sweet to do so once more. And Donnach believed banishment could keep him from his home forever! *Hah!*

He grinned and turned to Galan.

"I am home. And soon the lands of my birthright shall be in my hands once more."

Galan nodded and kicked his horse on.

"Bram!"

The mage nudged his horse beside him. "Aye, Lord Ciarán?"

"Your friends and fellow mages have done their work?"

"Callaghan sends a warband willingly. Retribution for the death of a brother, stoked by a mage's whispers. The young Duisdale warrior brings her company, although her father is ignorant of the fact. She lusts for battle, her patience worn thin at the traitor's tardiness."

"Mhàiri Duisdale regards the àrd rìgh as a traitor? How delicious." Ciarán laughed. "But why?'

"His wife, as Findlay has informed you, is from the Other World. Lady Duisdale views his allegiances as tarnished."

Ciarán approached the hills that hid his loch situated in the centre of Gallawain clan lands. On the island at this southern end of the small loch, his family caisteal would soon come into view. A messenger had reported the foreguard had reached it in the early afternoon, and Lorain now supervised the setup of camp.

"The cannon is in place?" Ciarán asked Bram.

Bram nodded.

"I wish to see it. Come, ride to the rise with me while camp is prepared." He kicked his horse onto the track that led up the nearest hilltop of the range encircling the loch.

At the top, the view spread wide and brought a tightness to his throat. An ancient, round grey-stone caisteal sat on the mound of island in the loch, as it had for centuries, its stone-edged parapet crenulations smoothed with age. The caisteal retained its permanence, solidity, and authority. Afternoon sunlight on the gentle waters lapping the pebbled shore glittered as the stars. An eagle flew over the loch, releasing its shrill cry.

Caisteal Gallawain. *Home.*

Here he'd grown. Here he'd learned to read and hunt and fight. Here he'd spent his early years with... Alana. The air was sucked from his lungs, the memory so sharp. Her sandy hair, kinked with waves glowing soft in the sunlight. Their play so innocent. Her thoughtfulness and care for him had touched the hard places of his soul. He blinked.

"Lord Ciarán, are ye well?" Bram's voice broke through the thrall of the past.

He cleared his throat. "Childhood memories. How time distorts them so." He coughed the huskiness from his voice. "The cannon is set for the north side of the loch, yes? Where the island lies closest to the loch shore. It will do enough damage to the caisteal to force submission but not place the structure in peril. I wish this fortress to be intact. It is strategic. One of many plans which will all lead to success. The master, my uncle, is in?"

"Nae lord, he has assisted the àrd rìgh and resided at The Keep for a time attending the war council. My mage nearby reports your uncle now travels towards this caisteal, returning home."

"Bah! Àrd rìgh," he snarled. *What a farce!*

"Be that as it may"—Bram's tone turned condescending— "with your uncle, Lord Adomàn Gallawain, not yet in residence, I believe this will be to our advantage."

"Yes, once they see our warbands, and the other two at each flank—"

"They will surrender without their lord."

He pierced Bram with his stare at the interruption. "My cannon may not be required to fire." He grinned. "A deterrent only."

"It would save the cannon balls, lord." There was humour in Bram's tone.

So, the mage displayed some mirth. *About time that dour-faced—*

A deep boom cracked the air around the loch. Overhead, the eagle flew away shrieking, and a puff of smoke rose from the side of the loch closest to the caisteal. A thud echoed from the caisteal on the side obscured to Ciarán's sight.

"What has happened? Tell me not they have fired the cannon before all is in place! Imbeciles!" Ciarán spun his stallion and kicked its flanks while it trotted warily down the track, moving no faster despite his pounding heels.

He reached the campsite, shelters half erected, and fires barely lit. Laird Lorain left off speaking with Galan, then strode toward him and bowed.

"My lord—"

"What have you done?"

"Lord Ciarán, our warriors overcame the outer defences with ease. Their number of warrior clansmen are small, many appearing absent from the caisteal. A light bombardment is all we need to subdue those who have sought shelter within the tower. We may spare warriors' lives, and this machine of war will do all for us. Fearing for their own lives, the caisteal will surrender. We have surprised them, for they jeered at our men as they set up the cannon. They mocked, throwing insults out the high windows, their ignorance of the power of our weapon obvious. We have surprised them with no siege works nor warbands. They will sit in shock and capitulate once they see the power of the cannon's blast."

"You are wrecking my home," Ciarán growled.

"We are strategic. It shall be an easy repair."

Ciarán narrowed an eye. Perhaps the man was anxious for the promised release of his family on completion of this task. Hastening when care should be taken.

"Bombard for a night," Lorain continued. "The explosive blast ripping the stone from the thick walls will hold them trembling. Tomorrow, surround them with our warriors, and they will return to you your home without protest."

Ciarán tapped his top teeth with a finger. 'Twas a grand plan. *If only it spares my caisteal.*

"Very well. But ensure as little damage as possible!"

Lorain bowed. "And the laird, your uncle?"

"Spy the road he travels. Arrest him on sight..." Ciarán sniffed. "Yes. Behead him in the caisteal's courtyard. Let all know who is laird now."

Thirty-One

— · —

I can't obliterate what you have done. It's part of my history and will always be so. But I can change the way I feel about the man who did it. I can choose to release myself from the hurt I feel. To be free of it so it will not enslave me.

LADY LEYNARVE OF MONSAE

Eastern Clanlands of Dál Gallain
Caisteal Monsae

It had been a hard ride, but Caisteal Monsae now came into Arlan's sight, and his friends would welcome his support. Not knowing what he would encounter, this morning he had ordered all into battle dress. The chain maille sat its weight on his shoulders and thighs. He wore a padded tunic between his skin and the cool, tight, iron-ringed tunic. The warmth of satisfaction spread through him, for it was a piece of workmanship by a master craftsman. A length of iron sat down the outer side of each boot to protect from sword slashes.

He glanced around at Findlay riding behind, his dog resting over the saddle in front of him. Eifion rode beside him. The journey was hard on the old mage. The lines of Eifion's face now creased deeper, but Eifion had insisted he travel with Arlan, for if Ciarán Gallawain was involved, he *would* be there.

Ahead, naught stirred at the parapet of the tall square rose-sandstone caisteal. At the base of its bailey wall, there were nae slain, nor churned earth, and no smoke arose from the caisteal, apart from that which floated languidly from its chimneys. The caisteal was unmolested, then? The scouts he'd sent ahead reported the same on their last return.

So, he had arrived in time with his warbands. They would help shore up defences and the other preparations for Ciarán Gallawain's onslaught. He sat into Mengus' canter. It would be braw to see Vygeas and Leynarve once more.

Hmm. Vygeas would sense the strain between himself and Rhiannon. Arlan rolled the tightness from his shoulders. *Nothing is sacred around that man.* Not even a silent argument between a man and his wife.

166

Rhiannon rode at her father's side on her pure white mare. She had spoken little through their five-day ride, although she'd snuggled close on the night camps, drawing warmth from him.

Impossible to him still, that Rhiannon had taken his bairn from him... and given her to *George!*

He gripped the reins tighter. No one in Dál Gaedhle would contemplate it. So much of the Other World still influenced Rhiannon's thinking. At times, it was though he knew her not. Would she ever fit in? Perhaps he'd misjudged her in the Other World and assumed, as her roots were in Dál Gaedhle, that she would slip into his life and the ways of his world without a hiccough.

He snorted a breath.

Forgive his wife—the hardest task assigned to him thus far.

But he loved her so. And he had pledged his love to her for the rest of his life.

Pledged it.

Naught could break such, nor the love that hurt so at the betrayal.

Nae. Give her and yourself time. Forgive.

Two figures appeared atop the battlements, peering in their direction, hands shielding eyes from the sun's glare. On a horse ahead of Arlan, Angus raised the banner of the Àrd Rìgh. It fluttered high amongst the riders of Arlan's warband. The lookouts on the caisteal's battlements waved to the emblem of a horse rampant surrounded by a chain of knotwork.

Angus need not have announced their identity though, for Drayce flew up and soared over them, coming to rest on the battlement walls, sending the lookouts hastening away. The gate in the bailey wall opened, the portcullis drew up, and Arlan's lead warband rode through.

"So, ye are still welcome, my Lord Àrd Rìgh?" Beside him, Douglas rode with a cheeky smile beneath his crooked nose.

"Aye, warrior, but they've spied you, and they are locking up their ale and their women as we speak." Arlan's chest shook with a laugh. He had laughed so little lately.

Arlan rode into the bailey yard now crowded with the warriors and horses of four warbands. Vygeas approached, still wearing the grey hooded cloak of his assassin days.

"Welcome." Vygeas' greeting came through the clatter of hooves, jingling of tack, and grunts of warriors dismounting.

Arlan slid off Mengus, landing as Vygeas reached him. Vygeas held out his hand for him to shake, and Arlan closed the distance then embraced him. "Sword-brother," he said into the lord warrior's shoulder. "We are not too late?"

Vygeas let go of him, then stepped back. "Ye are filled with concern and come ready for battle." He shook his head slightly. "But as you see, there is none and we are at peace." He faced Rhiannon, who had stood waiting silently by her mare with Eifion. "Lady Rhiannon, wife to my àrd rìgh." He placed a fist on his chest, then bowed low.

Rhiannon smiled, then Vygeas stood tall. She stepped forward and gave him a hug. He returned it, then held her at an arm's length, staring intently. She gave a half smile and shrugged, then Vygeas grunted and let go. Neither spoke.

Aye, it *was* unspeakable. A deep churning that knotted Arlan's stomach had kept the words of forgiveness he would say to Rhiannon coming out of his mouth when they should. He let out a slow, silent breath and willed his shoulders down from his ears. He would forgive. Nae, he *must* forgive. *Dragon's breath!* Rhiannon was his wife, by all that is good, he must resolve this strain between them, for he could bear it no longer! Even if their beautiful baby girl never returned to him...

Eifion stepped forward and nodded a greeting to Vygeas.

"My lord *sage*." Vygeas gave a bow, hanging on the word.

"Where is your lady wife?" Arlan asked, pushing aside the heaviness in his chest lingering from Vygeas' unspoken question to Rhiannon.

"Leynarve sits resting." He grinned.

"Resting? That isn't like Leyna... oh." Rhiannon's tone held a knowing.

"Come with me my friends," Vygeas said, "and see how fares the mother-to-be."

Arlan grabbed Vygeas in a fierce hug. "Congratulations, brother. When is the babe due?"

"Any day, or so the midwife tells me. So does my wife with unbearable regularity. Apparently, the last two weeks of carrying a babe cannot go fast enough." He turned and escorted Arlan and Rhiannon up the stairs. Arlan left Muir to organise the settling of the warbands in the outer bailey.

"Where is your true sword-brother, Lord Bàn Lùthas?" Vygeas glanced between him and Rhiannon. "He is well?"

"Aye, he is on a mission." Arlan let his stare linger on Rhiannon.

"And you will know all before long." Rhiannon kept her tone clipped.

Vygeas raised one brow, continuing up the stairs to the main hall. Arlan followed, with Eifion and Rhiannon not far behind.

A fire crackled in the large hearth at the far end of the room. Sunlight streamed in through the windows, catching the smoke that had escaped the chimney. An angled beam of sunlight rested on Leyna reclining on a long chaise-like seat, her large belly protruding. She swung her legs off the couch and sat up, pushing her hands into her lower back, and her curls spilling out of their clasp.

"Nae, Lady Leynarve, do not stir." Arlan reached her, knelt, and, taking her proffered hand, kissed it.

"My Lord Àrd Rìgh, I should kneel to you." A line appeared between her fine eyebrows.

"Not under these circumstances." Arlan chuckled and stepped away.

Rhiannon leaned in and hugged Leyna. "Congratulations. Are you keeping well?"

"Aye, she is robust." Vygeas spoke loudly.

"I am impatient." Leyna inclined her head to Vygeas.

Vygeas turned to Arlan and lowered his voice. "As I am reminded continually."

"I have nae sharp hearing such as yours, husband, but I know what ye speak." Leyna spoke in a gentle, reproving tone.

Eifion greeted her also, then moved closer to the fire and held out his hands to the flames.

"So," Vygeas looked directly at Arlan. "Ye fear we are to be attacked?"

"Nae." Arlan couldn't keep the questioning from his voice. "*Ye* did and sent for my help. Here." From within his armour Arlan produced the scroll the messenger had presented to him, then held it out.

At the same time Leyna said, "We have not done so. All has been quiet in these parts. Our patrols have not spied Ciarán Gallawain's warriors near our boundaries."

"This is a forgery of my lady's hand." Vygeas handed the opened scroll to Leyna. "And of the Monsae seal."

Leyna examined the scroll, and Arlan groaned, curling his fists.

"Misdirection," Rhiannon said.

"Gallawain is elsewhere, and we must discover it." Eifion voiced all their thoughts.

The door opened and servants brought in a tray of breads, cheeses and jugs of ale and placed them on the sideboard. Shouts echoed from the passage outside, and more came through the hall's windows, along with the clattering of arms gathered.

Vygeas' eyes widened. "It seems foes do approach."

The door to the hall opened wider, thumping the wall. A warrior entered, an older man with a sun-hardened face surrounded by tight curly hair common to Monsae folk, and weapons at his belt.

"We are readying, lord." He bowed to Vygeas, apparently used to his lord's pre-knowledge of certain things. "The warbands of our àrd rìgh join ours in preparation."

"How many are the enemy?"

"It appears but one warband, my lord."

Vygeas grasped Arlan's arm. "Come." He stepped to Leyna and kissed her, then turned to Rhiannon. "Please, my Lady Rhiannon, stay with my wife. She is in need of female friendship. Especially from one who has gone before on the path she now treads."

Arlan kissed Rhiannon, her shoulders tense beneath his hands. She was eager to fight, no doubt. "It is well. Please do as Vygeas requests." He nodded and left her with mouth open in mute protest. Eifion followed behind him.

"Come sit beside me, Lady Rhiannon." Leyna patted the seat.

Rhiannon let go a quiet sigh, turned from the door where Arlan had exited, and lowered herself to the seat. Leyna eased herself back into the couch, her pregnant belly jutting out in front of her.

"You must be getting excited." Rhiannon smiled, a slow ache forming in her heart, but she nudged against it.

"And how is your wee one? I must admit I am surprised to see you here." Leyna's deep brown eyes held hers, expecting an answer.

Rhiannon's throat thickened. She tried to swallow past the lump, but she only choked. Her vision blurred Leyna's concerned expression, and the tears she couldn't hold back tumbled down her cheeks.

"Rhiannon?" Leyna reached out and tugged Rhiannon to her.

She leaned her head on Leyna, her shoulders jerking.

"Your babe is well? I have not heard..."

Rhiannon let the tears fall until they stopped while Leyna rubbed her back.

"I'm sorry." Rhiannon sniffed and wiped her eyes with her hands, then looked up.

Leyna's forehead was a mass of crinkles.

"I don't know if my baby is well." Rhiannon's breathing hitched. "I don't even know for sure where my baby is."

The whites of Leyna's eyes showed all around for a flash.

"Oh, Leyna, I've been so stupid." She poured out the whole situation while Leyna sat and listened, her frown crinkling further.

"*Another* portal to the Other World?" Leyna's words were hesitant.

"Yes. I've hurt Arlan. Bàn hasn't returned, and he may be lost as well... if he can't get back... that's if he made it at all." She took in a shuddering breath. "That might be okay for Rhynne if he didn't, 'cos George still has her in his care. But not good for Bàn."

Leyna blinked, shaking her head slowly, then her arms pressed tighter around Rhiannon, holding her close. They sat in silence while coals popped in the fire.

"I do not wish to give ye platitudes." Leyna rubbed Rhiannon's back. "I know not what the outcome of your situation will be."

"Leyna, I've ruined things between Arlan and me, and he has every right to be angry. He may never see our Rhynne again and it's all my fault. He... might forgive me. Maybe. Eventually. But sometimes I'm not... so... sure." Her breathing hiccoughed and her tears spilled.

Leyna ceased rubbing between her shoulder blades and gently pulled her aside until Rhiannon could look into her eyes. She brought a small cloth from her sleeve and offered it to Rhiannon.

"There is something I must tell you." Leyna swallowed. "It was hard to learn, but one can do it. And your man, Arlan... well, if *I* can, he can."

"What?" Rhiannon blew her nose.

"You may not know this." A *v* appeared above the bridge of Leyna's nose. "But I had much to forgive my husband." She straightened and flicked a curl from her face. "You are aware he was an assassin?"

"Yes."

"He assassinated my parents." Leyna's voice grew soft. "Years before I met him."

"W... what?" Something like an electric shock sparked across Rhiannon's neck.

Leyna's lips thinned. "It wasn't until after we had become friends... well, more than friends, that I discovered this. And that I had also been a mark in that task. But here I sit, due to the kind heart that rested beneath his assassin's grey cloak."

Rhiannon cocked her head.

"Vygeas begged me to forgive him." She held Rhiannon's hands in hers. "It took time, and a willing heart. Plus, a growing love for Vygeas and a deepening knowledge that he was no longer the same man who worked as an assassin under Ciarán Gallawain's orders."

"Wow... you've forgiven him for..." Rhiannon shook her head. No more words came.

"Your husband is filled with love for you, and though it may happen in stages, he *will* forgive you. I am certain of it."

Leyna's tender words held a spark of truth, sending waves of calm flowing through Rhiannon's body. Arlan may eventually fully forgive her.

She'd hold on to that hope.

In a way, that was the easy part. The waves hit a wall, and she bowed her head against them, gripping Leyna's hands.

"But *I'll* never forgive *me*. How could I have thought it was a good idea? I took my husband's child from him. He accused me of not believing he could protect her." Her words came out hard. "Arlan could die out there"—she flung out her hand, pointing to the tall window that overlooked the bailey yard— "and never see his baby again. And it's all... my... fault." She spoke the last through her teeth, her breath staggering.

She slumped to the floor, sobs wracking her body.

Leyna's warm hands coaxed her head onto her narrow lap, then stroked her hair.

"Shush, shush, now."

A slow burn of shame ran through Rhiannon. Her breathing finally eased, and the fire crackled softly in the hearth. She opened her eyes. Smoke rose from the semi-blocked chimney to hit the roof and swirled around the rafters of the high hall.

"I must warn you, Rhiannon." Leyna's tone was so intense that Rhiannon took her vision from the ceiling to face her.

Shouts erupted from outside and Rhiannon knelt to get up.

"No, Rhiannon, hear me." Leyna gripped hard to her arm, keeping her face level with hers. "You must forgive yourself or it will eat away at you inside and eventually kill you, but not before it kills the love between you and Arlan."

Forgive myself? Oh, that will be impossible.

She bit her tongue between her teeth, stopping the words from leaving her mouth.

The shouting of war commands and the clatter of shod hooves on stone pavement grew in intensity.

"Answer me, Rhiannon." Leyna spoke with a passion.

"Yes, I'll try." *Am I lying?* She rose to stand. "May I see what's happening?"

Leyna relaxed back into the couch. "Please go to the battlements. I shall receive a report from your lips only. And I pray they will be the victors. I cannot bear to think either of us could lose our men this day. Especially you, my dear friend. You have so much to resolve."

Thirty-Two

I know him more than I do myself.
His actions and very thoughts
Before he himself conceives them.
Thus, the bond between sword-brothers.

POETRY OF THE WARRIOR
WARRIOR SAGE TAPAÌDH
(4009-4059 POST DRAGON WARS)

Eastern Clanlands of Dál Gallain
Caisteal Monsae

"We need not your four warbands, my Lord Arlan." Vygeas mounted his war horse, Dräger, as they stood at the drawbridge to Caisteal Monsae. "But it has been some time since you and I fought side by side, has it not?"

The opposing warband had halted a good way past a bow's range. Of the warriors who wore tartans, they were a mishmash of clans. A burly man led them, and a few in the rear held swords. Only two warriors looked like any challenge.

"Aye, my warband, one other and yourself, it shall be then." Arlan slid into the saddle.

"My lord." Muir pulled his steed beside him, his spear *Sleaghach* in his right hand. "May I suggest the body of our charge be spikes?"

Arlan nodded, then turned to the high battlement from where Eifion watched. Rhiannon appeared and stood close to her father. Drayce, who had perched near Eifion, lifted in flight. Arlan nudged Mengus, and Muir gave the orders. Swords remained sheathed, warriors took up shields and spears, then rode to the field, where Muir shouted commands. Arlan's warriors lined up, shields tucked tight and spear points bristling.

Drayce circled above. Faces along the enemy line tilted upward. Warriors jostled for position, some moving back from the front line. At the rear, a foot warrior turned and ran away. Another on horseback pursued and caught him, striking him down.

"This seems an inexperienced lot," Arlan said to Vygeas, who sat mounted beside him.

"Aye, and they send not one to parley." Vygeas looked into the sky. "Yet they still wish to fight despite your flying beast who only needs to be present, and their weakest loses their nerve."

Arlan grunted in reply.

Muir yelled a command, then the line of spears moved on at a trot. Arlan kicked Mengus to follow with Vygeas. They would pick up those who survived the spears. The opposing line ahead wavered, and their head warrior shouted them back into line.

The ground thundered with the horses' tread, and the enemy line became clearer the closer Arlan approached. Apart from their leader, the warriors wore no armour, some held pitch forks and others scythes. One or two swords wavered. Most of them were still in their youth.

It will be a slaughter.

"Vygeas," Arlan yelled above pounding hooves. "I call this off. Apart from the warrior in the lead and two behind, they are but farm boys."

"Aye." Vygeas returned his shout, now clearer to Arlan's hearing, for the body of Arlan's troop had advanced ahead of them.

Arlan halted Mengus, and beside him, Vygeas pulled Dräger to a stop.

"Most lads tremble. One or two are up for it. The one in the front seems a mean bastard. Look"—Vygeas pointed— "Douglas engages him."

Douglas had raced ahead, aiming for the burly one, who shouted his troop back into line. Only a handful of lads had lined up. Those with shields, knocked them together.

"I will stop this. I cannot bear useless deaths." Arlan kicked Mengus' sides and rode toward his troop, who were almost upon the line of rag-tag warriors.

Another commotion stirred at the back of the enemy line, where warriors fought behind the main warband of lads. Two showing skill were now engaged with two others who fought like *deamhans.* One warrior, a dark haired woman, wore a blue plaid tucked tight in her belt, the tartan unclear from this distance. The fighting style of the other, a man, was as familiar to Arlan as his own.

"*Bàn!*" To his line of spears, he yelled, "Cease!"

Muir spun to him, spear lifted upward and nodding, then shouted orders to Arlan's warriors who had already reached and impaled two of the enemy. Those who had not engaged halted their horses. The thundering of hooves and warrior shouts subsided. Douglas bent over a prostrate, motionless form: their leader now subdued.

"Round up the prisoners," Muir yelled.

Adele and another warrior galloped their horses past Bàn and his companion, then chased after those who fled. Bàn and the warrior with him were both engaged with the more skilled of the enemy warriors.

Angus, Morrigan, and others of Arlan's warband herded those on foot into a circle. The young captives stood close together, weapons abandoned, and hands held high in surrender. One had wet his breeches and others stared at bodies of their companions while Arlan's warriors held down the corpses with their booted feet and retrieved their spears.

The ring of clashing swords dominated the field with the grunts and cries of those engaged at the back of the enemy line. Arlan returned his attention to Bàn, who slashed the sword-arm of his foe, leaving it hanging by sinew and tendon. The man's blood spurted from the arm as Bàn ran him through.

Grunts now came from another Dál Gallain warrior near Bàn. Bàn's dark-haired companion thrust and parried and danced about the large man she fought as though teasing him. She spun around the warrior, his wide swipes missing her by inches, then stabbed him in the back, a mere touch accompanied by a flick of her head as if to say *see, I can!* The blade didn't go far, for the man wore thick-plated leather armour, but he grunted and jolted. He turned, his bloodied face wrenched in fury, and raised his blade to swing again. He slashed his sword down. She dodged and stepped away, grinning. The warrior gnashed his teeth at her, but she raised her chin in defiance. Behind him, Bàn yelled, calling the man's attention. The warrior spun to face him with sword high ready to strike. Bàn sliced his blade down, splitting the man's shoulder to the chest. The warrior dropped.

Arlan reached Bàn and slid from Mengus before his stallion had stopped. He ran to Bàn and threw his arms around him, almost knocking him over, and hooted into his sword-brother's shoulder. Bàn's laughter mixed with sobs as he pulled away from Arlan and wiped his blood-splattered face with his sleeve.

"Och. Ye are whole and returned to us." Arlan slapped Bàn's shoulder, and his smile grew wide. "But where is my babe? Who cares for Rhynne while ye slay our foe?"

Bàn's expression turned solemn, and he stepped back a pace, his Adam's apple bobbing as he indicated to his warrior companion who'd remained by the dying man. He wriggled his fingers to her in a come-here gesture. She wiped her face, sniffing, and lowered her sword. She walked toward Arlan, her eyes downcast on her path to him, and the breeze lifting her loosely tied long black wavy hair. A sword length from him, she dropped to one knee, head still bowed, and shoulders rising and falling rapidly. Neither Bàn nor the warrior spoke.

"Well?" Arlan addressed her.

"Lord Arlan MacEnoicht, my àrd rìgh"—the woman took a deep breath, then raised her head, her mauve eyes peering wide into his face— "and my father, I am home."

THIRTY-THREE

When ye were a babe, I held you
When but a child I carried you
Kissed away your scrapes, hugged away your aches
And told ye how things should be.
I comforted ye when they were not.
Through all of life I love you
Though imperfect, frail and inadequate, I am.
I have been and always will be, your father
A role of honour for any man.

POETRY OF A KING
ÀRD RÌGH RHONAN IUBHAR
(4030-4090 POST DRAGON WARS)

Eastern Clanlands of Dál Gallain
Caisteal Monsae

Arlan could not speak. He walked around the kneeling form of the tall, lithe warrior. Her skin the same paleness as his own, and her hair as black. Although, on closer inspection, it held streaks of grey. Her thin tunic clung to muscles toned from long practice. And the tartan she wore... was the blue of the àrd rìgh! Aye, this warrior had fought well and in chorus with Bàn. He returned to stand in front of her. Mauve eyes—Rhiannon's eyes—stared up at him, a crease forming above her long nose.

A beautiful young woman knelt before him, of that there was no doubt. And so reminiscent of his Rhiannon.

Bàn remained standing to one side, his stance held immobile. When they had fought, Bàn had moved in concert with this woman, and they had communicated like sword-brothers. No words required.

Arlan's mind spun, emotions whirlpooling in his chest.

"Where's my babe?" He spoke low and deep.

Bàn stepped in front of him then knelt beside the warrior woman. "My àrd rìgh, my sword-brother, my sworn lord, who has the strength of my sword arm, and the loyalty of my heart"—Bàn raised his head— "and my best friend. Believe me when I tell ye, this woman is your daughter, Rhynne, brought back from the Other World safely to your side." Bàn held his stare, unblinking.

Arlan slowly blew out through his nostrils.

Drayce circled above. Her wing flaps were drumbeats in his ears, in time with his heart pounding right up into his temples. Her flight became silent as she soared low and landed behind him. Gusts of wind stirred Arlan's hair, then his dragon clicked a vocalisation.

The young woman's eyes grew round, and she rose, her whole focus on the dragon, then stepped past Arlan.

"Rhynne!" Bàn hissed under his breath, but she ignored him and walked straight for Drayce.

Arlan followed her progress to his beast. She reached out her hand to Drayce, who shuffled forward and lowered her head to the young woman. His dragon nudged into the woman's stroke, which she smoothed down the dragon's back and ended with a pat on the animal's rump.

"Wow!" the woman yelled. "She's awesome."

Foot tread padded through the crowd of silent warriors that had gathered, and someone jostled the onlookers aside. Rhiannon pushed past Douglas, ran up to Arlan, acknowledging Bàn with a brief smile, then directed her eyes wide in question to Arlan.

He grunted and nodded toward the dragon.

Rhiannon turned, then halted, her hands going to her mouth. The young woman stood patting Drayce, who purred like a cat. She faced Arlan again, saw Rhiannon and dropped her hand from the dragon, then her sword fell to the ground.

"Mum?" she said in a childlike voice. She folded her hands and pressed them to her chest.

"Rhynne." Rhiannon's words were a mere whisper, then she ran and embraced her.

Nae, it is my babe. Arlan hung his hands limply by his sides. *It is Rhynne.*

His baby Rhynne was now grown.

Vygeas' grip sat strongly on Arlan's shoulder, fingers digging into sinew, as he directed him to the main hall. Arlan ushered Rhiannon, Bàn and Rhynne, along with Eifion—who had returned from the battlements, indicating he had seen all—to the couches by the roaring fire, then introduced Leynarve to Rhynne.

"We shall leave you to your reunions and discussions, my Lord Arlan." Vygeas' whisper came to his ear.

"Nae, I would disturb your wife not." Arlan indicated to Leynarve resting on the couch, her large belly prominent. Arlan's brow tensed, joining his shoulders. His mind was in parts numb, in parts a whirl. "I would also appreciate your... view on this."

"Oh, please my friend, nae. There are so many emotions thickening this air I can hardly breathe." Vygeas gave a quick bow. "I shall leave you with your family, for it is truly a matter for your family only." He helped Leynarve off the couch.

"What *matter?*" Arlan asked.

Vygeas walked out with Leynarve, his eyes engaging Arlan's but silently shaking his head as though to say he would elaborate nae further.

Eifion sat in the space on the couch Leyna had left, Bàn stood beside Arlan, and Rhiannon held Rhynne close, tears tumbling down her cheeks. She touched Rhynne's hair, brushed her thumbs across her cheeks, held her shoulders, and drank in every inch of her with hungry eyes. Rhiannon spoke quietly to Rhynne, and Eifion cleared his throat.

"Ye have done well, Lord Bàn Lùthas. Thank you for returning our girl to us." Eifion gave a reprimanding look to Arlan.

Bàn nodded to Eifion, then tensed beside Arlan.

The silence in the hall rang loud in Arlan's ears. He should rejoice, but now all was numb.

Oh, be not a fool, man! This beautiful young warrior woman is your daughter.

"Ye may report, Bàn," he said.

Bàn stood in front of him and bowed. "My Lord Arlan," he said, his voice stiff like his posture. "When I arrived in the Other World, I discovered it to be some years since Lady Rhiannon had presented Lady Rhynne as a babe to George Wilson, the language and history sage."

"So, she was grown when ye found her?"

"Aye, lord." Bàn frowned. "Therefore, I had to approach the situation differently. I befriended Rhynne through the martial art classes that she attended, and I sought for the right time to inform George of my need to return Lady Rhynne to yourselves."

Rhynne stopped speaking to Rhiannon and now faced Arlan.

"We were on a sword skills training weekend," Bàn continued, "when Dál Gallain warriors who had come through a portal attacked us."

Arlan clenched his fists, and Rhiannon gasped.

"During the fight, Lady Rhynne"—Bàn held out his hand to her— "saw a portal and led us through."

"She *saw* a portal?" Eifion exclaimed.

Bàn nodded briefly. "We arrived afore this winter past."

"And we couldn't come to you because I wasn't born yet." Rhynne's tone was one of defence for Bàn.

"Where did ye bide over winter?" Arlan asked Bàn.

A long winter.

Enough time to know my daughter well.

"A sage hold in the mountains of Dál Gallain," Bàn replied.

"Mage hold," Rhynne corrected.

Eifion rose from the couch and walked toward his granddaughter, smiling. "Ye... have the gifting of a mage?"

"Yes, Grandfather." Rhynne smiled, lifting her face to look straight at Eifion.

Arlan glared at Bàn, who held his mouth crookedly and lifted a shoulder. Arlan turned back to his women and Eifion, their gazes intent on him. Rhiannon's eyes pleaded.

Rhynne chewed her lip, and her moistening eyes slid to Bàn. Bàn swallowed.

"Lord Arlan." Bàn's voice gentled. "I ken it is a shock to ye that your child has grown. But she is home now. Are ye no' pleased?"

Arlan looked to the floor at his feet. A rug covered planks that were worn and stained with age. The rug's bright colours covered the evidence of years. Like the years he had lost with Rhynne.

"Aye, I am glad ye have returned my daughter, faithful sword-brother and friend." He coughed to clear his throat. "And what a lovely, brave and talented young woman she is." He opened his arms to Rhynne.

She rushed into them, wrapping her arms around his waist. The top of her head tucked under his chin, and her shoulders shook in their embrace. Tears fell down Rhiannon's cheeks. Eifion held his expression tight, nodding slowly.

He knows. For he too lost the years his daughter grew in the Other World, although Eifion knew not of Rhiannon's existence. Arlan stifled a groan.

He nudged Rhynne away a touch, then looked directly into her eyes.

"I have missed you, Rhynne. Missed out on you growing up. Missed so many things I wished to share with you. Years of your life we will never have together."

Her body tensed, and she gulped.

"No fault of yours, my daughter." For a heartbeat, he glanced at Rhiannon whose shoulders became rigid. He forced the smile that would not come of its own volition. "But I yearn to know you. What I see makes me proud." His voice came out a choked whisper. "And I look forward to discovering more."

Rhynne buried her head in his chest, her shoulders rising and falling with hesitant breaths. She spoke not. Perhaps she was overwhelmed. Had he said too much? Was she displeased with what she had discovered of her origins? Of him? He would not press, although he longed to know.

"But now, as ye are travel worn, I suspect your mother wishes to find the quarters our hosts have assigned to us and get ye washed and more comfortable."

Rhynne lifted her head to face Bàn.

Arlan narrowed an eye. "Aye, Lord Bàn and I have things to discuss."

"I shall leave also." Eifion placed his hand on Arlan's shoulder, his grip firm as he passed, but said not another word.

Rhiannon and Rhynne followed him, Rhynne's gaze lingering on Bàn until she could no longer see him without twisting her neck. Arlan turned to the fire and stretched out his hands to it, its heat bathing his face. Bàn stepped beside him, clearing his throat.

"Ye have more you wish to say to me, sword-brother?" Arlan kept his voice steady with much effort.

"Aye, my àrd rìgh." Bàn rubbed his thumb over his upper lip. "Arlan." His voice softened. "But ye may not be pleased."

"I am not pleased already. George has brought up my daughter. What has he said of me? For he held naught but jealousy toward me on his discovering Rhiannon and I loved each other. For two years he held the secret wish I would never bring her to Dál Gaedhle, and that he would in fact have her for his own love. Rhiannon told me of his urgings to forget me."

"Arlan, ye are too hard on the man. He loves your daughter like his own and has met"—he tilted his head to the side for a moment— "most of Rhiannon's requests. She speaks our tongue fluently, does she not?"

"Aye."

"He has never mistreated her. He did well, Arlan. Give the man his due. And now he has her not."

"My turn to be her rightful father." Arlan blinked against the smoke from the fire. *Or do my eyes sting from unshed tears?* "Well, I concede the report is good." He looked Bàn in the eye then. "But you have more to tell me."

Bàn gulped softly, then he stood taller. "I love your daughter."

Arlan let out a forceful breath. "I thought so."

"Be not angry with me, Arlan." Bàn's voice held firm.

Arlan blinked, shaking his head. His baby girl had just returned, and now she would be loved as a man loves a woman?

"Ye are my sword-brother," he growled. "Sworn to protect her—"

"Which I did—"

"From all that is..." Arlan waved his hand around.

"Bad? Ye think our love is bad?"

"*Our love?* She returns it? She knows not what she wants." He scoffed. "She clings to you, her saviour and guide through this world. It is a fantasy, not true love."

"I will not press her. She has told me of her love for me." Bàn crossed his arms over his chest. "Ye are the true brother of my heart. I have loved you from my youth. And Rhiannon, she is a woman of character and will to match no other." He paused, mouth working as if summoning strength. "How then, when I find your daughter, not a babe but a grown woman—"

"Ye could not stop yourself from lusting after her!" Arlan yelled.

Bàn never flinched but continued his speech, his words entangling with Arlan's.

"—a grown woman who is the best of the two people I love the most in this life."

Arlan shut his mouth tight on his next words that would spew out with a father's anger.

"How then could I *not* love her?" Bàn remained calm. "And it hurts me so for you to think I would make love to her out of lust, not a purer emotion. Do ye not trust me? Do ye not know me and how I would love and honour your daughter?"

Arlan could only glare.

"In truth, it was difficult." Bàn frowned above his crossed arms. "I have not taken your daughter to my bed, ye will be glad to know. Did ye register she is a mage? Those who follow the good began her training at the sage hold where we spent the winter. She would listen not to my attempt to dissuade her. Wilful. Obstinate. Once she has made up her mind..." He huffed. "Eifion will train her further, I guess."

The tightness around Arlan's eyes receded, and a heat came to his cheeks. "Forgive me, Bàn. I am being an over-protective father." He gave a short snort. "At least now I have a chance to be such. I ken ye would treat my daughter with respect."

"We have not seriously discussed... marriage. There's too much else to consider." Bàn paused, taking a breath, and examining Arlan's expression. "Just know I love her, and she will always be in my heart."

Arlan's own heart melted. "Come here." He grabbed Bàn in a fierce hug. "Sword-brother, loyal warrior, truest friend. I could not think of a better man for my daughter." He sighed. "Just give me time to digest it all, aye?"

"Aye, but she has one request. One I had to promise to ask you in order to keep her with me on this journey." Bàn pulled away from their embrace. "She wishes to see George again."

THIRTY-FOUR

Magic knows magic
Feels it in another body
Though it may dance to a different master
Magic's presence hails like a beacon.

MAGE MASTER FÀISTINNAECH
(3310-3380 POST DRAGON WARS)

Eastern Clanlands of Dál Gallain
Caisteal Monsae

I sunk deeper into the large tub, the hot water seeping into my bones and chasing out the perma-chill of the past few days. Steam swirled above the honeysuckle petals floating on my bath's surface, their oils smoothing my skin, and drawing away the grime. Muscles, stretched and fatigued from fighting—seriously fighting—now relaxed. I released a sigh.

I had met my father. My real father. Man, he was the opposite of Dad. And so awesome. Everyone around him looked up to him. Obeyed his every command. He was a warrior, alright. You couldn't miss him.

Dad, on the other hand... his students respected him, but you'd walk right past him on a street and not even notice. He was great in his own way. I guess I'd been selfishly blind to all he'd done for me, considering I wasn't really his. My mother from the Isles was just a story then. But why not tell me the truth?

I grunted. Would I have believed it if he had?

So, this was my true home. Bàn had said it, but now I actually felt it. It really was my world, and these people were my people. This king, my father. Rhiannon, my mother.

I knew she was my mum—was aware of it the moment she turned to me as I patted the dragon. In our first hug I'd smelled her, and baby-like recollections had come to me, as if I was an infant again, held close by strong but feminine hands.

Mum—Rhiannon—poured a jug of hot water over my head. It flowed through my hair onto my scalp, and Rhiannon's fingers massaged away the grease and grit with firm strokes.

"You may leave us now. Thank you," Rhiannon said to the servant who'd brought in the pails of hot water.

"Man, this is..." I blew air out between my lips. "Fully cool."

"Fully?" Rhiannon chuckled. "But you are *fully* beautiful, my daughter. You're *so* much like Arlan. You fought cleverly, and you and Bàn were a team. I knew the moment I saw the fight from the battlement, that the woman with Bàn could be no one else but our child." She huffed. "Not being able to line up the timelines between the worlds. It screws with your mind if you're not careful."

I held my mouth tight against a laugh, my shoulders hunching with my effort.

"What?" Rhiannon leaned forward, looking into my face.

"You don't speak like the others. It's more like..."

"You?" She laughed. "I've only been here a little over a year. I suppose I haven't entirely picked up the accent or the way they phrase things."

I frowned. "How old are you?"

"Twenty-six. Why, how old are you?"

"Nineteen"—I gave a half grin— "*Mum.*" I burst into laughter, and so did Rhiannon.

"We will look more like sisters than anything," I said.

"What every mother wishes." Rhiannon gave a soft chuckle. "Motherhood is held in high regard. And you only have one mother. Mine died when I was young. My adoptive mum, that is."

"I've never had a mum." I couldn't keep the wistfulness from my voice. *Oh, damn, perhaps I shouldn't have said it.*

"Oh, Rhynne." Rhiannon put her arms around my shoulders, pressing her face against my soaking wet hair. "I'm so sorry." Her voice cracked.

Her clamp-like grip held me in place. I couldn't move to return her hug, so I patted her arm, then held tight. She shook gently and her breathing staggered a little. I pressed my lips together, fighting against tears.

"It's okay. I'm here now."

"I'm so sorry," she said, her words almost choking.

I couldn't answer. Sorry for what exactly?

"For not allowing you to know your real father when you were growing up," she said, as if she'd read my thoughts. "For leaving you without a mother, although none of that was my intention. I've missed out on you too..." Her voice trailed off, then she coughed like she was clearing her throat. "And now, taking you from George."

"Dad loves me, and he looked after me. Now I can get to know my real father, Arlan. And you, Mum."

Rhiannon had loosened her hug, so I turned.

"You're so forgiving," she said, her eyes moist.

"Bàn explained you wanted me safe from a war. You were just protecting me."

"I thought I'd come back for you almost immediately in your timeline. When this war ended, but... it hasn't worked out that way." Her expression hardened a little.

Was she mad at Bàn for bringing me back all grown up? "It's okay. I'm in this really cool world now."

"There's a war on. The same one. You're still not safe." Rhiannon's words had an edge of defeat to them.

"But I'm an adult. I can cope."

"You're still my baby," she said, her voice softening.

"I'm a warrior. Just ask Bàn. He's trained me. I'll fight too." I leaned against the bath, reaching my hand out to her. Bathwater sloshed over the side and onto the floor. "I'm here now, so I'm part of it. Part of this family."

Rhiannon took my hand, frowning. "You don't want to go back? To George?"

"Bàn has promised he'll ask Arlan if I can see George again."

Rhiannon's frown grew deeper. "How would that work?"

Yeah, good question.

Someone tapped on the door.

Rhiannon sighed and let go, then wiped her hands on her apron and strode over to the door. She opened it, whispered to whoever it was, then came back, wiping tears from her eyes with a swipe of her finger.

"Your father wishes to speak with me." She placed drying cloths on the stool by the tub. "Once you're dressed"—she pointed to a gown draped over a chair— "come find us. Explore the caisteal if you wish. Don't worry, everyone knows you're the daughter of their àrd rìgh." She smiled and left.

Explore the caisteal!

"Oh, yeah!"

I got out of the bath, sloshing water over the sides onto the wooden floorboards and spraying droplets on the hem of the gown. I dried and dressed, then snuck out the door. There were many rooms off this passage. The walls were a dusky-pink sandstone peeking out from behind brightly coloured tapestries of warriors and hunts. Voices came from the room to my right, and I took a step closer. It was Rhiannon and Arlan. I squinted. Should I call them by their names or... Mum and... Father?

'Cos Dad would *always* be Dad.

I turned away from the door and their conversation. The tone sounded intimate. I cringed a little. I wouldn't interrupt that.

The wind whispered through the open window, tickling Rhiannon's cheeks, and teasing the muslin curtains of the fourposter bed. She followed Arlan's progress as he paced the room, his shoulders taut and his forehead like a furrowed field. He pierced the floorboards with his scowl, his fists clenching and unclenching with every step. All the lightness at Rhynne's return lifted from Rhiannon's body like the curtains in the breeze.

"Another man has brought up my daughter. He has told her of his dreams and beliefs," Arlan said in a severe tone. "What he wished for her. Taught her how to think. What to make of the world." His voice cracked. "You've denied me of this."

"Arlan, I'm so sorry." She pressed against the pleading in her voice. "I can't make it up to you. Can't change this. But please, don't hold it against Rhynne. Make the most of what we have. Tell her now what you think. What you feel. Show her how to be a great warrior, 'cos boy, she can fight. Or just show her the man she came from."

He stopped his pacing, his brow softening, and in a flash a look of pride came across his face .

"She's so like you." Rhiannon couldn't keep the awed inflection from her voice. "She's wonderful." More than wonderful. *Talented. Brilliant. Warrior-like. Beautiful. Natural...*

"She's so like *you*," Arlan said tenderly. "Bàn has told me she is stubborn and head-strong."

His mouth broke into a crooked smile. His curling fists had gradually unclenched, and now he lowered them to his sides, then took hesitant steps toward her.

Rhiannon ran to him, threw her arms around him, and buried her face in his armour.

"Please forgive me." Her words muffled into him, but his chin resting on her head told her he'd heard.

A sigh came from deep in his chest. "Aye, I do," he said, his voice a soft whisper. "If I can forgive you for taking her from me, then I must forgive you for all the consequences of it."

I wandered the tapestry-lined passage until I came to a stone stairway leading upward. Dim daylight shone down the steps. It probably went to the battlements at the top.

Climbing the stone stairs, my soft slipper-like shoes pattered on each step. I reached the top and leaned against the parapet, the stone cooling my arms, while the last of daylight sat around the rim of the horizon. A soft breeze flew through my damp hair, still loose from my bath and smelling of honeysuckle. The briny scent of the sea filled the breeze itself. The trees whispered in the wind, their fluttering leaves sang a quiet song, almost of welcome. I let the trees' music course through me.

I wasn't home yet, not to The Keep or that broch Bàn had mentioned—whatever a broch was—but I was with family, my *real* parents. I pressed my lips tight. Yes, they were my actual parents, and I couldn't deny that. My thoughts sped to Dad. He would be missing me. My heart curled inside me. Bàn had better find a way to keep his promise!

I shook my head, flinging away the ache of missing Dad, and tuned my hearing again to the tree song. It held a note of warning, and I strained to it. The song tuned out, then a man spoke.

"Aye, the warband has been thwarted." He spoke a little like me and Rhiannon. No, more like Rhiannon, with a real Scottish accent.

"And Lord Bàn returns with the daughter?" This voice sounded weird. Like you'd expect a dog to sound. Just like in a cartoon, or something. "Keep them all there. Our master has secured his clan lands and will soon head to you." A trail of power lingered in the air after the voice stopped. And a smell like... I strained to place it.

Oh, yeah! *Burnt toast.*

Power! Like magic. My insides jumped in recognition. But it wasn't the magic I'd used. This was... dark.

"Who is there?" the cartoon voice asked.

"No one," the man with the Scottish accent answered.

A shuffling came closer, then footsteps and... dog claws clicking on the wooden battlement floor. A man came around the corner of the square tower with his dog, a Staffordshire bull terrier, trotting beside him. The man's expression was tight but relaxed a bit upon seeing me.

I forced a smile. "Hi. Lovely evening. I was just having a look around. What a view."

"Aye, it's grand. And welcome to Dál Gallain." He tipped his hat and walked by me.

"I, ah, haven't caught up with everyone yet. Who's who and all that." I kept smiling.

"I'm Rabbie Findlay." He gave a brief bow. "Servant to your father and grateful for the high king's favour."

"Your accent...?"

"Aye. How perceptive of you. I'm from the Other World also, young lady. I look forward to catching up on that world's happenings."

"I'm not sure you will be."

He straightened, suddenly looking cagy.

"I mean, what year did you leave there?" I squirmed a bit, trying to keep the apologetic tone from my voice. "It's just that there was a plague a while ago. Not only in the UK, but absolutely everywhere. My dad, the man who brought me up, said it changed everything. So"— I shrugged— "it may not be the same world you left, I expect."

"Probably not." He tilted his head, walked past me, and hastened down the stairs, his footsteps rapid.

That was weird. *And not good.*

I waited till his footsteps faded, then took the stairs two at a time and went to the main hall. The door had been left open a crack, so I stepped in. Bàn stood by the fire, his damp hair slicked back. He wore clean clothes and he'd rested *Dileas* against the wall beside the fireplace. Findlay stood next to him. Bàn glared at the man, though he was trying to hide it.

He didn't like him? I didn't blame Bàn. Something about Rabbie Findlay was *off.*

And it was the *magic* dog.

I stepped further into the room. Eifion sat on the couch nearest the fire, and Vygeas stood next to Bàn, who'd spotted me and strode over, his mouth lifting in a grin as he approached. Bàn reached me, drew me into his arms and planted a kiss on my lips. I gasped into it. So it was alright to kiss me in front of them all?

"My father was okay about...?"

Bàn nodded, eyes alight.

"Bàn, I hate to break the moment," I whispered. "But I need to speak to Eifion without... *the other guy*." I mouthed the last three words.

Bàn frowned, then he nodded slowly. "Verra well," he whispered back, turned, took my hand, then led me to sit by Eifion on the couch. He looked directly at Vygeas, raised an eyebrow, then glanced sharply at Findlay and his dog, who hadn't seemed to notice.

A tingling wave passed over me. *Was that from Vygeas?*

"Findlay." Vygeas spoke like the lord of the manor. "They serve a meal for the staff now in the kitchen. Ye may go and eat."

Findlay nodded, sliding his vision to me for a nanosecond, then strode out of the room with his dog trotting beside him. I ran softly from my seat by Eifion to the door, then peered out. Findlay and his dog marched down the corridor.

I closed the door, then ran back to Eifion. Everyone in the room looked at me with curious expressions, except for Vygeas. That tingle came again. Bàn had said he could sense things. Maybe he saw something in Findlay. I crouched in front of Eifion, reaching for the old man's hands. They were hot and inviting, like I imagined love could feel. The warmth spread into me. *Oh.* I held my breath for a second, enjoying the sensation. Eifion's face broke into a smile.

"I love trees, Grandfather," I blurted out.

"Aye, of course ye do." He chuckled, his face crinkling further. "What troubles ye so, Rhynne?"

I glanced toward the door, then chewed my lip.

What I had to say would sound crazy, but not to Eifion.

"That dog holds a magic. Not like anything I've seen. Not like the light at the mage hold. It's dark."

"What do ye mean, Rhynne?" Vygeas stepped closer. "For I have sensed none."

"Nor I." The smile left Eifion's face, and he leaned forward.

I looked up at Vygeas. "It spoke."

"What?" Bàn breathed his question.

Vygeas grunted and Eifion *hmmed.*

I turned back to the mage. *Of course he gets it.*

"What does that mean?" I asked Eifion.

"What did the dog say?" Eifion's stare was intense.

"They were talking about Bàn coming back with me, the warband being defeated, like it didn't even matter, and that the master had secured his clan lands and was coming here. He told Findlay to keep us here."

"Ach! *Dragon's teeth!*" Bàn cursed.

Eifion nodded. "A mage is communicating through the dog."

"Findlay works for Gallawain," Bàn said. "I have just advised Arlan that on our way here, Rhynne and I saw Gallawain with three warbands heading north via the back way. Heading to Gallawain clan lands in Dál Gaedhle. Where's Arlan?" Bàn raced to the door and ran out, his footsteps banging down the hallway.

"Well done, my granddaughter." Eifion grasped my hands.

"Are we in danger?" A tremble sat beside my spine, but a slight tingle passed over me and I suppressed a start.

"No more than usual, Lady Rhynne," Vygeas said. "Have courage."

"Nae, not now ye have alerted us." Eifion brushed my hair back from my face with his heated hand. "Ye take after us, Clan Iubhar."

"Iubhar means yew, like the tree."

"Aye," he said gently.

Bàn soon returned, his face red from the neck up.

"Arlan comes?" Vygeas asked.

Bàn coughed. "I interrupted... something. But aye, Lord Arlan and Lady Rhiannon will join us. I have ordered my sister to keep watch on Findlay's moves."

"Do you think he could know that we know?" I asked Eifion.

"Only if he sensed your magic, my dear."

"Did he?" Bàn's question was curt.

"Ah... the dog knew I was there. But dogs hear things before humans." I lifted a shoulder, then let it fall.

Eifion scratched behind his ear and shrugged in a dignified way.

Arlan burst through the door, throwing his plaid over his shoulder, his body free of his leather armour, and his loose hair flying around him. The silver torc at his neck glinted.

"Tell me all, Rhynne," Arlan said, his voice deep and commanding.

I swallowed, huddling into myself a little. He looked enormous, all bulging muscles, and a little scary with his scarred face. He had a tattooed sleeve of Celtic knots like Bàn's, but a long scar ran through Arlan's.

Bàn had called him the *warrior king*.

Now I got it.

I relayed what'd happened, while Arlan squinted and frowned throughout. Rhiannon entered the hall, her hair roughly tied. Vygeas' wife, Lady Leyna, followed soon after. Arlan looked at Eifion and rubbed his hands through his beard.

"That *droch dhuine*, Gallawain! I wonder how fares my mother's cousin Adomàn, the current Lord of Caisteal Gallawain. And to think we made plans in that Findlay's hearing."

"Will ye execute him?" Bàn asked.

"What!" Ice flashed through my guts.

"That's what we do with traitors here," Bàn said simply.

"Nae," Arlan interrupted and placed his hands on his belt. "We will keep him out of our council and watch him closely to see what we can glean from him." He looked at me then, his navy-blue eyes stern. "Ye shall be our spy, Rhynne. He may know not of your gifting."

Arlan addressed the others. "We must keep to ourselves that she has mage abilities, just as your skills are not common knowledge, Eifion." He nodded and appeared to make another decision. "I shall secretly send messengers to The Keep calling Leuchars to engage our war host and approach Gallawain lands from the west and prepare to attack. We'll communicate further once we arrive. Thus, bringing the battle to the foe, and Gallawain shall see that Dál Gaedhle is not for the taking."

THIRTY-FIVE

The element the acolyte mage discovers to be their conduit will find them. Of this, they have no choice. It welcomes the new mage, though, like the return of a sibling long-lost. In its embrace, the acolyte finds their home.

MAGE MASTER FÀISTINNEAECH
(3310-3380 POST DRAGON WARS)

Eastern Clanlands of Dál Gallain
Caisteal Monsae

Soft sheets caressed Rhiannon. She lay tucked into Arlan's side, his warm skin connecting with the length of her body. Weak early morning sunshine beamed through the window, a block of light on the wooden floor. They lay in the same fourposter bed where she and Arlan had made love for the first time after the retaking of Caisteal Monsae—the time they'd conceived Rhynne.

A smile she couldn't contain spread across her face.

And now their daughter was here with them. What an amazing young woman. George had done well. Rhiannon took a sharp intake of air. She owed George so much, and Rhynne had spoken with nothing but love for her dad who, as a single-parent, had raised her. Yes, she hadn't made it easy for him. But he'd done it, and loved Rhynne well, according to Bàn. Rhynne spoke the Gaelic, fought like a Dál Gaedhle warrior, and had... magic.

"Wow." Rhiannon let the word out.

Arlan stirred, breathing in. Her arm across his chest rose and fell with his breath.

Make-up sex is wonderful.

Arlan sighed and mumbled softly in his sleep.

Rhynne loved Bàn. The way she looked at him. Relied on him.

And, oh yeah, he loves her. That was inevitable. What with his man-crush on Arlan and his secret love for herself.

She chuckled.

Warrior's voices and the whinny of horses echoed through the window from those sleeping in shelters in the bailey yard below. Drayce flapped at the sill and did her annoyed clicking, now too large to land on there, then flew away.

Arlan woke and rubbed his face, then turned and kissed her.

"I love you, my wife," he whispered.

"And I you, my husband."

He stepped out of bed and raised his arms above his head, stretching. Joints popped. He was all muscles, sinews, and taut healthy body. He faced her, a smile curving his lips and tugging slightly on the scar that ran along his cheekbone.

"We will meet and discuss much today. I would have you, Rhynne and Bàn there too, with Eifion." He lowered his hands from his stretch, leaned down, and, placing warm soft lips to hers, played with her mouth. "Then we head north to that *bassa* and rid ourselves of him." He dressed and left.

He had forgiven her all. The closeness and warmth she'd craved had returned. Her Arlan had come back to her. Rhiannon sunk deeper into the bed, pulling the covers closer to her heating face. Tightness curled in her chest, tying it in a knot.

She didn't deserve his forgiveness. She didn't have any for herself, so why should he?

Leyna's words replayed in her mind. Forgive *herself* or it would ruin her relationship with Arlan. She tucked her legs close and placed her chin between her knees. *Hmm*.

She got up and dressed in her breeches, then went next door to Rhynne's room, stopping a maid on the way and asking her to fetch clean suitable attire for Rhynne to wear for riding.

And fighting. She would travel with her, Bàn, and Arlan in the àrd rìgh's warband.

Rhiannon's insides tingled.

Then she squirmed a little. Rhynne was not much younger than her, and in some ways might be more like a sister. She shrugged.

But she'd always be Rhynne's mother.

She knocked and pushed the door open. Rhynne stood at the window looking out over the bailey yard. She turned as Rhiannon entered and strode to her, opening her arms for a hug.

"Dress quickly, you're summoned to the meeting," she said into Rhynne's shoulder. "We'll have breakfast then."

"Where's Bàn?" Rhynne asked, stepping from their embrace. "I don't see him with the warriors."

"He's a lord and has his own room, like you do."

A tap came on the door, and Rhiannon opened it to the maid with Rhynne's clothes. Rhynne dressed quickly, and Rhiannon took her to the main hall where breakfast was spread on a table: platters of bacon, smoked fish, eggs, and breads. A bowl of fruit sat in the centre. Arlan and Bàn stood in front of the fire, eating while they talked. Arlan laughed often.

Yes, he'd missed his friend.

Leyna, Vygeas, and Eifion were seated on the couches, and they'd all soon eaten breakfast.

"Friends, family, my close counsel." Arlan looked at them all in turn. "This morning, we hold a deception in order to call out the traitor in our midst." He indicated for Rhynne to come to him.

She glanced at Rhiannon.

Rhiannon nodded her encouragement and whispered, "You can't decline the invitation of the àrd rìgh. Or your father."

Rhynne stepped slowly to Arlan, who met her in a hug, pride filling his expression. "Good morning, daughter." He kissed her on the cheek.

Rhynne's shoulders relaxed, and she turned to stand beside her father, his arm gently encircling her. Rhiannon double blinked. *Man, talk about family resemblance.*

"We are about to bring in some warriors and Findlay. We have things to discuss, but one is a ruse, and ye have an important part to play in it. I shall order our warriors to prepare to return to The Keep"—he leaned into Rhynne and spoke softly— "but our plan is to storm Gallawain's caisteal. After I dismiss the warriors, ye shall follow Findlay, ever so quietly, and wait for him to *speak to his dog.*"

"I shall be nearby," Bàn said. "And ye shall testify against this cur, aye?"

Rhynne stood taller. "Aye."

Rhynne took a seat and Bàn strode to the door, where he called to the milling crowd of warriors whose chatter had muffled through. Arlan's troop walked in, Douglas the loudest and nudging Angus. Adele came behind Muir, both stern-faced. Morrigan trailed them with Findlay at her heels, his dog trotting beside him.

Vygeas' hounds bounded in and sniffed at Findlay's dog in greeting, then gathered around their master for scraps. Rhiannon frowned. Other dogs had never behaved otherwise to Findlay's animal.

The warriors finally settled along the wall.

"Muir," Arlan said. "Tell me of the youngsters whom we saved from battle."

Muir stepped forward. "Lord, those we captured were but sons of steading holders, as we surmised. Most came from a small village, Clachan Beag, which they tell me is just over the River Bàn-rìghinn."

"Och!" Bàn exclaimed.

"Ye know it, Bàn?" Arlan lifted his eyebrows at him.

"Aye." Bàn locked stares with Rhynne. "We stayed there before we headed up the mount. It's a fair way from here."

"Well, the lads who were the gamest for the fight were the oldest of that lot," Muir grunted. "The others seem to be from closer clans." Muir bowed, his report over.

"We would be pleased to house them here, my Lord Arlan." Vygeas looked to Leyna, who nodded. "We can train them and wait, if this war permits, till they are grown and can join our warbands, ensuring their allegiance is with you, of course."

"Excellent. Some may hold promise." Arlan turned to his warband. "Now, my warriors, we return to The Keep. Our friend and ally needs us not here at present. We go to resupply and plan our next moves. Ready yourselves."

I waited until the hall emptied and stepped over to Bàn, who stood by Arlan like his right-hand man.

Must be the sword-brother thing.

Bàn took my hands in his and looked me in the eye. "We will follow him close, Rhynne. When he settles on the place to do his magic communication, I shall be right beside ye. I trust the man not, although I have heard he is a poor swordsman."

Rhiannon chuckled behind me as she sat down on the couch next to Lady Leynarve.

"He needs a secluded place to do his thing with the talking dog," I said. "Now I've caught him on the battlement, he won't go there again."

I hurried out of the room, conscious of all eyes on my back. If I delayed any longer, I'd miss where Findlay went. I stepped out through the hall's double doors with Bàn a few paces behind me, and followed the backs of tall men and women. Findlay's head bobbed between the shoulders of the warriors. He stood a touch shorter than those he walked amongst.

The group headed out toward the yard where they'd kept Arlan's warriors' horses, and the grey. They'd put the teenagers of the warband we'd fought to work shovelling manure and grooming the war horses. Some traipsed back and forward from the door that led to the kitchens, loading bags and boxes of supplies onto wagons. Findlay walked casually in that direction, then sidled by the side of the caisteal wall and out of sight, moving like he knew the place.

I walked across the yard, avoiding the poop and the hind legs of the war horses, thankful I wore trousers and not the beautiful long gown Rhiannon gave me yesterday. I passed some of the guys who'd surrendered. They were so young.

They sent boys to war in this world!

Yeah, Ma Gabràn had said that.

I came to the corner of the caisteal wall and leaned against it. The sword I'd won from the warrior yesterday rested in a new baldric over my right shoulder and clunked against the stone wall. In the yard, Bàn made a show of instructing a boy on how to curry a horse correctly, but he glanced at me every few moments. I peered around the corner of the caisteal and looked along the line of the wall that led to a gate. Past this, a garden grew. Maybe a herb or vegetable patch. Findlay was just stepping through the gate with his dog slipping past him. I drew my head back from the stone corner where, with luck, he couldn't see me.

I counted to five, then checked again. The gate swung shut with Findlay's back moving out of sight.

I tried to catch Bàn's eye, but he stood with hands on his belt, frowning at a lad who reached up to brush the grey's mane. The horse was twice the lad's height. Bàn finally looked across to me, so I nodded. I hurried up to the gate and slowly opened it, holding my breath against a rusty hinge. No creak. The groundsman of this place did his job, then.

I stepped through to a walled garden filled with vegetables and herbs that greeted me in a splash of colour. Plants displayed their flowers of early spring. Bright green shoots clambered upwards for the sun. Sweet peas' heady perfume assaulted my nose and bees' buzzing droned into my ears. I tore my eyes away from the showy displays and searched for Findlay. The paths between the beds were soft sand and my tread, almost silent.

I halted to listen.

A mumble came from a slatted wooden boxed area. I crept closer. The scent of decomposing plant matter, new earth, and soil rose to meet me. It must've been the compost heap. But mingled through the healthy decomposing vegetable matter rose the stench of something gone off.

"Aye, they return to The Keep and plan to ready themselves for their next move." Findlay's modern Scottish accent mumbled from behind the compost.

"Which is?" The dog spoke like a cartoon again.

Wow, it was *weird*.

"I don't know. Get ready to defend their borders? Push further into Dál Gallain?" Frustration strained Findlay's comments. "Lord Bàn and their daughter, Rhynne, have just returned from that way."

"Aye, we know," the dog growled. "A key mage was severely injured in his pursuit of them."

The perfumes from the herb garden flowed over me, smelling strongly of lavender and thyme. They wisped about my face and shoulders, like silver fingers of mist pulling me away from the reek of decay.

Then I saw me.

I was squatting behind the wooden slats. Leaf litter, vegetable scraps, and horse poo rested on top of the pile in the wooden crate-like box. On the other side of it, Findlay sat on his haunches by his dog. A dark mist hovered around them both, but a blackness almost hid the bull terrier.

Footsteps padded behind me, and I fell back into my body, gasping and shaking. I spun. Bàn stood there, sword drawn and eyes wide, nodding.

He must've heard the dog speaking, too.

"We are found," the dog said.

Findlay gave a startled yell as the dog tore around from the compost bin and charged for Bàn, teeth bared and growling.

Bàn raised his sword.

"No! Don't hurt the dog!" I yelled, grabbing his sword arm. "It's not the animal."

"What?" Bàn's voice strangled around the word as he halted his sword strike and kicked out at the dog with his booted foot.

The dog skidded sideways into a pre-dug bed, its agonised yelp ringing through the vegetable patch. The blackness thinned, then rose like a mist from the writhing dog, lifting the rotten odour. Findlay jumped from behind the compost bin, sword raised.

He saw Bàn and faltered. Bàn stepped forward, swiping at Findlay's sword. Findlay blocked all Bàn's blows but made no attempt to attack. With a flick of his wrist, Bàn disarmed Findlay, his sword flying out of his grip and ending up beside his dog in the dirt.

The dog cowered, tail between its legs, shaking.

"Oh, poor dog. It's not fair." I turned on Findlay, my jitters now turning heated. "You've caught that innocent animal up in your dark magic. *You're* the beast. And the mage you work with."

"Careful, young lady," Findlay growled, never taking his eyes from the point of Bàn's sword now pressed to his chest. "It's a powerful mage you're speaking against. I'd watch my mouth, if I were you."

"And ye can shut yours," Bàn ordered, "until ye come before the àrd rìgh and explain yourself."

THIRTY-SIX

Those who trust the light need not fear the darkness.

BOOK OF LIGHT
MAGE TEXT. DATE OF SCRIBING UNKNOWN.
THE BOOK LOST IN ANTIQUITY

Eastern Clanlands of Dál Gallain
Caisteal Monsae

I stomped behind Bàn as he dragged Findlay through the bailey yard. He'd bound Findlay's hands behind his back. The young guys at the horses, plus warriors preparing to leave, stared at him as we passed.

Everyone stared as we marched all the way to the main hall.

The older warrior, Muir, had grabbed the dog and tied a rope around its neck. It cowered and its back legs trembled so much it could barely walk.

"Take the hound to the kennels," Bàn shouted over his shoulder. "We must keep these two apart."

Warriors and warband leaders followed us into the hall, then stood against the walls. Those who couldn't fit in peered through the doorway.

Bàn flung Findlay forward. Findlay thudded to his knees in front of Arlan, the wooden floorboards reverberating the thump and echoing it to the ceiling. He kept his head bowed.

The point of Bàn's sword sat at his neck.

Eifion stood by the enormous fireplace and watched me approach as I ran to him, shivering. He allowed me to snuggle up beside him to get warm from the fire and himself. A chill sat in my middle. With Eifion's arm wrapped about my shoulder, I absorbed the heat.

"We have discovered a traitor, my àrd rìgh." Bàn's voice sounded the coldest I'd ever heard it. "He used dark magic to do so, as Lady Rhynne will testify."

Findlay winced, then lifted his head briefly and, ashen faced, stared at me.

Arlan stood in front of the gathered warriors and crossed his arms over his chest.

"Findlay." Arlan's voice was a low grumble. "You, an Other Worlder, a stranger to Dál Cruinne, have committed a grievous crime. A betrayal of trust. Ye have lied and cheated on our friendship. You begged me to trust you and you repay me with treacherous duplicity. Do ye think me a *fool?*" He said the word with such force that I flinched. "I know you sent us here to Monsae. Gallawain is sneaking elsewhere, and *you* will tell me all." His shout filled the room.

Findlay rolled his shoulders, as much as he could with his wrists manacled, then lifted his head and looked past Arlan to me, a question in his eyes.

"Well?" Arlan shouted again.

Findlay hunched, his gaze flying to Arlan, then his shoulders slowly lowered.

"While Lord Adomàn Gallawain was away from his lands and caisteal," Findlay began, "Lord Ciarán—"

Arlan raised his hand. "He is no longer a *lord,* and has not been for over thirty years."

"Ciarán Gallawain has retaken Caisteal Gallawain, his clan's seat," Findlay said.

Arlan growled. "My father banished him. He has no clan. No lands. No *seat* to retake." Arlan lowered his hands to his sides and clenched them.

I looked up at Eifion.

"Returning after banishment is punishable by death," Eifion whispered to me.

"It is on." Arlan spoke to the warriors who lined the hall. "We go not to The Keep but straight to my mother's clan lands to assist my great uncle, Lord Adomàn, to regain what is his."

The tramping of boots filled the hall, almost drowning out the murmurs and comments of the warriors who left to ready for the journey.

I stayed next to Eifion, his body heat continuing to warm me along with the heat from the fire at my back. I glanced around at those who'd stayed. Apart from Bàn by Arlan's side, Rhiannon stood with Lady Leynarve, who, with her very pregnant belly, sat awkwardly on the couch. Lord Vygeas stood with Arlan.

"There is more," my father said, "and you will tell me all." His voice came out a harsh whisper.

I trembled at Arlan's tone, but Findlay looked him in the eye and closed his mouth tight.

A tingle came from Vygeas' direction.

"Ye need me not to tell you defiance pours from this man," Vygeas said.

Rhiannon got up from the couch and, standing by Arlan, faced Findlay.

"I... I can't believe you'd do this. You seemed such a nice man. A good policeman." She opened her hands to him. "What happened?" Her voice held hurt.

Findlay twisted his head slightly, eyes sliding to the side, his lips chewing over his next words.

"I *was* a good policeman. But it wasn't worth it. People still got away with shite and the string of thugs, wife beaters, and murderers just kept coming... no matter what I did." He looked at Rhiannon then. "And all my duty to service, all the hours I spent at work sorting out other people's traumas, got me a lonely life. My wife left me," he said, his voice flat and hollow. "Never had any kids." He dropped his gaze to the floor, his shoulders dipping.

What did this have to do with it all? And why deceive Arlan? He seemed a good leader. A powerful king and ... well. My chest warmed in that moment, and I held my head high.

"Why betray my father?" I stepped away from Eifion. Bàn stared at me like I should be quiet, but Arlan faced me and wiggled his fingers for me to step forward. "Why be so involved in"—a shiver coursed through me again— "evil magic?"

"Because spying for Ciarán gave me hope of another chance," Findlay said in a husky voice.

Eifion gasped and stepped forward. "What did he promise you? You have been deceived, for whatever it is, you will not receive it but end up in a dark place along with the one who made the pledge."

Findlay shifted on his knees, then looked at Eifion, his gaze including me.

"Ciarán Gallawain promised his mage would send me through a portal to a time before my wife left me so I could change my life and maybe she would stay. I'd give up *the job* and look for another. Fewer hours. Less stress. More time to climb Munros with her." His throat worked. "But now you've discovered me, that won't happen."

"Nae." Arlan's response was gruff.

"It would not have happened anyway," Eifion said. "The man you trust is a deceiver, and his lord is a liar."

"And there's Time Travel 101," I said, and they all looked at me. "His old self would be there." Huh? Was he that ignorant of time travel? "Didn't you ever watch sci-fi movies?"

Findlay dropped his head forward, and a tear splatted on the floorboards.

"So ye have spied and reported all to Ciarán?" Arlan's voice had turned hard.

Findlay nodded.

"What else?"

"The dragon attack on you, Lady Rhiannon. I made it up. The mage can control dragons. He had to do it then, although it wrecks him each time he does it."

Eifion leaned forward. "Tell us more of this mage."

"He's got a master. A bad one."

"A dark one," I said. They all looked at me again and Bàn's face hardened as he searched mine. "I've sensed it," I said as a shiver travelled right through me, sparking off the cold again.

"You have naught left to lose." Eifion said, his authoritative voice right next to my ear as he directed his words to Findlay. "Ye may as well tell all."

"Ciarán Gallawain is an evil, soul-sold, dissatisfied man, who'll willingly unleash all hell on you to gain control of this land." Findlay looked straight at Arlan, shaking his head, a tear rolling down his cheek. "Plus, he thinks a human sacrifice of some sort, like the old Druids did"—he huffed a cynical laugh— "will give him immortality."

"I know he plans his Armageddon," Arlan said.

"Oh, he's so looking forward to that." Findlay's voice held an edge. "He's got weapons and warriors lined up."

"He has cannon." Arlan grunted.

"*Ha*. From the snippets of conversation I've heard, cannon are the least of your worries." He glanced up at Arlan. "I'm not certain on specifics, but he maintains he has surprises in store for you."

"How will he accomplish this?" Eifion asked.

Findlay shrugged. "I don't know."

Bàn poked him with the point of his sword.

"I don't know!" Findlay raised his voice, flinching away from Bàn's weapon. "Portals somehow."

"Of his fascination with portals, we are well aware," Eifion remarked, as Bàn's blade pressed against Findlay's neck.

"The man never told me anything important." Findlay squeaked. "He's a user."

"Aye," Eifion said with conviction. "He has changed not."

"My brother?" Arlan asked.

Findlay grabbed his lower lip with his teeth and shook his head slightly. "He's enjoying father-son time with Ciarán."

Arlan let out an angry sounding groan.

"He's not all there, is he?" Findlay snarled.

"He suffered a head wound and is not the man he used to be." Arlan's voice came out strained, like he felt sorry and pained about it, though there was some relief in his tone.

So Arlan's brother is my uncle, but he's having father-son time with...?

Huh?

"Vygeas." Arlan's authoritative tone broke through my mental questions. "May we keep this man in your dungeon?"

Vygeas called his own guards, who took Findlay away. Findlay bowed his head and, with shoulders sagging, dragged his feet between his guards and never said a word as they led him out.

Bàn sheathed his sword. "Your plans, my high king?"

"Prevent Gallawain from establishing himself fully in Dál Gaedhle." Arlan frowned deeply.

"He is but two days' ride from The Keep," Bàn said.

"Aye, in good weather." Arlan rubbed the beard beneath his chin. "We will meet Leuchars and our war host at Gallawain lands. He can approach from the west. We shall approach from the southeast then attack Gallawain, who dares to enter Dál Gaedhle with impunity. And we must still block him from returning to his lands in Dál Gallain. We give him no choice. Fight him in Dál Gaedhle on lands we know." Arlan gave a sharp nod. "Send messengers in all haste to inform Lord Leuchars we are on our way to Caisteal Gallawain from the south east. Perhaps Lord Adomàn remains at The Keep and can join the war host. The marshes on the way to the loch where his caisteal sits will be sodden with snow melt from this past winter. It will be slow going for them and we may reach Gallawain lands at the same time they do."

Arlan placed his hand on Bàn's shoulder.

"Call our warbands. We shall plan further. Order Muir to hasten the loading of supplies and readying of warriors." He nodded to Vygeas. "Thank you, my friend, for your generosity to my army."

Vygeas acknowledged Arlan's gratitude with a bow.

"We could..." Bàn held up a finger. Arlan nodded, and he continued. "We could use Findlay to communicate still with the mage, find out Ciarán's moves and so on."

"Nae, I trust not the cur. The mage knows *we* know. And I'd rather be blind to his moves than have him know my every thought."

Eifion took my hand and led me back to the fire. I went willingly, leaving Bàn with Arlan to talk about war. Eifion would have the answers to the questions flying around in my head.

"Grandfather, about Arlan's brother?"

"Ah, Lord Kyle." Eifion's lips wriggled around like they were going to speak without his permission. Then he coughed. "Ciarán Gallawain fathered Kyle."

"What?" I stretched the word. Talk about family secrets!

"Therefore making Kyle Arlan's half-brother, but only recently revealed to be so."

I blinked. "Okay, so he's with the bad guy. Is he one too? Do we fight him?"

"No." Arlan broke from his conversation with Bàn. "My brother is now a simpleton. I will release him from Gallawain when I am able. He is still my brother, and I will fulfil my duty to him."

The room grew silent. Bàn looked at the floor and a crease appeared between Vygeas' brows. My father resumed planning with Bàn and the other warriors in his warband.

"You tremble still," Eifion said into my ear.

"I'm warming up now, but that magic left me cold." I lifted my head to his crinkled eyes, and a slow *v* formed between his bushy white eyebrows. "That magic is dark. Really, really dark." I trembled again and Eifion wrapped his arm around me in a hug. "It was black. Deep, solid blackness. I...just felt hate coming from it. It tortured that poor dog."

"You are safe, Rhynne, my precious granddaughter. You, like myself, are a mage in touch with the Light. We draw our magic from the life of plants, but our source is the Source of all Spirit. I will teach you all in due course."

"You mean the good god?" I asked.

"Aye, not the darkness. Not the evil from which the mage who speaks through that dog draws his power."

Arlan had spoken to Vygeas for most of my conversation with Eifion, but he turned now and smiled as he looked at me in Eifion's hug.

"I know this." Arlan's voice held awe. "The Source of all Spirit. The fountains of life. *Tobraichean na beatha.*"

Eifion held his breath for a beat.

"You *know* it?" I asked.

"Aye." Arlan spoke softly. "I met him at my kingmaking."

"You met a god?" I asked.

Eifion's soft cry of delight overshadowed my words.

Arlan nodded silently.

Eifion turned back to me, a look of anticipation in his eyes. "Ye know not of the lore of Dál Cruinne. Nor its histories, prophecies and beliefs."

I widened my eyes to encourage him. There was so much I needed to know. My father had met a god. Wow.

A warrior king who had met with a god.

"My father is someone special, isn't he?" I asked.

"Aye." Eifion's answer was heavy with a thoughtful wonder. "There is a legend," he continued. "A scroll in the Secret Sacred Writings of the Sages that promises an army will come to life when required." He leaned closer. "I fear the time draws near for your father to need such a thing. Even one as fantastical as resurrected warriors from our past."

"Where is this army?" I asked.

"I know not, only that the scroll records the warriors are hidden from time and people. A long green snake is involved."

"Huh? A green snake?"

"Aye, prophecy." Eifion grunted in annoyance. "Mysteriousness is a prerequisite." He stood tall, letting me go, then addressed the others. "I shall send a protection upon us all, for we shall surely need it." His voice ran through me and filled the hall. Everyone stood still and listened. "There is very much more to this war than what we see with our eyes, hear with our ears, and touch with our hands."

THIRTY-SEVEN

— · —

SAGE GLIOCAS
(2870-2962 POST DRAGON WARS)

Western Sovereignty of Dál Gaedhle
Loch Clach-Oilaire
Caisteal Gallawain
Lord Ciaran's Army Camp

Bram stepped back from the divination bowl, which rested on a sturdy squat log in his tent. Water dripped from his long fingers. The scrape of weapons sharpening, the pleas of prisoners, and the general hubbub of camp had muffled through the canvas, but now the patter of falling rain slowly drowned it out.

"Oh, Lord Ciarán will *not* be pleased."

He flung the tent flap open to a sodden view. A horse whinnied and splashed mud on the boy who handled it, its legs covered in brown muck well above the pastern. Bram grimaced. He possessed no assistant mage to set a *staying* in place to protect his body while he attended to his communications with Findlay through his mutt. A horse, a hound, an escaped prisoner, or any manner of intruders, could attack his undefended body. Thankfully, the truth of his manner of divination was not common knowledge.

Bram trod doggedly through the slush, his boots sticking every so often. He risked losing one as he applied force against the suction. He lifted his face to the soft falling rain and breathed deep, dampening the rising dread at the impending, inevitable outburst from Lord Ciarán.

The bombardment had achieved its purpose, with the caisteal surrendered. Although a hole the size of a wagon gaped with crumbled edges in the caisteal's wall. It looked like a crooked-toothed maw laughing at Lord Ciarán, who had put the castellan and his stone masons to work immediately, shouting that he would have his caisteal fit for habitation.

Well, he need not hurry them. Lord Ciarán would surely act on the news Bram would now bring him.

That was after he had finished the vindictive tirade he would spit in Bram's face.

Bram grunted and walked below the portcullis, raised beneath a gently arching gateway. The stone pavement was wet and slippery, and he steadied himself with a hand against the stone wall more than once on his journey. He entered the keep and climbed the staircase to the hall, where a fire burned brightly, heating the large room, and drying the clothing of the leaders of Lord Ciarán's warbands. Padded tunics draped over the seating by the hearth while boys dried and waxed leather armour. All weapons remained at the warriors' sides.

Lord Kyle sat by the large hearth, animated and eyes aglow.

"What a grand battle. The cannon is such a magnificent device." Lord Kyle spoke in his usual loud tones into the ear of the Callaghan warrior lord, who rolled his eyes, then stared into his wine cup.

Lord Lorain sat closest to the fire, huddled in a high-backed chair, and looking small. He held a cup in both hands and stared into the flames. The one disgraced, his eager battle plans the cause of the damage. That the man still breathed was a testament to his usefulness to Lord Ciarán. Next to him, Mhàiri Duisdale sat wearing a simple shirt over her leather breeches, her hair a halo of russet set aglow by the light of the flame.

Bram swallowed. He had no time for such notions. No energies for the physical delights a man and woman can share. Survival was now his one goal.

"Mage." Lord Ciarán sat by the solid table and took a draught from the bronze goblet he held, then set his glare on him. "I know you, boy. What is wrong?"

Bram stepped up to him, keeping just shy of two sword lengths from the lord and his warriors.

"We were discovered, Lord Ciarán. Findlay and I will no longer communicate."

"Tell me not that Findlay has turned tail and exposed us all." He thunked the goblet on the table.

"No, lord. The daughter of the àrd rìgh, newly arrived with Lord Lùthas, has the powers of a mage and spied on us."

Ciarán rose from his chair, mouth part open. He closed it slowly, his eyes narrowing.

Lord Kyle stood. "My brother's... my *niece* is a mage?" he squeaked.

Ciarán's narrowed eyes landed on Bram.

"She is untrained but has enough of the gift to discern our methods." Bram resisted the urge to shuffle his feet under Lord Ciarán's stare.

"A trifling child," Ciarán scoffed. "A gnat for you to swat."

"They detained Findlay and removed the dog to the kennels."

"But you can still spy." Ciarán's words were sharp.

"No, lord. All I see are other hounds. I doubt MacEnoicht would allow the dog to remain with humans."

"They will question Findlay." Ciarán released a low growl. "He will tell all. That Other Worlder is weak. I trust not his allegiances. We shall leave immediately. MacEnoicht will know I have my caisteal returned to me and he will head for us."

"Nae, he planned to return to The Keep and regroup with Lord Leuchars and the Dál Gaedhle war host he prepares."

Ciarán leaned closer, and Bram pressed his feet to the floor. A flicker of cool trickled through him as he tensed for the onslaught, but he would not let *that* face intimidate him.

"Then we shall ride and cut him off." Ciarán turned to his warriors, his tone tempered and level. "Gather your warbands. We ride as soon as possible. No! We ride now."

Callaghan bolted out of his chair and Lord Lorain grabbed a damp padded tunic and dressed hurriedly. Other warriors scurried to their armour and weapons.

Ciarán tapped his boot against the floor. "We must block the MacEnoicht pup from his main army." He spun back to Bram.

Oh, here it comes.

"Order your mages to deliver the message to their lairds. I will have more warbands come across through the mountains, out of sight of the *high king*"— Ciarán rocked his head in mockery— "and meet us just south of here." He stood tall, mouth drawing in a leer.

His hands rested on his belt, and he seemed in total control.

No thrashing for me, then?

"We shall push him east, away from home, allies, armies, and supplies," he continued. "Then we shall squeeze him to my Mòr Cath Làraich, the battle place of *my* choosing. There we will see and know who is truly king."

THIRTY-EIGHT

The elements of the universe—air, water, fire, stone, vegetation—hold power within themselves but more so, and of greater import to the mage, they are the conduit through which their magic will flow. Of the origins of the source, the choice belongs to the mage. This choice determines the power, service, life course and, aye, the very toll of magic upon the mage.

MAGE MASTER FÀISTINNAECH
(3310-3380 POST DRAGON WARS)

Eastern Clanlands of Dál Gallain
Caisteal Monsae

I walked with my grandfather through the trees.

My grandfather.

I'd never been close to grandparents. Dad's mother had died when I was young, and his father lived in Bournemouth. For some reason, that was a long way to travel from Oxford, according to Dad. More like he didn't get on with him. I'd overheard plenty of tense phone conversations.

A soft rain fell, pattering the fresh spring leaves high in the canopy with a gentle drumming. The tree trunks were close, and we walked on leaf litter toward the centre of the beech forest that grew to the right of Caisteal Monsae. A heavy raindrop hit my head, sending a cool trickle across my scalp. I followed behind Eifion—Mage Eifion, who was about to give me a lesson in *seeing*. I couldn't stop myself from grinning, and a buzz greater than I'd experienced in any sword fight ran from my neck right down to my fingertips.

"We have been gifted with an important task. Whether or not the leader you serve is aware you are a mage, your counsel and your magic are invaluable to them." He stopped at a tree and placed his hand on the trunk, smoothing his fingers over the bark with an affectionate stroke.

I placed my hand next to his, the grey bark cool and smooth against my palm.

"Your father's father, the previous àrd rìgh, Donnach MacEnoicht, knew not I was a mage." Eifion let out a deep sigh. "There have been millennia of prejudice against us."

"I know, Grandfather." I shook my head gently. "Bàn."

"Ah, but you are changing that for him." He smiled proudly. "Although there remains more distrust that he must shed." He returned his attention to the tree. "And the current àrd rìgh, your father, is brave enough to trust my gift for his purposes." He smiled down at me. "And yours, my granddaughter. Together, we shall *see* where our enemy is. We shall look far." He placed his hand over mine. "Once there, in the place in between, you will hold your spirit close to mine and not let go. I will *see*. You remain silent and watch. Do you understand?"

I nodded.

Closing my eyes, I *felt* the tree extending finger-like branches to me, with the perfume of fresh sap surrounding me. I saw myself, just like I had in the walled garden. Eifion stood beside me, his hand warm over mine. I could still feel his touch, even though I looked down on *us*.

A movement caught the corner of my vision, my *spirit vision*. It was Eifion, but young. Wow, so much younger. Dark hair, not a wrinkle. What a handsome guy!

He smiled and looked around, encouraging me to do the same.

The trees were all connected with golden threads of light running between them.

Eifion's spirit nudged me, inviting me to look up. So I did.

The sky looked different. Not the grey, rain-filled day. Not blue.

Bright. Shining bright.

I looked at Eifion's spirit form. He nodded, smiling.

The Light.

I gazed upward at it, stilled by its peacefulness.

Stay close.

Eifion moved, drawing me up with him, and we reached the treetops where we could see everything. It looked like Google Maps on satellite setting. He pointed to my left. Far in that distance, sat a big castle on a high rock.

The Keep. The caisteal of the Àrd Rìgh. Eifion's spirit spoke to me again, even though my ears didn't hear him.

Further past that, were mountains and lochs, and down to the left, the ocean and a squat, round tower. *Craegrubha Broch. The fortress of your father's clanlands.*

Eifion pointed north, where a thick mist sat around a loch with a castle on a small island.

Caisteal Gallawain. The lands of your grandmother's clan.

He then drew my attention to our right, the east of the land.

A darkness hovered. Thick darkness like I'd seen before. I sensed my body shuddering against the tree, and Eifion's physical hand clasp tighter over mine.

He drew us down and squeezed my hand. I jolted back into my body, my shoulders and feet thumping down, like I'd landed from a great height. Eifion looked intently at me.

"Why is it clear that way"—I pointed to my left— "but there's that darkness to our right?"

"Your father's lands are to our left in the west. Ciarán's mages cover the lands to the east. Did you also notice the thick darkness north of us?"

I nodded.

"It is Caisteal Gallawain. Ciarán's army is sure to be there for the man, according to the conversation you overheard between Findlay and his dog, has regained the Gallawain clan home. We cannot *see* any movements, nor discern the intentions of any who reside there."

"Why?"

"A strong mage covers him."

I swallowed. "The one I heard speaking through the dog."

"Aye." His voice was grave.

"Grandfather?" I couldn't help the tentative echo in my voice.

"Yes, child?"

"You are so young and handsome... in your spirit." I'd better not offend him.

Eifion chuckled, but said no more.

We walked out of the beech forest and beneath the wide-spreading branches of a lone oak tree, my feet crunching dry acorns. Clusters of new acorns, small and green, hung between the leaves. Eifion reached up and picked a cluster and spread it out in his palm, the lines about his eyes softening.

"The potential life of a whole great tree lives in each small seed." He passed the young acorns to me. "A vessel of power. Keep some natural life on you always, my granddaughter."

I nodded, then tucked the small nutty twig in the pocket of my breeches.

Eifion clasped my hand with his own. "Magic costs the mage, whether the magic be from good or evil." He glanced at my hair. Silver threads wove through my plait nestling at my neck and falling over my chest. "It will always exact its price. It *will* have the final say. The stronger the magic, the greater the toll on body, mind and spirit." He leaned closer. "Never forget this truth."

Arlan mounted Mengus, the stirrup leathers creaking. Eifion and Rhynne had swiftly returned from their *seeing*, reporting to him their blindness to Gallawain's movements. But a thick blackness gave Eifion a certainty of Ciarán's army's presence at the clan land caisteal of Mother's family.

Arlan ground his teeth.

"The messengers ye sent to Leuchars will barely be a third of the way to The Keep, Arlan." Bàn swung into the saddle of the massive grey. "Lord Leuchars will need time to gather arms, then journey to Caisteal Gallawain with the war host."

"They may arrive at the same time as we do, if we tarry not. We have a greater distance to cover." Arlan roved his gaze over the four warbands preparing to mount, and the wagons of supplies. "We must survey the lie of the land ahead of us with regards to Gallawain's warbands and those loyal to him."

Och, the beasts of burden and carts will make it a slow journey.

"These wagons will delay us," he said to Bàn, then called to Muir, who hastened to his side. "Order my warband and one other to load rations in saddlebags and ride ahead with us. Tell the battle chiefs of the other bands that they and their warriors are to travel with the supplies, keeping as close as possible. We will join them after our reconnaissance of Gallawain's warbands." He nodded to Muir, who hurried off, then turned to Bàn. "Two war bands will suffice for our spying. I wish to see for myself how Gallawain has fared from the taking of Caisteal Gallawain."

It had been two days' hard ride and now the border forts ran to Arlan's left. Drayce flew low over the newly pointed stonework of the closest tower. Arlan released a satisfied grunt. The clan lords had taken seriously their responsibility for repairing and manning the forts and walls near their caisteals.

In the distance and to his right, crumbled dwellings sat in clumps along the undulating landscape. He'd ridden his warriors by fields scarcely planted and many lying fallow. He recalled Bàn's recent description of Clachan Beag after Gallawain's warriors had finished with it. Arlan ordered the warbands to bypass villages. He'd prefer to not instil fear in the surviving inhabitants, fear not only due to Drayce. Two warbands of fully armed warriors on war horses would most likely be more than these people could take.

Nor did his warband carry enough supplies to meet the need of these poor folk. His warband had only enough for the rest of their journey north now that purchasing from the villages as they passed was not possible without leaving the locals even more impoverished.

He shook his head. That man Gallawain was *not* good for this country!

Arlan had sent scouts ahead. They'd returned regularly over the past two days with reports of no sign of enemy warbands.

All the journey so far, Rhiannon had ridden behind himself and Bàn, with Rhynne beside her. She'd given pointers on riding throughout the days, Rhynne still acquiring the knack.

He skewed his mouth to the side. He should be thankful. It was the only skill George had omitted from her education.

Eifion rode just behind the women. Arlan shook his head. The old man was determined. And faithful. A stalwart adviser to Father, and now to himself as high king in his time of dire need. Nae, not just an *adviser*. He'd placed a *protection* on the group and maintained it hid them from Gallawain's mage. He need not be here. But he was. And oh, how thankful Arlan was for his loyalty, his belief in Arlan himself and all he wished to achieve, and—dare he think it—for his magic.

Arlan's heart glowed. Such dedication and commitment surrounded him.

A smile tugged the corners of his mouth. Eifion and Rhynne had bonded. He would show her magic the right way. She brought joy to Eifion. He had seen it in Eifion's expression.

It was grand to have his girl with him. She'd hesitated not a jot at accompanying them in the reconnaissance of Gallawain's position and warband. He let his smile form fully. She was his daughter. Brave, bold, with an enquiring and keen mind.

Och, I have missed so much of her life.

He pushed down the hurt. He would make the most of being in her life *now*.

She would insist on fighting if required… He was still uncertain if he should place her in the vanguard when the battle arose.

Arlan sighed. It was a decision for another day.

Travelling north, a misty rain had fallen on them. Mengus shook his mane, spraying Arlan with wet-horse scented droplets. He cast his gaze around at his two warbands. Douglas, Angus, and the rest of his own personal troop formed part of his larger warband and rode close behind with rain-soaked hair and cloaks damp, but faces set in determination.

Muir had chosen the stronger of the other warbands to join them. Sent from clan lands by the coast next to Arlan's own MacEnoicht lands, the sea winds had hardened these warriors. A doughty one led them, looking more like he belonged with sail ropes and a rudder in his hands. Arlan had seen him fight, and he kept his warriors in line.

Pounding horses' hooves brought Arlan to face ahead. Two scouts galloped their lathered horses toward him, lashing reins on either side of their tired mounts' necks.

"Ho!" They pulled them up sharp. The older of the two spun his horse to walk beside Mengus. The gelding panted and coughed.

"Lord Arlan, my high king." The young scout bowed from the neck. "Warbands ride toward us." He took a breath, then swallowed.

"From Caisteal Gallawain?" Arlan gripped his reins tighter.

"Aye. We rode the first of the peaks as the mountains begin their rise and travel through to Dál Gaedhle."

"Ye can see for miles there, lord," the other scout interjected.

"There are five warbands, or so it seems, lord," the younger added.

"Five?" Bàn's stern voice held an edge, with plans flying through his mind, no doubt.

"Aye. About a hundred strong each." The young scout wiped his brow.

His companion kicked his horse closer. "Yet two more warbands, lord, or so we estimate, are making their way across the mountains."

"The back way." Bàn spoke in earnest. "Rhynne and I came part of this way from north Dál Gallain. It's hidden from us in Dál Gaedhle, and I doubt Monsae could see it also."

"Aye, lord." The scout nodded. "They are yet a ways off. It is possible they head towards these other warbands we spied."

Bàn rubbed his upper lip. "It is most probable they will join them."

Arlan's gut stirred. "Send me fresh scouts. Report more regularly."

The two scouts nodded, then rode to their companions in the warband, and two more on light swift horses set off ahead.

Arlan twisted in the saddle, shouting to Muir. "Get me a fresh messenger to send word to Monsae. I need my friend and sister in all things war. Her man, Lord Vygeas, will come to our aid once he knows of our need. And order the rest of my warband trailing us with supplies to hasten." He twisted back to Bàn. "We continue north with our reconnaissance, trusting our war chief, army and cannon to make their way to Gallawain lands as requested. Once we determine our enemy's true strength, we will plan the best attack."

THIRTY-NINE

There are the powers of magic, the methods of magic, and the inexplicable magic of the natural world. This alone fills my soul with the greatest wonder and awe.

CONTEMPLATIONS OF A TRAVELLER
GRAND MASTER LLEW
(POST DRAGON WARS 6000-CURRENT)

Eastern Clanlands of Dál Gallain

Tightness spasmed along Rhiannon's inner thighs, and her seat hurt just as much. In front of her, Arlan rode Mengus with Bàn beside him, both scanning the path ahead, brows dipping. Rhiannon twisted in the saddle, a twinge shooting down her right leg. Rhynne rode behind her, slumped on the gelding, and her forehead crinkling after another full day riding.

"Anything?" she asked Eifion, who rode beside Rhynne, grimacing and shifting in his position in the saddle.

"Nae, daughter." Eifion held a bunch of acorns. "A blank, dark mist covers the entire land ahead of us."

His reports had grown fewer while the landscape around Rhiannon had slowly changed to a deeply undulating grassland.

There had been no sign of Ciarán's warband on any horizon. The scouts returned with regular reports to Arlan, whose shoulders grew stiffer with each one. He had sent yet another pair of scouts ahead on fresher mounts.

The land beside Rhiannon dipped and rose. Smooth, treeless mounds of green became peaks the further north they went. And the rain grew heavier, soddening the ground beneath the horses' hooves.

"I'd hate to be the guys at the back." Rhynne spoke Rhiannon's thoughts. "They must be riding through mud."

Rhiannon kept her eyes on Arlan. "It's been some time since a scout returned."

"Too long." Eifion's deep voice held a note of warning.

Drayce left the large hare she'd caught, lifted into the air, then screeched.

A rumble came from ahead. Or did it? Rhiannon strained to listen.

"So, we'll fight, won't we, Mum—"

Rhiannon held her hand up to Rhynne, who closed her mouth on her words.

"Ciarán's warband," Arlan growled, his jaw muscles bunching.

"But the scouts—" Rhynne began.

"Return not," Bàn answered her. "Killed, I fear."

"You and Rhynne get up to that high ground and stay there!" Arlan looked Rhiannon straight in the eye, then nodded to Eifion. "Eifion, ensure they do."

"But we'll fight," Rhynne protested.

"Not yet!" Arlan yelled, his face hardening. He pulled Mengus back to Rhiannon. "Forgive me. I've just got you *both* back to me." He leaned over and kissed Rhiannon, his contact with her lips firm and jostled by Mengus, but holding love. "Stay safe." His voice softened. "I need you."

He lifted his shield from his saddle and slid his arm into its straps, then pulled his sword from its baldric. It took all Rhiannon's willpower to stop herself from grabbing her own sword.

The thunder of hooves came over a rise about a football field's length away. Arlan's warriors tucked shields and drew weapons.

"Mum?" Rhynne's voice came beside her. "We can—"

"Aye, ye can, but you will not," Arlan ordered, the force of his words directed at their daughter.

Rhynne cringed, then looked at Bàn, who gripped his sword and faced her. He returned Rhynne's stare, his blond brows set over determined features softening a fraction.

"Now go!" Arlan roared.

Rhiannon nodded to Arlan, her insides swirling, and glared at Rhynne. She turned Bridie toward the shallow hill behind her, nudging the mare to a fast trot. She threw a look over her shoulder. Rhynne had followed. Their men kicked their war horses' flanks, and joined by their warriors, headed along the track toward the source of the ground's vibrations. Drayce circled above, her cries filling the air.

Rhiannon reached the top of the shallow hill and pulled the reins round, spinning her mount. Rhynne and Eifion joined her, their horses' ears flicking and eyes widening. Arlan's two warbands cantered past, all with swords drawn or spears ready, with the banner of the Àrd Rìgh fluttering in the lead. Rhiannon had to pull Bridie back from cantering after them. Rhynne's horse whinnied and pranced, and Rhiannon grabbed the bridle.

At times, the horses of the warriors marching past slipped along the muddy track, but they soon regained their footing. The warriors kept on their mounts, knees clenched tight to their war horses now their hands gripped readied weapons. They crested the hill and disappeared over it.

At a far rise beyond where Arlan's warriors rode into a dip and out of sight, a long line of horsemen, leather clad, spears raised, and swords glinting dully in the drizzle, crested that hill then also rode into the valley and were lost from Rhiannon's view.

"Damn!" Rhynne's voice exploded in Rhiannon's ear. "We can't see anything from here!"

"I shall find a tree," Eifion said.

"Good luck with that, Grandfather. The nearest tree is miles back!" Rhynne groaned and her horse curvetted beneath her, stretching Rhiannon's arm as she held its bridle. "Ooh. Stay!" Rhynne said, pulling on the reins.

Cries of warriors and clashing steel, and the thud of metal on shields, rang over the rise leading to the valley hidden from Rhiannon's view.

"We have to go fight!" Rhynne shouted, and Rhiannon held tighter to the bridle of Rhynne's gelding.

"No, Rhynne. Your father needs us here. Protect Eifion. There are enough warriors out there."

"No, there's not. Did you see how many came over that rise?" Rhynne's voice rose so high in pitch it almost disappeared.

Rhiannon breathed out through her nostrils. There *were* more than their own numbers. But she knew why Arlan wanted them to stay here. She'd not make that mistake again and think she understood more than him about how things go in this world.

"I really want to see what's going on!" Rhynne spoke through her teeth.

A clicking squeal rose above the clamour coming from the battlefield hidden in the dip. Drayce flew up above the mêlée, thrusted spear points just missing her.

"Oh! Drayce, be careful!" Rhynne shouted.

Rhiannon's breath gushed out. Thank heavens something had taken Rhynne's mind off fighting.

The dragon flew away from the battle and circled above them, then landed beside Rhynne's horse. It shied and bucked, knocking Rhynne out of the saddle and jarring Rhiannon's arm. The gelding bolted, tearing the reins from Rhiannon's grip.

"Are you okay, Rhynne?" Rhiannon slid off her own horse and handed Bridie's reins to Eifion.

"Mm. Yeah, I suppose so." Rhynne got up, rubbing her rump.

Drayce stood nearby, creeping closer, clicking softly. She came right next to Rhynne and rubbed her knobbly head against her, just like a cat would.

"She really likes you, Rhynne." Rhiannon brushed down Rhynne's breeches.

"She is concerned for your welfare," Eifion said from his horse.

"Mum, don't fuss." She nudged Rhiannon's hands away. "I'm okay. I'm a warrior and I've got more than a sore bottom from a fight in the past." She rolled her eyes.

Drayce smooched her again, and Rhynne spun to her.

"What?" She patted the dragon's neck. "You want me to?"

"To whom do you speak, Rhynne?" Eifion asked.

Rhynne didn't answer. Grinning, she placed her foot on the dragon's bent front leg, then clambered up onto her back. Drayce lifted her head and clicked a few times as Rhynne settled herself between Drayce's wings.

"Rhynne!" Rhiannon's cry collided with Eifion's.

The dragon lifted into the air and Rhynne faced the battlefield, not turning back at Rhiannon's shout.

"No!" Rhiannon's scream drained her lungs.

Drayce circled above the battle, gaining height. Enemy spears sailed in the dragon's direction but missed their mark as Drayce flew higher.

"Father, do something!" Rhiannon yelled.

Eifion sat staring up, mouth open. Rhiannon ran to him, grasped his sleeve, and shook it.

He blinked. "She appears to be well and... smiling."

"Eifion! Call Drayce down." She gripped tightly to his sleeve, her fingers cracking.

"Alas, I cannot." He kept his gaze upward, eyelids narrowing.

Rhiannon flung her head back, searching the sky for the beast. Drayce circled the battlefield and was gaining height. Agonised cries, grunts, shrieks of horses, and clanging weapons still came from the field hidden from her view. Drayce circled wider, becoming smaller the farther she flew from the battle.

"What if she falls? She's so high."

"Nae, daughter. The dragon will keep her safe."

"How can you be sure?" Rhiannon's breath came in short, sharp gasps. "That's my baby up there."

"Hush, my own child. She is safe. The dragon invited her to ride. No harm will come to Rhynne while Drayce lives."

"Drayce... *asked* her to ride?"

"Aye." Eifion gave a brief shake of his head, one side of his mouth lifting in a grin. "So it seems."

"Don't mages get into a dragon's mind to control them? Isn't that what you told me?"

"Aye. But this is not the case. No control here. I see no magic other than communication between a beast and a young woman."

"Has this happened before? In the Dragon Wars?"

"I know not." Eifion shook his head, his hand now shading his eyes. "Look. They circle back."

Drayce came from the east, flying lower, skimming the gentle mounds of hills in her return path. It wasn't long before Rhynne's form sharpened.

The dragon cried and swooped lower.

"It's hopeless. They're way outnumbered," Rhynne shouted from Drayce's back. "Warriors are dying. Pointless! There's a good escape route and a place to hide back that way." Rhynne pointed behind her. "You've gotta tell Arlan. Tell him to follow Drayce to safety." Her voice dragged in the wind as Drayce passed. She now turned to swoop again. "Did you get that?" Rhynne yelled at Rhiannon. "Tell my father!"

Drayce flew off, Rhynne still clutching her neck, and circled high above the noise of battle.

FORTY

Look up.

VISIONS AND SAYINGS OF THE BLIND LADY SAGE

Eastern Clanlands of Dál Gallain
The Battlefield

Bram's horse nickered, side stepping and tugging the reins in his hands, jolting his arms to his shoulders. It released a shrieking whinny.

"Control your mount, mage," Lord Ciarán spat, never taking his eyes off the battle.

Bram drew his horse into line beside the lord, surveying the battle from the crest of the hill that edged their side of this small shallow valley, all activity clearer now the rain had eased.

"You missed it, mage." Lord Ciarán slowly turned to Bram, eyes narrowing. "How so?"

Bram steeled his tone. "They travel now with a protection as though covered by a mage. Their warband's scouts gave away their presence."

"They told naught. Yet the scouts headed for us. So, *they* were aware." Lord Ciarán's voice came out a mere growl. "Despite you owning you are now blind, we shall see with our own eyes the strengths of MacEnoicht."

Arlan MacEnoicht had led his warriors, with Lord Lùthas by his side, right onto the battle ground and straight to Lord Ciarán's warriors. The high king's warband then rode ahead of him, forming a barrier of mounted warriors blocking him from the frontal attack. The field in front of Bram was a churning mass of striving warriors, clashing their weapons and cutting each other.

Hmm. They guarded him faithfully. Bram glanced out of the corner of his eye and snorted.

I doubt Ciarán's warriors would do the same.

The dragon that had flown above them initially now returned. A medium-sized beast but still small, only slightly larger than the biggest war horse on the field, for it was the youngling who had hatched last year, winning MacEnoicht his Quest. The graceful beast had a darkening hide. The last he saw it was at night, when waist high in a burn holding a portal open, his body numbing with cold. Bram grimaced. The cough he'd gained from that venture had lasted all the winter.

The dragon's deep red hide was now tinged with black, with a bright red to its belly and throat. A handsome dragon. With a woman on its back.

"By Cernunnos!" Ciarán's stallion nickered at his shout. "A woman rides it! Who is she?"

"She looks like Lord Arlan's daughter."

Ciarán *hmmed* and scratched his whiskered face. "Get inside that dragon, mage," he snapped. "That whelp on its back will be no bother to you."

"I cannot at present. I require my divination bowl." Bram's gut clenched. Ciarán wished for more than *dragon control*. The death of the young king fighting like a deamhan would be his next command.

Nae. Not again.

The murder of the young man's father, that great king and brave man, still pressed on his soul like the evil of every world. And the guilt of every single wrong. No matter what this lord beside him ordered, while Bram had any choice, he would never again harm a human while in charge of a beast. His hands clenched around the reins, nails digging pain deep into his palms.

"There is a burn over there." Lord Ciarán pointed to their right, where late afternoon sun angled silver on a sliver of flowing water. "Go jump in it."

"But I require quiet to concentrate. The battle rages. The cries of the dying are too—"

Ciarán's scowl and popping jaw stilled the words in Bram's throat.

Bram gritted his teeth and nudged his horse forward, skirting a clump of striving warriors. Animal grunts and the dull thuds of swords landing on leather armour rang in his ears. A war horse screeched and pawed the air, landing hooves with a *thunk* on a Dál Gaedhle warrior. Bram kicked his mount to a canter and reached the burn, leaving behind him churned earth and horseshoe shaped divots filling with blood. He jumped off his gelding, left the reins dangling, then stepped into the water. He strode into the middle of the shallow burn, the current tugging at his calves and cold clamping his knees. Then he let his soul soar.

Drayce angled, turning to sweep over the battlefield. The wind flew through my hair and my body tipped in unison with hers. I gripped tighter on the ridge of scales between her shoulders.

"Go near Arlan," I shouted, the wind ripping my voice from me.

Fhéin. A sensation like admiration came from Drayce and, somehow, I could hear her in my head, though she didn't make any noise.

My mouth pulled in a crooked grin. To Drayce, Arlan was fhéin.

Self.

She thought of him as part of her.

I gripped tighter with my knees as we flew closer to the fighting. Arlan wasn't in the middle of the field anymore. His warriors had pushed in front of him, and Bàn sat on the grey beside him. The old guy, Muir, slashed and stabbed while the big woman, Adele, bashed a warrior's face with her shield. A group of Ciarán's warriors had got past Adele and Muir and engaged with Angus and Morrigan. Another two now slipped along past them to Arlan and Bàn, who set to with their weapons.

Drayce flew closer and screeched, vibrating my eardrums. The warriors who Arlan and Bàn pelted, flinched and looked up, facing us. Bàn cut one down, and the one fighting Arlan ran away, slipping and skidding in the mud.

Rhiannon rode over the rise and into the valley. Arlan turned to her and shouted. Bàn stayed with his sword ready while Rhiannon spoke to Arlan, face tight and pointing behind her. Drayce lifted, and we circled the field again.

"Scare the enemy."

Drayce flew across the middle of the fighting and screeched her loudest. It turned into a roar. Warriors flattened their bodies into the mud as we flew over. I glanced to the side where an old guy on a horse watched from the small rise on the other side of this shallow valley.

It must've been Ciarán. He had an authoritative air about him. Or perhaps just arrogance. His hooded eyes locked on me.

Then the wind grew chill, and Drayce grunted. I faced forward, her long neck now in my view. Cold covered my hand, and a stench tinged the air that flew past me. Drayce shook her head, jolting her body and tossing me from side to side. Gripping tightly to the ridge of scales on her back with one hand, I moved my other hand along Drayce's neck as far forward as I could reach to pat her and calm her like I'd seen Bàn do to the grey. Icy air, like the cold of the sage hold's mountain, hung over my hand. Drayce screeched and twisted, leaning me to the side. My vision flashed past a burn with a guy in it. He wore a mage's robe.

I drew the cluster of acorns from my pocket and held them tight, then released my breath and let go.

I was there, riding beside *me* on Drayce. A darkness hovered over her, near the back of her head.

A darkness I'd seen before.

No!

I sought the power of growing things, the potential in the seeds I held. Pressing against the black clamping on Drayce's neck, I moved the power, holding my mouth tight in the effort.

The dark wouldn't budge.

Not Drayce! Not our awesome, perfect dragon. I could sense love and trust in her. She was a warrior for my father, too. From how she'd spoken of him to me, I'd sensed she'd even die for him if she had to.

The mage in that burn was *him* for sure—the powerful one.

I looked up, pushing against a sigh of defeat. *It's hopeless!*

The sky above glowed bright in my spirit's vision. *The Light!*
Please. Save our dragon.

The brightness flowed down in a rush, like a stream falling over a waterfall. It poured over me and Drayce. The dark disintegrated and the mage in the burn cried out. His cry was so loud it tore at my ears as I came back into my body. The warriors nearest the burn stopped fighting and turned to the mage who'd bent over and collapsed in the water.

The old warrior on the hill, Ciarán, shouted an order. Mounted Gallawain warriors kicked their horses' sides while those sloshing in the mud grabbed free horses and jumped on, then followed their friends in retreat.

"Chase them."

Drayce roared, directing it at the retreating warriors whose horses shied, shrieked, reared, then bolted. We flew over Ciarán's head. He glared at me. Holding his reins tight and lifting in the stirrups, he raised his sword. Drayce beat her wings and rose in the air, twisting away from the sword point, then turning sharply in mid-air to snap at the man from behind.

He turned in the saddle, thrusting his sword again. Drayce dodged her head, and the point slid by her neck. A stinging erupted on my left forearm.

I drew my weapon.

A grunt came from the battlefield. Spears flew from that direction. I twisted on Drayce as a glinting point skidded across my back along my leather armour.

FORTY-ONE

For the currency of loyalty is blood.

SAGE GLIOCAS
(2870-2962 POST DRAGON WARS)

Eastern Clanlands of Dál Gallain
The Battlefield

"It's slaughter if you stay," Rhiannon pleaded. "Rhynne has seen their numbers." Blood's metallic scent filtered into her nose, closely followed by the nostril-closing stench of faeces.

Mengus pawed the ground. Arlan and Bàn were mud and blood splattered, and a disembowelled horse lay on its side, kicking beside its silent, crumpled rider.

Drayce roared and the battlefield fell quiet in seconds. Ciarán yelled an order and his warriors scrambled off the field.

"They retreat," Bàn said.

"Aye, and so do we." Reluctance laced through Arlan's tone.

"Live to fight another day, Lord Arlan." Angus stepped up to them, his war horse whinnying and trotting behind him, the banner of the àrd rìgh draped over the saddle with the emblem of the black horse rampant folded in on itself.

Rhiannon sheathed her sword and held tight to her reins, clenching away the trembles from her hands, and searched the sky for Rhynne. Drayce flew over a lone rider on the far hill.

Ciarán! He was drawing his sword.

"Rhynne! No!" she cried.

Arlan spun in that direction.

"Rhynne's on Drayce?"

"Yes."

"No!" Bàn's cry wrenched Rhiannon's heart.

She turned to where he pointed. A bloodied warrior stood among the dead in the middle of the battlefield and flung a spear. It went right for Rhynne at the same time

Drayce dodged Ciarán's sword thrust. The spear glanced off Rhynne's back, then the warrior picked up another spear.

"Rhynne!" Bàn's cry joined Rhiannon's.

Rhiannon kicked Bridie to a gallop, slipping and stumbling across the churned battlefield, dodging corpses and warriors. Tears blurred her vision.

The spear flew as though in slow motion. It tore through Drayce's skin-stretched wing. She limped away in an erratic flight, with Rhynne dangling from her neck.

Rhiannon headed for Ciarán, blood boiling. The ground rumbled ahead of her, and leather-clad riders arrived, surrounding Ciarán with spear and sword points bristling outward.

He saw her then and grinned devilishly. With his warriors shielding him like a hedgehog's spiked hide, he turned and galloped off toward the higher hills.

Arlan rode to the spear thrower, who slipped through the muddied, churned earth and clambered over dead bodies to a glinting spear resting by a dead horse. Arlan reached this warrior from behind as she pulled the spear shaft from another dead warrior's grip. He swiped, severing her head from her body with one powerful stroke.

"We'll pursue, lord?" Adele, gripping her sword, was hard on his heels. Muir and Morrigan also.

"The enemy still outnumbers us, and we face certain death if we do," Muir said grimly. "But if ye wish it, lord, we will go."

"Nae, man, I need you all," Arlan growled. "We shall face the deamhan again, no doubt. How far behind are my other warbands and supplies?"

"I shall send a scout to see where they are, lord," Morrigan offered.

"Where are my daughter and my dragon?" Arlan asked.

"Lord Bàn reaches them now, lord," Muir said.

The ground rushed up to me—a green blur. "Drayce!" I thudded hard against packed dirt. My vision went blank.

Warm arms held me. Sweaty-man smell surrounded me. Hot breath blew into my face.

"Rhynne." Pain surged through Bàn's voice.

I opened my eyes; blue intensity peered into me.

"Och!" Bàn pressed his face against my cheek, his stubble grazing me.

"I'm okay, Bàn." My voice didn't even convince me.

"Ye are blooded."

"Oh, no, that's just here." I pointed to my left forearm. "I'm okay everywhere else." Easing away from him a little, I struggled to a sitting position.

"Why?" There was a hardness to his tone, like he was angry, but it held more. *Surprise or pride?*

"Drayce asked me," I answered. "She showed me where we can regroup. Ciarán won't find us there. He's run off, anyway."

"Ye rode a dragon, Rhynne," he said more firmly.

"So much easier than a horse. Where's Drayce?" I scampered out of his arms and headed to Drayce's clicking. She'd turned back, then landed nearby. "She got speared!"

I be well. Fhéin comes. I heard her again in my mind.

Horse tread thundered behind me, coming to a halt followed by the thud of boots on the turf. Arlan and Rhiannon dismounted, and Eifion rode toward me also.

"Rhynne," Arlan ground out. "Are ye hurt, lass?" His brow knotted and jaw bunched, and his vision roved over my body.

"I'm fine," I said. "But Drayce is injured."

Drayce, who'd been inching toward me, nudged my injured arm.

"Ciarán stabbed you?" Arlan spoke low.

"It's not that bad. I'm going to check Drayce." I ran my hands over her neck and back. She knelt on her forelegs, and I smoothed my hands all over her. Rhiannon joined me and encouraged Drayce to open her wing.

Rhiannon examined it. "Not this one. Look at her other wing."

I spread the one on my side, and Drayce whimpered. Blood smeared across the skin of the outstretched wing and a hole the size of a side plate gaped near her shoulder, the broken skin sitting shrivelled to one side of the tear.

"Her wing's torn," I said. "We should be able to stitch it together. Does anyone have sutures? Know how to do this?"

Bàn lifted my hand from Drayce, pointing out the wound on my arm that I'd received from Ciarán. "You require stitching, also," he said then put his arm around my shoulder and tucked me into his side.

Eifion's horse nickered as it neared the dragon. "We are too far from the sage hold of the healers," Eifion said.

"I watched closely when they sewed you up, Arlan," Rhiannon said. "I could try."

"When we're in the safe place Drayce showed me." I tore a piece of my tunic and wrapped it around my cut arm.

"Drayce *showed* you?" Arlan asked.

Drayce hobbled awkwardly to be closer to Arlan, then rested her head against his chest armour, nudging her nose into his neck. He wrapped his arms around her head and leaned his cheek on her nose. "We shall repair your wing, my friend." He spoke softly, like she was his favourite pet.

"She loves you like herself," I said.

"Aye, she's a grand animal." He patted her neck, then rubbed his hand down her scaly back as far as he could reach.

"She sees you as part of her. She calls you *self*."

Arlan's hand froze on the dragon's neck. "Calls me?"

My lips tugged wide in a grin. "Yes, Father, your dragon speaks to me."

Arlan gazed down at Drayce, who then lifted her head and blinked at him, her reptilian second-lids jumping.

"She's so cute when she does that," I said.

Arlan shook his head, like he could hardly believe it, then patted Drayce.

"We must go to this valley ye say is safe until the arrival of our warband that follows us." He turned to Angus, who'd ridden up behind us. "Gather our wounded and strip the enemy dead. Who are our losses?"

"The warband from the coast, lord. They have lost many." Angus' brows drew together, and his voice wavered. "Their warrior leader among them."

Arlan looked to the ground at his feet, his shoulders lifting in a deep intake of air.

Damn. They were great guys. I looked around. Everyone's expression said the same.

"I honour their faithfulness, and we will make a quick burial here. So, we are down to one effective warband only until our other warbands arrive." He sighed deeply. "Take us to this valley, Rhynne. There we will tend our wounded and regroup."

FORTY-TWO

— • —

Give me thoughts beyond my own.

WARRIOR SAGE TAPAÌDH
(4009-4059 POST DRAGON WARS)

Eastern Clanlands of Dál Gallain
The Valley of Safety

Lookouts watched on either ridge. Arlan placed his hands on his belt as he stood with the sentries at the opening of the steep-sided, rocky valley.

"Those who spy above report the same, Lord Arlan," the warrior on sentry duty said. He was one of the surviving warriors from the coastal warband. "Gallawain warriors hover nearby to the north." He held a spear in his bandaged hand.

"I pray they are unaware of our presence in this hidden glen and wonder where we have fled." Arlan turned and wandered back to the fire. He had not spied the opening to this dusty valley until Rhynne, riding an injured Drayce, had hovered over the valley's mouth.

Arlan's remaining warriors settled down for the night. Campfires dotted a flickering glow through the widest section of this long, narrow valley. The cool night air wafted against Arlan's face. Their fires were small, not only due to the modest amount of charcoal they'd brought, but smoke would be a beacon to their presence. The place was secluded, that was for certain, but they had to be careful. He'd sent scouts further along into the gorge when the sun lowered in the sky, and they had confirmed this.

Arlan wandered back to his campfire where Rhiannon had sewed Rhynne's arm. Though small, the slice had needed closing. Both his women now attended the dragon's wing by the light of the fire. The task done, Drayce lay near the fire, clicking herself to sleep. Rhynne helped Rhiannon clear up, then sat with Arlan by the fire, their faces glowing orange in the lambent light of the coals. Bàn sat between himself and Rhynne, leaning over to her and placing a kiss on her lips.

A chuckle rose in Arlan's throat. So strange to see his sword-brother in love with his own grown daughter. It was... what did Rhiannon say?

222

Weird.

Eifion came through the shadows and sat on the far log, next to Rhiannon.

"Well, I'm knackered." Rhynne stood, pressing her bandaged arm. "Good night, all." She wandered over to Drayce and lay down, leaning against the dragon as a pillow. She closed her eyes and gentle snoring soon followed.

"Aye, an eventful day." Eifion gazed into the fire.

"Rhynne told me that tomorrow she'd fly Drayce to see where Ciarán is." Rhiannon wrapped her arms around her waist.

Arlan suppressed his instinct to shout *no,* and placed his gaze on Eifion, meeting his eyes.

"I am blind. Magic blocks my *seeing*." Eifion nodded. "Whereas our dragon rider can see as with the eye of a bird."

"And she may go further afield to see where Leuchars and your army are, Arlan." Bàn spoke with certainty in Arlan's ear.

"Ye are all well with Rhynne risking her life on the back of a flying beast?"

"Yes, even though I'd never forgive myself if she was hurt because of it." Rhiannon continued her self-hug.

"She is a gift to us." Eifion patted Rhiannon's knee.

"A strategic gift," Bàn said. "And willing to be of service to you, her father and àrd rìgh."

"What if we lost her"—Arlan pushed against the tightness in his chest— "falling from Drayce or impaled by spear or arrow?"

Bàn's dimple pitted with a grimace. "Either that or killed in a sword battle, for she will fight for you, Arlan. As we all will." His voice gentled. "I love her and could not bear to lose her to such, but I need not tell you we all risk much."

Rhiannon rose, stepped over to Arlan and sat close. He wrapped his arm around her, tugging her to his side.

"And we're all in this with our *all*," she whispered into his ear.

Arlan paced. Rhynne had left in the early dawn, and he'd tracked the sun's passage across the sky till it now neared the opposite horizon—what he could see of it above the high granite ridges of their secluded valley. Thank *Tobraichean na beatha* for this hiding place.

A sentry ran to him. "Lord, your daughter nears."

Everyone looked up. Drayce circled, then glided to land close to the entrance, her wing dripping blood. Rhynne slid off the dragon as Arlan reached her.

"Were ye attacked?" Bàn's foot tread thudded behind him.

"No. Her wound has reopened." Rhynne's gaze went past them both. "Mum, we'll need to sew her again."

"How long has she been like that?" Rhiannon joined Arlan standing beside Drayce.

Arlan reached out and patted Drayce's cool skin. She clicked, nudging his hand.

"Since about mid-afternoon," Rhynne replied. "She refused to turn back until we'd looked closer at Monsae."

"Monsae?" Arlan's neck cooled. "Ye must report all, Rhynne."

Rhynne brushed her hair from her eyes, her shoulders slack with fatigue. "It's not good, Father. But I'd kill for a drink first."

Bàn put his arm around her waist and guided her to the fire circle, where Morrigan waited with a wineskin. Rhynne took a long draught.

"I still can't get over how you all just drink..." She looked around at him, Bàn, Rhiannon, and Eifion. "Never mind."

"Sit, Rhynne." Arlan pointed to a log. "Tell your father-king and his warband all."

Rhynne nodded. "First, there are Gallawain warriors not far from the entrance to this glen, but north."

Arlan grunted.

"They didn't see me," she said and turned to him. "I'm pretty sure they have no idea we are here, or that this gorge even exists."

The tightness in Arlan's shoulders eased a touch. "We would have been attacked by now if they were aware."

"They know about our wagons. I flew low and behind hills until I found the supplies and the other warbands that followed us. A large group of Gallawain warriors were waiting for them."

"Och no!"

Those who gathered by the fire joined their exclamations of dismay to his.

Rhynne held up her hand. "I warned them, but it's too far for us to go and help them. We're too late anyway. Wait for it. It gets worse. Then we went north to where Gallawain's five warbands are." She paused as all grunted. "Plus, more coming through that mountain range." She took another swig.

"How many?" Arlan asked.

Rhynne swallowed, her eyes darting back and forth, as though she counted.

"Ah, it's hard to tell. They were all higgledy-piggledy in the mountains. Three warbands worth?" Her voice rose in question. "Then I thought I'd see where your army from The Keep was up to."

"Lord Leuchars, the war chief," Arlan said.

Rhynne nodded, a grim smile appearing on her lips. "We circled round the mountains where there's an island in the middle of a loch with a castle on it. I stayed close to the mountain and hopefully out of their view. But to the west of that a wee bit, there's been a battle, by the looks of it."

Arlan's guts clenched.

"Warriors who'd come from The Keep's direction were edging back," Rhynne continued, "and others who I can only assume are Gallawain's warriors, were beating them with cannons. There were bodies everywhere. It didn't look good."

Arlan closed his eyes and dropped his head into his hands. Silence surrounded him.

"We must go to their aid," Bàn urged.

"No, you can't," Rhynne said firmly. "There are too many. And didn't you hear me? They've got *cannons*!"

"Why did Leuchars not engage with our cannons?" Arlan lifted his head.

"Maybe they were surprised, like we were," Rhiannon said.

"Or the land was too sodden to traverse with heavy cannon, more likely," Eifion offered.

"And this other army probably has more." Rhynne widened her eyes. "We didn't go too close. Didn't want to go head-to-head, dragon to cannonball."

"So, there is more?" Bàn asked.

"Yeah, we did a circle. A wide circle." Rhynne sighed, annoyance wove through it. "This place is beautiful. Why on earth is that creep trying to wreck it?"

"Good question," Rhiannon said.

"Go on please, daughter." Arlan tried to keep the strain from his tone.

"From the tower in the east that you showed me." Rhynne looked at Eifion.

"Ciarán's tower and home base," Eifion said.

"There's a lot of warriors heading to Caisteal Monsae." She dropped the hand she'd been gesturing with. "How many warriors does Gallawain have?"

"Too many, it seems." Bàn huffed.

"Monsae," Arlan growled. "Gallawain wishes to attack our allies and regain what he lost. A reality this time. Nae ruse."

"So, my àrd rìgh." Rhynne's tone took on respect. "From what we saw, the only clear way for us is east, along this valley." She pointed behind her to where his warrior scouts were yet to explore. "We are way too small to fight it out that way." She pointed to the valley entrance, then her gaze spun to Bàn. "This narrow valley ends not far from that river in Dál Gallain we crossed. Twice."

"The Bàn-rìghinn," Bàn said.

"This narrow valley is really long though," Rhynne went on, "but once we're out of it, maybe we could go to the sage hold in the mountains and get some help. I'm sure Reece would get a warband together for us."

"We may be able to then double back, keeping clear of Gallawain warbands, and rescue our warbands with our wagons of supplies. Then aid our friends at Monsae and, with them, head to assist Leuchars to force Gallawain from the caisteal and lands he thinks are his," Bàn said.

"I need more warriors." Arlan ground his teeth. "This high king will be a leader of a roving diminished warband until I do." Arlan stood, then turned from his family.

He strode away from the campfire, the weight of their stares boring into his back. They wouldn't accuse, only look to him for orders. No footsteps followed, and the tightness between his shoulder blades slowly eased as he headed to the base of a steep rock face.

He required time to think.

For at this moment, he was short of a plan that even vaguely looked like succeeding. Ciarán had blocked him, and the only way of survival seemed to be to run.

Run!

He snorted, then strode to a quiet corner of the valley where the edge of the camp came to a granite cliff wall. He tilted his head back, a deep unbroken blue sky canopied above him. The sun had set, the moon not yet out, and stars just awakening.

Peaceful. When his world and his options were far from such.

What of Leuchars? A wise and skilled war leader, he would regroup and reinforce defences, then prepare for another attempt on Caisteal Gallawain. And Vygeas' own inbuilt early warning system would have him ready to defend Caisteal Monsae.

Aye, it wasn't as bad as it seemed.

Perhaps.

But the enemy barred the way home, the way to their wagons, supplies and other warbands. Also, to allies in Monsae. The Gallawain army outnumbered them. His own had only survived because Ciarán had called most of his warriors to retreat, except for those who searched for them nearby. That would be strategy, and his cousin would have more planned.

More attacks. More warriors. More weapons to direct at himself.

My warband is now small in number. And here we hide.

He closed his eyes, his skin cooling.

I have failed them.

What sort of king was he?

How would he ensure the victory of his warband—nae, the survival of his warriors and his family who rode with him?

It seemed the same as the beach at Craegrubha, where the surf would pound him to the shore, and leave him tasting sand while he waited for the next breaker to crash into his back.

He opened his eyes to a sky of deep navy blue.

"Ye wished me to be a warrior king." He choked out a laugh. "I need warriors to do that."

The breeze stirred, tickling his face with his loose strands of hair. It coaxed a memory and whispered to him.

You'll hear it in the wind. The words spoken to him at his kingmaking flew back to him.

The breeze grew stronger, jostling Arlan. Behind him, his people by the campfires stirred. Rhiannon and Rhynne's voices rose, and Bàn gave orders to weigh down loose objects. The horses side stepped and whinnied.

Heat filled Arlan's left forearm. He turned the underside to face him, then his mouth dropped open. The triskelion glowed golden amongst the blue inked symbols.

Just as it had at his kingmaking.

The wind blew stronger, whistling as it funnelled down the narrow glen, away from the entrance and toward the deep beyond, as if giving him directions.

"You'll hear it on the wind!"

Arlan spun and raced to the campsite. Rhiannon stared at him. Rhynne patted Drayce, who tucked her injured wing into her side and fought the wind's lift. Bàn stopped shouting orders and stood in front of him, expectant. Eifion sat still on the log seat, a smile curving his lips.

"Be ready to leave in the morning," Arlan announced. "We go to find... in truth, I know not what, but we follow this valley to wherever it leads. The wind will guide us."

FORTY-THREE

POETRY OF THE WARRIOR
WARRIOR SAGE TAPAÌDH
(4009-4059 POST DRAGON WARS)

Eastern Clanlands of Dál Gallain
The Valley of Safety

Drayce landed, her wing beats stirring up the dirt of the bare glen. Arlan coughed away the dry, choking grit and shielded his eyes from the dust. His warriors' horses whinnied and side-stepped around him, most still unused to a dragon so close. Arlan patted Mengus' neck, his war horse emitting a soft nicker.

Aye, all his warband's mounts must learn to be calm, like his own stallion. His dragon was now a weapon of war, even if only as a means of reconnaissance.

Rhynne slid from the beast like water down a graceful fall. His chest swelled with a gentle warmth he could only own as pride. *His* daughter rode and communicated with *his* dragon.

What a wonder.

And a gift.

"Gallawain's warriors camp not far behind us. That's why I headed out the back way so they wouldn't see where I came from and give away our hiding place. They man the forts where a road crosses the border." Rhynne caught hold of the wineskin Bàn offered her and took a swig. "It's all quiet at the caisteal on the loch."

"Aye, I wager Ciarán Gallawain concentrates his efforts on finding you, Arlan," Eifion said. "Knowing how the man detests you. He feels he has you cornered, and like a ferret in a rabbit warren, he will not desist until he has you."

"I believe Eifion," Bàn said. "Gallawain is blocking all ways to home and allies. Remember Findlay said Gallawain has plans for you. We must slip from his grasp. This valley will be the way. Then we can enlist help."

228

"Once we are through this valley, we will be so far east there will be no allies," Arlan said.

Silence surrounded Arlan for a moment, his companions' heads bowed in thought.

"There's something going on at The Keep." Rhynne broke the quiet. "They're loading carts, and it looks like they've got cannons on them. But I wasn't sure. I couldn't land or even get close enough to have a good look. They've got really big bows and arrows."

"Hunting bows." Bàn slid his gaze to Arlan. "They know not of Rhynne and that she rides your beast. It's not safe for her to approach closer."

"It sure isn't," Rhynne said. "I wasn't going to get speared by one of those arrows."

"Dragon's teeth!" Arlan ran his fingers through his hair. "Send another messenger," he said to Muir. "One crafty enough to find a gap in Gallawain's defences and get through to Leuchars to inform him of Rhynne and tell that our dragon is darker and larger than when he last saw her. More like a flying war horse herself. A huge one. Inform Leuchars he is to leave a warband to the west of Gallawain lands, then to come to *us* by whatever means with the cannon, for I pray that is what he loads on these carts. Gallawain is sure to enlist dragons." He faced Rhynne. "And our friend and ally, Vygeas?"

"A Gallawain warband is still blocking Monsae, though there wasn't any action that I could see." Rhynne shrugged.

Bàn lifted a finger. "From the Monsae battlements ye can see for miles. Vygeas is aware of our situation, I'm certain. By sea one can get to lands in the east and to the port past the mouth of the River Bàn-rìghinn."

"Do you think Leuchars will consider transporting army and cannon by sea?" Eifion asked.

"He may." Arlan cocked his head. "But we have had naught to do with Dál Gallain and her ports are not allied with us. Although we could secretly land ashore elsewhere." He shrugged. "I know not where. Inform our messenger we advise Leuchars to investigate the possibility," he ordered Muir, who then strode off to his task.

"But...?" Rhynne's mouth skewed to the side. "Surely that'd take longer than we have before..."

"We shall try." Arlan rested his hand on Rhynne's shoulder. "If the least Gallawain arms himself with is cannon... then we must as well."

"Hmm. Dad—George—knows a lot about cannons." Rhynne blinked away the lines that had formed beside her eyes. "The glen that way"—she pointed in the direction they would head— "opens up to a green valley. This dusty part of the valley stops just around the corner."

"We must go." Arlan nodded his order to all who had now mounted ready.

"I think I'll ride a horse." Reluctance edged Rhynne's tone. "Drayce needs a rest from my weight. I've probably pushed her too far already today."

"That's wise," Rhiannon said from her mount. "We don't want her wound splitting open again."

"Ride with me, Rhynne." Bàn reached down to her then lifted her up behind him on the grey horse.

Arlan kicked Mengus to a trot and led his warband out of the dusty glen into a narrow steep-sided cutting where tufts of grass grew from cracks in the granite. The ground-cover of wiry heather thickened as they journeyed along. The cutting floor was less rocky here and their mounts' *clip clop* echoed off the high grey walls either side. Drayce flew close overhead.

Arlan passed another bend, then the valley opened up a little. Its sides remained steep, but grass lined their path in a verdant green. Their horses' hoof tread now sounded a soft *clumping*, and emitted the scent of freshly crushed grass. Riders allowed their mounts to graze, for all saddlebags were empty of feed. The sky above turned a brilliant blue in the midmorning sun. Drayce's shadow criss-crossed the glen at regular intervals, flying in silence.

They moved on. Rhiannon, Rhynne, Bàn and Eifion rode behind Arlan. Angus rode with the standard of the àrd rìgh—the black horse rampant—billowing in the gentle breeze. Arlan's troop followed, along with those remaining warriors from his clan lands by the sea. Dust covered Muir's leather armour, Douglas' weapons glinted, and Adele's gaze roamed the tops of the cliffs.

The track widened to two abreast, and Rhiannon nudged Bridie beside Arlan.

"What are you looking for, Arlan?"

Arlan shook his head slowly, then shrugged. "An army."

Rhiannon's elegant russet eyebrow curled. "Yeah, but what kind of army exactly?"

"Ah, I know not. But I'll be shown. *We* will be shown. He promised me, and he will keep his promise."

"Who promised?"

"The one I met at my kingmaking. Source of All Spirit. But he wasn't a spirit. He came to me as a man who hugged me and spoke to me."

"Wow," Rhiannon whispered.

The track widened further and Eifion on his mount trotted up beside them. "There is a legend told that promises an army to save this world."

"Aye, of this I read when younger. A lecture from, ah, a sage who otherwise helped me sleep. Well, an army to replenish my warbands is what we need." Arlan repressed a cringe. Was he leading them nowhere? Deeper into a valley where Ciarán's warriors could line the ridgetops at any moment?

Nae. This was the way. And he could no more ignore the voice in the wind than stop loving the woman who rode beside him. He reached across and grasped Rhiannon's hand as she fiddled with her reins.

"Ye know I love you with all my heart, Rhiannon?"

Her hands stilled beneath his. "Yes," she said in a small voice. "I love you."

"I ken." He raised his brows and gave a firm nod. "I will do all I can to free us from this badness."

"Oh, how I know it. I'll never forget you leaning against the fireplace in my cottage and promising you would."

"I will do it with my last breath if I must. And be sure of this: I will love you beyond that."

She faced him fully. Strain lined her eyes, and her mouth quivered. "Me too," she whispered into the unspoken tension.

Surely, she knows I truly forgive her? She seemed uneasy about something. The moments he'd had alone with her were few, for the fate of a kingdom had monopolised his attention and private time with a wife had become rare...

"Wow. There it is, Father," Rhynne said behind him.

He lifted his gaze from Rhiannon's trembling lips and pulled Mengus to a stop. Grey granite mountains shredded the clouds passing over rocky peaks that shaded most of a long narrow glen running before him. A place where daylight would barely reach in summer, and perhaps never in winter. Burial tors sat in a line snaking through the middle of this green glen. Low circular drystone walls had conical roofs topped with turf. The valley rested in the silent quiescence of death. Drayce flew its length, her shadow passing along the tops of the tors.

Arlan's jaw slackened. "Eifion. What do you think? All I see are graves."

Eifion nudged his animal closer. "I have heard of this place, my àrd rìgh, but its location has been lost with time... until this moment."

"Tell me more." Arlan's eyelids strained as he sought to take it all in. The line of tors seemed to go on for leagues.

"It is said a great race of fearsome shield warriors, the Sgiathach Mìlidh, lived in the east in the distant past. They buried their bravest men in the *Gleann Tor.*"

"The valley of the burial mounds?" Rhynne peeked from behind Bàn, then jumped off the grey war horse and stood with her hands on her hips surveying the narrow winding valley. "Wow," she said, then she spun to Eifion. "A green snake!"

"Oh, aye." Awe filled Eifion's tone.

Mengus shifted beneath Arlan, lifting his weight from one hoof to another.

Tors full of brave fighters.

Dead brave fighters.

He'd trusted his kingship, his defence of Dál Gaedhle, and his life to *Tobraichean na beatha.* How were dead warriors *any* use to him?

Behind him came a rumbling. Riders turned to the mouth of the glen and horses nickered. The ground vibrated and travelled through Mengus, shaking Arlan in the saddle. Standing on the ground next to Bàn still mounted on the grey, Rhynne stumbled, losing her balance. Bàn reached down and scooped her into the saddle.

Waves of vibration, coming from deep within the ground, heaved along the floor of the valley toward Arlan, leaving soil and pebbles shivering like ripples on pond water. Their mounts shrieked, wide eyed, tossing their heads, and their manes flying. Warriors pulled reins tight and sought to settle skittish war horses.

Groundswells passed, shaking leaves from the scant gorse bushes, sending birds flying and calling out in alarm. Foxes scattered from the glen, and hare leaped along the rocky edges of the glen's walls. Rhiannon stared at Arlan, eyes round.

"Was that an earthquake?" she asked.

"A tremor." Eifion patted his mount's withers, whispering to it in the old tongue.

A breeze blew from the same direction as the origin of the grumbling ground, bringing with it the scent of familiar but distant. Of lilies and heather. Strands of Arlan's long black hair wisped past his face having escaped the leather thong. He yanked it back behind his ear and turned Mengus to face away from the strengthening wind.

The glen!

The once tidy tors now sat broken, their green turfed, conical roofs askew, and dry stonework dishevelled and crumbling.

The breeze blew stronger, gathering force with its passage funnelled through the glen's narrow neck. The squall nudged him, pressing his back and shoulders. Mengus curvetted beneath him. Arlan pulled his stallion tight as leaves and twigs flew past, adding pine's tang and holly's sweetness to the air. He glanced aside at his fellow warriors whose muscles bunched with their attempts to settle their spooked war horses.

His forearm heated. The same sensation as at his kingmaking and again last evening. He turned his forearm upper most. The tattooed triskelion glowed.

The wind gained in force, a tempest now on its journey past him.

"The Breath of the Ancient." Eifion's words lifted in the wind.

The wind now roared, sending a tormented swirl of leaves, dust, and twigs coursing through the broken tors in the narrow glen. Debris hit the back of Arlan's neck and left stinging stabs. Swirling leaves touched each tor and eddied at every entrance, then moved on. The wind travelled along and out the glen, leaving silence and stillness in its wake.

Horses nickered gently, leaves fell to the ground, and shafts of sunlight illuminated the glen, warming Arlan's back and head. A stillness came to his heart. The same peace he'd known encircled in the embrace of the young warrior he'd met on the mount of his kingmaking.

Oh, how he longed for that peace to be for all. To be the hallmark of his reign and war not even a thought.

Grunts of alarm from his warband broke the silence. Metal hissed like a roar in Arlan's ears as warriors drew their weapons in unity, magnifying the sound.

"Nae, my friends." Arlan held up his hand. "There's no threat here."

"Sword-brother." Bàn raised *Dìleas.*

Arlan followed the direction of Bàn's sword's pointed tip. The opened tors showed movement. Out of each one, tall skeletons, still in battle dress, exited their chambers of long slumber. Sinew covered bone, muscle bulked, and smooth youthful skin overlaid all. Restored sight gazed at the sky above, mouths gaping. Expanding chests breathed in the fresh mountain air, a scent too long forgotten.

The taste of a woodland breeze, blown past by the wind, now rested in Arlan's gaping mouth.

"Och!" was all Arlan could voice.

"The dead live," Eifion said.

"That was incredible!" Rhynne cried.

"And a wee bit scary," Rhiannon commented. "I'm glad I'm up here."

The warriors dressed in unusual garb. Each one wore a tunic covered in metal chest shields, reminiscent of the armour on display at Edinburgh Castle in the Other World. Their swords were longer, and they each held a large wooden round shield, much bigger than a targe or long shield.

"They're all men." Rhynne squinted, jumping from the grey. "No women warriors?"

"Nae," Eifion said. "It seems not, for they appear to be the Sgiathach Mìlidh. Famous shield warriors from our distant past." Drayce made another pass, swooping lower. "And they are unperturbed by our dragon."

Arlan took a breath to relieve the tightness in his chest. He counted the warriors coming out from their rest, restored and formed to life again in his very presence. Twenty to a tor! He strained his vision to the far length of the glen but was unable to determine its end.

What size is this army?

"Eifion, what do the histories say of the number of tors in this glen?" Arlan could not keep the excitement from his voice.

"My àrd rìgh, at least one hundred."

"Man, these burial mounds are massive." Rhynne spun to him, eyes wide. "They're still coming out."

Stirring continued to come from within each tor, animal grunts and cries echoing out of the one closest.

"But are they friendly?" Bàn gripped his sword tighter and slid his gaze to Rhynne. "'Tis magic, Arlan."

"Bàn." Rhynne sent a stony glare Bàn's way.

"They're a gift from *Tobraichean na beatha* to the high kingship," Arlan said. "It matters not if they are friendly, only that their loyalty is with me and against Ciarán Gallawain."

"History records the custom of the Sgiathach Mìlidh was to bury horses and favourite hounds with the warriors," Eifion said, his voice resonating for what seemed like the entire length of the valley.

A dog tore out from the entrance of the nearest tor, jumping up to land front paws on the chest of a warrior, who cheered and patted the lanky dog, his face splitting in a grin. Loud whinnies erupted from the tors, then horses trotted out to their masters.

"What language do they speak?" Arlan turned to Eifion.

"Our tongue," Eifion said reassuringly, then coughed. "But perhaps an older version. I shall seek to gift them with comprehension." He dismounted and walked stiff-legged to a nearby gorse bush, mumbling under his breath about small shrubs.

"Armed and mounted warriors, Arlan." Rhiannon leaned over to him. "Your army," she said softly. "Watch out, Ciarán Gallawain."

Arlan could not stop the smile spreading across his face.

Mengus nickered, stepping to and fro.

"Easy, mo dheagh charaid." Arlan patted his stallion's neck.

Mengus side-stepped and neighed loudly, as though a stallion calling his mares.

"What disturbs him?" Bàn sat on the quiet grey.

The valley echoed with answering whinnies coming from the mounts of the assembling army. The warriors held their horses' reins and grasped their long swords, directing the points to the ground beneath their boots. A sea of replenished faces, all looking at Arlan, filled the long glen.

Mengus let out a full-bodied neigh and reared on his hind legs. Arlan clamped his knees tight to his stallion and rode the lift as Mengus pawed the air.

"Laoch Rìgh! Laoch Rìgh!" Deep masculine voices, more than two thousand strong, roared their affirmation of their warrior king.

The ground vibrated with a thud as, in unison, warriors knelt, hands on sword pommels, heads bowed, and allegiances vowed.

"Laoch Rìgh! Laoch Rìgh!" The shouts of Arlan's warband rose beside him, surrounded him, behind and before, with voices strong in loyalty and trust.

Drayce flew over his head, releasing her roar so loud it shuddered to his bones.

Arlan's watery vision blurred, and a vital strength flowed from the glowing triskelion on his left forearm... and coursed right through him.

FORTY-FOUR

I saw you tomorrow,
Ye who belong to yesterday.

Eastern Clanlands of Dál Gallain
Gleann Tor
The Valley of Tors

The resurrected tor warriors had designated Óengus to be their leader. He towered over Arlan, was twice as muscled, and spoke clearly in Arlan's modern tongue. He smelled fresh like a newborn babe, and his blade's glint rippled in the sunlight, made of a folded metal Arlan couldn't fathom. His armour shone, though battle dints peeked through.

"Fifty will lead ye, some to scout ahead. The rest will follow behind ye, my warrior king." Óengus placed his fist on his chest and bowed low.

"Thank you, my friend." Arlan waited with his troop as the fifty tor warriors set off, then led his warband behind them, riding through the rest of the glen sandwiched between ancient warriors reborn.

"Our army moves as slowly as my nephew mucking out stables, lord," Douglas called behind Arlan. The sun had passed its zenith and only now the glen widened.

"Aye, but look." Bàn pointed ahead to where the glen appeared to end.

A meadow dotted with trees came clearer into view, and the rush of water reached Arlan's hearing.

"That would be the River Bàn-rìghinn." Rhynne peered over Bàn's shoulder as they rode beside Arlan. "I hope it's easier to cross here."

"Of what I recall from the geography of Dál Gallain"—Eifion's tone held a scholarly note— "there is a bridge north of the rapids that gives the white river her name."

Arlan rode for a league, then the river came into view, and he trotted Mengus to its near bank, Bàn and Rhynne, Rhiannon and Eifion with him. The body of water roared past, in spate, surging its sides with the last of the snowmelt. The water was brown here, too deep for rocks to churn and crest with white. It strained the banks, washing chunks of dirt away in its passage to the Muir Gallain, the ocean to the south.

Arlan dismounted and stepped to the riverbank. To his immediate left, upstream, a bridge spanned the water. The wing walls were intact, anchoring the bridge into the riverbanks, but sunlight hit the water beneath the road across the bridge in patches between these two stone structures.

"It looks sturdy enough." Bàn's voice came to his ear. "Sturdier than the one Rhynne and I crossed."

"Ah. Don't like the look of the road over it," Rhynne added.

"With our carpenters and siege workers travelling with Lord Leuchars," Eifion said, "we must cut the trees ourselves to fill the gaps and reinforce the road."

Arlan grimaced. "We have over two thousand warriors and war horses to beat their tread across it. It *must* be safe."

Arlan ordered the chopping of the tallest, sturdiest trees. Warriors hastened to their tasks, using war axes to fell trees, and glancing over their shoulders often. The tor warriors lined the road across with split logs, then with the road barely completed, they led the traverse across the bridge. Arlan waited on the near side of the river while tor warriors trotted heavy-footed war horses over creaking logs without incident. He breathed again and turned to Bàn.

"We should be next."

Warriors yelled, their cries funnelling along the glen behind him, accompanied by horses' neighs and the barks of dogs. A scout rode up to Óengus, who stood directing the tidy up of timber. He bent his head to his man, then turned and strode to Arlan.

"My warrior king." His forehead creased a touch, but his voice remained calm. "My scouts report skirmishes at the rear guard. It seems our foe has discovered a way into our valley of sleep. My men have held them off. Indeed, they report they press us, though without significant force." He bowed.

"Thank you, Óengus." Arlan pressed his lips together. "Move out!" he commanded once he and the others had remounted.

Óengus turned and gave orders to his warriors, who mounted up while Arlan led his troop across the bridge. The tor warriors who would travel close with them soon followed.

A steep mountain sat to his left and, far off, a small village lay nestled by the river. Past this, downstream, mountains rose right to the river's banks, then rippled to the seaward horizon, to the farthest Arlan's vision could take him.

"Oh, I know where we are!" Rhynne said from behind Bàn on the grey war horse.

"That's the mountain of the sage hold, Arlan." Bàn pointed to the steep mountain on their left. "They lost many due to a plague this winter past." Bàn, twisting in the saddle, exchanged a look with Rhynne. "If requested, they would supply warriors, though it would be a warband small in number."

"We need all the assistance we can get." Arlan rubbed the back of his neck.

"It is worth asking," Bàn said. "Although if we are pursued, as it seems we are, they would be only a small band to attack our enemy from behind."

"We must ask this of them. Perhaps Óengus can spare a warrior to journey up the mountain to obtain their help."

Bàn pointed to the wee village on their left far ahead of them. "That is Clachan Beag."

They rode further. The remains of a small steading stood in the close distance; its thatched roof collapsed. Rhynne and Bàn spoke in low tones, and Rhynne wiped her eyes.

Arlan inclined his head to Bàn.

"Ma Gabràn lived here. We spent most of summer and autumn with her." Bàn's voice was thick. "We discovered she gave her life for us, Arlan. For your daughter's safety."

Arlan's heart pinched. That a stranger would give the ultimate price for his daughter. Nae, they were not evil people this side of Dál Cruinne, and they deserved better than Ciarán Gallawain served them.

Distant shouts from the valley now behind them, and the clash of steel against steel, filtered through the clop of hooves. A rider approached from that direction on a swift horse.

"My warrior king." It was one of the tor warriors. "Lord Óengus wishes me to tell ye that his men guard the rear as ye hurry ahead." He bowed.

"Is the fighting fierce, man?" Arlan pushed against the alarm rising within at the nearness of Ciarán's warband.

The tor warrior shook his head and snarled. "Nae, Warrior King. They harry us like dogs nipping the heels of cattle. But slip back when we advance, disengaging like cowards."

"Ciarán herds us like sheep," Arlan ground out, then steadied Mengus, who jostled and tugged on the bit. "That mountain range to the south hems us in and funnels our path in only one direction—to his Cath Mòr Làraich, I'll wager."

"I ken where that would be, Lord Arlan." Bàn's deep voice came sharp to his ear. "I have mapped it. We must head there."

"What?" Rhynne's tone was incredulous. "And be right where he wants us?"

"Nae," Arlan said. "So we are there first and well prepared. Where else is there to go, my daughter? The land lies against us, and we have no means of gathering ourselves to travel down this river before Gallawain sets upon us from behind." He glanced over his shoulder at the distant clamour. "We wouldn't obtain barges enough in time."

"Aye, there is but one ferry. It carries one goat at a time," Bàn said. "Remember, Rhynne?"

Arlan turned to Bàn. "Ye have mapped it, ye say?"

"Aye. I have determined places for defence and offence. Found sources of water and shelter." Bàn spoke quickly. "There are a few narrow mountain passes, scattered along the glen, which are potential escape routes if required."

"Verra well." Arlan ran his hand through his hair. "We shall not be pushed but hold them back with my tor army until we are prepared for Gallawain. If we're going there, we'll dig in and be ready to fight, know the land and have strategies planned." To the messenger he said, "Relay my wishes to your lord, if ye please."

Bàn communicated the information about the sage hold and the request for aid to the messenger, who nodded, turned his horse, then galloped off.

"We need that cannon." Arlan huffed and scratched at his beard.

"I'll go to The Keep." Determination laced Rhynne's voice. "If I fly a white flag, they'll not fire on me. Maybe," she added less confidently. "Surely they'd recognise Drayce. It's the fastest way."

"Och, it's probably the best solution for us." His scratched his beard with vigour.

"Wave the tartan of the àrd rìgh," Bàn suggested.

She leaned past Bàn and looked at Arlan. "I'll find the war chief, Lord Leuchars."

"Ye'll ken which one he is." Bàn gave a low chuckle.

"I'll tell him to hurry with the cannon to the coast and ship them around this way." Rhynne frowned, opening her mouth as though to speak, but hesitated.

"What, Rhynne?" Arlan dropped his hand from his beard and bore his stare into her.

"You need Dad. He'll know how to make your cannon more useful. You're gonna need it against Ciarán. Dad knows all the medieval war stuff. And, well, you're even behind *that* sort of weaponry here." She widened her eyes, nodding. The grey side-stepped beneath her and Bàn pulled him back into line. "He'll know how to make it into a tank with the primitive options you have here... sorry. He'd know how to build a mechanism out of wood, enabling it to move without using a horse... which can get killed, and then it's useless." She shrugged and spread her hands.

Arlan stifled a groan. *George...*

"We will discuss this when ye return. Ye have less than half a day to fly to The Keep and back."

Rhiannon pulled a white cloth from her saddlebags. "Approach slowly, Rhynne. Be careful. Be sure they're okay with you before you get right up to The Keep."

"Yes, Mum." Rhynne jumped off the grey, her tone one of impatient youth. She tugged the white cloth—a chemise—from Rhiannon's hand.

Arlan chuckled and slipped off Mengus. "Come here."

Rhynne approached, and he gathered her into his arms in a hug. "Fly safely, daughter of mine."

"I will," she said into his chest. "Please think about... Dad can really help, you know?"

He held her slightly away from himself. "Ye miss him." A statement, not a question. "Bàn informs me he made a promise that depends entirely on me to keep."

Mauve eyes looked straight into his, full of hope and touching his heart.

"On your return. Now go. Be safe." He kissed her crinkled brow.

She turned to Bàn, who wrapped his arms around her, then kissed her. "Wave the white and the tartan!"

"Okay, guys! I know what to do. *Man!*" She whistled and Drayce glided down to her, landing neatly by the horses.

Rhynne mounted, then Drayce lifted. They were soon small in the sky, like a high-flying bird, heading west.

Arlan waved Morrigan closer. "Assign two warriors to accompany you and follow the line of the river to reach the coast. Ye may have to hire a barge. Guide Lord Leuchars to us when he lands."

"Aye, lord, but how will I know where you are?" Morrigan asked.

"I will ensure Rhynne keeps you informed of all our plans."

Morrigan nodded to two warriors close by, gave a brief, wistful look to Angus, then galloped away with them. Battle clamour echoed behind Arlan, nearing the other side of the bridge.

"Over that rise is the way to a wide valley." Bàn pointed eastward.

Arlan jumped into the saddle then headed his companions in that direction with a contingent of tor warriors riding behind and ahead. The clash and cries of skirmishes, which had continued to come from their rear, now faded. The clatter of their mounts' galloping hooves continued for some leagues, then, with the racket of battle far behind, Arlan ordered them to slow to a fast walk.

"I agree with Rhynne." Rhiannon broke the silence sitting between them all. "He gave you the right advice about gunpowder, remember?"

"George is a good man, Arlan." Bàn stared straight ahead.

"He appears learned, and well... he probably has the knowledge you require." Eifion snapped his mouth shut at the glare Arlan sent his way.

"Don't shoot yourself in the foot, Arlan," Rhiannon said.

He frowned.

"It means don't not do something that you need to do just because you're still jealous of the man who can help you." Rhiannon's mouth twitched. "Or something like that."

"I'm not jealous of the man. He is jealous of me—"

"You're jealous that he brought up Rhynne, but it sounds like we could do with his help right now."

"When I spoke to George"—Bàn squinted as if recalling something— "a booklet with pictures of war-like objects on the cover sat on his table."

"What if he wishes not to come? And who"—Arlan turned to Eifion— "will travel through the portal to get him?"

"The most skilled amongst us." Eifion twitched his lips. "I will look for the nearest portal, then assist with magic to ensure accuracy. Remember—any place, any time, from any portal."

Arlan slid his gaze aside to Rhiannon, who had hung her head, fiddling with the reins, the comment sure to have sparked a memory of her personal mission through a portal. The beginning of their hurt.

You are forgiven, though a part of my very soul still aches for the lost years of fathering Rhynne.

"Rhynne can see portals." Bàn's voice beside Arlan broke through his misty reflections. "So now with her magic, she may be able to go to George, convince him to come and aid us, then come back here to *now*." Bàn shook his head in short rapid shakes. "I... cannae believe I offer this information, nor do I like her using magic, but Arlan, George's knowledge may be a great help to win this war."

Arlan stared straight ahead at the approaching valley.

"Yes"—Rhiannon lifted her head, her voice husky— "because Ciarán's cannon will mow down your warriors no matter how brave they are."

Arlan swallowed, his shoulders sinking. "Aye, it is a good idea. But Rhynne must agree." He turned to Eifion. "And you must instruct her well in the ways of a portal. She *must* return. I will not lose her again."

Eifion nodded an *of course*. "Rhynne is a gifted mage."

"She is untrained, Eifion."

"Rhynne can see portals, therefore they are her natural bent. Her forte. She, along with my assistance, will manage her journey. I am confident of this." Eifion grunted, folding his hands before him as he sat his mount.

"But we must discover a near portal." Arlan's statement hung in the air. They could only add a search for one to their many other battle preparations.

The sun sat in its mid-afternoon portion of the sky and a range of mountains to the south continued to herd them eastward. They passed a pond fringed by water reeds, and Bàn looked at the still water, a smile creeping across his face.

"Mòr Cath Làraich is over this rise, Arlan."

FORTY-FIVE

Aide me, O Fountain of Life, to fight against the chaos in your strength and not mine own.

SECRET SACRED WRITINGS OF THE SAGES

Eastern Clanlands of Dál Gallain
Mòr Cath Làraich

Shafts of sunlight angled through the low-lying clouds and pierced the wide long glen with fingers of silver, illuminating boggy moor and clumps of purple heather sitting beside a long sinuous burn. It was as though an electric lamp of the Other World directed its light on the scene. Wooded areas dotted along either side, with craggy outcroppings of rock at strategic intervals. The glen went on for quite a ways, ending in a deep forest growing at the base of a wall of rocky grey mountains. Beyond these, more mountains covered in white extended past vision's telling.

Arlan let his breath escape him. Not only was it a beautiful long glen, but a death trap for any army caught in its blind end.

Aye, they must take advantage of the positions for strategy, dig in, and ensure all would be set for the upper hand in this battle. For surely Ciarán Gallawain would plan his own strategies down to the last detail.

Perhaps arriving before him would thwart those plans. Well, that was *the* plan...

Mengus snorted and stomped beneath him. Arlan turned to Bàn, who raised an eyebrow at him.

"Most of Óengus' men can continue to hold off Gallawain"—Bàn lifted his chin, pointing to the field— "while a couple of hundred assist us in securing redoubts, cutting timber and making palisades, gathering supplies, setting defences—caltrops and such. And finding access for Lord Leuchars and the cannon." He took a rolled cloth from inside his armour, opened it and handed it to Arlan.

"A map." Arlan blinked at the detail in blue ink on a hide patched to cloth, scribbled in Bàn's own hand. "I would say you're worth your weight in swords, but ye are not heavy enough for this bounty ye have given, sword-brother." He reached over and clapped Bàn on the shoulder. "Douglas!"

"Aye, lord," Douglas answered behind him.

"Please request Lord Óengus to come and consult with me. We have much to discuss. We will be down there when ye return with him."

A line of warriors guarded the rise. Arlan stood with his back to the campfire, the warmth slowly seeping through his breeches. Warriors had caught rabbits, and now the aroma of roasting meat tickled Arlan's nostrils as he stared to the west. The sky slowly dimmed from vibrant blue streaked with mauve and argent, to the monochrome of evening. Rhiannon slipped her arms around his waist and leaned into him.

"She had a lot to do." Rhiannon's soft voice drifted up to him. "It may take her till tomorrow."

He snorted. "This is one of the rare occasions that I wish for a gadget of the Other World. A mobile phone would be helpful here, would it not?"

Rhiannon chuckled. "You sound like any parent of a young adult. She'll be fine. Your dragon will look after her. They've a connection."

"Aye, but now Gallawain is aware, he's sure to enlist his mage..." He closed his eyes and breathed in deeply, the clear scent of the moor mixing with Rhiannon's natural perfume filling his head and pushing out the dread lingering there. "I cannot dwell on the worst that can happen. I must hope for the best. Our daughter is wise and clever. Och. How I love her already though in truth I know her but little. She is mine own flesh and I see my people in her so strongly. I wish to know her more." He looked down at Rhiannon, whose eyes were moist. "If I do not survive this and miss time I could have with her, please tell her all ye know of me. Let her know how much I admire her, how pride fills my chest at her every action—"

Rhiannon's fingers pressed against his lips. "You'll tell her yourself, Warrior King."

"There will be losses."

"Yes."

He shrugged, then pulled her close. "I love you, my wife."

"And I you, my husband."

He held her in silence. The cool evening breeze stirred, wafting camp smoke, the sappy scent of freshly cut timber and the all-pervading odour of horse into his nostrils.

"It's not something you can entirely sort out in your mind." Rhiannon's voice held a wistful note. "You think you've got the idea of death, but then if someone you know dies, it hits you in the face again. Or you hear so and so's got cancer. Or you're in a car accident and you survive. You think you've got it straight in your mind—that everyone dies and you're just like everyone. But it jolts you back to the fact that each day is precious. Each moment may be your last. Each time you hold the person you love... knowing you will die... should make you live stronger. Love more deeply. Choose more carefully. Like what you decide to believe in. That what you live for is worth dying for." She tilted her face to his. "Dál Gaedhle is worth dying for. *You* are worth dying for." Her soft breath brushed his cheek.

His throat closed in and, unable to swallow or even comment, he held her tighter.

Axes *thunked* against the nearby wood. Bàn directed the securing of the nearest redoubt, his shouted commands travelling over to Arlan from the southern side of the wide glen. Bàn had sent two warriors seeking a gap in the steep sided glen, one he'd noted previously. It would be the escape route if needed, and where they would bring in the cannon if Leuchars had initiated the plan to carry them by sea. He trusted Morrigan, and the two tor warriors with her, would reach the coast unmolested and in time.

A cry rose from behind the rise of the hill where, out of Arlan's sight, Óengus and the tor warriors shielded the valley from Gallawain's army, keeping them at bay.

"They attack at dusk?"

"No, lord," Angus yelled, turning to face him from where he stood halfway up the rise. "A dragon approaches from the southwest." His grin widened. "It looks like Drayce."

A dragon's cry came from the south, close. Drayce brushed over the treetops of the small wood to Arlan's left, glided and dipped into the glen, then landed in front of an almost completed redoubt.

Arlan let go of Rhiannon and they both ran to Drayce, with Eifion grunting behind him to keep up. Bàn met them by the dragon as Rhynne slid down Drayce's back, landing awkwardly and flexing her fingers as though she wished to feel them again. Arlan approached with Rhiannon at his side.

Bàn hugged Rhynne, smiling, then he placed a kiss on her lips.

"You smell like sweaty man," Rhynne said, when Bàn's lips left hers.

"Aye, and ye smell like sweaty dragon." He kissed her again.

"That's impossible," she said into his face. "Reptiles don't sweat."

"We have all worked hard at preparing this valley to be to our advantage." Arlan smiled at their affectionate tones, and the burning tension in his neck muscles eased a wee bit. "Please tell us all."

"We didn't land at The Keep." Rhynne patted Drayce absently, like she would a horse. "Good old Leuchars. Great guy, by the way. He's a softie under all the red hair and scars. He'd already thought of going to the coast to avoid the blocked borders. There are warbands and some rough-looking guys—"

"Bandits," Bàn offered.

"Yeah. Anyway, Leuchars was almost at the port when I caught up with him and his load of three cannons and a mound of cannon balls on barges going down that river that runs past The Keep."

"The River Ruairidh," Bàn said.

Rhynne nodded. "I told him about maybe landing somewhere past the Bàn-rìghinn on a quiet bit of coast. I checked it out and spoke to Morrigan on my way back. They should meet up in a couple of days." She gave Arlan a look, a silent question.

Would that be soon enough?

Arlan grimaced. "We must hope." Hope was all he had. "And the army? He takes the army by sea?" Arlan couldn't keep the concern from his voice.

"He may. If there's enough time to organise that." Rhynne took the offered waterskin from Angus. "I told him about the mountains and that this river was the only way to this valley, but the coast seemed the best for the cannon. Leuchars seemed to know but sent for a map. He muttered something about getting the most effective weapons to you in time. Some warriors are riding out to meet Ciarán's army to try their luck against them at the border. They're planning surprise guerrilla tactics of some sort. The rest plan to sneak past, cross the river, then get to you here"—she screwed her mouth to the side—"somehow. Leuchars said they'd lost a few in that battle I told you about, and two clans from the north have joined Ciarán."

"Who?" Arlan's guts ground at the betrayal.

"Duisdale and Callaghan."

"Ach! Why am I nae surprised at that?" Bàn rubbed his upper lip with his thumb.

"So, Leuchars has called further into Dál Gaedhle for more warriors?" Arlan asked.

"Iubhar clans have pledged more. My relatives, apparently." Rhynne's lips cocked in a half smile so like Rhiannon's.

Eifion joined them, and Rhynne took another swig from the waterskin, her eyes roving the scenery. Coughing on her drink, she pulled the skin away from her mouth.

"Wow. Look!" She pointed out to the glen. "It's full of them!"

"Of what?" Rhiannon spun to face the glen behind her.

"What do you see, Rhynne?" Eifion asked.

Bàn grabbed her shoulders as she turned to face Eifion. "Portals? Rhynne, do ye see portals in this glen?" he asked.

"Don't you?" she asked Eifion.

"Nae." He shook his head briefly. "But ye must tell us all and mark them out."

"How many?" Arlan asked.

Rhynne narrowed her eyes, peering along the glen. "At least half a dozen. Man, why are there so many in one place?"

"I know not." Eifion came and stood beside her, looking in the direction where she pointed out the portals. "But we must make the best use of these resources."

"They're disappearing." Rhynne turned back to the tops of the eastern mountain range where the last of daylight glowed.

"Mark the closest one, my daughter," Arlan said. "For at tomorrow's sunrise you may go and, if the man wishes, ye may bring back George."

Rhynne squealed.

FORTY-SIX

—·—

VISIONS AND SAYINGS OF THE BLIND LADY SAGE

Eastern Clanlands of Dál Gallain
Mòr Cath Làraich

"Rhynne, ye will land in the Godstow Nunnery ruins." Bàn adjusted my sword belt, ensuring my coat covered my sheathed sword, his golden hair glowing where the pre-dawn's faint light touched it. His crumpled brow, and his obvious concern, tugged at my heart.

"Come back to me," he continued tightening the sword belt at my waist.

Is that doubt in his tone?

My stomach hardened. "Do you think I'll stay there with Dad?"

He shook his head vigorously. "I know not what ye will think... What ye will feel once you are back in the Other World."

"Bàn, I'll be here, fighting beside you. Fighting for my world. For my father's kingdom." I grasped the sword belt that crossed his chest, the leather worn and smooth beneath my fingers, and my knuckles pressing into the warmth of his body. "To be honest, I don't know or fully understand the big picture here. But like you, I see there's something else going on, and it's larger than all of us. And I want to be in it, even though I can't see it all. I know I'll just have to trust those who do—and do my bit." I locked my gaze with his. "And come back to the man I love."

There. I'd said it without my previous hesitation. Of course I would be with Bàn, no matter what we were about to face.

I lifted my chin and reached his mouth with mine, pressing hard against his soft, full lips. He opened his mouth and surrounded my lips with his own, holding warmth and love, his quiet moan of longing escaping into my mouth. He broke away, resting his forehead on mine.

"Be quick, will ye?"

"Of course. I don't want to miss out on the fun here." I gave a gentle laugh, but it choked a bit.

I'd noted at the previous sunset that the closest portal to our camp opened by a copse of ash, and now we gathered by the place. Eifion leaned beside the nearest tree with his arm around it like it was his best buddy. Rhiannon and Arlan were a step away, faces mirroring each other with creased brows and tight mouths.

"I'll be okay, and I'll see you all soon." I may as well have been a nanny reprimanding kids.

Drayce clicked behind me, and I turned at her nudge.

I be waiting.

"None of you will wait long. Eifion has told me everything I need to know." I rubbed Drayce's knobbly black head. Her hide was darker. Or maybe I imagined it.

"It should be time, granddaughter. Do you see it?" Eifion spoke, and Arlan and Rhiannon stepped back.

"You'd better join them," I told Bàn. "You're right where I think I saw the shimmer at last evening's sunset."

He nodded and slowly stepped backward to where the others stood.

I clasped my hands in front of me to stop them from trembling. *Soon I'll be with Dad.*

"I'm not looking forward to travelling through again." I looked at Bàn. "I nearly threw up last time."

Bàn opened his mouth, like he was about to speak, and if he did, I never heard him. In front of me, a wall of water shimmered, like a swimming pool on its side.

Awesome.

Taking a breath, I stepped through.

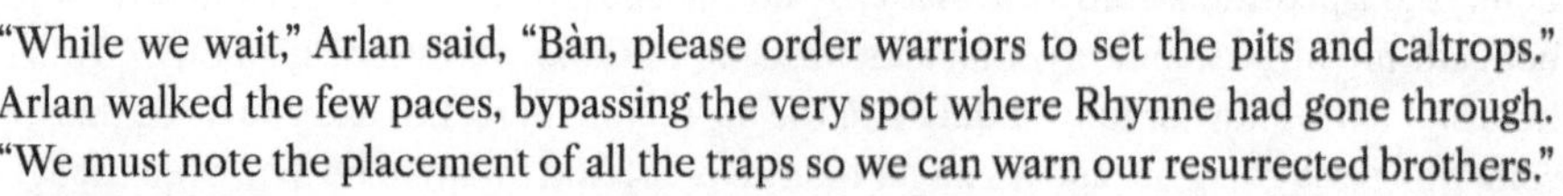

"While we wait," Arlan said, "Bàn, please order warriors to set the pits and caltrops." Arlan walked the few paces, bypassing the very spot where Rhynne had gone through. "We must note the placement of all the traps so we can warn our resurrected brothers." He raised his vision to the horizon where the rim of the world awakened in the shining orb's silvery light.

"Oof!" A familiar voice came from behind him. "Wow." The word dragged out, spoken by a male with a distinct accent of the Other World.

"Told you I wouldn't be long." Rhynne's voice held an unfamiliar cockiness.

Arlan spun, unable to stop his mouth from gaping.

"Ah, hello, Arlan." George stood there, head slightly bowed, a bundle of books tucked under his arm.

"George! We're so glad you agreed to come." Rhiannon stepped up to him and gave him a hug. "Aren't you, Arlan?"

"Aye." Arlan coughed. "The army of Dál Gaedhle is grateful"—he glanced at Rhiannon, who frowned at him— "as am I. We trust your expertise will assist us in making our cannon more effective once they arrive."

George gave a slight nod and looked around the glen, resting his gaze on the nearby redoubt, the partially erected palisades, and the line of warriors on the rise. His mouth slowly gaped, corresponding with his rounding eyes.

"Ah, Lord Arlan." George choked on a cough and wiped his mouth. "I have only the theory. I draw heavily from the record of Leonardo da Vinci's war machines." He looked Arlan in the eye and cringed a little. "I haven't ever actually made one."

Arlan raised an eyebrow.

"But ye have the books." Bàn, who had kissed Rhynne in greeting, now let her go and pointed to the papers under George's arm.

"Dad, I showed you what I meant." Rhynne placed her hand on his shoulder. "The guys here will cut the wood. You just tell them what to do with it to make the tanks."

Eifion had barely let go of the tree he'd embraced during Rhynne's departure, attending to his magic. He now stepped forward to George, his voice orotund, and his appearance its usual *commanding*. "May I see the parchments, Master George?"

"This is my grandfather, the Mage Eifion." Rhynne's voice resonated with pride.

George double blinked at Eifion, then bowed. He took the books from under his arm and handed them to him. Arlan peered over Eifion's shoulder at George's books, which Eifion had opened at a page with a detailed sketch of the tank to which Rhynne had referred. It was a wooden covered cart with a conical shaped roof. The cannon fitted inside. The cart had four wheels driven by a set of cranks, and the side had holes through which the cannon barrel pointed out.

Hmm. It looked complicated. *But I am a warrior not an engineer.*

George tugged at the straps of the backpack over his shoulder, looking around at the glen, examining the whole length of it.

"The ground looks boggy." George chewed his lower lip.

"Aye, it is in places." Bàn approached George while he spoke. "I shall show ye the map."

Bàn took the map from where he kept it in his leather armour, then showed it to George. They spoke together for a time, Bàn pointing out the dry areas good for tracks that wouldn't catch a wheeled cart in a bog. Or a tank. George spoke the tongue well, as he had when Arlan was with him in the Other World.

Arlan lowered his eyes, his cheeks heating. He should not be jealous of this man. He'd protected and nurtured his daughter to grown womanhood. Here George was, in a strange world, assisting *his* cause. The man seemed to manage the transition well, engrossed in conversation with Bàn, his comments showing an understanding of the ways of war in Dál Cruinne—plus a warfare with more complex war apparatus such as cannon.

Och! I would be stupid to hold anything against this one from the Other World. And a worthless king to deny my army the knowledge he provides.

Rhiannon walked toward Arlan, eyes alight, as though reading his mind. He nodded gently, locking her gaze with his own as she stepped right up to him.

"He'll do well," she whispered. "He'll make you a tank that will be ready when the cannons arrive," she said in a louder voice.

"Yes, how long do I have?" George asked.

"A couple of days maybe," Rhynne answered.

"Actually, ye have as long as we can hold off the Gallawain army." Arlan looked at Rhynne. "Ye have told George all of our situation?"

"Yeah." She looked at George then. "If things get hairy, I'll take him back through a portal."

George skewed his lips to one side. "Where will your cannons come from? I mean, how will you get them into this valley?"

Bàn sucked air through his teeth and rubbed his thumb over his upper lip.

"Bàn?" Arlan asked, and all turned to Bàn's concerned expression.

"Och. We have nae found a track through the side o' this glen that could be wide enough and reaches the way from the sea. There are tracks we could escape through—" Bàn lifted a shoulder— "but a cannon traversing..."

"Drayce can carry them." Rhynne gave a short nod. "I've seen them. They're smallish."

"Are ye sure my wee beast is up to it?" Arlan asked.

"She's not that wee, and she's stronger than you think." Rhynne straightened. "I mean only one cannon at a time, though, and not all the way from the coast. Just over this peak." She pointed to the trackless hillside beside them.

The breeze blew the early morning air, changing direction and sending the clash of distant battle their way. George looked to the rise, and Arlan turned. Cries and clanking steel grew in intensity and a lone rider, a tor warrior, crested the rise. Arlan braced his hands on his belt and waited for Óengus' messenger. The man rode close, his horse lathered, and he pulled it up sharp.

"Lord Arlan, my warrior king." The tor warrior bowed.

"Tell me, man." Arlan gripped the handle of the short sword at his belt, its leather-bound wood digging into his palm.

"The enemy presses us." He wiped sweat from his brow. "My Lord Óengus wishes ye to ken we hold them back, but we suffer losses."

"They have attacked at night also?"

"Aye, they harry us still both day ¡end night, but pull back on our advance, only to come again with full force. Those we knock down are quickly replaced. Gallawain has a seemingly endless supply of warriors to sacrifice to his cause."

Arlan bowed his head, rubbing the back of his neck. The tor warriors die *again*.

And for him.

I had counted them immortal.

"Tell your lord I cannot express enough my gratitude for the sacrifice his service means to me. Do ye think ye can hold out two more days?"

The rider shrugged. "My warrior king, that depends on the enemy. I shall inform Lord Óengus of the need for time."

Eifion stepped forward. "Please, young man, do you know how many mages are with Gallawain?"

The messenger frowned.

"Those who wear the black robe in the same fashion as mine?" Eifion clarified.

The man blinked, as though recollecting his view of the battlefield. "Nae. But perhaps one, who is at Gallawain's side."

"Ciarán remains on the field?" Arlan asked.

"Aye, Lord Warrior King. Most of the day. He watches all with hooded gaze roving everywhere."

"Is there a younger man with him bearing a strong resemblance?"

"Aye." The man's mouth hardened. "He seems to see a lighter side to the battle, lord. For he claps and cheers often."

Arlan dismissed him and spun to Bàn and George behind him. "Ye had better get to cutting the timber required," he said to Bàn. Then to George, "Make the tank ready to the point of fitting the cannon. With *Tobraichean na beatha's* help, perhaps our cannon will arrive in time. If not..." Those he loved most dearly turned to face him.

His next words refused to come out.

FORTY-SEVEN

*An angry heart bares its teeth
And tears through a foe like a lion.*

*SAGE GLIOCAS
(2870-2962 POST DRAGON WARS)*

**Eastern Clanlands of Dál Gallain
Mòr Cath Làraich
Lord Ciarán's Camp**

"Come, mage!" Ciarán curled a finger at Bram, then strode through the churned ground toward the mage's tent. He took a deep breath, the aromas of an army camp swirling up his nostrils: horse sweat, leather's earthy tones, the oily hint of metal honed as warriors sharpened weapons, and the distinct stench of human waste wafting from hastily dug latrines.

Ciarán cast his gaze up at the steely sky before throwing aside the rustic canvass flap of the mage's tent, pinching his nostrils tight against the cloy of herbs. He glanced around the small space. Bram had brought the stone bowl with him, and it sat on a flat, round log in the centre of the tent.

In pride of place. Bram loved the thing.

Saddlebags lay in disarray on the camp cot, their contents spilled on the woven rugs, dried herbs mixing with parchments and scrolls. The tent door flap swished open, and the mage entered, wide eyed and shoulders tense.

"You wish something, Lord Ciarán?" The lines around his mouth deepened.

"Yes, mage. I enter your lair uninvited because now is the time for you to do your work."

"I have summoned the mages, lord. They await the command."

"Very good, but that is not the work to which I refer."

"I am concocting the potion you requested." Exasperation frayed the edges of Bram's voice.

"Still not the specific task I desire you to perform." He cast his vision over the mortar filled with a pungent smelling substance. "Nor the reason I enter"—he closed his nostrils against the stench the herb emitted—"your makeshift workshop."

Bram stood taller, his long dark hair framing a perfect face, one which women would swoon over. The grey streak had thickened of late. The mage attributed it to his work with magic. It aged him, but in an endearing way. The young man's eyes narrowed slightly.

"You wish me to call my master, lord?"

"Yes. But as you may recall, that one is also *my* master. And my time of service is greater than yours. We have an agreement, he and I. He owes me a debt, and now it is time for him to settle." Ciarán clipped his words through a tight mouth.

Bram's throat worked.

"You are afraid, mage?"

"The one of whom you speak is powerful." Bram's tone held a warning. "I myself had spoken lightly of him until I met him."

"Oh, *I* have met him." Ciarán held his breath, fear ruffling through his words at the memories of that meeting pouring into his mind. "He came to me in the form of a foppish young man, tricked me into signing a contract of service, then revealed his true self to me." He leaned into the mage, surprised at the control in his own voice. "A revelation I will never forget."

So near now... he could taste it—the culmination of a lifetime of promises.

"I know you think me callous when it comes to your magic. But I was blood-sworn to your master before I was weaned. Your magic is a tool. Another weapon in my armoury."

The mage blinked, eyes narrowing further.

"Yes, you abhor my attitude to your magic, but I wait for the power promised me. The immortality assured for services rendered while I enjoy my role in the grand plan."

"If you wish me to call the master—" Bram regained his deep tones— "I must perform my summoning in private."

"No."

Bram's eyebrows rose and his mouth opened.

"I will be here." Ciarán spoke low. "I will address him."

"You—" Bram shook his head almost imperceptibly. "Very well, Lord Ciarán. I shall prepare." A resigned sigh escaped his lips as he picked up a jug by the door and poured the water into the carved stone bowl.

"You can do nothing without this?" Ciarán waved his hand over the water-filled dish.

The mage did not answer, continuing his preparations, then kneeled by the bowl so his hands rested comfortably on its rim. Bram cricked his neck and shuffled from one knee to the other.

"Come now, mage, you test my patience. Do your magic. Get along with it!"

Bram slipped his hands into the bowl, closed his eyes, and mumbled to himself. His face tilted back, and his features softened.

The mage was enraptured, but Ciarán could hear not a word.

"Out loud, mage!"

The mumbling ceased and Bram's eyes flew open, skin pinching white around flared nostrils.

"You will speak aloud so I may hear," Ciarán ground out.

Bram's lips became a thin line. "Very well." Harsh reluctance laced through those two words. He closed his eyelids.

"O Great Power of the Air

Lord of those who would meet ye here.

An audience your servants seek

Here we wait to hear you speak."

Bram's eyes remained closed.

Ciarán tapped his foot. "Must it rhyme?"

Bram took a breath and lowered his shoulders. "I have done this but once. I beg you please"—his eyes flew open— "Ciarán Gallawain, be silent!"

Ciarán took a short step back, right eyelid flicking, but held his tongue.

Bram closed his eyes again, tilted his head and became very still. So still, Ciarán held his own breath, waiting for Bram to take another. Warriors chatted outside, horses nickered, mallets thudded as servants hammered tent pegs in place, and the wind stirred the tent flaps. The glow of sparse sunshine, hitherto lighting the canvas, now dulled.

The poor light within the tent dimmed, and the leaves in the trees at the side of the camp played with the wind. A breeze ruffled the tent, the canvas sides now in constant movement. It sent chill air through the door flap and under the canvas walls. The cool clamped Ciarán's arms to his sides.

Bram grunted, but remained with upturned face, now with an expression of ecstasy.

A presence crept into the tent and Ciarán strained his vision to see it as it swirled around the mage, danced over the bowl, then became a mist.

It rose vapour-like, tall and long, hovering over them, a shadow in the darkness.

Formless.

Sentient.

It looked at Ciarán.

Ciarán swallowed, proving to himself that he could, indeed, move his mouth.

"Cumhachd adhar?" he asked the roiling steam-like presence hovering above Bram.

"You will call me Master," it whispered. Though it spoke from vapour, the voice was dark and solid, as though it came from the depths of the Abyss.

A shudder walked through Ciarán, stepping on every nerve in its way, and a trickle of sweat followed its path down his spine.

"Master." Ciarán spoke, his voice a husk of itself.

"You are here to do my will. You will perform your task." The whisper tickled his ears, pricked his neck, and pressed on his shoulders.

"I have one question." Ciarán's voice scratched out.

"Speak." The word itself, coming from the whisper, thickened the air.

"Are you the one I met many a year ago? The one who promised me all?"

"You will be rewarded. As promised." The whisper now held form. It felt like a lie. Looked like deception. Smelled like dishonesty.

And yet it continued to hold out hope to him.

"But so far, you have not fulfilled your side of our deal." Ciarán choked. He *would* ask it. "I will be king from this? I will have eternity, yes?"

"If you submit." A force pressed him, so physical in nature his joints cracked.

"I submit," he yelped, then bowed the knee.

The swirling solid mist enveloped him... and entered.

It spread fear through him, sending his heart pounding and his breath shrivelling in dread. The weight and shame of a lie pressed upon him and choked him. The hunger and dissatisfaction of greed filled him. His soul darkened with hate and the red-bloodied rage of every violence known to him.

Yes. He welcomed it—right into his soul.

The tent billowed and spun around him. Horses shrieked and warriors yelled. Bram's eyes flew open.

And Ciarán crashed to the ground, thwacking his face in the coarse rushes covering the tent floor.

The maelstrom ceased. Horses settled. Bram stood, locking his glare on Ciarán.

Ciarán scrambled to his knees, then jumped to stand, creaking joints of age replaced with the suppleness of youth. He clenched a fist, relishing the strength of his arm. An energy vibrated within him. A grin tightened his lips, then changed to match the scowl he gave to the mage who stood gawping at him.

"Get to your work, mage. We have an àrd rìgh to usurp."

FORTY-EIGHT

— · —

And the very trees lay down their lives in sacrifice.

FOREST OF STRATHRÌGHINN

Eastern Clanlands of Dál Gallain
Mòr Cath Làraich

A steely sky sat in silence above the glen. No sun shone. I blinked at the clouds that just hung there, not a breath of wind stirring. Arlan and Bàn were convinced this glen would be the place where Ciarán Gallawain would choose to have his battle to end all battles.

I traced Drayce's silhouette off in the southeast. She dived suddenly, catching her prey, probably. She'd told me she was hungry, and she needed to keep up her strength. Arlan and Rhiannon stood in a huddle with Eifion. Dad and Bàn looked at the map and discussed something I couldn't quite catch. The noise of constant battle came over the rise that bordered the mouth of this glen. The tor warriors held Ciarán's army at bay and continual waves of shouts, ringing metal, and horses' whinnies came over the rise.

Dad looked up from the scroll that he and Bàn pored over, then scanned the whole long glen. "Those older trees at the far end, near that—stone slab, is it?—look to be our best option."

"Nae, they are too thick for the job, Master George," Bàn said. "We require younger trees, straighter and easier to fell in our current circumstances."

Dad pushed his glasses up his nose like he'd always done. It was one of my earliest memories.

My chest tightened.

"Dad!" I ran and wrapped my arms around him. "I've missed you." I sniffed back tears.

His arms held me in a grip. "Rhynne, to me, you're still at the HEMA weekend. I haven't missed you yet." He shrugged, bumping our hug. "I guess I'm the lucky one."

"So, what do you think? Awesome, isn't it? And my... father? He's..." I searched Dad's face. The lines beneath his eyes sharpened.

"Yes, your father is a special man." His tone had an edge, and he coughed it away. "And this man"—he pointed, smiling with fondness at Bàn— "protected you and got you here looking like a warrior."

"She *is* a warrior, Master George," Bàn said.

"Well, I approve, whatever the case." Dad's grin wavered. "That's if my opinion holds any weight here." His words were barely a whisper.

"Of course they do, Dad," I said.

Arlan and Rhiannon's conversation with Eifion finished, then they walked over to us with serious expressions.

"George Wilson." Arlan spoke all kingly-official-like. "We wish to thank you sincerely for bringing up our daughter." He paused and looked at me, the serious tilt to his mouth softening. "Rhynne is a wonder, and I am indebted to you for keeping her safe." His voice broke then, and Rhiannon gave George a hug. Arlan stared at me, his eyes moistening.

I hurried to him and wrapped my arms around him. "I love you, Father," I whispered into his chest. His large hand touched the back of my head, stroking my hair, and his lips pressed a kiss to my forehead. "And I love you, my precious daughter," he said softly.

My heart swelled and I held him tighter. How could I be so lucky? To have two great men for fathers.

"We must hasten." Bàn held up the map. "We have much to do before Gallawain's army crests that hill."

"Wood," Dad said. "For a multi-cannon tank da Vinci style we'll need some trees felled."

"How many?" Eifion's voice was strangled. "Please leave the older mature trees, particularly of that ancient forest at the glen's end." He pointed to the very forest Dad had just indicated.

The small wood grew thick with ancient oaks and beech there. A group of granite slabs, like tipped over gravestones, lay on the ground in front of the trees at the dead-end of this valley.

Bàn gave orders to the nearest tor warriors, and they ran to the copse beside us, war axes in their hands, then started chopping down the tallest tree. It was younger and thinner than the ancient trees at the end of this valley.

"Very good, I shall leave you with Lord Bàn." Arlan turned away with Rhiannon and headed toward the warriors preparing weapons and checking their horses' gear.

Dad opened his books and studied the pages with the diagrams of those funny round wooden tanks that could go in almost any direction. The wooden wheels didn't look simple to make. Dad smiled to himself and... *hummed?*

"You're loving this, aren't you, Dad?"

His humming stopped, and he looked up, his lips breaking into a grin. He surveyed the surrounding glen, the sky, the warriors, glanced at Rhiannon and Arlan, then let out a deep sigh.

"This may sound stupid, but I feel like I've come home." He chuckled and stuck his nose back into his medieval war machine books. Bàn peered over his shoulder.

Warmth bubbled up in my chest, so I let the laughter escape. Maybe we wouldn't laugh for a while. Then I closed my eyes, swallowing.

What if the cannon didn't get here in time? Or if Dad didn't have these complicated machines ready when they did?

"I need to scout," I said.

Dad frowned. "Rhynne, where're you going?"

"To the coast. I won't be long." I whistled for Drayce.

"But is it far? You'll be exposed. In danger." Dad looked from me to Bàn and back again. "The other army will attack you."

"Rhynne will be fine, George." Bàn's cheeks dimpled. "She has Drayce."

"What's that? Her horse?"

"Nae. Rhynne?" Bàn called behind me as I searched the sky. "Have ye no' told George about your dragon?"

"Dragon!"

I turned at Dad's shout. His glasses slid right off his nose.

"She's friendly," I said, as her screech filled the air.

Drayce soared low over the glen, skirting its mouth and the edge of the skirmish there, leaving a rise of shouts and a thunder of battle noise in her wake. She landed gracefully near me.

Arlan spun to the increased volume of battle and ordered the young warrior, Angus, to go look over the shallow hill that separated us from them.

"Father," I shouted, "I'll see where Lord Leuchars is up to."

Arlan nodded, dark brows meeting in the middle. "Aye, take care."

"Yes, be careful." Dad's voice trembled.

He stood back from Drayce, clutching his books to his chest. I mounted, and we lifted into the sky. I looked down at him, his mouth open and shaking his head slowly, and I blew him a kiss.

"To the coast, Drayce."

FORTY-NINE

He gives the gift of battle song
Lauding loyalty and strength
Of warriors and heroes
Who give their very breath.

He gives us gifts of stories
Of courage true and rare.
Of bravery in battle
A prize beyond compare.

POETRY OF THE WARRIOR
WARRIOR SAGE TAPAÌDH
(4009-4059 POST DRAGON WARS)

Eastern Clanlands of Dál Gallain
Mòr Cath Làraich

Sunlight glowed the cloud-filled sky to silver, the glare hitting Arlan's eyes. Shielding them with his hand, he followed Rhynne and Drayce's flight south until they were out of sight. Battle cries increased. A far-off war horn's threatening call reached Arlan's hearing, and moving through his body, landed like a fist in his stomach. Warriors crested the rise, and Óengus' men spilled into the glen.

Och, his tor warriors were retreating. Arlan bound his hair back, tugging at the roots. *The battle turns.*

He counted barely three hundred riding or running toward him, Óengus' shout to regroup travelling clearly to his ears. On the rise, leather-clad warriors sat mounted. Behind them rose the spikes of spears. Further back, the tips of the weapons held by foot soldiers—pitchforks and scythes. The breeze brought to Arlan the potent smell of battle-blood and sweat, and those long in the saddle unwashed.

"Mount up, all!" Arlan ordered, then looked to the tor warrior standing near George and Bàn. "Ye go with Master George," he ordered the warrior. Then to George he said, "Continue making our tanks, George. We may yet get a chance to use them. Bàn, with me."

"Aye, Arlan." Bàn flew into the saddle of the grey, Rhiannon following suit on Bridie, with Eifion close behind on his steed.

Arlan grabbed Mengus' reins, his tall black stallion curvetted as he mounted, eager to be in the fray. The rush of warriors and their war horses, plus the jeers of the Gallawain army lining the rise, with a carnyx now above them trumpeting a call to war, all beat at Arlan. Adele and Douglas were close beside him. Arlan pressed down on his teeth and spun Mengus to face the horde along the rise. Two horsemen galloped to him from the mound where Gallawain's army stood ready. Long hair streamed behind the youngest riding in front.

"Lord." Angus' breathless cry came to him first. "We held off as long as possible. The tor army and our warband are overwhelmed. Gallawain outnumbers us."

What? Were the tor army not the ones to win this war for us? Why then did To-braichean na beatha send me to them?

Óengus' cries urging his mount on, carried over his war horse's thudding hooves. On reaching Arlan, he pulled the stallion to a halt, tack jingling and foam flying. The man himself was dirt flecked, shield dented, and blood sprayed.

"Ciarán Gallawain calls for a parley with you, Warrior King. He orders no weapons. Their leader stands ready to lower his own."

"I will attend." Bàn placed his vice-like grip on Arlan's arm.

"He will only speak to the warrior king, Lord Lùthas." Óengus dipped his head.

"Even so, I will be there," Bàn said, his voice like gravel and his face as fierce as a sword.

"It will be a one-sided parley, my àrd rìgh. I am certain of this." Eifion touched the handle of his short-sword at his belt. "I shall attend."

"I'll come too," Rhiannon said.

"Nae, Bàn will suffice." Arlan nudged Mengus past the rows of tor warriors, their barricade parting to let himself and Bàn through.

Angus raised the standard of the Àrd Rìgh; the black horse rampant surrounded by a chain of knotwork lifted in the gathering breeze. Remaining behind with the others were the warriors of his original troop. They had continued faithful and true to him, even though they could lose everything. Their gazes were heavy, like the maille tunic he wore beneath his leather armour.

He walked Mengus along the avenue lined with the tall tor warriors on grand war horses. Many of their brothers had lost their lives to buy him precious time. Though depleted in number, their looks remained stern and held admiration, and their very presence was a testimony to their determination to fight beside him, and for him, now.

I must be worthy of it all.

Ahead, a lone horseman trotted forward. Behind him, four sleek, white cannon pointed at Arlan from the centre of the mound where the Gallawain army lined up. The tartans of Callaghan and Duisdale flickered in the wind, flanking the front line of warriors. A young man in a black mage robe sat ahorse beside an older man in an unfamiliar orange tartan, who held himself like a warrior of experience.

"The one next to Ciarán, wearing the orange tartan?" Arlan leaned toward Bàn.

"The laird of Lorain," Bàn answered. "Aye, must be his war chief."

A cry came from the line-up behind Ciarán, Kyle's voice catching in the breeze, and a warrior in full leather armour grabbed Kyle's waving hand, pulling it down.

Arlan's gut clenched.

Perhaps Kyle's ransom would be part of this parley. Ciarán must return Kyle. He belonged to his family, despite his real paternity. Arlan would have him near and safe in his now diminished state. Not under the influence of Gallawain. Who knew what lies Ciarán had fed him?

Closer now, Arlan ran his gaze along the cannon. Warriors, lightly armoured, stood beside them, no tapers lit. Arlan slid his vision back to Kyle as the wind tugged at his hair, lifting a lock to reveal a silvered, round scar from the trepanning where the sage healers had relieved the pressure of a blood clot. Saving Kyle's life, but aye, he would never be that man again. Kyle's chin lifted with an arrogant tilt, and his hooded eyes fixed on Arlan—the expression of disdain Arlan had borne all his youth now flew at him. Sharper than any spear, it pierced his chest, catching his breath.

Kyle still despises me.

The grey-haired warrior approaching bore no obvious weapons, but metal armour clad his torso. It was Ciarán, and he halted his war horse then dismounted, landing lightly on the ground despite the weight of the metal breastplate he wore. Arlan pulled up Mengus and, slipping his leg over his stallion's neck, dropped to the ground. He raised his hand to Bàn.

"Stay mounted, sword-brother." He slipped his baldric from his shoulder and handed *Camhanaich* to Bàn.

He shortened the distance between himself and Ciarán Gallawain until he stood only three paces away.

The tall, lithe stature of the man brought flashes of remembrance to Arlan's mind. A dark evening, a dance of swords, a searing pain on his arm and cheek, Drayce screaming like a deamhan, then the man was gone. Arlan suppressed a gasp. Wave kinked hair, long nose, and the same oval-shaped face as Mother's—the family likeness was unmistakable.

Ciarán's chin tilted, and Arlan glanced at Kyle.

"I would prefer to end this conflict with negotiation." Arlan held his voice firm, ignoring a tremble in his belly.

Ciarán's fingers clenched and unclenched, a dark hardness coming to his hooded, grey eyes.

"Ha! You know you lose before you begin." His cousin's well-spoken voice held the sharp edge of cut ice.

"I wish to avoid bloodshed. And I require my brother's return."

"It is far too late for such. To avoid more blood spilled, you will surrender."

"I will not give my people over to your rule. They will remain free."

"Then I will take them." Ciarán bent down and grabbed a handful of dirt, the breeze stirring loose strands of long, grey hair across his face. "Come, boy king, and I will crush you," he said, his voice like grinding rocks as he forced out the words. "I let you go once, but no more. You will be as dust borne on the wind. All will look for you, but you will not be found."

He raised his hand, releasing the dirt. The air caught a fine silken spray, carrying it away, each grain disappearing in the breeze. Ciarán looked through his brows, lips curving upward.

Arlan ground his teeth, heat radiating against the shudder in his belly.

This man cannot win.

Will not win.

He had no exceptional senses as Vygeas, nor the magic his daughter held. Only the perceptions of any mortal.

And one thing I do perceive—evil fills Ciarán Gallawain.

"Very well." Arlan backed away, his stare never leaving the dark, hate-controlled eyes of his cousin's.

Once out of sword reach, he spun, ears sharpened to any movement behind him, and ran to Mengus, jump mounting him as best he could in his maille, then grabbed his sword from Bàn.

"Come, Bàn. We have a battle to fight and a war to win."

FIFTY

— • —

Where are your tears!
Dál Gaedhle is moor grass flattened by the wind.
An ancient oak fallen, its trunk splintered, acorns scattered.
Where are your tears?

WORDS OF RIEINMELLTH
ANCIENT WARRIOR QUEEN OF DÁL CRUINNE

Eastern Clanlands of Dál Gallain
Mòr Cath Làraich

"Tell us all." Arlan stood with Óengus and two lower-ranking tor warrior leaders, plus his faithful troop, Rhiannon, and Eifion. Sweat trickled down his temples and his torc's cool touch surrounded his neck. His maille sat heavily on his shoulders, along with the responsibility of leading his warbands against...

He flicked his head in a slight shake. Nae, they battled not solely against Ciarán. There was more to the man now. Perhaps there had been all along and, with a perceived victory eminent, the *true* man emerged—or the true force behind the man. Arlan let his breath out through his nostrils.

Óengus pursed his lips, his hand gripping his sword pommel. "The warriors who harry us be not from the Dál Cruinne *I* know. Unless much has changed in three thousand years since my death."

Arlan blinked and Bàn's thumb rubbing his upper lip froze.

"Explain yourself, man."

"They wear strips of leather for kilt, and sandals. Their shields are square and long, and their swords short. They collect together, shields covering afore, above, and behind, and ram into my warriors like an armoured turtle—but faster." The corner of his mouth flickered in a flash of a smile. "They speak a strange rhythmic tongue. Disciplined and organised. I have never seen their like."

261

"Oh!" Rhiannon exclaimed.

"What, daughter?" Eifion had leaned forward, intent on the description given by the tor warrior. "You know who these are who thwart our bravest warriors?"

"They sound like the Roman Legion." Rhiannon's expression screwed in disbelief.

"Dragon's *Damainte* breath!" Arlan shouted, flaming heat coursing through his veins. "The bassa has secured armies from your world." He glared at Rhiannon.

"From the Other World's past. Hundreds of years ago. Can he do that?" she asked Eifion.

"It would seem so." Eifion slid his hands into the sleeves of his robe and his vision turned inward as though seeking to recall what he knew of such.

"Eifion." Arlan suppressed a groan. "We have not our cannon and Gallawain's front line has four." Arlan pulled his mouth to the side, cringing slightly. "Can ye magic ours here?"

Bàn grunted, Rhiannon's eyes widened, and Eifion snapped his gaze to Arlan.

"Nae, my king. Magic works not like a portal."

"A portal!" Rhiannon cried. "Didn't Rhynne say there's a dozen here in this glen? What if there's one on the coast? Rhynne can get them through!"

"At this day's sunset, if she returns in time to tell us that Leuchars is at the coast." Bàn's voice was low and clear. "If he *is* at the coast and *if* there is a portal there." He crossed his arms.

Rhiannon's shoulders dropped. "It was worth a thought."

"Does the mage hold on the mountain agree to assist us, Bàn?" Arlan asked. *I grasp at straws.*

"I have heard naught of a reply, nor if our tor messenger even reached them. If we were to send another message now, it is over a day's ride to their mountain. That way." Bàn pointed to the mouth of the glen where the Gallawain army stood facing them, cannon silent, and a stirring breeze tickling their standards and horses' manes.

Silence hung around his group of faithful warriors. Rhiannon's drooping shoulders lifted, and she placed her gaze on Arlan. Eifion looked mid-distance, like he scoured his mind. Bàn rolled his shoulders, flexing muscles. Indeed, Angus, Adele, and Douglas straightened, gripping sword handles. Muir stood stern-faced.

"We await your commands, Warrior King." A grim smile crept across Óengus' lips.

"To the defences," Arlan ordered. "We fight off their approach. Each guard the other's back." He tilted his head. "Mayhap we can hold them till our cannon arrive, and George's journey to us will not be for naught."

"Ah, Lord Arlan." George spoke from behind his close warriors, and Arlan peered past them. *How long had the man stood there?*

"You'll need to move your palisades back and make barricades maybe half a mile from their cannon. That's their possible range. Ah, that's one sixth of a league, I think. And move them back more every time Ciarán moves his cannon forward." George looked out of place in his clothing from the Other World, but the man showed his worth.

"You heard him," Bàn said to the tor warriors who stood next to George. "And get the man some armour!"

With one eye on the army behind him, Arlan moved with his warriors to the distance suggested by George further into the glen and ordered the resetting of the palisades. He would leave the caltrops already set in place. George hurried back to the tor warriors preparing the timber.

"Your daughter returns, lord." Douglas looked into the sky, shading his eyes from the glary grey. "On yer wee beast."

Arlan turned to the south. No dragon flew through the clouds.

"Nae, lord, she comes by way of the west, skirting the enemy."

Arlan spun. Rhynne flew high by the southern edge of Gallawain's army, Drayce emitting a shriek. From where George stood by the cut wood he turned to face her, his glasses glinting, then he headed to Arlan. Drayce landed behind the warriors laying defences then Rhynne slid off and ran to Arlan.

"Father," her voice choked. "Leuchars is still at sea. Nowhere near landing. I returned the long way. The Dál Gaedhle army is held back, flanked by guys in ancient armour. They look like they're closing in on them on either side."

George reached them. "The pincher movement of the ancient Greeks," he said.

"Ciarán's warbands still block Vygeas and the Monsae warbands," Rhynne continued. "So, not good news here, either? I see the guys on the rise haven't moved."

"Nae, not as yet," Arlan said.

"But Gallawain made demands on your father," Eifion said grimly. "We defend ourselves."

"To the death," Douglas said.

"Dad!" Rhynne spun to George. "I'll get you through at sunset."

"No, Rhynne." George wiped his forehead with a neatly folded handkerchief. "I'll stay and get these cannons set up when they arrive."

"But..."

George shook his head.

"Rhynne, ye can keep lookout for us." Bàn then looked at Arlan. "Tell us of their movements, aye?"

"Keep a safe distance," Arlan said to Rhynne, then faced Bàn. "Gather our warriors. I wish to speak to them."

Rhiannon remained staring at the warriors on the rise, and Rhynne followed her mother's gaze.

"What, Rhiannon?" Arlan clasped her elbow as he passed her, then turned.

Ciarán sat upon his horse near the cannon. The lightly clad warriors, who appeared to be those manning the cannon, stood stock still. The breeze stirred standards and loose plaid, while along the line-up of warriors, horses shifted from hoof to hoof and shook their heads, their manes flicking.

"Why aren't they moving?" Rhiannon's eyes narrowed. "What are they waiting for?"

Arlan focused. Ciarán nodded to the mage in black beside him.

The young man turned his horse then galloped away.

FIFTY-ONE

My hands are trained for battle
My heart prepared for war.
Like a ferocious boar, I gore my enemies
My foes lie dead in my path
Their weapons strewn aside
And war horses flee like shaky-leggéd colts.
Lairds bow at my feet
They grovel for mercy
From the victor of kings.

POETRY OF A KING
ÀRD RÌGH RHONAN IUBHAR
(4030-4090 POST DRAGON WARS)

Eastern Clanlands of Dál Gallain
Mòr Cath Làraich

Arlan sat in the saddle, stirrup leather creaking and Mengus snorting and stomping a hoof. Sweat stuck his padded tunic to his back, and he tugged at the front with his free hand, lifting it away from his chest only for it to sink back, stuck again. Ahead of him, the Gallawain army with its cannon sat menacingly on the rise that lined the mouth of this glen. The caltrops and pits Bàn had set were between his warriors and Gallawain's army, ready to pierce the hooves of the foe's mounts or break their legs with a stumble into a shallow, narrow pit.

Arlan spun Mengus to face behind at the blunt end of the glen where the sea of warriors he had called to him stood attentive. He should give them a rousing battle speech, but in truth, he needed to muster his own courage. His band of less than four hundred now faced a horde of warriors, some with tactics unknown to him. He could not plan strategies against those he'd never encountered. His heart threatened to sink.

No. He would not allow himself such despair. His warriors were brave and faithful. He touched the torc at his neck, nestling cool at his throat.

He was their king. *They* his faithful people. He would *not* fail them.

"We fight not for ourselves but for Dál Gaedhle. For our people to live in freedom and peace. To grow crops, herd stock, wed, bear children and nurture them to live lives of contentment." He looked at the surviving tor warriors. "You fight for a warrior king. I promise I will fight with all my heart and be worthy of your service, and of those who have already given their all."

He closed his eyes. What hope could he give them? Outnumbered. Tor warriors dying a second time, diminishing his army's strength. Cut off from the support of the Dál Gaedhle army and Vygeas' ally warbands. No chance of Leuchars and cannon arriving in time.

The odds are truly against us. He opened his eyes wide, including all in his view.

"Nae friends, we fight for our very lives this day. Be brave. Know my love and admiration are with all of you."

He turned to those beside him. Two pairs of mauve eyes full of trust looked back at him from the faces of the women most dear to him in this or any world. Bàn dropped his hand, ceasing the thumb scratch across his upper lip, and raised his head and shoulders high. Eifion, and those remaining of his warband, plus George, all set their focus on him.

"I wish ye were not here," he said quietly to them all.

He leaped from the saddle, as did Rhiannon and Rhynne. He pulled Rhiannon close and pressed his face into her hair. Above the odour of sweat-stained leather, the perfume that was *her* filled his head.

Rhiannon raised her face to him. "Well, we are here. And here for you, our warrior king."

Rhynne ran to him, then clasped her arms around both of them. "I would never have missed this, Father."

"Aye, Arlan. Sword-brother," Bàn said from the grey, then cleared his throat. "We are for you. Know this as a surety. We will not turn, nor faint, though the battle be against us. We will stand firm."

Bàn's words received affirming grunts from Eifion, the others from Arlan's remaining warband, and even George.

"Aye." Arlan breathed out the word, the only one that would come in that moment. Then the unnerving stillness on the rise nagged at him.

"Rhynne, please see what's happening. Why they move not," he said over Rhiannon's head.

Rhynne nodded, then spun to Bàn, who dropped from his horse and ran to her. They met in a crushing hug, though their lips met in an earnest gentleness. Arlan blinked back the tears that would come.

There must be a future for them. And all those he loved.

He must make it so.

Rhynne eased back from Bàn, who drew aside the hair from her face and tucked it behind an ear. He leaned into her, forehead on forehead. Arlan turned from their private moment, Bàn's deep whisper barely reaching his ears.

Arlan looked at Rhiannon, still in his arms, then kissed her. His chapped lips to her soft mouth pressed hard. Then he let go, releasing her from their embrace.

Bàn stood back from Rhynne, then nodded. She whistled to Drayce, who had flown to a redoubt and perched there, raising her nostrils to the wind, and flicking her forked tongue in and out, tasting the air. The dragon turned her head to Rhynne's whistle, double blinked, swished her spiked tail around behind her, but didn't move.

"Huh? That's the first time she's ignored me." Rhynne placed a hand on her hip and whistled again.

Drayce lifted from the redoubt and glided to land right next to Arlan. War horses nickered and side stepped away. She creeped the few steps closer and nudged him, smooching like she did when she desired a scratch.

"Very well, my dragon." He patted Drayce's head.

His dragon snuggled close under his chin, and he hugged her neck and leaned into her knobbly head. Her cool black scales were smooth beneath his fingers. She clicked, the noise she made when content, but this time with a mournful ring to it.

"Wow, Drayce is clinging to you," Rhynne said, then she shook her head. "Something's going on. I can usually hear her thoughts, but I'm not getting anything coherent."

Drayce clicked and grunted, then sprung into the air, gusting Arlan's hair into his face.

"Hey, wait!" Rhynne shouted, but Drayce kept flying.

Arlan looked at Eifion. "My mage, can ye determine if you can see for me?"

"I shall try, but I shall require"—Eifion faced the trees at the very end of the glen, a quarter league's distance— "I shall ride to that ancient forest." He stepped to his horse, mounted, and rode off.

"Angus, guard him, please," Arlan ordered.

Angus kicked his war horse after Eifion. A loud pop came from the rise, followed by a *whoosh*, then a spray of dirt exploded from the ground in front of tor warriors in the middle of the glen. Horses shrieked and two fled riderless.

"We need to move back!" George shouted.

Warriors on foot clambered to grab either end of the palisades, then ran back in the direction Eifion had gone. Arlan jump-mounted Mengus, and so did his close troop onto their war horses. Adele pulled George onto her mount, the man all limbs and awkwardness as he settled behind the warrior woman who dwarfed him. Rhynne slid behind Bàn, who yelled to a small group of tor warriors, ordering them to man the first redoubt. They were to throw the gathered pile of rocks at the oncoming warriors. Those tor warriors still mounted brought up the rear behind Arlan.

So, Ciarán has finally made his move.

Arlan kicked Mengus to a canter, his troop joining him. He passed George sitting behind Adele.

"Beside that next rock outcropping should be a safe distance." The horse's gait thumped George's words.

Arlan rushed past clumps of wood, his pulse quickening and the green foliage a blur while Mengus tore the distance beneath him. He pulled up his war horse just after the place where tor warriors responsible for honing timber for suitable use worked quickly. Adele lowered George off her horse, and he joined them, barking orders. Tor warriors on foot came behind Arlan and set the mobile palisades in place once again.

Muir and Douglas set about with other warriors building barricades from whatever dead branches and rocks they could find. Arlan turned back to Ciarán's army, where smoke from cannon fire lingered and a cry arose from the rise.

Dál Gallain warriors moved forward. Those tor warriors who had stayed behind and were now on the front line, stood in a protective row, forming a shield wall. The clunk of wood on wood, as they knocked their shields together, rang through the war cries.

The ground vibrated through Mengus, touching Arlan. It grated louder, but wasn't coming from near the mouth of the glen where Dál Gallain clashed with ancient shields. Arlan faced the nearest side of the valley where a glow appeared.

White sand blew through this glimmering. Warriors on ponies charged out, dressed in baggy breeches and all holding bows. A rain of arrows flew from the close-riding bunch encircling a group of tor warriors like a swarm of wasps. Their stings flew before warriors of Sgiathach had a chance to raise their shields. The riding archers skirted yet another group, arrows flying. Arlan's jaw slackened at their accuracy. Even those who shot their arrows while twisting to aim behind, passing the tor warriors, hit their targets. A tor warrior shouted a command, and their hounds gathered as a pack and gave chase, nipping the ponies' heels. Dogs yelped and dropped, arrow fletching spiking from their backs.

"Archers from the ancient Mongolian steppes." George's tone held awe.

Smoke billowed out of another glow and with it, men holding... *guns*. Named *rifles* in the Other World, if Arlan recalled correctly from a documentary of their First World War. These had short swords attached to the ends. A dark-robed mage holding a large smooth stone in each hand walked among them, incongruous in his flowing black against their tight-fitting khaki garments and round metal helms. Behind and through the circle of smoke, sat a boggy field of dug trenches, sandbags lining their tops. Wire of barbs wound round palisades.

A mule pulled a cart through. Two men in khaki clothing stood on it with a gun... aye, a large gun... tripod mounted on the cart. It flashed rapidly.

Och, no. This one's bullets hit the closest tor warriors. Some jolted and fell. A continual barrage pelted those quick enough to raise their shields, but some bullets pierced the thick wood, leaving warriors grunting or slumping to the ground.

Arlan spun to another, closer, grating vibration. A round opening stood nearby. A portal, no doubt, for yet another mage carrying a flaming torch guided people through. These were clad in a thin, sleek cloth, with gadgets buckled on belts around their waists and across shoulders. Helmets with clear face shields covered their heads, and each held a gun like none Arlan recognised from the Other World. The view through the portal showed no land, only sky with floating boat-like vessels but without sails, dotting the dark behind them.

"What is this?" Bàn shouted in his ear. "Strange warriors pour from the portals, yet it is still day."

"The mages hold them open," Rhynne said from behind Bàn.

Along a section of the burn that ran through the glen, the water stirred. Its flow stopped and lifted like a whirlwind, swirling in a circle on its end.

Another portal?

The bow of a longship peeked through. A mage stood on the foredeck behind the prow adorned with a carved dragonhead, holding a miniature swirling water circle. With its shallow draft, the ship entered the burn, but then ran aground. Undaunted, warriors clothed in leather and furs, and wielding battle axes jumped off the narrow vessel and onto the pebbled bed of the water course. They roared and shook their weapons, turning this way and that, then headed as one toward a group of tor warriors, spittle flying and shouts spewing from their mouths like angry gods.

"Oh, no!" Rhiannon pointed to the warriors approaching from that near portal where the night sky sat behind these the strangest of warriors. "Spacemen?" She choked on her words.

"Laser guns!" George's voice strangled, and light darted to the lifted shields of the nearest tor warriors. "They'll be cut in two."

The deep throated cry of a warrior came from beside another holding a charred shield. The stench of scorched flesh wafted over to Arlan. Flashes flew from the guns of these clear-helmeted warriors, many in only moments. Solid wooden shields and swords alike were severed in half. Tor warriors doubled over, abdomens gaping, limbs severed, but with little bleeding. They writhed in agony.

More shields cracked, smashed by berserker warriors laying into tor men. Dogs nipped at the sea-faring warriors' heels, but they shook them off like rags.

"Stop them!" Rhiannon's voice held an ache. "We've no hope against this!"

Arlan surveyed the scene. Gallawain warriors pressed toward them along the valley. The clash of swords and battle axes battering wooden shields rang from the opening end of the glen, accompanied by the hoarse cries of warriors. The rapport of machinegun fire came from one side of the glen as bloodied brave men crumpled on the heather. Cannon fire rang and warriors exploded in a mist of dirt. Mounted archers corralled and harried small groups of his own warriors. Battle axes cleaved heads from bodies. And a soundless light burned through tor warriors like a hot knife through...

"Retreat! To Eifion! We can regroup near the far forest." Arlan dug his heels into Mengus, shooting a glance behind to ensure all who could follow, did. His ears rang from the gunfire, competing with the thunder of hooves and pounding pulse in his temples, his mind scrambling. He gritted his teeth.

Father had said there was *always* a way.

And so, he must find it.

FIFTY-TWO

When chaos beats me,
Inundates me, sweeps over my head, leaving me in the deep.
This truth I grasp with the grip of a drowning man:
Ye are with me... and you will never slacken your hold.

POETRY OF A KING
ÀRD RÌGH RHONAN IUBHAR
(4030-4090 POST DRAGON WARS)

Eastern Clanlands of Dál Gallain
Mòr Cath Làraich
The Ancient Forest

Arlan, son of my heart, Warrior King, your high kingship is tested.

Eifion lowered himself from his horse, ignoring the streak of pain down his thigh. Battle's din pounded his back. No need to secure the reins, lest the beast die in battle. Let the creature flee.

He strode to the nearest tree, a thick-trunked, ancient oak and sturdy with age. He embraced it. The aromatic and comforting scent of oak, like a well-aged whisky, filled him with a headiness.

Then his spirit soared.

Grasping the treetops with his spirit's fingers, he faced the battle. The horde of Dál Gallain warbands had surged forward. Doors to the Other World had opened wide and warriors poured in.

In his state, in this *other* plane... the spiritual plane... the *real* battle lay before him.

Darkness heaved and laughed, seething with joyous pleasure at death, and grinned in absolute delight as warriors hacked and souls lifted or sank.

Eifion shook his head at the incomprehensible weapons that burned with a touch of heated spear-light. Chaos surrounded Arlan and filled the battlefield. A chaos untouchable and unseen by Arlan.

Neither by my child nor my precious granddaughter.
A blackness so thick it was solid sprang into being just in front of Arlan.
Eifion shuddered in both spirit and body.
Then raised his vision skyward.
O Fountain of all Being...

The thunder of war horses' hooves surrounded Arlan while battle cries and cannon booms battered his ears. Arlan faced the end of the glen. Eifion had dismounted and strode to the wood, his horse trailing the reins over lying stone slabs. Angus had pulled his horse up in front of the trees and faced out toward the fray. A *whoosh* pierced Arlan's hearing. A long pointy object flashed by him, and the forest to the right of Eifion burst into flames. Eifion flinched, then grasped tightly to the nearest tree, and Angus' war horse whinnied as he pulled the rearing creature into line. Eifion's mount shrieked and galloped toward Arlan's approaching warriors. Arlan slowed Mengus, then twisted in the saddle to the origin of the sound.

Not cannon.

Warriors in grey uniform stood hastily from a squat, one with a large tube over her shoulder, and retreated to yet another portal held open by a mage with a small shrub in a pack strapped to her back. The costume of these warriors was familiar: the material pattern of urban-camo from the Other World.

"He has hunted every time in the Other World for any mercenary game for the adventure," Bàn spat.

"And the money," Rhynne shouted. "Bet he's promised them riches."

Arlan and his troop continued toward the granite slabs that lay by the forest where Eifion stared up at the trees that had escaped the flames.

"No! Another portal's opening." Rhynne pointed. "There, just in front of those rocks that look like a dismantled Stone Henge!"

"Where?"

Figures emerged from nowhere. One, dark-robed, stayed at the open portal, his cloak flapping, swirled by the wind. Arlan pulled Mengus up sharp, Rhiannon halted beside him on Bridie, and Bàn on the grey with Rhynne, stopped close by. Adele, Muir, and Douglas skidded their horses to a halt, mounts tossing their heads, and shocked cries emerged from all riders.

Ciarán Gallawain, still dressed for battle, dragged Kyle along by the collar and stood just behind a prostrate slab. The Laird of Lorain in his orange tartan stepped through, followed by more Gallawain warriors, a younger one a mere step behind Ciarán. The portal slowly closed, the view of the wind-swirled mage closing like the curtain on a troubadour.

"Come, boy king, I have a proposition for you." Ciarán's commanding voice drew Arlan.

Ciarán led Kyle to stand just behind the granite slab.

"Hello, little brother." Kyle's wrists were bound in front of him, but his condescending stare remained, despite the sweat trickling down his brow.

"Hush." Ciarán's sharp tone matched his drawn sword, which he now pointed at Kyle. Kyle flinched, the whites of his eyes prominent. "Be still," Ciarán ordered, his words ringing out unnaturally loud in the natural arena, and the battle behind Arlan quietened.

"Do not harm him!" Arlan's voice came out strained. "He's your son!"

Ciarán sneered, white teeth glinting. "Your life for your brother's. What do you say? Is a brother who is only half a brother truly worth it?"

Deep murmurs of disgust from behind Arlan tweaked his ears, but Kyle's stagger filled his view.

If I decline, I'd be free of Kyle's derision. Free of this bully. The thought took half a second. Arlan's face steamed, and he dropped his gaze to the ground. He would not be so low. So selfish.

How could I think such a thing of my brother, my flesh and blood? It was tantamount to fratricide!

He returned his stare to Ciarán.

"Your life for this simpleton." Ciarán pressed his sword point onto Kyle's throat. Kyle yelped. "Come now, such a straightforward decision should not take so long for one who leads an army." Ciarán raised a sardonic brow. "A kingdom."

Kyle whimpered, his eyes locking on Ciarán.

"No, Arlan." Rhiannon's tremulous voice came to his ear, soon followed by Bàn's.

"Nae, sword-brother. Listen not to the deamhan," he hissed.

Rhiannon nudged her horse closer, then her long fingers gripped his arm, tight despite the padded tunic and maille he wore. A low growl came from Bàn.

The man could demand worse.

Ciarán lifted his chin, letting go the scruff of Kyle's neck with such force that Kyle stumbled back, waving his bound wrists around to regain his balance.

"No. I have something better. Your life for *your people*." Ciarán rolled his tongue over the words. "Ah, now there's a notion. I will keep Dál Gallain—return my clan lands in Dál Gaedhle to my Uncle Adomàn's son"—Ciarán's mouth turned to an uncomfortable sneer— "retreat and leave your people to live their miserable, ignorant lives. I could rule my eastern kingdom and pursue its expansion in another direction." A fine, greying eyebrow curled. "It will stay the slaughter." He lifted his chin to the battlefield beyond Arlan.

Arlan need not look to the churned glen strewn with bodies, mangled and torn beyond recognition, and lying still. The silence stretched on the stone platform, threatening to rip, as Arlan's mind whirled in a tangle of thoughts.

Had Ciarán really just demanded this? His own life for that of his people? Arlan shook his head briefly. *Nae, I should not be surprised.*

"No!" Rhiannon whispered harshly in his ear.

"Or"—Ciarán spoke in a level tone, as though he negotiated the price of a steed—"you live and I send my armies, my dragon, and my cannon and other weapons throughout the land of Dál Gaedhle. These devices from the Other World are marvellously destructive, are they not? And"—he tipped his head— "I shall begin with those who stand by you now, of course."

A dull repetitive thunk battered Arlan's brain—his own heartbeat. Ciarán's demands gave short time to ponder. He would go with what his heart held, and not his instinct.

The swell of alarmed voices rose at the rise where Ciarán's army had gathered, and rippled through the valley and by every portal, followed by a roar, the timbre and depth prickling Arlan's skin. Ciarán's leer stretched and the lines on his forehead deepened. Arlan turned at the astonished cries of his warriors, Mengus stirring beneath him.

It was a dragon. Massive and totally black bar a red breast. The wake of its wing strokes gusted against his tor warriors gathered to one side. It lifted its head, opened its mouth, and belched flame into the copse at the edge of the glen beside them. Trees burst into fire, crackling loud and pouring heat over tor warriors who lifted their shields to cover themselves. Warriors' mounts whinnied and shied. Spacemen, Mongols, urban fighters, and First World War soldiers all stared at the sky, mouths dropping open.

Ciarán gritted his teeth. "Imbecile! Why does he waste his flame on wood!"

It had been a struggle. The beast was a wild one, strongly wilful. It had taken all of Bram's skill to enter and wrest control.

He'd soared over the cannon, then along the battlefield, now strewn with the twice-dead of MacEnoicht's tor army. Gallawain warriors lay also among the ruined bodies of men, women, and horses. The mêlée heaved. Warriors from the Other World's wars, given access through open portals, strove with MacEnoicht's warriors. Although, those nearer the lying stones where Lord Ciarán stood, now set their attention there.

The forest beside the old mage, Eifion, was ablaze, but the mage flinched not, intent on his task.

Bram breathed deep and forced out a dragon roar. Flame burst forth, and he aimed it to consume the forest to the other side of the mage. Trees were the old one's source of magic; he would be powerless without them. Lord Ciarán, miniature on the battlefield below, shook his fist in Bram's direction. Bram soared on and turned, readying for another swoop across the field.

FIFTY-THREE

War chiefs will negotiate. As far as possible, as much as it depends upon you, keep your army from battle. Diplomacy is always preferential to combat. It is a shame to needlessly spill the blood of faithful warriors. Champions may combat to resolve disputes.

ADVICE TO WAR CHIEFS
WARRIOR SAGE TAPAÌDH
(4009-4059 POST DRAGON WARS)

Eastern Clanlands of Dál Gallain
Mòr Cath Làraich

Arlan's chest constricted, his temples tumultuous. He forced himself to breathe. Fresh moisture trickled a line down the side of his face. He wiped it away, blood-tinged sweat staining his glove.

"Ye cannae trust him, Arlan." Bàn's deep voice travelled to him above the astonished cries of warriors, his words as though through a snowstorm.

"I must trust the word of one who, although now has no title in Dál Gaedhle, was once a nobleman-warrior." *No matter how low my cousin has sunk, a warrior's vow is his bond.*

A mist came in front of Arlan's vision as he stood at the fallen stones. A swirl of chaos buffeted him and the space between himself and Ciarán. This man was chaos itself and sought to push against him. Push him away. Give him no choice in his destiny, nor that of his people.

A wind stirred the leaves in the tree Eifion now stood so close beside. It was an ancient tree with a wide trunk, and it grew beyond the monoliths arranged at this end of the glen. Although filled with smoke that stung Arlan's eyes, the wind blew a recollection his way—the arms of love holding him at his kingmaking.

He held onto the remembrance and looked around at those he loved. His sword-brother. His father-in-law and adviser now in what remained of the forest. His brother who returned little of the love he'd ever sought to give. His own close warriors, and even George, to whom he owed so much.

And his wife and daughter... He looked Rhiannon in the eye as she sat beside him on Bridie, then he silently took her hand from his arm, where she held it in a tight grip, and gave her hand a gentle squeeze.

Arlan returned his attention to Ciarán. The man's steel-grey eyes deepened.

Ciarán meant it.

My cousin will kill them all if I decline.

Ciarán would order his warriors with superior weapons to slaughter his. He would then move to Leuchars coming via sea. He would demolish Monsae and kill all allies. Then work his way to The Keep—flattening the Dál Gaedhle army on his way—take control of The Keep and, with his mages and the weapons his warriors carry—ones without answer in this world... Leuchars, Vygeas... none would withstand Ciarán's onslaught.

Arlan let go of Rhiannon's hand, then grasped his sword handle. It dug deep into his palm.

I am a king, am I not? And kings kept their people safe. Lead by example.

If he wanted his people to live in peace, love would have to go with it.

Love—an essential ingredient in such a life.

Selfless and sacrificial. Father had shown him how. He had been a great clan king and àrd rìgh. An ache for him pierced his soul.

So now, as their king, *he* would show them how to do it.

He dismounted Mengus to the cries of protest from Rhynne and Rhiannon, and Bàn's deep warning growl. Off in the forest, Eifion still embraced a tree. Arlan glanced over his shoulder at the strained faces of his close warriors. George peered from behind Adele, pushing his glasses up his nose, taking in all.

"I will fight you to the death, Gallawain, as is our tradition." Arlan held *Camhanaich* tighter. "I, myself, will be my army's champion."

Ciarán may best him, for he had done so in the past at that jagged stone circle by a portal.

But if I die, it will be with a sword in my hand.

The ring of his warriors unsheathing their weapons surrounded him, their mounts stirring. The warriors with Ciarán stepped forward, blades threatening. Arlan threw a glare behind to his own. They halted, faces hard, eyes creasing.

"This is the way," he whispered. *You will have a chance if I submit.*

"You are a king, you say. And a high king at that." Ciarán's greying eyebrows were a line. "Galan, remove from him his royal torc," Ciarán ordered the young warrior, who then stepped forward.

Arlan baulked, stepping back.

"Now, now." Ciarán tutted. "You will allow it." He bit off every word.

Arlan yielded his neck, and Galan widened the silver ring, only marginally, then tore it from his neck, leaving a burn in its wake. Galan handed the torc to Ciarán, who prised it apart and secured it around his own throat.

Kyle trembled and sent furtive glances Ciarán's way. Ciarán reached out and gripped Kyle's arm, holding him steady. "No, you will see this." Authority rang in his voice.

A single bead of sweat trickled down Arlan's face, mirroring the moisture tracking between his shoulder blades. Images flashed through his mind. Mighty angelic warriors gifting him with sword skill and agility. A glowing triskelion imbuing him with strength. Heat rose from his arm once more and spread throughout his being.

He could do it. He could win.

Arlan stood taller, shoulders straightening, then turned to his people. "Enough warriors have already sacrificed their all. You will die if I don't fight him."

"Oh, how noble." Sarcasm dripped from Ciarán's tongue.

Rhiannon's face crumpled, and a red flush climbed Rhynne's cheeks.

"But ye cannae trust the cur," Bàn repeated, his expression hardening, jaw muscles popping.

"Lord Lùthas." Ciarán curled his lip at Bàn. "He trusted you with his wife on many occasions—the secret love of your life until you found their daughter. If he can trust you, he can trust me."

"No." Rhiannon's plea was barely a whisper as she slid off Bridie and thrust herself into Arlan's arms.

He sent a look over her head to Bàn. *Kill him if I lose and he's rejoicing over my body.*

Bàn nodded silently, his face hard like flint, and by the tree, Eifion grunted.

He held Rhiannon at arm's length, seeking to hold her tear-streaked gaze. "I have forgiven you. Tell me now that you forgive yourself. I hold naught against you. Do the same."

She didn't answer, her mouth trembling as she drank him in with her eyes, as he did her.

"Tell me. Promise me. Torment yourself nae longer."

She nodded, her lower lids filling with tears.

"I love you, my wife." His voice held a slight tremor.

She swallowed, the quiet gulp reaching his ears. "And I you, my husband." Her voice was as soft as thistledown. "Now, go kill him."

Bàn and Rhynne dropped from the grey with swords drawn and set a fighting stance. He released Rhiannon and held his free palm up to them.

"Nae." The force of Arlan's words halted them, and Rhiannon's expression tore.

Readying to fight, he wiped his nose with his maille sleeve, only to graze it.

Galan stepped forward. "Nae swords today," he growled, reaching for Arlan to surrender his sword.

What?

"Ye may sheath your weapons," Ciarán commanded those close to Arlan, his voice steel-edged. "Arlan, cousin"—now the man spoke like they were long-lost friends— "ye need not yours. You agreed—your life for theirs. But the manner of your death is mine to decide."

No fight? No chance to beat him? *Then why did the mighty ones at my kingmaking gift me, if not to save my people?*

"I can't believe you're doing this!" Rhynne shouted at Gallawain. "You're a crazy bastard."

"Rhynne," George hissed.

Rhynne directed her venom at Ciarán. "I wish I wasn't related to you!"

"Hush, Rhynne." Arlan faced her, his heart stilling at her lined forehead and quivering lip. He gathered her into his arms. "There is more going on here than you see, my child." He whispered. "Trust me. And trust the one who sees the whole plan."

"Come, come." Ciarán tapped his foot and lifted his hand, wriggling his fingers. "The family farewells are touching but cause such delay. Tarry no longer!" He snapped his fingers.

A screech reached the glen. A dragon's call, but not from the large dragon soaring in circles overhead.

"Drayce!" Rhynne faced the sky, her voice held strain.

Drayce soared over the rise and headed straight for the big, black beast who had torched the wood.

"No. Don't!" Rhynne cried, then ran from Arlan's grasp and headed for the forest where Eifion stood.

FIFTY-FOUR

The attractive flower of the perennial known as the foxglove, like all substances holding healing value, is therapeutic in correct dosage. Deadly poison to the heart and its beating when administered in too large a quantity.

SAGE PHELAN'S HERB LORE

Eastern Clanlands of Dál Gallain
Mòr Cath Làraich

A screech rent the air, piercing the ears of the dragon Bram now mastered. The animal cry belonged to a younger, smaller dragon. Bram had heard her before with his human ears. The one named Drayce.

MacEnoicht's beast.

His pet.

The diminutive dragon sped toward him like an arrow released from a longbow. Bram flapped the dragon's massive wings and veered to the right. He would turn to make another pass of the battle and dodge the youngling. The battlefield's chaos returned to his view and a sharp pinch caught his tail. He turned the colossal beast as the smaller dragon darted beneath him.

Drayce has nipped this giant?

She left his view, and so he moved the beast's head from side to side. No dragon. The acute hearing caught the soft wing flap coming from behind. A nip and a shriek in his right ear.

This monster of a dragon was so encumbered with size and age! Impossible to manoeuvre as was required for battle. Lord Ciarán had insisted—ordered on pain of punishment—that Bram find the largest beast in the land. Did Ciarán not comprehend the *torture* it was to control one!

Bram followed the wake of the small beast, his focus on her tail. She darted here and there across the wide glen. He snapped at her, grabbing a mouthful of air. She flew on to the end of Lord Ciarán's Mòr Cath Làraich, over the sharp knuckled mountain, and on to ice-thickened peaks that sat between the ancient glaciers.

He grunted. *The sooner I rid myself of this annoyance, the sooner I can return to Lord Ciarán's task of harrying Dál Gaedhle warriors.*

He pursued.

Arlan stared at his hand, his grasp empty of his daughter. The warrior, Galan, ripped his sword and his dirk from him, then threw them aside. Grabbing Arlan's leather chest armour, he dragged him to Ciarán, who stood by the granite slab. The younger man was surprisingly strong... and determined.

Ciarán's knuckles were white as he held Kyle close to him; his metal breastplate and the short dagger at his belt glinted dully in the cloudy sunlight. With his free hand, he pulled a vial from a pouch at his belt.

"Of a warrior's death, you will not have the honour." Ciarán flipped the cork open with his thumb and held the vial out to him. "Drink." Ciarán's hard voice echoed in the small arena of slumbering sarsens.

Arlan pressed his lips together, willing his heart rate to settle and his breathing to an even rhythm.

If he must die for his people, he would do it with dignity.

Through his thunderous temples, Bàn's growls and Rhiannon's weeping came to him.

"Is there no other way?" Rhiannon said through a sob. "Take me instead."

Ciarán threw back his head, laughter bursting from him. *"Take me instead."* His mocking voice took on a high impersonating note. "You, woman tainted by the Other World, are a worthless harlot. I need a purer sacrifice to achieve my purposes. As much as I hate to admit it—and *hate* it, I do—this young man is more... acceptable."

"A Druidic human sacrifice?" George's accented speech came from the back of Arlan's gathered warriors.

Ciarán lifted his sight to George. "Yes," he hissed. "A sacrifice, though I am unaware of the *Druidic* nature of it." His gaze flew back to Arlan. "Drink!"

Horses reared behind him, and a string of curses flowed from his close warriors. Galan paced back, pushing Rhiannon aside, and joined by the other Gallawain warriors, barred the way.

"Do not harm her!" Arlan shouted. "Stop, my warriors. Desist!" he commanded them, then faced Ciarán. "Do not hurt them! Your bargain was for me. Do not *touch* my people!" His words tore from his mouth.

From his heart.

"Ensure your warriors are in line," Ciarán snarled.

Arlan faced those dearest to him. Bàn stepped to Rhiannon, his face like flint, and held her close, her sobs continuing. Arlan gave them all a curt nod. They returned frowns, Adele's eyes moistening while Douglas coloured the air with expletives.

"Are we behaving now?" Ciarán thrust the vial at Arlan. "Drink!" He flung his words at him.

Arlan took the vial, his fingers trembling around the tiny vessel. He faced his people for a moment, taking in their faces. Rhiannon's, usually the face of love, but now torn with painful emotion. Bàn, mouth tight and nostrils flaring. If only he could look upon Rhynne and Eifion once more.

Placing the vial to his lips, he drank the thick liquid—a mushed vegetable matter. It poured cool down his throat and the vapours, like the stale urine of mice, rose into his nose. He winced and the thudding pulse in his head slowed a touch.

I pounded toward Eifion, my teeth clunking together with each footfall. Eifion leaned against the wide-trunked oak, fingers stretched to cover as much of its circumference as he could. I crunched through dried acorns and thudded against the trunk, the rough bark grazing my cheek, and the fingertips of my right hand touching Eifion's.

"Grandfather?"

His face was a determined stare. He was already there. *With* the tree.

I closed my eyes—and let go, flying through the calming scent of sweet wood. Young, handsome Eifion hovered above the upper canopy, surrounded by a glowing light. I rose to meet him.

Very good you are here, granddaughter, but very grim. Your dragon fights for your father, set against a mage-controlled beast.

What do I do?

Eifion nodded toward the standing stones that weren't standing.

More dire things overshadow in importance.

Darkness hovered around Ciarán as he thrust something into Arlan's hands.

Thick and sharp. I could taste it!

Poison.

No, Father!

Arlan drank, then the darkness thickened.

FIFTY-FIVE

Remain not silent when time to speak the truth.
Though great the cost
Omission's price the dearer.

SAGE GLIOCAS
(2870-2962 POST DRAGON WARS)

Eastern Clanlands of Dál Gallain
Mòr Cath Làraich
The Stones

"Yes." Ciarán's eyes locked on Arlan, his tone holding a satisfied note of triumph. "Thought you could be an àrd rìgh, did you? Follow in your father's footsteps? *Fannlag.*" He spat the word. "You consider yourself noble in this act as your father was in showing mercy and pardoning me. You are a *weakling*, such as he. Embracing the simpler way. Not willing to spend hours on a battlefield exhausted, bruised, cut and bleeding, maimed. Watching those loyal to you spill their entrails and have my warriors stomp on them. Your women warriors raped and torn apart. Yes, even that wife of yours. You're leaving them all to their vainglorious deaths!"

"I told ye he cud nae be trusted!" Bàn cried, joined by the other voices of Arlan's close warband.

Galan and the other Gallawain warriors ran past Arlan, and sword clash erupted behind him. Rhiannon's grunted effort combined with Bàn's and the others. The cries and clash of the battles at open portals recommenced, dimming from his hearing by the moment.

Numbness touched Arlan's fingers and toes, and his thudding heart slowed its beat. His guts knifed pain, his stomach rose and heaved, a black fluid spewing from his mouth, leaving an acid burn on his tongue.

Ciarán jumped back, splashes of vomit just missing his boots, and dragged Kyle with him. "Never mind. The mage assured me the dose would be sufficient, more than required, even in one the size of you."

Arlan staggered, his legs losing their strength. Kyle stared at him, forehead crumpling as his gaze followed Arlan's erratic movements.

"Donnach was content in his own small piece of Dál Cruinne. Never seeking more." Ciarán spoke low, though Arlan heard above the ring of swords close by. "He had it all," Ciarán continued. "He had my kingship. My Alana... Your mother was a treasure. A goddess." Ciarán placed an affectionate arm around Kyle, who cowered beside him. "She gave me you, though I knew it not," he said to Kyle and raising his voice with pride. "Your mother and I had something unique." Ciarán turned his face from Kyle and looked into the mid-distance. "Though her passion was not as great as mine... reluctant, she yielded in the end and soon saw the benefits of our love—"

"What do you mean, *reluctant?*" Arlan's voice croaked, pain wracking his body with every word.

Kyle stiffened and flew his gaze to Arlan, then back to Ciarán. "Did you take Mother by force?" Kyle's voice rose above the striving surrounding Arlan.

"He raped her!" Rhiannon cried. "I saw it... I... had a vision."

The clatter of arms and nearby grunts quietened. Both Kyle and Ciarán looked beyond Arlan to where Rhiannon spoke.

"I've always had visions." Her voice, sounding small, came from behind Arlan.

Arlan's legs weren't there anymore, or so it seemed, and his vision was yellowing. He blinked. *Must be the poison.* He fell to his knees, then the ground rose to meet his face.

Kyle spun to Ciarán, his scowling face hard and determined. "Did you?"

"Would I do such a thing?" Ciarán's tone filled with confidence in Kyle possessing a positive opinion of him, and through Arlan's hazy vision, Ciarán held his head in a cocky tilt.

"Well, yes." Kyle straightened. "You're not a nice man, even for a father. You bully the mage and order all around like you own them." Kyle glanced at the Laird of Lorain standing two paces behind Ciarán.

"Ha!" Ciarán replied in a dismissive tone, then returned his intense stare to Arlan.

The glint of metal flashed from Ciarán's sheath at his belt, Kyle's movement a blur. A dagger handle now pressed neatly between Kyle's bound hands.

"You hurt Mother," Kyle said as he thrust the pointy blade into Ciarán's side, between the metal chest plate and back shield of his armour, his face contorting with the effort.

Ciarán grunted. "What!" He opened his eyes wide, then his hands flew to Kyle's throat.

Kyle slumped to the ground, landing on his knees with Ciarán's hands locked around him. Blood gushed from Ciarán's flank, spurting bright red on the vivid-green grass.

"The sacrifice is done. See, your younger half-brother moves not. I shall not die." Ciarán glanced across to Arlan, his face ashen, and letting go of Kyle's throat, withdrew the dagger from his side, increasing the flow of his crimson life-blood, then cast it aside. "I am promised life immortal."

"You wished to beat death, cousin." Arlan gripped his belly, now tightening in the poison's grasp, and lifted to his hands and knees, limbs shaking with the effort. Ciarán twisted to face him, mouth contorted in alarm.

"Do you really think my demise will save you?" Arlan forced the words out, leaning back to kneel. "Your own actions seal your condemnation."

Ciarán's labouring breath grew heavier. He turned to Kyle who had picked up the dagger.

"Give me that, you imbecile!" He groped for the blade, stumbling to his knees.

"No!" Kyle stood and took a step from Ciarán, holding the blade high and out of Ciarán's flailing reach. Kyle looked to Arlan.

"Help me, little brother." Sweat dripped from Kyle's brow. "You are high king. You must judge this beast of a man who hurt Mother. As well, his life was forfeit the moment he broke his banishment and crossed into Dál Gaedhle lands. Is that not so, my àrd rìgh?"

Ciarán raised his pallid face to Arlan and snarled. Kyle kicked Ciarán's knees, but the man didn't budge. A flash of orange tartan caught the edge of Arlan's vision. Lorain stepped forward and grabbed Ciarán's arms, restraining him with his hands behind his back. Lorain looked to Arlan, a pleading and justified expression on his face. Ciarán gnashed his teeth in his weakened efforts to free himself from Lorain's hold.

Arlan staggered forward on his knees and Kyle stepped to him, the dagger handle secure in his grasp. Arlan stumbled, grabbing Kyle's hands around the dagger, steadying himself.

"No." Ciarán's growl was low and deep. "Pointless." He let out a derisive, husky laugh.

Blood poured from Ciarán's side; floods of it soaked the grass at Arlan's knees.

Why was the man not dead yet?

Arlan directed the dagger point to Ciarán's throat, to the thin gap between his gorget and jaw, then thrust it in deep. It would cut the man's voice box but not his life. Kyle pressed on the dagger from the side, sliding its edge along beneath Ciarán's jawline, combining his strength with Arlan's weakening thrust, severing vessels vital to life. Blood poured in a stream from a gurgling Ciarán. All the while Lorain held the weakening man steady.

Arlan fell back, his body tightening, his throat closing in on itself and his breath a mere wisp. His heart rate not much more. His vision misted as he collapsed, his bones shuddering on the granite slab.

Why had the god of this world led him here?

Why does he not break through those clouds, reach down, and save me?

Save my warriors? Save my people? For though I die, their future remains uncertain.

Soft thoughts invaded his foggy mind. He had a part to play. A major role in the history of his people.

Was this why he made me warrior king—not to fight a battle, but exchange my life for theirs?

Lorain thrust Ciarán to the ground in front of him. He bled from side and neck. No way back for him... *or me.*

Arlan moved, rose, floated, but he felt different. He looked down. A tall warrior had collapsed on a lying stone, his black hair splayed behind him. Two men were sprawled beside the stone. One was Kyle. The other, older man, Ciarán, lay in a pooling red. The Laird of Lorain looked on.

Arlan gasped.

It is I on the slab.

Beside his body, his warband and Ciarán's warriors had ceased their striving. Rhiannon took a pace back from the stilled group, who now stood slack-jawed, staring at Ciarán and Arlan's own body. Bàn darted a glance in Rhiannon's direction, his sword still trained on his opponent.

With our spirits above the tree, Eifion faced me.

This is your gift, granddaughter. Time to use it.

I stretched out my spirit. Darkness shielded those who stood at the stone slab. But not Rhiannon and Bàn. Rhiannon had broken away from fighting one of Ciarán's men. She radiated a glow. It surrounded her.

Grandfather? I pointed out my mother.

His eyes rounded. *Call her.*

Rhiannon, we need you. Come. I sent my words to her. Would it work?

Rhiannon! Come!

Arlan hovered out of his body. The view below him was like a scene from a troubadour's performance.

"Let me go, Bàn. It's okay," Rhiannon said. The strain in her voice spoke of a grief mixed with hope. "I'm going to Eifion and Rhynne." She turned and ran toward the trees at the end of the glen.

Bàn wrenched out a cry, pelting the foe with blows, while Muir, grunting, thrust his sword at Galan. Adele held back Dál Gallain warriors who had approached the small mêlée, and Douglas mowed more down with his war horse.

Their anguished cries floated right through Arlan.

Rhiannon had left Father and now raced to Eifion and myself at the tree, then looked at our bodies hugging the ancient oak. She pressed herself to the trunk, touching our fingertips with hers. The three of us together encircled the oak exactly. I shifted down, in my spirit form, and held out my hand. Her spirit looked up at me and grabbed my hand, rising. Her face illuminated, eyes alight, and mouth gaping.

We need you, Mum.

Aye, daughter. Eifion spoke in his spirit. *Though ye only now recognise your gifting. Come, assist us.*

Rhiannon held on to us in her spirit, while we all held hands around the tree trunk below in our physical bodies. Eifion looked up, and I followed his lead. So did Rhiannon. It was there, again. The golden light. Or maybe it had always been there. I yearned for the gilded glow above, and Rhiannon joined me.

A waterfall of light, like a river of molten gold, engulfed us with power. The warmth of love surrounded me. Energy surged right through me, shaking my soul to its very centre.

Purity. Goodness. Everything that was *right*.

I looked at Eifion. He nodded.

I flew to Arlan. His body still held a little warmth, but no breath moved through his lungs, and his heart didn't beat. Someone floated above me, so I turned.

Arlan! Father!

FIFTY-SIX

The enslaved shall be free.

BOOK OF LIGHT
MAGE TEXT DATE OF SCRIBING UNKNOWN
BOOK LOST IN ANTIQUITY

Eastern Clanlands of Dál Gallain
Saw-toothed Mountains

Bram passed over a quiet, white world, the rumbling clash and anguish of battle far behind him, icy cold touching an already cool hide.

The wee dragon stopped her flight, and turned back in mid-air, scraping past, claws scratching scales in her pass. Bram turned, his flight much slower. Drayce had spun once more and faced him, diving again. His dragon was a majestic stag dive-attacked by a chaffinch. A gnat. He would swat it.

If only the wee dragon kept still long enough!

She flew circles around him, dizzying him to keep his eye on her. She dived low, landing on a platform of pure white. He pursued, down to a narrow ice-sided glen enclosed in a snow-filled space. He landed, claws sinking deep in the soft snow topping—

He slid, clawed feet splaying.

I've landed on ice!

Drayce screamed. It held pain. Did she know what his lord intended for her master? There existed a bond between the high king and his dragon. What strength the connection? Not of magic, for Bram had spied none, but a bond, nonetheless.

And his daughter who rode this wee beast... another bond there for certain... perhaps that was a magic of sorts.

The wee dragon screeched again, hovering out of snapping range. The cry deepened and became a roar.

MacEnoicht had consumed the poison for certain, then.

This slippery ice beneath him held not enough purchase for lift, and he would need to run to take flight, but the narrow glacial glen was too short for such. If he *could* run on such a surface with sharp talons.

Ifrin. Deamhan's home! The wee one was smart but had not his weapons.

He drew in a breath and belched out flame on the hovering, whimpering wee dragon. She darted away, leaving a slight singe in her wake.

She roared again. And glowed. A flame burst forth from her. She shut her mouth tight after it, her flight stumbling mid-air.

So, she had surprised herself. Perhaps she had not yet breathed her fire. She had pluck, he would admit. 'Twill be a shame to kill such a one like herself—

Flame seared his left eye, melting orb and lid. Stabbing pain ensued, right to the dragon's brain. He blinked against the burn, now with only one window able to see this world of white.

A mirror of flame glowed by his right eye, scorching pain and dark now his vision.

Evil beast! *I am blinded!*

He pricked his hearing. Wing flaps darted either side of the great beast he controlled. Soft roars of flame came, alternating between either wall of the narrow glen, up and down, and along the deep, icy chasm. He took a breath and, waiting for the next whoosh of flame, aimed, and sent forth his own.

Drayce squealed while wing flaps flurried about him.

More soft bellows of heated breath came. He followed them with fire of his own. His feet were now wet in a cold puddle, claws slipping further.

The ice beneath him cracked—split beneath Bram's dragon feet, then warmth gushed through the crevasse. He fell, rushing to meet the hot air rising from below. Deep, deep down to an infernal heat.

Drayce snapped from above. The wee beast bit with a vengeance and howled like a grieving wolf. Her frantic attacks blocked the way above him. Bram opened wings to spread and lift.

No space—such a narrow crevasse.

Sulphur's sharpness hit his nostrils at the same time scorching heat touched his talons.

The heat increased. He pressed wings and claws on the side walls, burning both.

He slid lower. Drayce's attacks continued, biting his head, his wings, his tail.

He snapped back, but still he slid.

No way out. The dragon would die in a subterranean volcanic hell.

He sought exit, his soul searching for the access out of the dragon he'd controlled by his magic. The words of Drostan, his first master, rang in his head.

To retain the control of a dying beast means a mage's death also.

The beast shut tight the walls within its mind. No door apparent, though Bram scrambled to find one.

What! It would hold me in? Not release me from its mind?

He sought again, his efforts as frantic as the wee dragon's attempts to force this older, larger dragon to the flowing heat below.

Trapped in a volcanic crevasse. He let out a sardonic laugh. How pitiful. Trapped in life, duped by a sinister force into service out of love for his former master, Drostan. Enslaved by the self-centred Lord Ciarán.

How I wished not to kill. Strove to keep the people safe. My only guilt is the old high king—the death of that grand man.

And now his magic impotent against an inescapable beast.

No! He beat against the mind-walls. He would pummel his way out.

No give. No budge. No gap. He'd underestimated the intelligence of the aged dragon who would take him to the grave.

His soul sobbed. How apt he should die without escape in a place fit to be hell. Maybe it was hell. *'Twill be the abode of my deserving.*

I will soon know for certain.

His dragon fell.

'My Fhéin dies!'

Bram ceased his pummelling. Who spoke, invading his mind with primitive thought?

'Ye harmed them not.' Again, the thought-voice came to him.

The claws of the massive reptile touched molten stone, seared then shrivelled.

'Ye can go.'

Bram stilled his straining, blocking out the pain from the dragon's burning, and attuned his spirit to the origin of the voice.

The wee dragon? Drayce?

'Thine master is evil. Of the physical and of the spirit. But ye can be free.'

This monstrous beast has jailed me. I speak to a dragon?

'Ye have the power. Ye hold goodness. Find your liberation from all that masters you.'

The wee dragon wished him to be free?

The stench of burned flesh enveloped him, the will of the beast incarcerating him slipping away. Its demise drew near, and soon he would follow.

'Leave the dying old one... go rebel from the ancient spirit. Go!'

Bram pressed out. The walls were down, and his spirit escaped. He rose through glowing rock, radiating intense heat many times greater than a smithy's forge. Burnt rock's stench pinched his spirit's nose. Now charred flesh followed. He glanced down. The gargantuan animal slipped into the molten lake, an underground lava flow.

Bram's spirit fled.

He lifted his head, the side of his face wet from dipping in the divination bowl. He grabbed his arms, patted his mage robe where it covered his legs, wiped his cheeks and chin. Fresh air blew through the tent flaps, filling his nostrils with the odours of camp. The unsullied perfume of rain came on the wind. No scent of incendiary.

"The wee beast saved me?"

No. Told him of freedom, aye. One more thing he must do to truly gain his liberation.

Ye have the power, she had said—*nae*, she had thought *into my soul.*

Now his mind was clear. The veil ripped, the false image shattered, the grimy looking-glass polished. His master—the spiritual master of his master Drostan, which Drostan had passed on to him on his death—had held him enthralled by his power. That one was a slave owner. All his plans were of destruction. Bram squeezed his eyes shut, blocking out the vision he'd received when he first summoned the spirit—a long line of death and hate trailing behind it—what it named the grand master plan.

"Well, I want nae part in it. I relinquish my consent. Retract my will from yours!" Heart thundering, he speared his gaze around the tent. "Do you hear me?" he yelled.

The tent flap snapped with an icy blast, and thick smoke flew into his tent, filling the tiny space until Bram could barely take a breath in its choke.

"You will address me as master." The solid whisper spoke with echoes of agony floating between the words.

Bram shuddered. Burning needles stabbed every inch of his skin, moving deeper.

"I resign my contracted service to you."

"Ha." The laugh cut like the cold slice of a honed-edged knife. "You cannot. You are mine."

"Nae." Bram had to force the word out. 'Twas as though a mighty hand gripped his jaw shut. "I am not. Not anymore. I. Will. Not. Do. Your. Bidding."

The deep black mist snorted. "You cannot."

"My will is mine, and I will not serve you." Bram spoke and the hand gripped tighter, digging sharp talons into his cheeks. "You. May. Leave."

"You belong to the darkness, murderer. There is no goodness"—it spat the word in his face like icicles— "in you. At all. You cannot relinquish my lordship!" The icy blast swirled, lifting herbs and scrolls, dizzying them around Bram.

It is a lie—that the bonded cannot go free. Yet another untruth to fill this spirit's spectral mouth.

"I. Can. And. I. Will." With each word, the grasp on Bram's jaw lessened. "I am free from you. There is some good in me. And I will nurture it."

He would take the antidote to MacEnoicht. Lord Ciarán would try to stop him, but he would wade past the man, seek the help of MacEnoicht's warriors.

"Too late. Your worldly master is gone. You are alone in this world. MacEnoicht's warriors will slay you."

"I forbid you to read my thoughts! Leave!"

At Bram's shout, the dark smoke drew in on itself, blackening in intensity, then springing outward and expanding, it knocked the tent pole, lifted the canvas upward, taking bedding and scrolls with it. A shriek rent the air as herb pouch, inkpots, and mugs flew, and for a moment, black fog blotted out the silver sun. The boys and pages in the camp cried and covered their heads, then ran. Screaming camp prostitutes followed in their wake. The pack mules and garrons snapped tethers and galloped away.

In the ensuing silence, Bram slumped to the ground, limbs heavy and jaw bruised. Quills, seeds, and furs fell to the ground, a clay pot stoppered with a cork landing just beyond his head. He flinched, rousing himself.

"The antidote!"

FIFTY-SEVEN

The Light of Life.

BOOK OF LIGHT
MAGE TEXT DATE OF SCRIBING UNKNOWN
BOOK LOST IN ANTIQUITY

Eastern Clanlands of Dál Gallain
Mòr Cath Làraich

My spirit hovered over Arlan's body. He and I were both there, above him—his body, that is.

Man, it was... *awesome*.

He looked back at himself lying by the stone slab. His forehead scrunched—his *spirit's* forehead scrunched—and his gaze flicked everywhere, like he tried to take it all in.

I covered his body with my spirit, embracing the physical with the spiritual, and held tight.

Please! Please, light that is good. Source of life and everything that holds meaning. Save my father.

The life of the trees reached out to me, giving me the same sensations of healthy peace, like when I've walked on a forest trail. Golden threads streamed from the remaining trees spared of the bazooka or dragon's flame. The light from above poured down, following the streams, flowing to me, then through me.

Golden warmth infused every sinew, nerve fibre, joint—filling me with lighted heat that built to a crescendo. To a point of pressure so great I could've exploded. But wonderfully nice. I held on tight, my breath so taut in my body hugging the tree, my lungs might burst.

Mirroring this, my soul erupted with vigorous life. Pure. Untamed. Strong.

It gushed out of my hovering spirit.

And poured over Arlan.

Arlan's cooling body heated beneath me, his physical form's solidity pressed against my spirit.

"Oh!" His startled cry came from behind me, then he flew right through me and back into his body.

For a nanosecond, I sensed *him*. A whole world that was Arlan. More stuff than I could ever have imagined about him. I shuddered with the intensity of the sense of his love for me. And his willingness. He was okay with dying for his people. For Mum. For me. For Bàn. He wanted us and his people free of Ciarán—and whatever it was behind Ciarán—no matter what it cost *him*.

I pushed back the tears. My job wasn't over yet. The darkness hovered over his body, and I held on tight.

Please. My body hugging the oak whispered it too.

The golden light flooded his body, forcing out—wringing out—the poison that sat in his cells, *around* his cells, glutted his liver and lungs, clogged his kidneys, and strangled his heart. I saw it all, like one of those animated You Tube clips they made us watch in high school biology class.

Then the dark drifted away, extinguished by the wind.

Light filled Arlan with gentleness, and wholeness returned. He opened his eyes, his chest rising with a deep inspiration.

"Rhynne?" He rolled over, lifting himself to stand and moving right through me.

Ciarán lay on the ground, surrounded by darkness. Images—shadows—scrambled around him. Smoky dark beings grabbed his spirit, which rose from his body, then dragged it down through the ground. His soul's eyes widened as his mouth twisted. Then he was gone.

Kyle stood, frozen, staring at Ciarán's now empty body.

Bàn grunted behind me, racing forward to Arlan, thrusting aside the stunned Gallawain warriors.

I flew away, back to my body by the tree.

Drayce's roar rang over the mountains.

FIFTY-EIGHT

The breath of life flows through the trees.
My voice vibrates the air.
Ageless stone remakes my bones.
Soil of the land shields me with flesh.
My blood flows like a gentle burn.
But my heart is spirit,
Forever free.

SAGE EIFION IUBHAR
SAGE ADVISER TO HIGH KINGS
(6020 POST DRAGON WARS-CURRENT)

Eastern Clanlands of Dál Gallain
Mòr Cath Làraich

Arlan breathed in deep, blood's ferrous scent and human stale sweat filling his nostrils. But his heart beat strong within his chest, and leg muscles held his stand, sturdy and firm. Drayce circled close above, flapping her wings, seeking a place to land, startling riderless war horses and emitting a roar that sent gusts of sulphur-scented air his way.

Bàn raced past him, then stood with sword raised over Lorain, who stepped back from Ciarán's cooling corpse and raised his hands, palms outward. Arlan faced those around him. Muir pointed his sword at Galan's throat. Dál Gallain warriors, both on foot and mounted, stood with weapons stilled, held back by Adele and Douglas, but with wide eyes directed at him. George and a handful of tor warriors were a few paces back. And further behind him, skirmishes beside portals stilled.

All looked to him, eyes round and expectant.

Except for Kyle.

Kyle leaned over Ciarán's body, his lips held tight.

"He was a wicked man," Kyle stuttered. "He was my father." His voice trailed to a whisper.

Arlan strode to where Galan had flung his weapons and picked up his dirk, then cut Kyle free of his bonds.

"But he didn't love me." Kyle's voice grew stronger, and he lifted his face to Arlan. "Not like Father did. Or you, my little brother." He leaned into Arlan, and Arlan placed a hand on his shaking shoulder. "I heard you," Kyle whispered, "when I lay wounded with an incredibly sore head. You said you forgave me. Forgave me for treating you like Ciarán has been treating me."

Arlan swung his gaze to Galan, then the Laird of Lorain, the glen of battle as quiet as death behind him.

"We wish for peace, Lord Arlan," Lorain said, glancing at the point of Bàn's sword. "I want you and all to know Lord Ciarán had my service under duress. My family languishes in his tower dungeon, and he used my lands, warriors, and people by force."

Galan lifted his sword in Lorain's direction, seemingly oblivious to Muir's sword pointing at him. "You...!" he growled.

"Halt!" Arlan cried while Muir kicked out at the younger man and dropped him to the ground.

"May I speak, Lord Arlan?" Lorain bowed. "I wish to address Lord Ciarán's army. To halt this."

"Aye, ensure that is all you do." Arlan gave a brief nod to Bàn, who kept his sword pointed at the Laird of Lorain.

"Do you not trust me, Lord Arlan?" Lorain asked. "After my assistance rendered just now?"

"Forgive me if I still ponder where your loyalties lie."

A flash of hurt crossed the Dál Gallain war chief's face, then he turned to the field, his gaze roving over Gallawain warriors, those from the Second World War and spacemen alike.

"I order you all to cease," he shouted, then bore his stare into the nearest mage. "Remove those from the Other World. Send them back, mages, they belong not here. Close the doors to the wars from whence they came. We need them not. Nor have we ever."

"We'll take no orders from you, nor the High King of Dál Gaedhle," a black robed one shouted back.

"Then you will take this order from Grand Master Llew!" A mage rode through the crowd of bleeding warriors, both Gallawain and tor, on a small, light-footed beast.

The crowd parted, allowing him close access to where Arlan stood. Drayce, who had circled, finding no place to land near him, now dived toward this mage, who ducked.

"Call off your dragon, Lord MacEnoicht! I come in peace," the mage said.

Drayce! Och, to know if this mage is friend or foe!

Drayce hovered near, stirring dust, and pushing nearby warriors away from Arlan. She landed with grace beside him and crept ungainly to him, then nudged her head to his chin. He grabbed her to prevent stumbling over, a waft of scorched hide rising from her.

"I'm well, Drayce." He ran his hand over her scaly skin, nicks and scrapes nobbling beneath his fingertips.

Arlan faced the mage, who had halted his horse at Adele and Douglas. They gave the mage their direct attention, weapons drawn.

"Where is Eifion?" Arlan spoke low, his words for Bàn only.

Bàn searched the field behind them where Rhiannon and Rhynne had run to Eifion. Bàn gave a startled grunt. Arlan turned to the trees at the end of the glen. Rhiannon and Rhynne hovered over Eifion's slumped form, then Rhiannon knelt and drew him into her arms. Angus dropped from his mount and hurried to them.

"Och, no! Douglas, go discover what has happened to Sage Eifion," Arlan ordered.

Douglas bounded past on his war horse, divots flying.

"They wrap him in their plaids, Arlan." Bàn faced the trees while Arlan returned to eye the mage.

"I surprise myself to say this"—Bàn whispered close to Arlan— "but by my sword, I'm glad your daughter is a mage. She healed ye, aye?"

"Not just your daughter, Lord Àrd Rìgh of Dál Gaedhle," the mage announced from his mount, "but your wife and father-in-law also."

Arlan spun to look at the end of the glen. Douglas arrived there as Angus dragged thin logs to Eifion. Both warriors removed their plaids and strung them between the charred poles, forming a makeshift litter, adding the plaids his women provided.

"Sage Eifion has used great magic." The mage spoke in authoritative tones. "It now extracts the cost of such."

Eifion!

"Bring him to me with all haste!" Arlan lifted his voice to the group at the trees.

Adele left Muir standing guard over Galan, mounted her horse, and thundered past toward those milling around Eifion. Swirling portals, with distant battle noise blaring through, varying from cannon fire to laser *zings*, brought Arlan's attention back to the mage.

"State your name and purpose."

"I am Talorc, mage in service to Grand Master Llew of the Isle of Innesfarne." Talorc dismounted a little awkwardly, favouring one hip. "My purpose is to send these mages to Innesfarne for discipline after they have returned to their own worlds and times those warriors whom they induced into Ciarán Gallawain's service." He turned to the gathered crowd of stern-faced mages and restless warriors. "Do as I order. Return your charges. Pay them well from Lord Ciarán's hoard."

Mages gave grim and begrudging nods, then ushered their respective warriors toward the sides of the glen where portals glowed with life. Warriors filed out followed by mages closing portals behind them, leaving a quiet calm only broken by the hoarse, emotional shouts arising from those running beside the horse-drawn litter carrying Eifion.

The party soon drew near and stopped by Arlan. Eifion's face was pale, his eyelids partly closed, and his chest barely rising for a breath. Rhynne and Rhiannon stumbled to a halt by the litter, their red-rimmed eyes riveted on Eifion. Rhiannon raised her head, and seeing Arlan, ran to him, wrapping her arms around him and leaning heavily upon him.

"Oh, you're alive," she breathed.

"Was it... because of me?" Arlan asked. "Because you healed me?" *What a price?*

"Father, we all worked to heal you." Rhynne looked up from the litter, tears streaming down her cheeks. "To return you from death. But Grandfather seems to have taken the greatest toll."

Holding Rhiannon by his side, Arlan stepped to Eifion, whose breath rasped between his dry lips as he lay on the litter.

"Water! Get some water," Arlan ordered.

Rhynne stood up in a rush. "I killed you." Surprise rang through Rhynne's tone as she directed her statement to Talorc, who had limped closer. "With a heavy branch."

The mage returned a rueful smile to her. "Fortunately, no. Only further injured one already maimed."

"Ye sought to kill us." Bàn's voice hardened. "Or your warrior wished to do so for me."

"You fought to protect your charge. I wished only for the young and very gifted mage you guarded."

"What else do you wish to ask of the Àrd Rìgh of Dál Gaedhle, Mage Talorc?" Eifion said, his voice a husk of his usual commanding strength. "You who represent the Mage Masters of Innesfarne?"

Although Eifion spoke in almost a whisper, it was as though all in the glen silently listened to his speech. Having ceased their striving, warriors now seemed to strain for every word.

"Sage Eifion Iubhar." Talorc bowed from the waist. "Ye are well regarded among the mages of Innesfarne. They watch you and are aware of your true gifting that you guard with secrecy. Although"—he gave a wry smile— "your actions of today have revealed it to all."

"Why are you here?" Eifion's voice was a little stronger. "You see we have only now overcome our great and dire struggle. What more do you wish to inflict upon us?"

"You trust me not, Sage Eifion, but I assure you your mistrust is misplaced—"

"Allow me to make that judgement." Eifion had rallied and now glared at the mage.

"The knowledge of portals with the magic to transport us from our world to others has been hid—locked away—for millennia. The awareness of their existence is dangerous in the wrong hands." Talorc spread his own hands wide. "To which the events of this very day attest. The mages connected to Innesfarne are to be... re-educated in their use. The mage masters wish not this to be a skill common to mages, nor one in use"—his mouth twitched— "at all."

"This information relieves me greatly." Eifion's frown deepened. "Ye have more to request. Be about it." His head flopped back onto the garment rolled into a makeshift pillow. "I would hear it while I still can." His words trailed to nothing.

"Eifion?" A chill dropped into Arlan's guts.

Eifion raised a hand, but his eyes remained closed. "It is well." His voice was but a whisper. "I will hear him."

"But we must get you to a..." *Deamhan's Ifrinn!*

"We will heal him, Father," Rhynne said, kneeling beside Eifion.

"Ye are well aware of the extraordinary gifting of your granddaughter," Talorc said to Eifion. "But even so"—Talorc now looked directly at Arlan— "your daughter requires training—"

"Her grandfather will attend to it," Arlan said over a gasp from Rhiannon, his own heart squeezing.

Talorc bowed his head. "It will take much more than the skills of those present to reverse the cost of your resurrection, Lord Arlan."

What?

"No!" Rhynne and Rhiannon spoke in unison, each grasping one of Eifion's hands.

Arlan stepped closer to the litter and knelt on one knee. "Eifion..."

"Rhiannon." Eifion breathed her name.

"Yes, Father?" Rhiannon leaned in.

"Ye must tell your husband you do, indeed, forgive yourself."

Eifion released Rhiannon's hold and lifted his hand to Arlan's face. Bony fingers stroked Arlan's cheek, cool fingertips tracing the scar.

"It is well, son of my heart. Saving you was my honour and your very worth," he rasped. "Go, be the àrd rìgh this land needs." His words were so faint Arlan leaned into hear them.

Eifion's hand fell beside him. His gaze turned skyward, then his breath slowly trickled out.

Arlan's shoulders trembled, shaking his inhalation. The strength of his body, renewed on his rising, now diminished to heavy limbs, as though the exhaustion of the days of battle had returned. The clouded sky above deepened in grey. The air stilled. Silence filled the long glen. Small raindrops fell, their patter gentle, pooling the slackening creases of Eifion's face with soft water.

And Arlan's heart tore.

FIFTY-NINE

In the whisper of a lover's voice
The wind through the glen spoke to me.
It sang the melody of the mountains
The music of the flowing burn
The firm sureness of the ancient peaks.
Recounting tales of warriors past
Of blood shed and lives spent.
Of clan kings great and noble.

POETRY OF A KING
ÀRD RÌGH RHONAN IUBHAR
(4030-4090 POST DRAGON WARS)

Eastern Clanlands of Dál Gallain
Mòr Cath Làraich
Lord Ciarán's Camp

If only I could spirit my body there. Bram's journey from his tent in the camp to the battlefield was taking too long. Not a horse to be found. All fled with the angered cries of his spirit master.

"*Once* spirit master. But no more." Bram ground the words out as he clutched the clay pot of antidote, and yet his soul was uncoiling.

"Freedom," he whispered to no one but himself.

He ran over churned ground, the battlefield less than a league away from the camp. Blood filled tracks where the cannon's wheels had left ruts, the sun silvering the sky's reflection. Horse's grunts and whinnies, the clang of sword on sword and the cries of men should reach his ears and grow louder at his approach to the main battlefield.

But they did not.

Surely the weapons of the Other World would drown out the cries of warriors. Cannon, fiery darts from the bazooka, and beams from those who walked the skies? Yet all seemed subdued. Bram strained his senses.

Portals lay open... but diminishing in magical energy.

They are closing?

He ran on, past those mortally wounded and crying in pain. Past bodies, motionless and abandoned. Weapons strewn. Swords lay with broken shields, like children's toys forgotten after play.

He faced the rise, over which he would spy the MacEnoicht defence lines.

And Lord Ciarán dead, or so his old master said. But what to believe? Lying, the true nature of *that* spirit.

Bram slowed at the rise. All those ahead of him stood still, backs to him, intent on a cluster of warriors ahead.

Surrounded by his close warband and bent over a lying form on a litter, the Àrd Rìgh of Dál Gaedhle lived and breathed.

Arlan MacEnoicht!

Bram skidded to a halt, bumping into a broad-shouldered warrior of Lorain.

Gasping for breath, useless clay pot clutched tight, he stood, thigh muscles trembling joined by his guts.

"The man lives. Did he not take the poison?"

"Aye. He took it." The warrior on whom he leaned spun to him. "We saw all. He were dead. His mage brought him back. Ha! Thought they did nae believe in magic in Dál Gaedhle."

"Mage don't look sae healthy now." Another pointed with his bloodied sword to the body on the litter.

Àrd Rìgh's Camp

Arlan's warband set up a small pavilion. A hasty tent erected from the stores of the cowed Gallawain warriors. Eifion's body lay on a camp cot, set out in a regal pose, like a monarch on a tor slab, surrounded by heather gathered from the hillsides. Purple heather matched his purple mage robe and hid the pasty pall of death imbuing his skin.

Arlan swallowed, wiped his eyes with the heel of his hand and turned from Rhiannon and Rhynne, who fussed with the sprigs of heather surrounding Eifion's face.

"It should've cost *me*." Rhynne's voice was barely a whisper.

Arlan turned back.

"It is my gifting... to heal. He took the price for me." Rhynne bowed her head and rested it on Eifion's cold form.

Rhiannon slid to her side and wrapped her arms around her shoulders. "He loved you. Loved us." Her voice broke.

"My Lord Àrd Rìgh." Bàn spoke in sombre tones at the doorway to the tent. "Ye have much to attend. The honouring of your bravest warrior"—he flicked his chin towards the bier— "must wait a while yet."

Arlan lifted his head to those gathered by the tent. His warband, dusty and blood-stained, looked at him with shoulders broad and chests puffed. Tor warriors moved with purpose through the jumble of human forms, finding those injured and covering those dead. Gallawain warriors milled at the rise. Some had approached and waited in line, supervised by his own warriors. Laird Lorain stood to one side, removed of his weapons, and insisting on the validity of his own surrender.

"Aye, we have negotiations to make, enemies to imprison, and wounded to attend."

"Talorc awaits your attention," Bàn said.

"I will see him first, then send him on his way."

The man stepped up behind Bàn as if awaiting that moment.

"Lord Arlan." Talorc bowed. "The Mage Masters of Innesfarne wish to train your daughter—"

"No!" Bàn growled beside Arlan.

Rhynne rose from Eifion's bier, wiping her eyes on her plaid, her brow creasing as she looked up at Bàn, who frowned and shook his head.

"Lady Rhynne, what do *you* desire?" Talorc asked.

Rhynne looked to Arlan, then to Bàn. "I wish to be taught by those who love the Light." She faced Talorc then. "How can I trust you? You sent warriors to the mage hold, killed warrior sages, and chased us down the mountain. Hell, you probably killed Ma Gabràn!"

Talorc held up a placating hand. "Nae, 'twas not I, but Gallawain's men who harmed the old woman. Please, I wish for you to have a training far greater than the one you would receive—"

"Enough. Go!" Arlan's voice ricocheted around the glen.

Drayce lifted from her place near the tent and hovered, roaring with flame bursting from her mouth into the air above Talorc, threatening to set the tent on fire.

Talorc didn't flinch, only smiled and lifted his hand toward the flame.

"Drayce, no!" Rhynne shouted, and Drayce closed her jaws, then lifted and circled above them.

"I comply with your wishes," Talorc said. "Lady Rhynne, if ye reconsider, the offer of training with the masters stands open for you." He mounted his horse and rode away through the warriors sorting the dead.

The small dragon who had saved his life flew overhead. Bram stood away from the Gallawain warriors discussing amongst themselves their next move, their voices vague murmurs around him. He stood focused on the mage now leaving Lord Arlan and his family.

Talorc trotted his horse away from the warriors who guarded the victor of the battle, nudging his mount closer to Bram, eyes growing wider while clustered warriors parted to allow him passage. "What are you doing here?" His question was a harsh growl.

"I came with... too late," Bram said, holding up the clay pot.

"And you will come with me now before you are discovered," Talorc hissed. "Get up behind me."

"I must make amends—"

"Hush! Pull up your hood." Talorc grasped his free hand and hoisted him into the saddle behind him. "You must make your escape. That is what you *must* do," he growled his whisper over his shoulder into Bram's face. "You controlled the dragon who killed the previous high king."

"I must confess."

"You what?"

"I have been set free. I must make amends for my actions performed while under the lordship of my previous spirit master."

"*Previous spirit master?*" Talorc's whisper scratched. "There is no such thing. What have you done, lad?"

"I have renounced my spirit master. I am freed. But I must acknowledge my guilt."

"Hush again, I say. Let no one hear you. Those who wish to gain favour in the victor's eyes would send you to him for justice without a thought."

"I deserve justice."

"You are invaluable to Innesfarne, and I will not see you hanged for your deeds done with exceptional magical skill. Be silent. Pull up your hood, I said! Cover your face. You will come with me. Grand Master Llew awaits, and we will discuss your... *renouncing*."

"Come here," Arlan said to Rhynne and encircled her in his embrace. Her taut, muscled form trembled in his arms.

"I was sure Talorc would make me go with him," Rhynne said.

Rhiannon came out from the tent and leaned into Rhynne's back, putting her arms around her.

"And... the man's conduit is fire," Rhynne said with awe in her tone. "Drayce wasted her breath."

"Och, aye." Arlan blinked. "My dragon breathed fire!"

Douglas approached, concealing an object in his grip, silver glinting between his fingers.

"My àrd rìgh and warrior king." Douglas bowed and held out the silver torc he had removed from Ciarán's corpse.

Arlan released his women from their hug, and took the proffered torc, placing it around his neck, where it sat cool against his throat. A cheer rose from the gathered warriors, those remaining from his warband, and the surviving tor warriors. Drayce, circling above, let out a roar.

Near the rise where the Gallawain army had lined up, the crowd cleared and some warbands rode away, their plaid flapping at their backs. A troop of warriors approached, brushing past Arlan's tor warriors while nodding respect to them. Mhàiri Duisdale stepped forward, followed closely by young Callaghan.

Mhàiri bent the knee. "We beg your forgiveness, Lord Arlan." Mhàiri shot a quick scowl aside at Callaghan, who then lowered to one knee. "We deserve a traitor's death," she continued. "But we trust ye will be as forgiving and merciful as your father once was, for we pledge our undying obedience henceforth."

Beside Arlan, Bàn let out a grunt of caution.

"We shall consider your case and your promise in due time." Arlan nodded to Douglas. "Keep these two under guard and arrange for their warbands' supervision."

Douglas and Muir led them away, along with Galan, now manacled, and the other Gallawain warriors.

"Please Lord Arlan, I wish to stay"—the Laird of Lorain stood attentive— "and be part of the negotiations."

"Ye were his war chief," Bàn accused.

"Out of necessity and under duress." Lorain sent a pleading look Arlan's way. "I am for you, Lord Arlan MacEnoicht. Surely my actions in Gallawain's execution bear witness to this and exonerate me?"

Arlan nodded to Bàn. "Let him be."

Out of the milling crowd, a group of warriors in the garb of warband leaders of differing clans, wearing their respective tartans, came with heads bowed. They stopped by Adele and spoke to her in low tones.

"What is it, Adele?" Arlan asked. "Bring them here."

Adele took their surrendered weapons and nodded them forward.

"Aye?" he said to those who came with lowered gazes.

"Lord Arlan MacEnoicht, we are warlords of Dál Gallain." The tall, bloodied man who spoke glanced across to Lorain. "We are not all who fought, mind. Some have fled." He straightened, looking Arlan in the eye. "We saw what happened. Most of us. The rest, well, they heard as warriors passed it along the line. That Lord Ciarán demanded your life for your people's freedom... and ye gave it." The man's throat worked, and he lifted his chin in the direction of the stone slabs. "We saw ye dead upon that stone, lord. But now... here ye are. Alive." The warlord's face softened in awe.

His companions nodded to him, and he continued. "We have not conferred with other lairds of our land"—he glanced at Lorain once more— "but we wish ye to know we are for you, Lord Arlan MacEnoicht. We also beg your pardon and your favour, for we have kin held by Gallawain in surety of our cooperation who we wish to be set free of that dead lord's imprisonment. Our desire is for you to be our àrd rìgh. Please consider us and ours to be part of your rule. For we know ye are loved, and fair, and a man of honour and... Och, well, Dál Gallain has sorely lacked these qualities in a leader for many years."

The Dál Gallain warlord fell to his knees, his companions following suit. "I do not hold my sword, but it means nae less when I say, Lord Arlan MacEnoicht, ye have my sword arm, my loyalty, my oath. We submit to you as *our* high king... if ye wish to be so, lord."

Lorain fell to his knees and bowed. "As do I, Lord Arlan."

Arlan swallowed, blinking the mist of tears from his eyes. "I accept your pledges, warriors and lairds." His voice came out husky.

The warlords stood, bowed, then walked back to the crowd and headed to groups of warriors wearing their respective tartans. Smiles greeted them, and cheers erupted throughout the glen from the remaining warrior bands.

Rhiannon's arms slipped around him, and her face lifted to his, a slow smile broadening.

"So ye have visions, daughter of the Blind Lady Sage?" he said softly, for her hearing only.

"Aye," she said shyly. "I'll tell you about them sometime."

"Ye had better."

"I love you, my husband."

"And I you, my wife."

"You are a grand warrior king, Arlan." Rhiannon cupped his cheek with her warm hand. "You have rescued your people from that monster. Freed your enemies, too. And you've saved me." She lifted her face to his, and he bent forward to receive her kiss. She released their embrace, then stood back. "But you must promise me... and all of us"—she raised her voice— "to not die again too soon, hey?"

A chuckle rose in Arlan's chest, drowned out by the cheers arising from all standing nearby. His heart, now beating strong and healthy, glowed in his body full of life and breath. He gazed around at those he held close to his soul, and what he could only own as gratitude filled him.

"I thank you, my family and friends. You were there for me."

"Nae, lord, ye were there for us. And for all of Dál Gaedhle." Angus led the cheer, sword thrust skyward. "Laoch Rìgh! Laoch Rìgh!"

The glen rang with the roar of warriors echoing the shouts of Arlan's close warband.

The cheering finally died down, then Bàn stood tall in front of Arlan, his leather armour mud sprayed, and his hair sticking to his sweat-streaked face. George stood beside him, smiling crookedly as he pushed his glasses up the bridge of his nose. He wore leather armour, and his muddied jeans were sweat soaked. Rhynne stood between them, holding the hand of each man. Arlan slid his gaze to one side of the glen where cut timber sat in readiness to be made into George's tank.

"Ye have done well, George Wilson, but at this time we require not your tank."

George gave a shrug, the crooked smile still on his face. "I am here, Lord Arlan, and I wouldn't want to be anywhere else."

Bàn straightened and looked to Rhynne beside him. Bàn—his faithful sword-brother, who had remained by his side all battle, as ever. The look on his best friend's face could only mean one thing.

"Aye, sword-brother," Arlan asked. "Ye have a boon for me to grant on this victorious day. An apt request to aid our celebrations on winning the freedom of Dál Gaedhle and freeing the land of "—he looked across at Ciarán's body now covered with a stained Gallawain standard and lying next to a pile of the slain— "the one who would destroy all that is good and true." He turned back to Bàn. "How do ye wish to celebrate *our* victory? The victory of all Dál Gaedhle, wrought by all its warriors and friends. Those who fought well and gave all. Some the ultimate price." His words caught in his throat. The tent flapped in the breeze, giving him a glimpse of a supine, mauve-robed figure.

He pressed his lips together and inclined his head to Bàn. "Ye have a request? State it, man!"

"Aye, Lord Warrior King." Bàn's cheeks dimpled through the grime. "One I cannae wait any longer to ask."

A smile curled Rhynne's mouth, and her eyes glittered, her head gently nodding.

"Well," Arlan said. "It seems I must say, aye."

— · —

EPILOGUE

I left my world, my home, my dad. Dragged from them by a stranger. A handsome one.

I travelled through a portal I could see—but no one else was able—leaving behind microwave ovens, mobile phones, social media, and the hope of my dreams fulfilled in a world grown dim, darkening by the moment. I pined for the realm I came from, and the dad and friends I left behind.

But my warrior kept me safe and brought me to a place he maintained to be my real home.

A strange place, where beauty was clear, loyalty solid, and one's word worth dying for.

I came alive. I felt more. Saw more. Fought for more.

And we won.

I discovered myself, my gifts and talents, and found other people. The people who made me, would nurture me, love me.

Here now is my home. Here now is my life. Here now, my blood surges through my veins—along with my magic.

Here is Dál Cruinne.

THE END
If you enjoyed the Arlan's Pledge Series, please leave a review.
Thank you.

THE CLANS of the SOVEREIGNTY of DÀL GAEDHLE

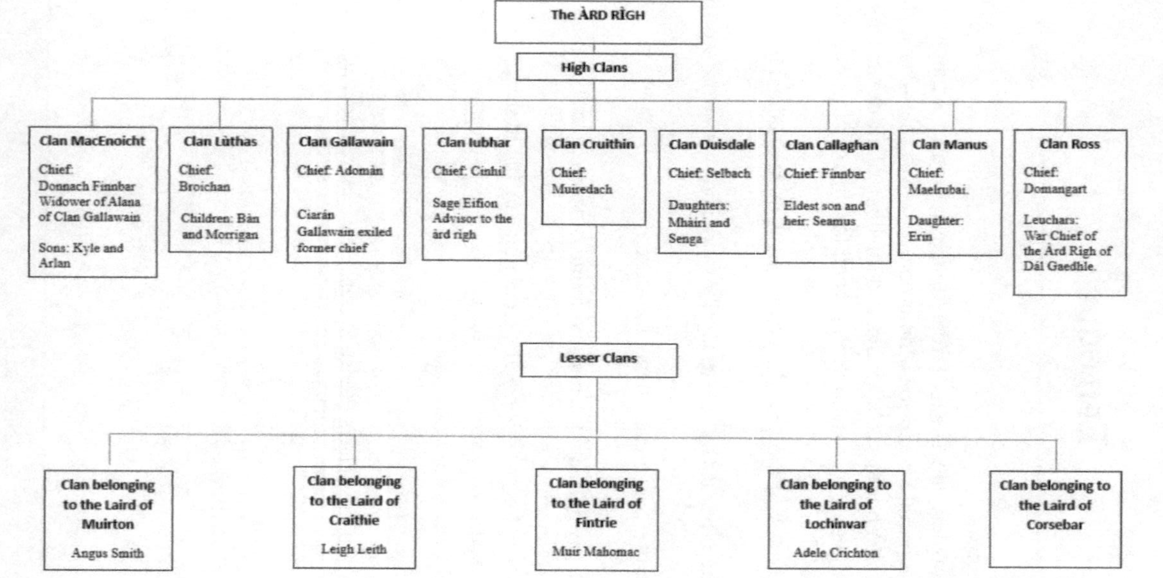

GLOSSARY of GAELIC and SCOTS WORDS

A gràidh chridhe	love of my heart
Am fuath	the fae
Àrd Ghliocas	high wisdom
Àrd Rìgh	high king
Bayrd	sings
Beul an latha	the dawn of the day
Beul na h-oidhche	the dusk of evening
Boireannaich	woman
Braw	Scots for good/great
Broch	round tower of iron age construction
Burn	a small watercourse, creek, brook
Cernunnos	Celtic god of beasts and wild places
Creagrubha	rocky outcropping
Cruinne	the globe/world
Cumhachd Adhar	power of the air/bad spirit
Dál	denotes belonging or ownership
Damainte	damned
Deamhan	demon/evil spirit
Dearg	to redden/draw blood
Dreich	Scots for dreary/ bleak

Droch dhuine	bad man/reprobate
Eilean	island
Fàistinnaech	wizard/prophet/diviner
Fannlag	weakling
Giorsal	grey hair
Gliocas	wisdom, prudence
Heid	Scots for head
Murtair	assassin
Muir	sea
Oidhche mhath	goodnight
Phelan	wolf-like
Ruairidh	red king
Sàsaichean	council
Sleaghach	spear
Stramash	Scots for disturbance, uproar
Tapaidh	clever smart brave heroic
Tobraichean na beatha	the fountain/source/issue of life
Tòireadh	a quest, diligent search
Trobhad	come here!
Uisge beatha	malt whisky
Weesht	Scots for *shush*

AUTHOR'S NOTE

It's no secret I love castles.

I always have, and probably always will.

My earliest memories of painting—apart from the very early splashes and daubs melding the primary colours into a full page of brown—are of the pink (yes, pink) castles I painted one after the other in grade three art class. Crenulations, towers, turrets, drawbridges and portcullises featured even before I knew the names for these particular structures. And so, when I began to write fantasy, castles became an essential item.

History, Scottish history in particular, fascinates me. I am blessed to live once again in Scotland, and I breathe in the air thickly infused with its past, and relish it.

I find history inspires my fantasy writing, and Scotland's history and geography has inspired many settings and doings in my novels.

The caisteals of Dál Cruinne in particular. Also, the brochs of the past (see author's note *Of Warriors and Sages*). There are two castles I'd like to mention here and the reasons I chose to mimic these buildings in Arlan's world.

Stirling Castle, Stirlingshire, sits high on a prominent outcrop of solid rock and gazes down at the town of Stirling, the meandering River Forth, and the many roads travelling up and down Scotland. The area is the site of battles past, the Scottish victories of Sir William Wallace and King Robert the Bruce. Old Stirling Bridge was the safest and easiest way to pass from north to south and vice versa in days gone by, and crucial to the battle strategies of those mentioned above.

It was mainly Stirling Castle's situation that inspired me to imagine The Keep in a similar geography.

The seat of the High King of Dál Gaedhle, The Keep, sits on a high, rocky mount that is surrounded by a meandering river, the River Ruairidh. One sole bridge crosses this river, giving the only easy access from the east to the west of Dál Gaedhle. Boggy banks surrounded by marsh make traversing this river difficult for some, treacherous for others. Those who wish to cross must pay a tax to the àrd rìgh, and every trader's wagon and farmer's cart has done so over Dál Gaedhle's millennia, making the position of high king coveted for its wealth.

Castle Campbell is a historic fortress above Dollar Glen, Clackmannanshire. It hides behind hills with narrow gorges on either side, and is surrounded by forest. I have visited Castle Campbell twice. On each occasion I approached this fortress, I experienced the same awe and surprise as the stone fortification appeared seemingly out of nowhere, a high square fortress standing proud on a mound, viewed through the tree-lined road.

Once inside Castle Campbell, a circular stone staircase takes you right up to the top where you can walk out onto the roof perimeter safely behind the chest-height, stone wall-head, with the view of forest and burns roaring by (Burn of Care and Burn of Sorrow). Here you sense the squareness of the building with views in all four directions of the compass.

Whenever writing Caisteal Monsae in the *Arlan's Pledge* novels and in *Murtairean: An Assassin's Tale*, I envisioned Castle Campbell... but in (you guessed it) pink—dusky-pink—sandstone. I have situated it on the Dál Gallain coast with rooftop views of the Muir Gallain on the south side. At a similar roof and stone wall-head to castle Campbell, I envisioned Findlay viewing the initial attack in the retaking of Caisteal Monsae by Leynarve and Arlan's warbands (Of *Warriors and Sages: Arlan's Pledge Book Two*). Then running back down to the kitchens for his escape route beside the enormous hearth. On his way, he looked into the main hall and witnessed the skirmish occurring there. The morning after the battle, Rhiannon runs to the top of this fortress and, again from behind the wall-head, she spies the beauty of the sea—which I positioned Caisteal Monsae close to—also witnessing the harshness of her new world as she looks down to see Arlan execute a prisoner.

In this novel, *Of High Kings and Mages: Arlan's Pledge Book Three*, Rhynne experiences the view on the wood-ward side of this rooftop as she settles into the caisteal and hears warning in the trees of the forest right before experiencing Findlay and Bram communicating through a dog using dark magic.

I have used other ancient structures as springboards for settings in my stories. In the novella, *Running with the Stags*, (available for free as a welcome gift on joining my newsletter) the ancient deer trap on the Isle of Rum inspired me for both setting and plot.

I trust you enjoyed my use of castles in these novels. Please, if you ever are in Scotland, visit these structures that were once homes and fortresses of safety in days past... and then, go dream yourself there.

Acknowledgements

Thank you for reading *Of High Kings and Mages: Arlan's Pledge Book Three*.

As with the second book in this series, this third book also seems to have taken an age to bring to publication.

I started the first draft in August 2020, when like most of us, I had more time at home, although I continued to work as a nurse throughout the pandemic. I still find it interesting that I have written a plague (subconsciously) into this story.

I also find it interesting that when I conceived the idea of Arlan and Rhiannon's story, (when it was one long story now divided into a trilogy) in 2016, Romantasy wasn't even a word. And now that it is complete, I see that's exactly what I have written.

The interruptions related to the pandemic plus moving from one side of the world to another added to the delays, but here it is: the final section of Arlan's and Rhiannon's, and now Rhynne's and Bàn's, story. Although I am feeling wistful at the completion of this tale, there is a nagging in the back of my mind that these characters haven't finished with me yet.

It's time to thank people and, due to the gaps and time delays, if I have omitted anyone involved, please forgive me.

Firstly, Candida Bradford of *A Place of Intent*, thank you always for your editing skills and believing in me and my stories.

Fiona of Fionajayde Media for the wonderful covers.

J I Rogers, author and graphic artist, for the third map in this world, and also your friendship across the miles and support in so many other ways, including your mega skills in graphic art.

To my critique partners, Word Menders (part of Realm Makers) authors SL Dooley, KT Sweet, Philip Wilder, MB Heywood and PS Patton, you have questioned, advised, been dead honest and helped make this novel what it is today. Love you, guys.

ARC/beta readers: Claudia, author Elizabeth Klein, Twany Molina, Beatrice Grasso, Heidi Farmer, Joanne Smith and Frank Lees

To author Eliza Hampstead, thank you again for your tips and corrections when it comes to the finer points of HEMA. Much appreciated.

For all those who believed in me, followed my progress and put up with me talking about my writing... again. Thank you.

Thanks to my supporters on Patreon, whom I am mentioning here as your financial support in the expensive business of independently publishing a novel is invaluable:

Estelle Gallagher, Joanne Smith, Stephanie Dooley, Geoff Russell, Gail Balfour, Elizabeth Miller, Jennefer Rogers, Gillian Lister, Rebecca Dawson, Sue Jacka, Nancy Davis, Tammy, Claudia, Crystal Stewart, Karen Sweet, Roger Fauble, Diana.

Special thanks to Joanne and Robert Smith, friends, fellow writers and published author (Robert J Smith), who have taken me under their wing and supported me no end in the Scottish part of this endeavour.

And to you, the reader who has purchased, read and told others about this world and these characters. Thank you.

I do it for you.

Thank you, always, to my husband, Frank. My writing wouldn't be possible without you. Thank you for supporting me, believing in me, reading endless manuscripts over and over (and over) and putting up with a wife with imaginary friends, enemies and beasts, all in a fantastical world in her head. You keep me grounded.

ABOUT THE AUTHOR

DESTINY RELATIONSHIP COURAGE

Award winning author Jenn Lees latest release, *Of High Kings and Mages: Arlan's Pledge Book Three*, reached the Semi-Finals in the OZMA Book Awards for Fantasy Fiction 2024 CIBAs (Chanticleer International Book Awards).

Of Warriors and Sages: Arlan's Pledge Book Two reached Semi-finals in the OZMA Book Awards for Fantasy Fiction 2023. Long Listed in the Realm Awards 2025 Fantasy Section. As the manuscript *The Quest* reached the Top 10 in Ink & Insights 2021.

Jenn Lees' Best Selling novel, *Of Myths And Portals: Arlan's Pledge Book One* achieved First Place Award (Gold) in The BookFest Fall 2024 Fiction-Romance-Fantasy, Second Place Award (Silver) in The BookFest fall 2024 Fiction-Fantasy-Magic, Myths and Legends, and Fiction-Christian-Fantasy

The Crossing: Arlan's Pledge Book 1, (Re-released as *Of Myths and Portals*) achieved the finals in the OZMA Book Awards for Fantasy Fiction (previous draft manuscript) CIBA 2021 . *Restoring Time* (Book 4 of the *Community Chronicles Series*) reached the finals in the CYGNUS Awards for Science Fiction 2021 CIBA.

An Ink & Insights Competition judge says of *Arlan's Pledge*:

'Beautifully crafted, full of rich setting descriptions, tension that caught my attention and kept it, and characters that leapt off the page. This author is a skilled storyteller.' (Melody Quinn. Ink & Insights 2021 Competition Master Category Judge)

Retired nurse, Jenn has travelled extensively and lived on three continents. Scotland remains her source of inspiration.

Jenn loves walking through a forest and climbing a mountain to experience the view.

Her only disappointment in life is that time travel is not possible... apparently.

Find out more about Jenn Lees and her novels.

Sign up for the newsletter and receive *Running with the Stags,* a free novella in the *Arlan's Pledge Series.*

www.jennleeswriter.com

Want more of Jenn Lees?

Support Jenn Lees Fantasy Author on Patreon. https://www.patreon.com/c/jennle esfantasyauthor/members

Discover Vygeas' and Leyna's story in *Murtairean: An Assassin's Tale*, another novel by Jenn Lees set in the world of Dál Cruinne.   Recommended reading prior to *Of Warriors and Sages Arlan's Pledge Book Two*.

ALSO BY JENN LEES

OF MYTHS AND PORTALS

ARLAN'S PLEDGE BOOK ONE

DESTINY MUST CLAIM THEM

OF WARRIORS AND SAGES

ARLAN'S PLEDGE BOOK TWO

THE HEART QUEST MUST WIN

**Also in the World of Dál Cruinne
MURTAIREAN: AN ASSASSIN'S TALE**

AND
The Community Chronicles Series
A dystopian time travel romance set in a possible future Scotland.
All novels are available in audio book